Pamela Hart is an award-winning author for both adults and children. She has a Doctorate of Creative Arts from the University of Technology, Sydney, where she has also lectured in creative writing. Under the name Pamela Freeman she wrote the historical novel *The Black Dress*, which won the NSW Premier's History Prize for 2006 and is now in its third edition. Pamela is also well known for her fantasy novels for adults, published by Orbit worldwide, the Castings Trilogy and her Aurealis Award–winning novel *Ember and Ash*. Pamela lives in Sydney with her husband and their son, and teaches at the Australian Writers' Centre.

To find out more about the true story behind the book and to sign up to Pamela's newsletter, visit:

www.pamela-hart.com
www.facebook.com/pamelahartbooks
@pamelahartbooks

THE WAR BRIDE

PAMELA HART

piatkus

PIATKUS

First published in Australia and New Zealand in 2016 by Hachette Australia
An imprint of Hachette Australia Pty Limited
First published in Great Britain in 2016 by Piatkus

1 3 5 7 9 10 8 6 4 2

Copyright © 2016 by Pamela Hart

The moral right of the author has been asserted.

*All characters and events in this publication, other than those
clearly in the public domain, are fictitious and any resemblance
to real persons, living or dead, is purely coincidental.*

All rights reserved.
No part of this publication may be reproduced, stored in a
retrieval system, or transmitted in any form or by any means, without
the prior permission in writing of the publisher, nor be otherwise circulated
in any form of binding or cover other than that in which it is published
and without a similar condition including this condition
being imposed on the subsequent purchaser.

A CIP catalogue record for this book
is available from the British Library.

Cover design by Christabella Designs
Cover photographs courtesy of Getty Images and Trove

ISBN 978-0-349-41020-3

Text design by Bookhouse, Sydney
Typeset by Bookhouse

Printed and bound in Great Britain by
Clays Ltd, St Ives plc

Papers used by Piatkus are from well-managed forests
and other responsible sources.

MIX
Paper from
responsible sources
FSC® C104740

Piatkus
An imprint of
Little, Brown Book Group
Carmelite House
50 Victoria Embankment
London EC4Y 0DZ

An Hachette UK Company
www.hachette.co.uk

www.piatkus.co.uk

For my mother

PROLOGUE

13 January 1920

There didn't seem to be a band playing. And only a few people on the wharf at Dawes Point. A handful of Army types, a man in a suit waiting with a taxi, and the normal number of stevedores lounging around, grabbing a smoko while they waited for their cargo to arrive.

Frank was surprised. The last time a war-bride ship had docked – when his mate Smitty's girl came out – there had been crowds, an Army brass band, streamers and shouting and crying – even a man with a placard saying, 'Welcome to your new home, Mavis'. He'd thought about making one of those for Margaret, but now he was glad he hadn't. He felt silly enough, clutching a bunch of roses in a sweaty hand.

He hoped he'd still recognise her. Two years and four months was a long time, and women did things with their hairstyles. Clothes were different. But surely Margaret's tall, slender form would stand out the way it had at Reading train station, when they'd said goodbye. Surely he couldn't mistake that lovely, soft smile of hers for anyone else?

It was hot already, and humid, as Sydney summers always were, but he was ruefully aware that the sweat running down his back wasn't only from the heat.

Wound tighter than a watch spring, he was. Two years and four months and no giving in to temptation, no matter what. A married man, and he'd stuck to it, and God hadn't it been hard! But today ... the house he'd found for them was all ready, the bed made with brand-new sheets. A thorn pricked his thumb and he loosened his grip; not long now.

The SS *Waimana* loomed closer; still painted in its camouflage colours, even now, fourteen months after the war had ended. Frank blinked, confused. There weren't any passengers lining the rails – no, wait, there were a couple on the top deck, holding up some kiddies to see. Where were the women? This was supposed to be a war-bride ship. It should have been packed to the gunnels.

The ship was tied up and the gangplank put across the gap. A trickle of passengers came down, but the only young woman who emerged was a redhead. She winked at him as she went past, her hand tucked into a corporal's arm. That was all – the others were a family group and a couple of men in suits.

Where was Margaret? He checked the letter from the Repatriation Committee again, for the tenth time; yes, the *Waimana*, arriving January 1920, check shipping news for arrival date. Which he had. Surely she hadn't got off at Fremantle or Melbourne? Maybe most of the women had been going to Melbourne, and that was why the ship was nearly empty. That would be it. But where was Margaret?

Who could he ask? An Army sergeant was checking off the corporal and his redhead from a list. With the enlisted man's instinctive avoidance of authority, Frank went instead to a sailor who was securing the mooring ropes at the bow of the ship.

'My wife was supposed to be on this ship,' he began.

The sailor hawked and spat into the greasy Harbour water. 'Soddin' women.'

Frank ignored his comment.

'Margaret Dalton?' he asked.

The sailor looked at the sky and sucked his teeth, thinking.

'Brown hair? Good looker? About so high?' He measured against himself. Frank nodded.

'Yerse, I remember her. There were only a couple without their blokes. She came on board, but she took herself off again. Women – always changing their bluidy minds.'

He'd felt cold like this when he'd been shot, at Passchendaele, in the streaming mud, trying to crawl under barbed wire. The shock had gone through him the same way, exactly.

'Took herself off . . .' he managed.

The sailor shrugged and made fast, then circled him to get back on board.

'Life's a shit, eh?' he said as he climbed the gangplank.

•

Frank threw the roses into the gutter as he walked away. Walked and walked, hot in his good suit (his only suit) and his shiny shoes.

Part of him wasn't surprised. He'd always known that Margaret was too good for him. Too beautiful, too kind, too loving. He wasn't worth that kind of girl; a nameless orphan with nothing more than what his two hands could make. But she hadn't seemed to realise that. Had seemed to think they were on a par, that she was making a good bargain. Had seemed to look forward to a life in Australia.

When she'd walked with him to the station to see him off to the front, she'd cried silently, surreptitiously rubbing the tears away from her face, not wanting to make him feel any worse. They'd only been married a month, then, and parting had been so hard. When they'd kissed goodbye, her soft mouth had been salty with tears.

She'd loved him then, he was certain.

Two years and four months was a long time. Long enough, it seemed, for her to change her mind, even if it was at the last moment.

He'd had letters; but not for a while, now he thought about it. A few months. Maybe that should have made him realise. Made him prepare himself, instead of being side-swiped like this.

She should have warned him. Told him she'd had doubts. He could have reassured her. Hell, he would have gone to England to fetch her if he'd had to.

Unless someone else had changed her mind for her.

The thought of Margaret with another man hit him low and hard, and left him gasping.

He needed a drink. There was a pub on the corner. Not one he'd been in before, but it was open. He went in and hesitated, then ordered a whisky. Beer wouldn't chase away this shaking feeling inside him; wouldn't put him solidly on his feet again.

One whisky didn't, either. He had another, and another. A vague sense that he was spending too much money sent him out the door, jingling the coins in his pocket, along with the key to the house he'd prepared so carefully for Margaret.

It made him sick to think of living there alone. Made him walk faster, as if to outdistance the thought.

He stopped for breath and realised that he'd walked a long way; had taken a familiar path, to Stanmore, and Gladys.

Well, why not? Hell, he'd been faithful the whole time, and what did he have to show for it? Anger rose up in him, finally chasing away the cold, sick dread. If Margaret didn't want him, there was one who did. Who always had. And there was no reason now that his daughter couldn't have a proper father.

That thought was the first good one he'd had. It would be wonderful to see more of Violet.

He turned into Cavendish Street and walked up to number 64, Mrs Leydin's boarding house, where Glad had a room for her and Violet. For a moment, before he knocked, he was afraid that she wouldn't want him, either. That she'd throw him off because he hadn't chosen her over Margaret, despite the fact that Margaret was his lawful wedded wife. He was frozen with that fear, for a moment; that he'd be back to being alone in the world, as he always had been until that miraculous day that Margaret had said she would marry him. Alone and forsaken. But he wasn't alone. Violet would always be his.

His knock would have woken the dead.

It was still early; Glad was on second shift at the biscuit factory, and she hadn't left for work yet. She answered the door and put her hand to her heart as she saw him; did he look that bad?

'She didn't come,' he said.

Her pale little face flushed and she took his hand almost shyly. 'I'm sorry,' she said. That was Gladys. She was sorry, always, at anything that caused him pain. She really loved him. Tears came to his eyes but he didn't want her to see, so he pulled her into his arms and hugged her. Violet came running out of their room and crowed with delight to see him.

'Papa!' she yelled. She barrelled into his legs and he swept her up with one arm, still holding Gladys tightly with the other.

He kissed Vi's cheek and she threw her little arms around his neck. There was nothing like that feeling.

Gladys leaned her head against his shoulder; her love and acceptance soothed the raw wound of Margaret's rejection.

'You and Vi should move in with me,' he said. 'We'll be a proper family.'

'Yes,' Glad said. She smoothed his hair back and smiled at him. There was a hint of sadness at the back of her eyes, but he concentrated on the smile, mirroring it until the sadness disappeared. 'A proper family.'

1

26 January 1920

'Passport and marriage lines.'

Margaret handed over the small green book and carefully unfolded her marriage lines before laying them on the desk. Excitement bubbled up under her ribs; an hour, maybe less, and she would actually set foot in Australia. And Frank would be there, waiting for her. She wanted to skip from foot to foot, but she tried to school her expression into one of patience. Perhaps some of her anticipation showed, because the Immigration Officer – a nice old man with very clean fingernails – smiled at her.

'Been a while since you've seen him, then?'

'Two years, four months,' Margaret said. 'He was wounded at Passchendaele in 'seventeen and shipped straight back here from Belgium.'

'By golly! That's a time.' He stamped her passport and handed her back the marriage certificate. 'You've got your clearance from the quarantine doctor?' She nodded. 'No need to keep you any longer, then, Mrs Dalton. Welcome to Australia.'

She beamed at him, then made her way to Mrs Murchison, who was travelling with her husband, a sergeant in the Light Horse.

Most of the war brides on the SS *Borda* were travelling with their husbands, and often children too. A year and two months after the war had ended, and already some of these couples had two or even three children. She wished she and Frank had met earlier in the war. A couple of months together before he was sent off to the front hadn't given her nea 'v enough memories of him.

She pushed through the crowds to the handrai. nd stared avidly at Sydney Harbour. So much bigger than she'd expected! Busy with ferries and yachts and what she supposed were fishing boats, all dancing across white-capped waves under the brilliant golden sun. It was hot already, despite the sea breeze. She hugged herself in self-congratulation. She would never be cold again!

Tall golden cliffs guarded the entrance to the Harbour; their ship had been at anchor off the northern headland since just after dawn, when the quarantine doctor had come on board. Most of them had been given a clean bill of health, but two women and three children had been taken off to the Quarantine Station, a long low timber building at the base of the headland.

Thank God she was healthy! She couldn't have borne yet another delay. A year apart from Frank during the war. A year waiting for notification that the Australian Repatriation Committee had a berth for her on a war-bride ship. Three weeks at anchor at Tilbury in that disgusting old scow the *Waimana*. Then the change of ship to the *Borda*. Then the long, exciting but frustrating sea voyage.

Finally, finally, they were here. As soon as the doctor was finished checking the crew, the ship would make its way to the dock. And she would see Frank again.

It was silly to feel butterflies. It wasn't nervousness, just sheer excitement. She had left nerves and fear and grief behind her, together with death and horror and cold grey despair. A new life in a new land. She and Frank, together at last.

The ship was moving so slowly, its little tug boat valiantly pulling through the wide open Harbour, past docks full of ships, steamships and schooners and sailboats, small and large. There were many more sailboats than she would have expected on a weekday.

'Anniversary regatta,' Sergeant Murchison said. He waved a folded newspaper at her – the pilot ship had brought the day's papers on board and they'd rapidly gone the rounds of the men.

A regatta! How nice of them to put on a show for her, she thought, laughing. She turned for a moment to tilt her face up to the sun. She was lucky, because although her skin seemed fair, and freckled easily, it tanned to a honey colour; not exactly like a lady, but better than burning under this blazing southern sky. She looked up only for a moment: she had to turn and watch the Harbour again, all its movement and life and colour.

Margaret felt greedy for every impression, every sight, every sound. She'd imagined this so many times, but she'd got it wrong. She'd forgotten to imagine the sea smell, and the trees – so many, many trees on the headlands and foreshores, all a dull shade of green, almost olive. And the gulls. They didn't mew sweetly like gulls in England. They positively squawked and shrieked as they tussled over scraps the kiddies threw to them.

She laughed aloud. Good for them. Good for everyone and everything who reached out and held onto life. Everyone who

3

looked forward instead of back. That's what she would do, from now on. No more grief or regret. The bad times were over, the dead were buried, and it was time to enjoy life. With Frank.

It felt just right to hear an Army band play 'Waltzing Matilda' as the ship drew into the wharf. Some of the men on board started to sing, and she joined in, her voice rising above theirs. She'd learned that song, and a few others, on the journey. The men had taken it upon themselves to teach their wives how to be 'real Aussies', and they had included her and the three other women travelling alone in the lessons. She knew the difference between New South Wales and Victoria, 'outback' and 'back of beyond', a privy and a dunny. At least the currency was the same, although the Australian money was much prettier than the English.

The dock was full of people waiting, waving, laughing and shouting. She searched the faces of the men – why wouldn't they take off their hats so she could see properly! Frank was tall; but all these Australian men seemed to be tall. There weren't *that* many younger men. Mostly older people and younger – parents, sisters and brothers, she supposed. A man in a flat cap held up a brace of beer bottles, and one of the NCOs further along the rail yelled, 'You bloody beauty, Micko!' Micko made the bottles dance in the air, and everyone laughed in sheer good spirits.

Where was he? For a moment her gaze was caught by a tall man, but he was in uniform; an Army sergeant with a sheaf of paperwork. She kept looking, face after face, none of them Frank's.

She held back once the gangplank was set up. Let the families with babies go first, she told herself, but knew she was hoping that as the crowd thinned she would be able to see better, to find Frank. Setting foot on Australian soil without Frank waiting for her wasn't right. Just wasn't right.

The families left, then the couples; not all of them were greeted by friends or relations. Some of them had hundreds of miles to go still before they were home. Each was checked off a list by the tall sergeant and collected their trunks, caught taxis from the line at the dock gates, and left. The wharf emptied of everyone except the Army personnel. The band began to pack up.

The sergeant checked his list and looked up, straight at her. Nothing for it, then. She had to move. Of course, this man would know. There would be a message for her. How silly she'd been. She walked briskly down the echoing plank and smiled at him as confidently as she could.

He blinked and smiled back; a redheaded man, pleasant to look at despite a tight white scar on one cheek, going as high as the corner of his eye.

'You'll be Mrs Dalton, then?' he asked, checking his list. 'I'm Sergeant McBride.'

'Yes.' She swallowed. 'Have you a message from my husband?'

He shook his head. 'No, sorry. But don't worry. Things happen. It'd be a bad boss who wouldn't give a man the day off to meet his wife, but some bosses are like that. I'm sure he'll turn up.' His voice was reassuring, yet he wouldn't quite meet her eye. 'Best for you to come up to the barracks and I'll check his contact details, send a messenger. He might have had the day wrong.'

He saw her into a taxi and got in after her, settling his long legs with difficulty in the cramped car. 'Victoria Barracks,' he told the driver.

•

Victoria Barracks was surrounded by a wall of the same golden stone as the Harbour headlands, and inside the compound the long Georgian-style buildings were a matching colour.

Troops were drilling on the parade ground in front of the main building, but Sergeant McBride directed the cab up the hill to the left, to a smaller building in a more colonial style, a bit like the government buildings she had seen in Colombo on the journey out, with a verandah along the front.

'Headquarters,' he said as he ushered her into a surprisingly well furnished waiting room. Mahogany table, upholstered chairs. Aspidistras. It smelled of furniture polish. The building blocked the heat, and she shivered with a sudden chill. But that wasn't a goose walking over her grave. No. All she had to do was wait and this competent man would sort things out for her.

'I'll check his records,' McBride said. 'Would you like a cup of tea while you're waiting?'

Margaret didn't know what to say. Tea. Yes, of course she would like tea. She was English. That's what you did in a moment of crisis. You had tea.

'Thank you.'

She was conscious of trying to sound posh, as though that could change the outcome. An old habit; it was certainly true in England that you were treated better by officialdom if you sounded educated – that was why her mother had scraped and saved to send both Margaret and her brother to elocution lessons. During the war, she'd been grateful not to sound like a hick from the Black Country; but when she went back there, when her parents fell ill, it had stamped her as an outsider and made it harder to find work. Who knew how people were supposed to speak in Australia? Any way she spoke would mark her as a real outsider here.

There were typewriters clacking and doors opening and closing, the sound of men's voices, someone shouting orders on the parade ground. The armchairs were deep and looked comfortable, but she didn't want to be comfortable. She paced, still clutching her purse, with its passport and papers tucked safely inside.

A young private – surely only a schoolboy? – brought her a tray of tea, so she sat on a hard chair near the side table. Silver tray, just like on the ship. A silver pot, heavily polished. She was glad the boy had left because her hand shook as she poured and the tea spilled onto the tray, dulling its shine. Panic struck her, unreasoning panic. She grabbed her handkerchief from her purse and mopped it up and then didn't know what to do with the dripping linen. In the end she stuck it into one of the aspidistra pots. It was a good hankie, too.

This was ridiculous. She was overreacting. Sit still, she told herself. Drink your tea.

Sergeant McBride came back and stood for a moment in the doorway, his cap gone, a paper in his hand. His face was grim, set as if for an unpleasant task.

No. No. No more death. Please God, don't let him be dead.

'Frank – is he all right?' she managed to ask.

Anything but dead, please God.

'As far as we know, he's – he's fine.'

Relief flooded her. Yet the sergeant was looking at her with such compassion.

'I checked his file. Frank Dalton, correct? Nineteenth battalion?'

'Yes.' The relief was gone. Something was wrong.

'I'm afraid . . .' He hesitated. 'I'm afraid I have some . . . difficult news.'

He proffered the paper. Enlistment papers. Australian Imperial Force. She saw Frank's name. Yes, that was him. There was a list of questions, and Sergeant McBride pointed to them:

What is your age?   *22 years, 3 months*
What is your occupation?   *Railway blacksmith*
Have you ever been an apprentice? *Yes*

Some details about his apprenticeship. Then –

Have you ever been married?   *Yes.*

Her mind stuttered. Of course he was married – but this was his *enlistment* paper. They hadn't been married then.

Who is your next of kin? *(wife) Gladys Jane Mortimer*
        64 Cavendish Street, Stanmore

Wife. Gladys Jane Mortimer.
Wife.
'But . . .' she said. 'But he signed the form! He signed the form to get me to come out here!' It couldn't be true. Perhaps this Gladys was dead. Dead before they'd ever met. That must be it.

'Yes,' McBride said. He sighed, and rubbed the back of his head. 'They do that.' He paused. 'I've sent a messenger to the address on this form, and another to the address we had for him after he was demobbed. They'll take a little while to get back.'

'She must have died,' Margaret said. She could hear the ridiculous certainty in her voice.

'Mrs Dalton,' he said, and then hesitated again. 'I have to tell you, I see quite a bit of this. It was lonely, being so far away from home, and if the marriage wasn't going well before they left, sometimes the men . . . looked for consolation.'

She didn't believe it. Couldn't.

'But . . . but why sign the request for me to come out here, then?' She clung to that. He'd signed it before he went to the front, to make sure that there could be no hold-up after the war was over, that she could get the first available ship.

'Heat of the moment, optimism that they'll be able to keep it all quiet even after they get home.' McBride shrugged. 'And then sometimes they get home, and the real wife is waiting for them, and . . .'

'He would have told me.' She couldn't imagine it, even now with the weight of McBride's experience against her. Frank couldn't have – *wouldn't have*. He was a good man. She said so. McBride looked at her with compassion and a surprising degree of understanding.

'The ones who do this, they're not villains. They're mostly just – weak. They take the path of least resistance.'

Weak. Was that possible? That Frank had been weak?

The day before their wedding, he'd taken her for a walk along the river. They'd kissed under the bare branches of an elm, and then he'd held her hands.

'Margaret, I have to tell you – I haven't been a saint.' He'd been sheepish, ashamed. She'd laughed. She was a working-class girl, not some sheltered debutante.

'You don't expect men to have been saints,' she said. 'But you'd better toe the line from here on in.'

'You betcha! I know when I'm well off.' He had kissed her again and she had never been so happy.

Not a saint. That covered a lot of possibilities, but surely not *this*?

•

Two hours later, *this* was looking certain.

The messenger from Frank's address was told that he had moved out without leaving a forwarding address.

The messenger from Gladys Mortimer's address said that she no longer lived there. That she'd moved back in with her fella.

Most damning of all was a copy of Frank's will, which he'd lodged with the battalion, as many soldiers had. A handwritten scrawl, it left everything he had to his daughter, Violet. The will was dated five weeks after his marriage to Margaret. The week after he'd gone to the front. He had known he had a daughter. When they got married, he had known and he had chosen to bequeath everything to her.

Margaret sat, hunched over as though recovering from a kick to the stomach. She couldn't cry. Mostly she felt dazed. It reminded her of the week after her parents died, when she had walked through the house randomly picking things up and putting them down again. Nothing had seemed to fit, to belong, even the mantelpiece clock, which had sat there her entire life.

Now she was the thing that didn't fit.

'I'm sorry,' Sergeant McBride said.

'It still doesn't make any sense to me,' she said. 'I understand why he might have married me – but why wouldn't he have told me the truth before I came out here? It – it's *bizarre.*'

'Yes,' he said. 'It is. But you're the third woman it's happened to in the past four months. And there've been six more just abandoned – the men don't turn up at the ship, and if we can track them down, they've joined up with some other woman, or they've gone upcountry droving, or they've dived into a bottle when they got demobbed and never climbed out again.'

'Will . . . will you try to track Frank down?'

'I suppose we could try the railways, see if he's gone back to work for them. Do you want us to?'

She thought about it. Did she want to confront him, see him shuffle and lie and look ashamed? Or worse, watch him brazen it out and laugh at her for being gullible? The very thought of it made her want to vomit.

'No,' she said. Panic climbed up and caught her around the throat. Alone in a foreign country. What was she to *do*?

Sergeant McBride's voice was gently reassuring. 'The Army has a house; a hostel. I'll take you there.'

She let him lead her to a taxi. It was a short trip, through winding streets full of two-storey terraced houses until they stopped at a larger house and the sergeant paid the driver. At least this place had a front garden and a wall around it, and was well maintained. White cane chairs were set out on the front porch.

'What is this place?'

'A hostel for . . . well, for women whose husbands don't turn up at the wharf.'

She looked around. Across the street were more terraced houses. Different from English terraces; these each had a balcony on the upper storey. She saw women sitting there, in kimonos or housecoats, legs apart and elbows on knees, faces rouged and powdered. A couple of them called out to the men who walked past below. Not a salubrious area, by the looks of it. Why did the Army put women here? Damaged goods, she thought. They think we're damaged goods.

'Deceived wives,' she said, unwilling to step through the gate and brand herself one of them.

'Not all. Sometimes the men have died. We got a lot of that in early 'nineteen with the Spanish Flu. And sometimes the bastards just abandon them.' He didn't apologise for his language and she didn't blame him.

'And the women stay here?'

'Until we can organise a passage home for them.'

Her attention caught, she stared up at him in alarm. 'Home? Do I have to go back to England?'

He studied her silently. 'Mostly they want to.'

'Not me. Not for anything.' It was the first real feeling she'd had since she saw that will. Desperation. Frank couldn't take this too. She wouldn't let him steal Australia away from her. Images of grey, rainy, grimy streets filled her head. Her parents' faces as she pulled the shrouds over them. The names on the roll of honour at their church: almost all the boys she had gone to school with, picked out in gold. Death and horror, cold and dreariness; she had no good memories of England to draw her back.

For the first time, Sergeant McBride smiled warmly, a genuine, amused, admiring smile. 'Don't worry,' he said. 'Australia's not going to turf you out if you don't want to go. We need girls like you.'

•

The hostel was run by a middle-aged, organising woman, Mrs Pritchard.

'Come on in, now. All your things are here.'

Margaret followed her into a small room, where her trunk sat at the foot of the single bed.

She shot back out of the room and confronted Sergeant McBride.

'You had them bring my trunk straight here from the ship.' It hadn't even occurred to her to wonder where it was.

He looked abashed, folding his cap in his hand and fiddling with it.

'Mostly, if they haven't sent a message, and they're not there at the wharf, the women end up here.'

Humiliation burned through her; she could feel herself blushing furiously, and hated him suddenly for being the witness to it.

'Men!' Mrs Pritchard sniffed. 'Don't you worry about any of that, now. Come in and wash your face before lunch.'

'I'll check back tomorrow,' McBride said. There was too much understanding in his eyes, as though he'd seen other women react as she had.

Her emotions were up and down, all over the place. Just as suddenly, she was sorry she'd hated him. He'd been kind.

'Thank you,' she said.

He nodded and left.

'Now,' Mrs Pritchard said. 'What do we call you?'

'Margaret.' She didn't want to think about what her name really was, now. Margaret Adams, she supposed, like it had always been, but she had no documents in that name. Her passport said Margaret Dalton. Would she have to apply for a new one? She imagined explaining to someone at the British Consulate why she had to revert to her maiden name and wanted again to vomit. Bigamy. Ugly word.

'Go and wash your face,' Mrs Pritchard said again. Her tone was firm, as though she spoke to a child. 'It'll all sort itself out.'

Margaret sat on the side of the narrow bed and stared at the whitewashed wall. She unpinned her hat and laid it on the bedside table, and then finally dragged off her gloves and threw them there too.

Her wedding band mocked her. She tugged it but her hands were swollen in the heat and it stuck on her knuckle. The fight with the inanimate object was the last straw, and she began to sob. She fell sideways onto the bed and curled up like a baby, like a hedgehog, burrowing into herself as though she could shut the entire world away if only she kept on crying.

2

Perhaps she fell asleep; it was almost dark when Mrs Pritchard tapped on her door, and a wind was howling and battering at the windows.

'Time to eat!'

It struck her that she had missed her first day in Australia – she had looked forward to it so much, and Frank had stolen it from her. As, she realised, he had stolen her virginity, her innocence. Did that make her a fallen woman? She'd lain with a man who turned out not to be her husband, after all. She rinsed her mouth with water from the bedside jug, but it didn't take away the bad taste.

The dining room was utilitarian. It reminded Margaret of the railway restaurant at Reading Station and smelled of boiled cabbage and fresh bread. The long pine table was polished and at one end sat two embroidered placemats near a bread board and some steaming baking dishes. Mrs Pritchard sat at the head of the table and beckoned Margaret to the seat on her left.

'Sit yourself down and tuck in.'

Margaret sat and stared at the embroidery on her placemat: wattle, she thought it was. Bright yellow and green, almost shockingly vivid. A plate appeared in front of her. Grilled fish, peas, potatoes, carrots. A wedge of lemon – a whole wedge, not a slice, like she would have had at home. She picked up her fork and ate without thinking. The fish was delicious, but different. Not cod. They didn't eat cod here, did they? It seemed strange to her that she might never eat cod again. Suddenly it hit her, how far away from home she was. Her empty fork stopped in mid air.

As though her stillness were a signal, Mrs Pritchard started to talk. 'Just as well you came in early this morning. We had a real southerly buster come through an hour or so ago. Pity the poor sailors in that regatta they were having.'

'Southerly buster?'

'It's the wind we get in summer. You'll learn. Here, have some bread.'

The bread was fresh and white, but Margaret laid it aside on her plate. The smell made her feel a little hungry, at least.

'You're my last, you know. The *Borda* was the last war-bride ship. Any that are left will have to make their own way. It's like the war's finally over. I've had to find myself a proper job.' She said it with a mix of satisfaction and nostalgia; a mix Margaret had heard many times before, at the end of the war.

Job. Margaret would have to get a job. The fork moved again, onto her plate, and she swallowed.

She looked up to find Mrs Pritchard regarding her with a shrewd eye.

'They're all bastards, love,' she said. 'Better off without any man. Sooner you look for a job for yourself the better. Got any money?'

'A bit.' She'd saved – oh, how she'd saved – in anticipation of making a home with Frank. She thought about the sheets and the tablecloths folded so neatly in the bottom of her trunk. An odd glory box. They seemed pathetic, now. 'What a fool I've been!'

'Yerse,' Mrs Pritchard said. 'Young women *are* mostly fools where men are concerned.'

'I trusted him.' That was the worst. That she could have been so *wrong* about him. So deluded, so deceived. Idiot. She was a stupid, trusting idiot.

'You'll know better next time, then,' Mrs Pritchard said without a shred of sympathy. She laid down her fork and knife and observed Margaret with a detached air. 'I've seen a few come and go here. Most of them are too soft. Ripe for being taken advantage of.'

Margaret looked at her properly for the first time. Mrs Pritchard's face was full of scorn. A face that had seen too many women betrayed.

'You mean I was gullible.'

'I call it as I see it,' Mrs Pritchard said. 'Up to you what you do next. Now, eat your tea before it gets cold. Nothing worse than cold fish.'

Her matter-of-fact cynicism was surprisingly bracing. Up to her. Margaret considered a life that was entirely under her own control, as it never had been before. It was terrifying. She had seen poverty and desperation up close in her childhood, and she never wanted to see it again. She could feel that fine tremble start again under her breastbone, and forced herself to take a deep breath. On the other hand, there was no one depending on her; no one for her to look after, or to take orders from.

Single again. No, not again, because she'd never really been married. Single still.

She ate, helped clear the table, went to collect her towel. She bathed – at least the house had a real bathroom, with a wood-chip heater – and went back to her room and dressed, with deliberate irony, in the frothy lace-and-cotton nightgown she had bought for her reunion with Frank.

All she had in the world was in that trunk. He might have tricked her and lied to her and deceived her, but if she let him spoil the little she had left she was even more of a fool than he'd taken her for.

She had pinned such hopes on him. On the move to Australia. A way of leaving grief behind her, of running away, running *to* a better life. One free from grief, from care. A child's dream, maybe, and she'd been roughly awakened from it. Because here she was, with a different kind of grief and a whole new lot of cares, including how to support herself and simply survive in this new land. She had to find a way to put her shoulders back, keep her head up and act as though she was fine, as though she could cope with anything. Her mother hadn't raised cowards.

The worst was that she had *believed* in him so. How could she ever trust another human being again? Trust her own judgement? Mrs Pritchard was right. She'd been gullible, tricked by a warm smile and nice brown eyes. No. Forget him. She would wear her lovely nighties and use those embroidered tablecloths and be damned to him. But it was a hollow kind of defiance, a thin shell over pain and humiliation.

'Never mind,' she said out loud, to make herself believe it. 'It will get thicker over time. Like a pearl.'

She clung to that idea. Her name, Margaret, meant 'pearl'. Frank would be the small irritant that made her create a pearl of a new life.

And she would never trust another man as long as she lived.

•

The next day Margaret ventured out to a corner shop to buy a newspaper. How strange the products were: Arnott's biscuits instead of McVitie's, Omo soap instead of Lever's, the *Sydney Morning Herald* instead of the *Reading Times*. It gave her a surprising spurt of relief to see a yellow Keen's Mustard tin on the shelf.

She had changed some money on the ship and carefully counted out a penny-ha'penny for the newspaper. The man behind the till had one sleeve of his shirt pinned up; a veteran, no doubt. He was incurious about her, his attention on two of the 'young ladies' who had followed her in and were chatting amiably about 'trade' being good thanks to the fine weather.

She'd been brought up to look down on prostitutes, but there had been a time when she'd feared she might have to turn to that herself. She'd gone home to nurse her parents. After their deaths, the station-master at Reading had told her that her job had been given to a returned soldier. That moment of panic, of not knowing where her next meal might come from, had scalded all judgement out of her.

Back at the hostel, she and Mrs Pritchard spread the paper out on the dining table and went over the Positions Vacant ads. Margaret was qualified as a clerk and a typiste; but most of the jobs for clerks specified a man, and the ones for typistes also wanted shorthand, which she didn't know. She could work a switchboard, but there were no vacancies for telephonists.

'Have to apply at the GPO for that,' Mrs Pritchard said sagely. 'General Post Office, in Martin Place.'

The rest of the jobs that were open to women, depressingly, seemed only available to juniors. Girls were in demand, but not women.

In the end, there were only three suitable.

WANTED, experienced LADY CLERK, competent to do ledger work, salary 47/6 week. Permanent position. State age and qualifications.
3024, Herald Office, Pitt-street

WANTED, TYPISTE, with knowledge of Filing Systems. Good position for competent young lady. Salary to commence £3 per week. Apply, with copies of references, to BOX 2109, G.P.O.

WANTED, Typiste good at figures. Apply by letter to DAVIDS, BERTRAM and CO, Auctioneers, 44c Belgrave-street, Manly.

'The first two are in the city,' Mrs Pritchard said. 'T'other's away to buggery.'

'Manly?'

'Other side of the Harbour, out to North Head,' she said, as if that were halfway to England. 'Have to get a ferry and then a tram. Take you all day.'

'Well, I can't pick and choose.' Margaret looked at the advertisements. Three pounds didn't seem like much, but it did say 'to commence'. Perhaps she would get more with time. But there was another, more immediate, problem.

'Mrs Pritchard, I don't suppose you have a typewriter?'

'I don't,' she said. 'But the Army does.'

•

Sure enough, an hour later an Army wagon rolled up to the front and Sergeant McBride got down carrying a typewriter.

He brought it into the dining room and set it down carefully on the felt mat Mrs Pritchard had placed at the end of the table.

'There you go,' he said. 'The Colonel's away for a month, inspecting the barracks up in Brisbane. Have to have it back by Sunday, though. I'm getting demobbed on the Monday.'

'Thank you ever so much,' Margaret said. Today she was conscious of how big Sergeant McBride was – not just tall but wide across the shoulders.

'Demobbed?' Mrs Pritchard asked. 'Where are you off to, then?'

'I've got a job over in Berry's Bay,' he said. Now he had his hands free, he pulled his cap off and ran a hand over his short-cropped hair. 'Sawmill. I'm to be leading hand.' He made a face. 'Used to be the foreman at my old place, but beggars can't be choosers. Lucky to have a job at all.'

'Your old boss doesn't want you back?'

He shrugged, seeming a little uncomfortable. 'Best not to look back.'

A good attitude. Margaret thought that perhaps he was like her, and had too many bad memories. Maybe people he'd worked with were dead, like her friends at home.

'Thing is, Mrs Pritchard,' he continued, and now he looked apologetic, 'I've had orders to close this place down in a week.'

'Oh, I've seen that coming, don't you worry. Got myself a nice little place being housekeeper to a man widowed by the flu. Over at Rose Bay. Quite posh. I start in two weeks' time, and I'll take a holiday with my cousin in Young before that. But what about Margaret?'

He looked at her, his eyes assessing.

'I'll be all right—' she began, at the same time he said, 'Well—'

They both stopped and smiled and waved each other on, but it was he who spoke.

'I've organised with the Army for Mrs . . . for Margaret to be paid the war widow's pension for two months while she finds her feet, in lieu of providing accommodation here,' he said. 'Now, I've found myself a place in a nice boarding house over at North Sydney. There's another room available there, and I thought it might interest Margaret?'

'That's very kind of you,' Margaret said. Relief warred with a kind of annoyance at being so patently 'managed'.

Mrs Pritchard had fallen silent, her lips pursed. Then she nodded. 'Well, it might be all right. Rent'll be cheaper over there, and if you get the job in Manly it's only a tram ride away.'

'I'm off duty at four,' Sergeant McBride offered. 'I could take you over there, to have a look, if you like.'

She felt as though she were being swept along by a windstorm, as though the world were disposing of her as it saw fit, without her having any say in it. But it was all so sensible. It would be silly to refuse just because it was someone else's idea. She had to live somewhere.

'Thank you,' she said. She would visit the boarding house, once she had spent an afternoon practising her typing. She was pretty rusty after her time at sea, but she had to brush up quickly before she typed out her job applications.

He grinned, his face changing oddly, the scar pulling his mouth to the side.

'Don't you worry, Margaret,' he said, and it was a shock to hear her name in his mouth in such a warm tone. 'We won't let you down.'

•

All very well to say, she thought as she waited for him to pick her up. But what did she know of him? Far less than she'd known about Frank, and look where that had led her. She'd had enough experience with digs in England to be able to assess this place for herself. She would examine this boarding house with a fine-toothed comb and make her own judgement. Her first decision in this new life.

She'd half expected a taxi or an Army car, but he came walking down the street, cap on his head, hands in his pockets, at ease with the world, whistling. The girls on the balconies called out to him but he ignored the invitations.

He smiled when he saw her sitting on the porch and she took a deep breath and went to meet him, fixing her straw hat on her head with a hat pin.

'Ready? Good girl. Come on, then. The tram stop is down this way.'

She fell in with him on the footpath and they walked in silence down to a wide road, busy with cars and trams.

'William Street,' he said. 'We can get a tram into Circular Quay from here, and then get a ferry to Milson's Point and another tram up to near the house. Or we can walk from the ferry.'

It was another hot day, but overcast with high silver clouds she couldn't take seriously. They didn't look quite real. She was beginning to feel warm, and she relished it. She'd never been really warm in England. As though the winter cold had got so far into her bones that they could never unfreeze. On the ship, coming through the tropics, she had felt that ice start to melt, drop by drop. If she stayed here long enough, she might get warm right through to the marrow. She wished she could walk bareheaded, as some of the 'ladies' in the area did, to let the heat bake into her skull and her neck.

The tram came, and Sergeant McBride tried to pay for her when the conductor came around, but she forestalled him, though she made a hash of it and gave the man far too much money. She had to take the change in pennies, and it weighed her purse down terribly.

'Save those,' McBride advised. 'The house has gas heaters in each room, but you've got to put your penny in.'

'Heaters? Why would you need heaters here?' she laughed.

'It gets plenty cold enough in winter. No snow, but a sharp wind, straight off the Antarctic.'

As long as there was no snow, she wouldn't need pennies for the heater.

Despite still feeling as though she were caught in some odd dream, Margaret studied the city with great interest as they went through it, stopping every block or so to let passengers off or on. People moved differently here. It wasn't just that they were dressed more lightly – men were still in suits, after all, and women in proper dresses or blouses and skirts, even if there was more cotton and less wool in their frocks. It was the way they walked. Head up, looking life in the eye.

She thought of the evenings at home in winter, when the men from the factories and the mines trudged back to their houses, heads down against the wind, feet careful on the icy road. Even in summer, those heads didn't lift much; perhaps the relentless toil had its effect. Or the centuries of pulling the forelock.

That was the thing. When she was at home, she could tell, just by the way they walked, who was a toff. A mill master, a mine owner. They walked as if they owned the earth.

Everyone walked like that here, as if they owned the earth. But without that extra attitude the bosses had, as if everyone else had better get out of the way, quick smart.

She raised her own chin, practising. Look life in the eyes, she thought.

As she looked up, she caught Sergeant McBride's gaze, and he smiled at her. A blush started in her cheeks. She hadn't been posturing to attract his attention, and she was mortified that she had. Still, his eyes were filled with warm approval, which just made her blush more deeply. As if he understood her confusion, he began to talk.

'It's going to take some time to get your papers amended,' he said. 'I think you're better off introducing yourself to our landlady as Mrs Dalton.'

'But—'

'A widow,' he added.

'I can't pass myself off as a war widow!' she said. That would be a truly shocking lie. An insult to all those women who *had* lost their loved ones to King and Crown and duty.

'No,' he allowed. 'But your husband – I mean, Private Dalton – could have died after the war, but before you arrived here. As I said, we had a number of cases like that, with the Spanish Flu.'

Margaret thought about it, and thought hard. It was repugnant to her. To lie. Especially about something as sacred as marriage. To deceive and keep deceiving, because once she'd told that lie she'd have to keep telling it. On the other hand, all her references were in the name of Margaret Dalton.

'I'll never get a job without references,' she said. 'And they're all in . . . I'm Margaret Dalton in all of them.'

'There's no reason you should suffer because Frank Dalton is a blackguard,' McBride said. '*And* it's harder in the world for a single lady. No doubt about that.'

No doubt at all. As a widow, she'd be respectable. And enjoy a lot more personal freedom than would an unmarried girl.

Her maiden name, or a name she didn't have the right to claim? But how could she pretend to be a – a maiden? That was far behind her. A tremor shook her, a mixture of shame and grief and horror. What had *happened* to her? How did she get to be this deceived, hoodwinked fool of a woman?

Damn Frank to hell.

'Yes,' she said, trying to keep her voice steady. 'Mrs Dalton. You're right. That's the most sensible thing.'

Hesitantly, he patted her hand. 'It'll be all right.'

Tears sprang to her eyes and she blinked them back as the tram lurched to a halt and the conductor cried out, 'Cir – cu – larrrrr Quay! All out, all change, please!'

3

The ferries were two-storey single-funnel boats, seeming very small and slight after the bulk of the SS *Borda*. But as they pulled out onto the Harbour, heading straight across for the point of land opposite the Quay, Margaret felt the same light-heartedness she had felt on the boat.

Not quite the same. This was a small lift of the heart, not the fizzing happiness she had felt then. But there was something about the salt wind in her face, the dance of the waves, the great arch of blue sky, which spoke to hope. To the new start she had planned. The ghosts of the past might be with her always, and Frank's betrayal might corrode her present, but she wouldn't allow them or him to control her future.

'That's Milson's Point,' Sergeant McBride said, pointing to the approaching ferry wharf, a large structure with a rounded roof. She could see a tram travelling towards it, down the steep hill. 'And up the hill is North Sydney. My job . . .' he pointed to the left of the wharf, 'is in the second bay along from Milson's Point. Berry's Bay.'

All along the foreshore were docks and narrow piers, lined with every kind of boat imaginable, and men loading and unloading, carrying goods into the timber buildings behind, or working directly on the boats themselves. Painting them, scraping off the barnacles, doing arcane things to the rigging. It reminded her of reading Jack London's *The Sea-Wolf* as a girl, where sailors were always springing for the rigging, or trying to climb to the cross-trees.

She had a book in her purse now, a small edition of Joan Conquest's *Desert Love*. She had swapped *The Sheik* for it with one of the women on the *Borda*, and was liking it much better. It was just as exotic, but the main character was one she could admire. Margaret smiled ruefully. She didn't need to read about exotic locations and exciting adventures anymore. She was living one! She wondered what Joan Conquest would make of her current predicament. Probably use it to show that the heroine was undauntable. Pity she felt so daunted.

She was surprised by the size of the ferry terminal. It was a big arch of glass and steel, rather like one of the London railway stations, complete with clock tower. The ferry drew right in underneath it to dock and they waited for the gangplank, then made their way into what she now realised was not a ferry terminal, but a tram interchange.

'Walk or tram?' Sergeant McBride asked.

'Oh, walk, I think.' Time to get her land legs back.

The hill ahead was covered with cottages and two-storey houses, low enough to the ground that the shape of the land beneath was clear. It was noisy; the tram pulled past them with a clatter and creak that echoed the horses' hooves on the road, the creaking of cart wheels.

It was a steep climb and she had no breath to talk, which was just as well, because she didn't know what to say.

An odd situation, to say the least. Sergeant McBride kept his gaze on the footpath but as they turned into Lavender Street, he spoke.

'Mrs Burns is a bit of a character but she's the right sort.'

What did that mean? Margaret thought, a frisson of apprehension sliding through her. After Mrs Pritchard's scorn, she wasn't sure she could cope with a 'character' for a landlady. Her last landlady had been a tiny arthritic Welshwoman who only came out of her overheated room to grab the rent for her bedsit with gnarled hands. Dismay crept into Margaret, an image of sitting alone in her room night after night sending a chill across her shoulders.

She could picture it too clearly: no job, no money, no friends and no way of meeting people. Perhaps she'd been a fool to turn down that offer of a berth home. She was pathetically grateful that Sergeant McBride, at least, would be a familiar face at this new lodging.

They turned up a side street and Sergeant McBride pointed to the house on the next corner.

It was big, a two-storey brick building, each level boasting a deep verandah and separated from the other by dark green shingles. The front door – solid, with stained glass – was reached through an imposing brick archway, and the rooms on either side had French doors that opened onto the bottom verandah.

Next to the door was a brass plate: The High House. Looking back down the road, Margaret realised why – the hillside stretched steeply away until it came to the Harbour. The air was full of the smell of the sea. You could sit on this verandah and just watch the boats go by.

Sergeant McBride twirled a little handle set into the door, and a bell trilled. The door opened almost immediately, to reveal a heavyset woman of fifty or so, dressed in a plain wrap-around pinafore, the blue perfectly matching the floral design of the print frock beneath. Her tight brown plaits were secured across her head and she looked like she didn't suffer fools gladly. But as soon as she saw the sergeant, she broke into a welcoming smile that lit her face and showed a deep kindliness.

'Tom!' she said. 'Come on in.' She cast a look at Margaret as she moved back to let them enter, and though it was quick, Margaret felt thoroughly inspected nonetheless.

'This is Mrs Dalton,' Sergeant McBride said. 'Her husband didn't make it through the flu, but it was too late to let her know before she left England.'

As simple as that. The lie on which her new life would be built.

Mrs Burns looked her up and down again, and sniffed.

'Turn sideways and you wouldn't see ya,' she said in a broad Australian drawl. 'Skin and bones. Didn't they feed you in England?'

Her tone was abrasive but her eyes were kind, and she led them through a hall to the parlour on the left of the door quite readily.

Margaret had been expecting something like Mrs Pritchard's house – bare and functional, as most boarding houses were. But this house hadn't been furnished by the Army. It was pure Art Nouveau. She had been to a lecture once, at the Reading Women's Institute. The speaker had used magic lantern slides, and here was that furniture, those vases and decorations, in the flesh.

Tall Tiffany lamps stood at either end of long peacock-blue sofas with wooden arms and backs; the mantelpiece was carved cedar in flowing depictions of lilies growing around an oval mirror; even the windows had stained-glass panels showing roses and lilies. There was a side table in the bay window with a big gramophone on it, the brass horn shining with polish, and a telephone right next to it. A piano on the opposite wall, pleated green silk behind its carved screens. Every surface was covered in . . . Margaret tried to think of the word. Not knick-knacks . . . object art. It was *sumptuous*!

Any thought of 'inspecting' the place went out the window.

'Nice, isn't it?' Mrs Burns said with satisfaction. 'Mrs Shelley – I was her housekeeper here – left it all to me, lock, stock and barrel. "Just look after it, Daisy," she said, "for I've no kith nor kin to call my own."'

'It's beautiful,' Margaret said.

Mrs Burns stooped to pick a fleck of lint from the carpet – a Chinese rug, with pile so thick it cast a shadow at its edge onto the wooden floor.

'That's why I won't have just anyone staying,' she added. 'But if Sergeant Tom here thinks you're all right, you'll do me.'

Margaret was highly doubtful that she could afford this kind of luxury. She cast a wary glance at Sergeant McBride, which Mrs Burns interpreted with no trouble.

'Don't you worry about money. I was hard up once, before Mrs Shelley took me in as housekeeper, and I don't charge above the going rate. But I have to be careful, see? I have to protect what she left me.'

'Of course,' Margaret said. She smiled, suddenly. 'It'll be like living in a palace.'

Mrs Burns looked round complacently, and nodded. 'Isn't it? Just like a palace.' She became businesslike. 'Two pound ten a week bed and board. Breakfast at seven. Dinner at six-thirty and if you're not here, your loss, there's no leftovers. Find your own lunch. Sheets once a fortnight, towels once a week, and you do your own—' She glanced at the sergeant, and lowered her voice. 'Your own *special* washing. I'll give you a bucket.' She took a breath. 'No overnight guests, male *or* female. No inviting guests home for a meal unless you've cleared it with me first. There's a roster for the bathroom. Men shave in their rooms, so it's not so bad.'

Margaret nodded. She could feel the routine of the place settling on her comfortingly. She might not know who she was or where she was going, but she could be certain of that clean towel at the end of the week. The churning in her stomach began to settle down. Perhaps it would be all right.

'Now, come and have a Captain Cook at your room,' Mrs Burns said and stumped out the door and up the stairs. They followed meekly. Captain Cook, Margaret thought. What can that mean?

'First on the left, that's mine. I like my zeds, so no loud music after ten o'clock. Other side is our Jane. And here's yours, Sergeant.' She flung open the third door, a room at the back of the house, past the bathroom, which faced the hill behind. The sergeant stuck his head in and whistled.

'Bonzer, Mrs Burns.'

'Burnsie'll do from you, my lad.' She turned to Margaret. 'You're next to Janie.'

Margaret opened the door Mrs Burns indicated. Sunlight streamed in through a big window that looked out over rooftops to the Harbour. She made straight for the window without even glancing at the rest of the room.

Past the slate roofs she could see a small patch of blue where ferries chugged along, and trees along the foreshore, green, waving in the breeze off the water. The window was open, its lace inner curtains pushed back so that the breeze could cool the room, bringing with it the salt of the open sea. There was a large tree just outside, so she looked at the view over a carpet of dark green.

Smiling, she turned back to Mrs Burns. 'Oh, it's wonderful!'

'Haven't even had a gecko at it yet,' she grumbled, but she was smiling. 'This used to be my room. I loved that view, and the angophora tree.'

The room wasn't as grand as downstairs, but it was still the nicest bedroom Margaret had ever been in. It had a lovely Turkish rug in rich colours of red and blue, and a big bed – three-quarters size, with a white coverlet.

Tears came to her eyes. She didn't deserve this. Not a place as nice as this. She remembered her own cherished bedroom in her parents' house. She'd been lucky to have a piece of painted canvas on the floor, and a couple of faded blankets. Three hooks to hang her dresses on, a small tin chest for everything else. This room . . . there was a washstand with a marble top, a chest of drawers, a wardrobe with an oval mirror carved in a way similar to the mantelpiece, all lilies twining upwards. The whole place smelled of beeswax and the sea.

'I'm just a foundry-worker's daughter,' she said to Mrs Burns, gesturing helplessly.

'And I'm a drover's wife!' Mrs Burns declared.

Sergeant McBride leaned against the doorframe and grinned. 'Welcome to Australia!' he said.

4

Getting her trunk across the Harbour the next afternoon was easier than she had thought. Sergeant McBride and a friend of his called, apparently, Chilla, simply carried it on board the ferry. She insisted on paying for a taxi to take it up that long hill, though, and they laughingly agreed. But they wouldn't take any thanks after they'd deposited it in her room, not even enough money for a beer to cool them down.

'Can't take a shout from a sheila!' Chilla said, shocked. She had no idea what a 'shout' was, but she got the general idea. Sergeant McBride just grinned at her.

'Oh, I almost forgot,' he said. 'The Army will send your money orders here for your widow's allowance.'

She felt guilty about that, but it wasn't as though she had deceived the Army – they knew the truth.

She went with them down to the door and watched as they walked to the gate. Sergeant McBride said a word to his friend there, and came back.

'I just wanted to tell you . . .' He seemed uncomfortable. More bad news? Her stomach twisted in anticipation. 'I had the local police make more enquiries at the address Dalton gave us. One of the other boarders there said . . .' He looked away, briefly, unable to face her. 'Dalton got the letter saying you were coming, and he cleared off the next day. Didn't leave a forwarding address.'

Cold settled on her, moving down her body. 'So, he didn't want to face me?'

'Seems like it,' McBride said. 'I'm sorry. Well. I'll see you Monday.'

She went back upstairs and closed the door behind her, safely alone in her room. She hadn't realised that part of her had been hoping there'd been a mistake, some mix-up that would be resolved in a flurry of relieved laughter. No mistake. He didn't have the guts to face her; he'd run away rather than look her in the eye. What a coward. That cut across the love she'd felt for him like nothing else had. A shirker.

She wondered what had happened to his wife and child, if he was living in a boarding house. He'd probably abandoned them, too. She felt a flicker of pity for that unknown woman.

It took her only a few minutes to lay everything in the drawers. And then there was nothing to do but look out the window and wait for a reply to the job applications she had posted that morning, complete with her new address and telephone number. Mrs Shelley must have been really well off, to have had a telephone.

She wandered downstairs and back to the kitchen. Here was the clean functionality she'd expected, but it was still a peach of a kitchen. It stretched the width of the house, with a scullery to the left. Two dressers on either side of the door she had entered were full of crockery. Willow pattern in one, plain blue-and-white stripes in the other. There was a large porcelain sink and a draining board, underneath which were pots and pans on open shelves. Pantry cupboards to the right of the sink. And in the middle, a scrubbed-white pine table. Mrs Burns was busy at a big range, feeding the firebox with wood and adjusting the damper.

'Scones'll be ready in a jiff, dearie,' Mrs Burns said. That was the smell. Scones. It reminded Margaret of the bakery she had worked at after her parents died and her old job at Reading Station had been given to a returned soldier. It had been a big concern, for a family business, and she had been the general office manager, in charge of everything from ordering the flour to paying the wages to manning the till when the shop got busy. A bustling life, dreaming of Frank and of Sydney, and surrounded by the smells of yeast and slightly soured milk. She hadn't been happy there, but nothing could have made her happy in those months. Her brother's death on the Somme, followed so closely by both her parents from flu, had carved out of her any ability to feel normal. Every so often she'd been knocked sideways by a wave of grief, but mostly she'd felt numb. Distanced from the world, like looking through a piece of gauze – she knew that the colours and movements she glimpsed were real for the people outside, but for her it had been misted over.

She had gone about her business because she had to, because she could look forward to being reunited with Frank and a new life in Australia. Night after night she'd put herself to sleep with plans and dreams for the two of them, together once more, here in Sydney. Night after night she'd dreamed of golden sun and love and laughter. That was all that had got her through the bad times, the only times she'd felt alive.

She put the memories of those dreams aside. This was here and now, and she had to get on with things.

'I don't usually make afternoon tea,' Mrs Burns said, setting the table with swift efficiency. Margaret tried to help, but she was too late; it was all done: three cups and saucers in the blue-and-white stripe, three bread-and-butter plates, milk and sugar, knives, jam and butter. One large plate, empty. Mrs Burns regarded it all with satisfaction.

'I do like everything to match,' she said. 'Put your sit-me-down on that chair and tell me all about yourself.'

The interrogation. She'd known it was coming. Margaret sat down and clasped her hands on the table. Ready.

'So . . .' Mrs Burns prompted.

Margaret put on her best voice. 'I'm from West Bromwich. That's in the Midlands, but during the war I worked at Reading Station. That's where I met Frank.'

The first time she'd said his name since she'd realised the depth of his betrayal.

'He was an Aussie?' Mrs Burns took the scones, golden brown and fluffy, out of the oven and slid them onto the waiting plate. 'Help yourself, love.'

'Yes. With the nineteenth battalion. He was a railway blacksmith before the war, and he was working on the troop trains, repairing the couplings, that sort of thing. I worked in the scheduling office.'

It was easier than she'd thought it would be. It was as though she were telling someone else's story. As though this Margaret and Frank were two different people; people far away from the here and now. Mrs Burns nodded, and Margaret wondered: if she told the truth, would Mrs Burns look at her with the same scorn that Mrs Pritchard hadn't bothered to hide? Perhaps a lie *was* better.

'And you got married over there?'

'A month before he was transferred to the front.' She looked down, still upset by that moment, that memory of saying goodbye, and then of receiving the dreaded pink telegram. 'He was wounded in a big push, and they took him to a hospital in Belgium, then shipped him home from there.'

'Badly wounded?'

'A shoulder wound. They said it would take a long time to heal, but he was all right eventually. By that time the war was over.'

'So, you haven't seen him since a month after you were married?'

'October of nineteen seventeen,' Margaret confirmed.

'Godstrewth! You poor little blighter, excuse my French. Only a month, and now he's dead!'

Looking at it from that point of view, it was a sad story. So, it was all right to look sad, to look disappointed and betrayed – by fate, if not by Frank. With some thankfulness, Margaret let tears rise to her eyes.

'I haven't even got my blacks,' she said, realising it for the first time. She'd bought a black skirt and jacket in England after her brother had been killed on the Somme, but they were far too heavy to wear in this heat. But she'd have to do the right thing. Although rules about mourning for other family members had loosened during the war, rules for widows were still strict. A year in black, and a host of social expectations to follow about what she could do and not do during that year. It was going to cost a lot to fit herself out as a widow.

'Oh, I can sort you out there,' Mrs Burns said cheerfully. Margaret blinked. 'Mrs Shelley, she was a widow, and so genteel. So fashionable. I reckon we can put something together out of what she left. Doesn't go near me – I'd need two of everything to cover me up! But you're the same shape, near as, and she did have the loveliest clothes.'

Margaret had visions of herself arrayed in some Victorian lady's widow's weeds, and hesitated. She was no seamstress, to remake them to be more modern.

'Wasn't Mrs Shelley a . . . an older woman?'

'Lord no!' Mrs Burns laughed, a big belly laugh. The kettle began to whistle, and she got up to make the tea. 'She was only a few years older than you. Not twenty-six when she died. Lost her man at Passchendaele. Orphan she was, but lovely brought up. This was her parents' house before it was hers. That was the thing about the Spanish Flu – it took the young and left the old biddies like me.'

'My parents . . .' Margaret said, with difficulty.

'My, you have been in the wars, haven't you?' Mrs Burns said with ready sympathy. 'Never you mind. It's all behind you now. Have a scone.'

She poured tea and Margaret milked and sugared it, marvelling at how much sugar there was in that one bowl. No rationing here! The first sip was like a blessing, the aroma fresh and comforting. She took a bite of scone and butter and licked her lip clean of the crumb that clung there. Delicious.

The back door in the scullery slammed open and shut and a girl came in – a girl with fair hair and red lips and a skirt halfway up her calves. And a figure to be envied.

'Scones? Bonzer, Mum.' She bent to kiss Mrs Burns's cheek, then sat down and helped herself to tea and a scone. 'G'day,' she said to Margaret. 'You must be Mrs Dalton. I'm Jane.'

'Margaret.' The reply was automatic, but the next moment she wondered what had possessed her to offer her Christian name as though they'd known each other for years. She'd only just

met the girl! But there was something in Jane's clear blue eyes
and ready smile that disarmed her. Besides, every 'Mrs Dalton'
set her teeth on edge.

'Nice to have another girl around the place,' Jane said. She
grinned at her mother. 'Mum likes to fill the house up with
her tame soldiers.'

'Nothing wrong with my boys,' Mrs Burns said complacently.
'When you've finished that, we'll go up and find something in
Mrs Shelley's boxes for Mrs Dalton to wear.'

She just couldn't bear to be called that any more than
she had to. 'If I'm going to be Margaret to Jane, Mrs Burns,
shouldn't I be Margaret to you, too?'

Mrs Burns smiled magisterially upon her, her chins sunk
into her neck. 'Well, that will be very nice and homelike. And
you can call me Burnsie, like the boys do.'

•

Half an hour later her bed was buried beneath piles of the
late Mrs Shelley's clothes. Jane peacocked around the room,
buttons undone down her back, in a bright yellow satin that
clashed terribly with her blonde hair, giving an impression of
a society lady dying to go to the toilet but too polite to say
so. Margaret and Burnsie, sitting on the bed, were crying
with laughter.

'You should go on the boards!' Margaret said.

'That's what I reckon!' Jane agreed.

'Don't you go filling my daughter's head with that vaudeville
nonsense. She's got a good job already. At the *council*.'

'I'm just the tea lady, Mum,' Jane complained.

'It's a good job. A *government* job. No decent man's going
to marry a woman who's been on the stage.'

This was clearly an old argument, and wasn't going to be settled here and now. Margaret fingered the clothes, all fine linen and lawn and the lightest of wools. If she dressed in these, would she even recognise herself? But could she resist?

'Mrs— Burnsie, you'll let me buy these from you?'

'Not on your life, love,' Burnsie said. She heaved herself to her feet and shook her finger at Margaret. 'Mrs Shelley would have wanted you to have them – same as her, orphaned and widowed. Besides, seems to me you've had enough bad luck. Time for things to go your way, I reckon. It's not like they'll fit Jane.' That was true. Jane was shorter and rounder and a good deal curvier than Margaret or the late Mrs Shelley.

Margaret climbed out of her dress – astonished that she should feel comfortable enough to do so with these strangers – and put a simple black linen dress on over her slip. It fell to mid-calf, and the wide sleeves just touched her elbows. It had a sailor collar and a pleated skirt. It fitted her to perfection.

'Like it's been made for you!' Jane said, enviously. 'Wish I could wear them. But Mrs King, round the corner, she said there just wasn't enough material in the bust to make them fit me.'

'Don't you worry,' Burnsie comforted her. 'Men like a woman with a bit of meat on her. Saving your presence, Margi.'

Margi. Not Marge, as Frank had sometimes called her, which made it sound like it was short for Marjorie, but Margi, with a hard G. No one had ever shortened her name like that before. It sat oddly on her for a minute, but then she decided she liked it. No memories of Frank in that name. Margaret the Englishwoman. Margi the Australian.

It made her feel even more guilt-ridden that she was lying to them.

'Don't mind me,' she said. 'You're right. They like curves.'

'Well, dinner in an hour,' Burnsie said. 'Jane, help her pack away the colours; they'll still be in fashion next year. Then come on down and peel the potatoes.'

They packed the yellow satin and the pale green velvet and all the other lovely colourful dresses and blouses and skirts back in the trunk.

'Nice to be wearing real clothes again,' Jane said.

'You were in uniform?' Some women in the railways had worn uniforms when Margaret worked at Reading – all the station staff – but the girls in the office had worn mufti, thank the good Lord.

'VAD,' Jane said. 'The apron made me look like a pouter pigeon.' The Volunteer Aid Detachment girls had assisted nurses in war hospitals, Margaret knew. A hard job. Margaret looked at Jane with new respect. Not such a flibbertigibbet as she seemed.

'Next year you can wear all these,' Jane added, laying down a lovely turquoise blouse.

Next year. Her husband was supposed to have died in the flu epidemic – it had hit Australia later than England, Sergeant McBride had told her, and he could have died as late as November, after she'd left her West Bromwich digs to go to Tilbury to wait for the ship. So, in November she could put off her blacks and take up colours again. God alone knew where she'd be by then. She found, in the pile of lovely things, a plainer black skirt and blouse, and put them on, laying the other widow's clothes away in the wardrobe and drawers.

'Lucky you're the same colouring,' Jane said. 'Even if they fitted me, I couldn't wear these. Mrs Shelley, she was a brunette, too. There!' She closed and latched the lid and Margaret helped her carry the trunk back to the storage cupboard at the end of the hall.

'It's very kind of your mother.'

Jane smiled with rueful affection. 'She loves to spoil people, does Mum. Mind you, she's got a pretty sharp eye, so she generally spoils the right sort, though she doesn't put up with any nonsense. Well, me for the potatoes.'

Margaret went down with her and, over Burnsie's protests, helped with the vegetables.

'If you're going to treat me like a member of the family, giving me so many lovely things, then you're going to have to take help from me like a member of the family, aren't you?'

Burnsie put her hands on her hips and stared at her. 'Yair. You'll do all right here.'

'I'm glad you think I'll fit into the house.'

'Nah. Not the house, love. Australia.'

•

At dinner she met the other three lodgers. Two young men – barely twenty, and yet they'd both served in northern Africa – who shared the last room on the right and who were students at the Sydney Conservatorium of Music; 'But don't worry, love, they practise at school.' A cellist and a tuba player, apparently. They were full of praise for their headmaster and conductor, Maestro Verbrugghen.

And there was an older man, Mr Lewis, around forty, who worked on one of the ferries – not the one that went across to Circular Quay, he explained, but one that went up the river to somewhere called Parramatta. He kept his head down and ate steadily. Yet another of Burnsie's 'tame soldiers', no doubt.

'And on Monday,' Burnsie announced as she carved more corned beef for the boys, 'we'll have a new gentleman boarder. Tom McBride.'

Tom was starting a new life too. They could keep each other company.

•

Her first night in a new home. Not what she'd expected. It was silly of her to miss Frank, to wish he were here, to remember how they had planned to meet in Sydney when the war was over. Why had he *done* that? She would never understand. Best not to cry; she'd cried enough at Mrs Pritchard's. She just wished she could confront him, ask him *why?* But maybe she wouldn't like the answers. It would be horrible to see Frank's face turn into that of a spiteful stranger.

She went to bed with the window open and the curtains pulled back, the breeze cooling her but not making her cold under the sweet-smelling sheets. It wasn't a smell she knew, not lavender or lilac . . . something tangy and sweet with a hint of lemon. She would ask Burnsie tomorrow. It had helped, telling her story again to the men at the table. They hadn't cared, hadn't been curious. It reassured her that she wouldn't have to lie and lie again and again. Not everyone would interrogate her as Burnsie had done.

She might get through this thicket of confusion and grief yet, and find her way to the life of golden simplicity of which she had dreamed.

5

Tom McBride signed his name firmly at the bottom of his discharge papers. Technically, he would be on leave for another ten days, but he had been 'finalised', and he didn't have to come back after his leave allotment was over.

The clerk, John Bradley, had worked under him in the building section before he'd been sent to France.

'You want a new uniform, Sarge? You're entitled to one.'

Tom looked down at his well-worn khaki. It had been new only a year and a half ago, when he got back to Britain from France and his colonel had seen the state of the uniform he'd worn in the trenches. That had gone into the rag-bag at HQ in London, along with the uniforms of most of the battalion. The uniform entitlement had been a way of protecting those at home from too much knowledge about the real conditions of war; the men being demobbed preferred to go home clean and neat, so they could pretend the whole thing had been a bit of a lark. They'd all had to protect their families from nightmares as well as from Germans.

This uniform had no blood or mud or shit stains on it. And if he never saw another bit of khaki it'd be too soon.

'No thanks, Jack. Civvy street for me.'

He handed in his weapon, his greatcoat and some other bits of kit, settled his slouch hat on his head and grinned at Bradley.

'What about you? Staying in?'

Bradley shrugged. 'Suits me,' he said as he handed over an envelope.

Tom signed the receipt book and stuck his demob pay in his pocket. Not his full payout – only ten pounds to tide him over until his leave pay and his final payout was authorised to his Commonwealth Bank account. The Army had 'reserved' a shilling a day during his stint, set aside for his post-Army life. By now, that would add up to more than sixty pounds, which he would get in due course. He knew what he was going to do with it, too: find a block of land and build himself a house. And maybe a family.

'Well, good luck with it,' he said to Bradley. 'Keep your head down.'

'You too.' They shook hands, and Tom walked out the door into the heat, the blazing blue sky above him.

He was out.

He let that thought rest in him for a moment. He'd made it out alive. So few of his battalion had. France had devoured them, slain them with German shells and mustard gas and pneumonia and the thick, killing mud of the trenches. They'd died by enemy fire – and some had suicided that way, too, although fewer of the Australians had taken that route out of hell than the British. Mind you, the British had been conscripts. The Australians had all put their hand up for the job, and they'd always carried that sense of having to see it through.

That didn't stop the odd bloke from shooting himself in the foot to get out, though.

Alive. He touched his cheek, where the scar was tightening under the sun. A piece of shrapnel from a land mine had almost taken his eye out. Three dead, four wounded, and he was the lucky one. Mitty had lost an arm, Le Touche an ear, Sleeton half his foot. At that point he'd envied the ones who'd died. Soul sick with loneliness and lost love and what his lieutenant called 'the general malaise'.

He'd had two weeks in a hospital in England, in Brighton, and when it came time to be discharged, to head back to the front, he'd been given three days' leave. Mostly the Aussies went to London for their leave, but he couldn't be bothered spending a day on the train and a day back just for a look at the sights, so he'd stayed at a local boarding house, and walked on the beach. Though the 'beach' was covered with stones and the water was grey and uninviting, the hiss on the strand, and the roar of the breakers as the wind picked up, was the same as at home, the same as Sydney.

He spent his last night not at a brothel, as everyone expected him to, but lending a hand on a fishing smack that was venturing out, despite German submarines, to bring back herring for breakfast. He relished the hard physical labour after so many months stuck, waiting, in the trenches.

Going back to France wasn't too bad, until he was posted forward and realised how few of his company were left.

He'd made it out alive. He'd have to do a novena in thanks.

•

He had a bit of shopping to do before he reported to Burnsie's. Couldn't work a saw in this clobber, and while he'd put his good clothes in storage at his aunt's house when he enlisted, his old work gear hadn't been worth saving.

Rather than catch a tram, he walked into the city. Before the war he'd shopped at Lassetter's, the big department store that covered two whole blocks. Cheapside, they called it. But David Jones offered ten per cent off to demobbed soldiers buying their first civilian clobber, so he went there instead.

Work clothes were easy to find, but more expensive than he'd expected. He'd saved a good bit of his pay, though, knowing he'd have to bridge the gap between being demobbed and getting his first pay packet.

Two pairs of trousers, two shirts, two vests. Army underwear would do. He had socks but needed a pair of work boots, with steel caps to protect his feet.

A waistcoat. A jacket. A hat.

'Most of the returned soldiers prefer an Akubra, sir,' the clerk said, and no wonder. Akubra had made the slouch hats for the Aussie diggers, and Tom knew first hand how durable they were. But he went for dark grey, not khaki.

He went into the fitting rooms and changed, stowing his uniform and the rest of the parcels into his duffel, crushing his Army hat down ruthlessly. It wouldn't take any harm; it was tougher than that.

Then he went out of the store and made his way to the ferry. It wasn't until he was walking down George Street that he realised that being in plain clothes changed how people reacted to him. They didn't look at his face, and moved only just far enough aside to let him pass; no respect for a civilian. He could live with that.

•

Finally, standing at the ferry's bow, he could think ahead to his new life.

A life with women in it. After four years of men only, he looked forward to meals with women. It would be refreshing just to have a woman say, 'Pass the salt, please.' Burnsie was like a second mother to him, and Jane the little sister he'd never had. And then there was Margaret. A friend, he hoped. She'd had a bad knock, but her gallant courage despite the destruction of all her dreams, all her faith, had caught his admiration.

Margaret's chestnut curls and Jane's blonde prettiness were as different as could be from Ruby Hawkins' dark beauty. He didn't think about Ruby much; what was the use? She'd been married when they met, and she loved her husband, even when he was away at Gallipoli, with a fierce and devoted love. No room for him there, which was why he'd signed up in the first place.

And why he wasn't going back to his old job, although his old boss had offered it. Because Ruby was still working there, at least for another six months or so, until her husband finished his training as a stock auctioneer. It was more than three years since he'd seen her last, and he was pretty sure he was over her, but working with her day to day . . .

Yep, better not to go back to the old pain, the old longing. A fresh start.

He walked up the hill with a lightening heart. A free afternoon, before he started work the next day. Maybe he'd take Margaret out for an ice cream.

•

When he got to the High House, Margaret was out, at a job interview in the city.

So he unpacked in his comfortable little room – odd not to be in uniform ever again – and then sat in the kitchen and chiacked Burnsie while she did the Monday washing. He chopped some wood for her, carted a few buckets of water, turned the mangle on the sheets, and stood the prop up under the full washing line so the clean clothes didn't dip into the dirt.

A domestic day. A jewel of a day, bright and shiny and ordinary, like a new-minted penny.

Margaret came home at three, disappointment written all over her. He stared for a moment at her slashing dress. She almost looked like a different person, she was so fashionable. Out of place at the kitchen table, if it hadn't been for her ease there.

'They wanted shorthand. Why bother to interview me in the first place? I said I could type, not take dictation!'

'Maybe they thought you could just pull it out of your garter!' Burnsie said.

He laughed, and Margaret smiled, visibly putting her disappointment behind her. She wouldn't let herself worry for long, he could see.

'You'll find something,' he said.

'I have another interview tomorrow, at Manly,' she said.

'Cross fingers,' he said, and she smiled at him.

Gosh, she was a looker. He wondered if it was being demobbed that had made him susceptible to female charms. No need to go overboard, though. It might be that she was just the first pretty face he'd seen in a while who wasn't an honest-to-goodness war bride, with a husband waiting anxiously for her. Yes, that'd be it.

'They were fools not to take you,' he said.

6

In the early post was a letter from the Manly business, saying they had found someone for the job and regretted, etcetera, etcetera. Margaret felt a pang of fear, just like the one shortly after her parents died. It had been a bad time. Their house was a tied cottage, owned by the foundry, and the foundry manager had asked her to leave as soon as the funeral was over. She'd had no job – just the week before, her boss had told her he'd given her job to a recently demobbed soldier, a man with only one leg. And still she was waiting for her ticket to Australia, to Frank.

Nowhere to live, no job, and only her savings – not much, at that stage – and the little she got from selling off their bits and bobs of furniture. She'd even had to sell her parents' clothes to the rag-and-bone man. When she came to pack her possessions for the trip to Australia, she'd realised that she had nothing of her mother or father, except a studio portrait of them on their wedding day and a pair of gloves her mother had lent her when she started her job at Reading.

It had been three weeks before she got the job at the bakery in West Bromwich. She'd stayed at a transients' hostel, where most of the other 'guests' were travelling salesmen. She'd learned to scurry to her room when she came in, head down. One moment of pause and someone would proposition her. She'd never felt so alone.

Those were the hardest days. She'd lied in her letters to Frank, saying she was fine. Putting it all down on paper would have made it worse. She'd found the best way to get by was to put her chin up and look ahead to the next possibility, no matter how scared and lonely and sad she was. At least she'd had Australia and Frank to look forward to then. Now he'd betrayed her, it was time to put her chin up once again.

She had an interview in the city the next day. She would look forward to that.

It was at an importer's, in an area near Circular Quay called The Rocks – by the look of it, an oldish part of the city, if anything in Australia could be called old. There were rows of warehouses and bond stores along the foreshore; her appointment was one street back, on George Street, more or less, in the Malcolm Building, third floor.

She walked up a dingy but well-scrubbed stairway to a glass door with 'C. Horace, Manufacturer's Agent' on it in gilt letters, and went through.

It was a small reception room with a secretary's desk guarding another doorway, no doubt the inner office. There was no secretary there, which gave her a spurt of hope. It looked like a respectable place. The furniture was old enough for it not to be a fly-by-night operation, but new enough that it wasn't shabby. The typewriter was a recent model, and the two armchairs for visitors were deep-buttoned green leather. Should she sit down and wait or make herself known? There didn't seem to be a bell.

Hesitantly, she knocked at the inner door.

'Come!'

Opening the door, she pasted on her professional smile and went through. A man got up from the desk and came around it to greet her. About forty, good-looking, with curly dark hair and blue eyes, a full moustache – Black Irish, her mother would have called him. He smiled at her with a question in his eyes.

'Well, hello. Can I help you?' It was clear he wasn't expecting her. Margaret's heart picked up pace. Had she made a mistake?

'I'm Mrs Dalton . . . I'm here for the interview?'

'Oh!' He was taken aback. 'I'm sorry. I wasn't expecting . . .' He focused on her clothes with an assessing stare, lingering. 'You're in mourning?'

'For my husband,' she said stiffly.

'Well, I'm sorry, but you won't be suitable.'

'You haven't even interviewed me!'

'Sit down, sit down,' he said, waving her to a chair like the ones in the outer room, smiling rather patronisingly. 'That must have seemed very abrupt.'

'Just a little.'

'My secretary needs to do a lot of liaison work with the buyers and the salesmen and so on, and I've found in the past that it's much better for business if she isn't too pretty.'

Pretty? She was being denied a job because she was *pretty*?

'It wouldn't matter so much if you were married, you see, but a widow . . . oh, that's just asking for trouble. The only thing more distracting than a pretty widow is a pretty divorcée!' He chuckled as though she ought to find that funny.

'I'm very businesslike, Mr Horace. I can assure you there'd be nothing . . . untoward.' Her stomach was roiling with anxiety. This was her last interview. Without a job, she had only the widow's pension coming in, barely enough to pay Burnsie. She desperately didn't want to dip into her capital.

'Oh, it's not you I'm worried about! It's the men. Although . . .'

Mr Horace got up again and came around to sit on the desk beside her. His leg brushed against her thigh. She moved away. Was she imagining his intention? His eyes weren't salacious; more calculating, as though she were a potential client with a big bank account.

Again his leg rested against her thigh. Again she moved away.

On the bookshelf behind the desk was a photograph of him with a woman in a bridal gown.

'You're married, Mr Horace,' she said. Her mouth felt stiff and clumsy.

'Doesn't bother me,' he said.

'It bothers me,' she said, moving to get up.

He put a hand on her shoulder. Panic flared through her. No one knew exactly where she was – she hadn't given the address to Burnsie. If he, if he . . .

She pushed him away violently and scrambled to her feet, cursing the deep chair.

'Get your hands off me!'

He was affronted, as though she and not he had crossed some invisible line.

'No need to overreact,' he said. 'You've got to expect men to try. You'll find it hard to get a job with that attitude.'

Now she was on her feet and next to the door, her courage flooded back. She gathered every bit of her self-possession and looked him up and down as though *he* were a piece of meat.

'And *you*, Mr Horace, ought to expect women to say no. You're a slimy piece of work.'

She managed to get all the way back to Circular Quay before she started to shake. Thank God the ferry to Milson's Point was due in only a few minutes. She waited on a bench and stared fixedly at her shoes, in case any of the men waiting near her saw her looking around and misunderstood it to be an invitation.

She was filled with a hot mixture of anger and fear. Anger was easy. How dare he! Fear was more difficult. What if he were right? What if widows were expected to . . . Perhaps she would have been better going back to her maiden name after all.

Poverty stretched out before her. No job meant nowhere to live, nothing to eat. It was just as hard to get a job in England, but at least there she had known people and, more than that, known how everything worked. Known what those invisible lines were, and how to react if someone crossed them.

The poorhouse seemed a long step closer than it had this morning.

By the time the ferry came she had stopped shaking. She sat on one of the benches at the bow, and listened to a couple of men, clerks by the look of them, who had their sandwiches in brown paper bags and were eating while they talked. If she could hear enough Australian conversations, would she understand her new home better?

'Yeah, last year. March. The whole lot went right over,' one of them said in a broad Australian drawl that reminded her, piercingly, of Frank.

'How many then?' his companion asked in a pronounced Scottish accent.

'Five, just younguns. Bloody idiots!' He glanced quickly at Margaret as though only just realising he was in mixed company, and made a quick apologetic grimace to her. She nodded and looked away, but she couldn't help listening as he went on. 'Serve 'em right. Fancy boating without knowing how to swim!'

'I can't swim,' his friend admitted. Neither could she. Her brother and his friends had played around in the river, but girls weren't allowed because the boys swam naked.

'Gawdstrewth, man, can't have that! If you're going to be an Aussie you have to learn to swim!'

'Och, laddie, I'm not one for water.'

'You're in Australia now!'

The ferry began to turn in towards the wharf, so she got up and left them arguing, wondering if it were possible for her to learn to swim. It seemed unlikely, even here. So often, when people said 'Australians' or 'Britons', they really meant just the men.

She was getting used to the hills, and she arrived at the High House with a little breath left. She found Burnsie in the kitchen, darning a stocking.

'Well?' Burnsie demanded, putting the stocking down and coming around the table to her, as though ready to pat her on the back if the news was bad.

'No good.'

Burnsie did pat her back, gently.

Margaret felt tears prick her eyes. She had so looked forward to living with Frank, being his wife, having his children and raising them. And now she was back to the everyday grind, the worrying about money – well, of course she and Frank would have worried about money, but they'd have done it *together*.

For the first time, she was hit by anger with Frank. True, deep, scarifying anger. If he hadn't misled her – *lied* to her! – she might be back in Reading this very minute, married to some nice English boy, with a couple of kids. Or married to one of those kind men on the *Borda*, the ones who cared enough about their families to sail with them.

She didn't care if Frank *had* been shipped home to Australia as a wounded soldier. He had been demobbed for a year, now – he could have come to England and fetched her, for heaven's sake, if he'd really wanted her. One man on the *Borda* had done just that.

But he didn't want her. He never had. He'd just wanted a comfortable bed and some warm arms when he was on leave. The anger rolled up in her, and almost burst her eyeballs with fury. He'd treated her like a prostitute. Like a drab – worse! He hadn't even bothered to pay her. That was her: cheaper than a brothel. The same way Mr Horace had seen her.

She was overcome by a wave of self-loathing. Such a fool, such an idiot, such a stupid, naïve, gullible *girl*.

'You'll find something,' Burnsie said.

'Oh, I could have had *something* today – if I'd been prepared to, to . . .'

Burnsie straightened. 'Oh. One of *those*, was he?'

Margaret nodded.

'Never mind, love. Worse things happen at sea.' Her grandmother used to say that; it struck some long-silent chord in her, and she laughed brokenly. 'That's the spirit,' Burnsie said. 'I'll make a cup of tea.'

As they sat companionably drinking the tea, Margaret decided that as soon as she was finished she would pop back out to get the day's paper. Time to scan the employment ads again.

Surely there must be *someone* in this city who needed her skills?

7

Walking up the path to his old home shouldn't have felt any different just because he was in civvies, but it did. He'd been based in Victoria Barracks for six months, and he'd visited his mother and aunt plenty of times, but still . . .

Tom opened the door and called, 'Hoo-roo!' into the house, moving down the corridor into the lounge room. His mother came through from the kitchen, wiping her hands on a tea towel. Her face lit up at the sight of him, as it always did, but then it crumpled into tears.

'You're out!' she said, voice choked. 'You're out and you're safe!' The first time she'd seen him in civvies since he joined up. Even though the war had been over for more than a year, it still made a difference. He'd felt it himself. She threw her arms around him and hugged as much of him as she could – a thin woman, his mum, and of course much shorter than he was. 'Theresa! He's here!'

Tom kissed the top of her head and swung her off her feet, whirling her around until they were both laughing. Then did the same to his aunt as she came in behind him from the front bedroom. For a moment afterwards they stood and beamed at each other, simply happy.

'I'll put the kettle on,' his aunt said.

They all went through to the kitchen and he sat at the table as the two women busied themselves. There was nothing for him to do – their household habits didn't include him anymore. Until tomorrow, he had nowhere he had to be, nothing he had to do. After three-and-a-half years of having every second of his day organised for him, it was a profoundly odd feeling; like being suspended in mid air.

'The oven's not hot enough for scones,' his mother said. 'Why didn't you tell us you were coming? Never mind, I've got some shortbread I made on Thursday for the Red Cross meeting.'

In two shakes of a lamb's tail the table was set and the tea was made. The two women, so different in looks, gazed at him with the same satisfaction and affection. His mother was thin, spare and upright, mind like a trap but with a surprising tolerance for human foibles. His aunt, roly-poly, soft on the outside but prone to quick judgement. There weren't many who could fool the two of them together. He often wondered how his uncle had dealt with the women of the family – he'd died in the nineties, in a railway accident. The compensation had paid off the mortgage on this house and allowed his aunt – and, later, he and his mother – to live off the small wages a woman could bring home. As soon as he'd turned fourteen he'd insisted on leaving school to help.

Sometimes he wondered where he would have been if his father hadn't died. If he could have stayed at school and become – something. He didn't know what. A plumber like his dad? Or something posher? He couldn't imagine himself working in an office, but he'd enjoyed supervising the building of the barracks out at Liverpool when he first went into the Army. Maybe a builder.

No tea tasted like the tea you got at home. He drank and ate shortbread and they just talked. News about his aunt's Red Cross work. News about his mother's job at the bottle factory; she was foreman now.

'I've got a new job!' his aunt announced. His aunt had worked in a lot of different jobs. She was good at all of them, but easily bored.

'A new one!' he repeated with a smile.

'Yes indeed. I'm the Parish secretary now.'

'I didn't know they had a Parish secretary.'

'Well, they didn't. But they do now!' She paused for effect. 'I'm learning to be a typiste!'

He let out a shout of laughter and she hit his arm, but she didn't take offence.

'Rude boy,' his mother said. 'She's teaching me at night, too. There's a company that pays you to do typing in your own home. We're saving up for a machine. For when I get too old for the bottle factory.'

'I'll be looking after you when you get too old for that, Mum.'

She shook her head, the bun at the back of her neck wobbling with the strength of the movement. 'No. By then you'll have a family to look after. You know I don't like being beholden. Even to you.'

That stubborn independence was what had kept them fed and clothed. His aunt had it too. So many Australian women did; he'd noticed that, in England. The girls there seemed more subdued than the Australian women he'd known. But it was his job to look after his mum and aunt. Tom felt a twinge of guilt. He'd sent back money from the front all through the war, but now he could only afford to help them if he moved back in. And he just couldn't bring himself to do that.

'You're not coming back here, are you?' his mother asked. Quick as ever. No flies on her.

'I've taken a room over in North Sydney,' he said. 'Close to work.'

'Mr Curry'd have you back,' his aunt said reproachfully, glancing at his mother to emphasise where his duty lay. 'He said so at church last week.'

'Oh, leave the boy alone, Theresa. He doesn't want to come back and have the same life he did before he went away.'

'I can still help a bit,' Tom said. 'But I won't be earning as much as I did at Curry's. I'm leading hand at Cobbin's, not foreman.'

'You'll be foreman soon enough,' his mother said. 'In any case, we don't need your money. We can look after ourselves.'

She got up and went into her bedroom, the second room off the corridor, and came back with a bank passbook. She gave it to him, opened on the last page to show the balance.

One hundred and fifty-six pounds and three shillings. And the name on the passbook was his. This was the account he'd set up so they could draw on his earnings while he was in the Army.

Open-mouthed, he stared at them both sitting there like cats that had got the cream, looking startlingly alike.

'We left your money in it, apart from any little things we bought to send to you.' Aunt Theresa was cock-a-hoop, jiggling in her seat with happiness at his surprise.

'So, you see, we don't need your money,' his mother said. 'We get along just fine on our own.'

'And when you meet a nice girl and get married, you can buy a house straightaway!' his aunt added. 'Have you met anyone yet?'

Involuntarily he thought of Margaret Dalton.

'He has, Dot. Look at his face. He *has* met someone!' Aunt Theresa slapped her hand on the tablecloth.

But his mother reached out and gently stroked back that one lock of hair that always fell on his face.

'Leave him alone, Theresa. Let him find his feet as a civilian before you start pushing him into marriage.'

She smiled into his eyes and he felt the familiar thankfulness rise in him. Other fellows had mothers who were smarter, better dressed, better educated. But no one had a mother who understood things the way his did.

•

Cobbin's timber mill was like every one Tom had been in – the one he'd worked in before the war, Curry's, over in Annandale, and all those he'd visited since as an Army representative. His colonel had been sure that he was the only man in the battalion who knew what he was doing when it came to acquiring trench timbers. Maybe he'd been right. They hadn't had as many collapses as others did.

Cobbin's was a thriving concern. A big shed where the sawn timber was stacked on rows of shelving. A spacious yard where drays and lorries could pull in for loading and unloading. Another large shed where the buzzing saws turned logs into planks. But this yard specialised in fine-faced timber, not the rough lumber that had been Curry's stock-in-trade.

There was only a small wharf at the edge of the yard. Right on the point, it wasn't big enough to take the huge logs that sailed down the coast from the timber-getting country, as it had been at Curry's. But here, unlike Curry's, there was a shed where boards were cut to size, routed or turned if needed, sanded and finished so a builder had nothing to do but put a nail into them. They made balustrade spindles, carved fascia boards, lots of speciality items.

He'd done a bit of all of that, in his time, but he had to admit he needed to learn if he was going to work his way back up to foreman. He didn't feel much enthusiasm for it, which surprised him. He'd always been someone who put his whole heart into his job; it was the only way, he reckoned, to give the boss value for money.

But now, he sighed. The war was a long time over, and something had gone out of him. He found it hard to care about anything as much as he had before. Maybe he was just getting old. Thirty was only two years away.

He took off his hat and walked into the office. All men there, older men who'd worked through the war and held onto their jobs when it was over. Good luck to them, and to the foreman, Ernie, who must have been only a boy when Tom joined up but who'd grown into his job and his authority. He'd have to be careful not to seem like a know-it-all, he thought. Can't undermine the man in charge.

Tom entered his details in the sign-in book and nodded to the head clerk, who had employed him, then headed out to the yard.

'McBride!' the foreman said, just a little nervously.

'G'day, boss!' Tom said, and hunched his shoulders as though nervous too.

Ernie relaxed and waved at the saw shed. 'I've put you as second on the big saw. Till you find your feet.'

'Fair enough.' So it was, fair. He'd do the same with a new man.

'We've got good blokes. Just one thing: don't ever put Bingo on the big saw.'

Tom quirked an eyebrow.

'He can't take the noise. Shell shock. But he's fine on the lathes and the hand finishing.'

It was common enough. God knew the noise of the shells got in your head and rang there, even after a raid was over. He dreamed about them still – they all did, whether or not they admitted it.

'No worries,' he said.

The shed was open and caught the breezes from the Harbour. They had a big spotted gum on the table, being cut into four-be-fours to act as floor joists.

He and Ernie did the first run together, the important one that set the grain for the rest of the cuts. He returned to the smell of sawdust and pine and put his hand to the logs and the saw as though he'd never been away.

In the past, seeing the big trees reduced to useable, useful timber had been a source of satisfaction to him. He'd always felt he was part of something bigger, something more important than himself. Civilisation, maybe, the striving of mankind to climb out of the mud. To make homes and factories and even sheds.

Today, seeing the log make its smooth run onto the saw and out the other side as joists, as bits of itself instead of a whole thing, Tom was reminded too vividly of what metal could do to flesh. For the first time he was afraid of the saw. It was only a moment, and it puzzled him. He wasn't afraid of hurting himself; he'd never done so, not once in all his years working.

There was something else there.

Ernie shouted, 'And again!' and there was no more time for thinking. He had a job to do and he did it.

The men took their lunch on a swathe of grass and rock down by the water, where Ernie said it was safe to smoke. Tom joined them with a sandwich Burnsie had made. Despite all her protestations that they'd have to find their own lunch, his paper bag had been waiting for him at breakfast time. Corned beef and chutney, and the odd-job boy made a billy of tea on a circle of rocks by the water's edge.

There was always something to watch on the Harbour. This time of day was too late for the fishing boats, but there were tugs, barges and the ever-busy ferries. They could see right past Blue's Point, and across to Dawes Point and its long row of wharves, full of tramp steamers loading and off-loading, tug-boats and barges. He couldn't help it: he smiled. So much life, so many people just going about their business.

Berry's Bay curved behind them, a collection of boatsheds and boatyards. He could hear hammers and the dull hum of hand saws floating over the water. It was soothing, the sound of something being made instead of destroyed. He tucked that thought away for later and swigged back the last of his tea.

As always when a new man joined a team, the others felt him out. Before the war they would have talked about sport; football, maybe, or cricket since it was summer.

Now they talked about war service.

Following custom, the oldest man started the interrogation. His name was George.

'Got yourself a nice one there, mate,' he said, touching the side of his face to indicate Tom's scar.

'Ypres,' Tom said.

'Ah.'

A few of the men relaxed a bit, pulled out the makings and rolled themselves a smoke, handling their matches with the care he'd expect from men who were sitting only feet away from what was effectively a yard full of firewood. Not to mention sawdust, which could catch like the dickens.

The rollcall went around the group.

'Anzac,' said one whose left hand was missing two fingers. 'The Somme.'

'Toulouse.'

'All over bloody France,' said the larrikin of the group, a monkey of a man with bright brown eyes and weathered skin. 'And back round again.'

'G'arn, Bingo,' the old bloke said. 'You was just looking for some French mamwozelle who could stand staring at your ugly mug.'

They all laughed. So, this was Bingo. He looked all right, thought Tom; but then, shell-shocked men often did, until the shakes started.

Ernie leaned against the side of the cart they used to make deliveries and listened. Tom thought he did it well, this being with the men who'd served. A lot of young blokes in his position would cut in or show how much they knew.

Ernie brought out his own sandwich, roast beef and mustard. The smell cut through the air sharply, and most of the circle flinched, a couple of hands going to throats. Remembering the smell of mustard gas, all of them, and what it did to human flesh. No one said anything, though. Tom wasn't sure if that was because they didn't want to seem weak, or if they didn't want to bring the memory closer to the surface.

Tom refused the offer of a smoke from George; his old boss had never allowed smoking on the job, so he'd never got in the habit. The others smoked like all soldiers did, with the cigarette held backwards so their cupped hand shielded the tip from the wind. It worked just as well for a stiff Harbour breeze as it had in the trenches.

They'd all picked up habits that would mark them for a lifetime. He wondered what he did that pointed him out to others as a returned soldier.

He wasn't sure he wanted to know.

8

At eleven on Thursday morning, the telephone rang. Margaret was sitting outside on the verandah, watching the boats go by but not enjoying it as much as she had expected, because of the gnawing worry of unemployment. Her father had been out of work, once, and she remembered, too clearly, eating nothing but scant porridge for a week until he was taken on at Halley's.

She had received more 'no thank you' letters that morning from enquiries she had sent out. Three sent out, three sent back. It was getting harder to convince herself that she would get a job with the qualifications she had. Perhaps she should do a shorthand course while the Army was paying her the widow's pension.

Perhaps she should look for a cheaper boarding house. The High House wasn't expensive, but there were cheaper options. Her stomach curled at the thought of leaving what felt like a safe haven – a beautiful, luxurious safe haven – but she might be better off getting out before she got used to all this comfort. Her father would have said she was being spoiled, made soft. He'd be worried about her losing her fighting spirit.

'Mrs Dalton! Telephone!' Burnsie called. That was odd; not only wasn't she expecting any calls, but why would Burnsie speak so formally?

She went into the parlour through the French doors and took the receiver from Burnsie, who smiled encouragingly at her.

'Hello?'

'Mrs Dalton? This is Mr Bertram, from Davids, Bertram and Company. In Manly?'

It was an educated voice, with beautiful vowels that reminded Margaret of her elocution teacher back in West Bromwich saying, '*Niii*ne, not *noi*ne'. How she herself had striven to sound like that, but the accent she had ended up with was neither Black Country nor upper class. It was hard to place, which allowed her to act as though she were middle class, and that was all her mother had ever wanted. This voice was the real thing.

'Yes, Mr Bertram?' Perhaps they'd forgotten they'd already informed her she wasn't successful.

'I'm in a bit of a spot, Mrs Dalton, and I hoped you'd be able to help me out of it.'

'I'm sorry?'

'You applied for the typiste's position, if you remember.'

'Yes, that's right.'

'Well, I know we told you that we had found someone for the job, but the fact is, the girl never turned up. Her family says she's run away with – well, with a married man, not to put too fine a point on it.'

'Oh.' What did you say to something like that?

'So, I was hoping that you might still be available for an interview.'

'Oh. Oh, yes! Yes, of course.'

'Perhaps even this afternoon? Could you come at two?'

'Yes, yes, of course.'

'Excellent. I'll see you then. Goodbye.'

'Goodbye.'

For a moment she stood there, dazed, but Burnsie popped her head around the door and said, 'Good news?'

'Yes! It's the Manly job. They want to interview me after all.'

'I told you something would turn up.'

She raced up the stairs, sorting her clothes frantically in her mind. Should she wear widow's blacks again? Surely not everyone was like Mr Horace. Mr Bertram had sounded very nice on the phone.

Bother it! She *would* wear her blacks, if only as a riposte to Mr Horace.

•

The tram ride to Manly was unexpectedly picturesque. Margaret had thought that there was just one Sydney Harbour, but apparently there was Middle Harbour as well, and beaches all along the coast. The tram travelled the ridge for the first section, so she could still see down to the Harbour she knew. Then it turned north along the coast, still on a ridge, and in some spots she could glimpse Middle Harbour to the right of her and another body of water – a river? – to the left.

The tram dipped down a steep hill with a prolonged screech of brakes, on the shore of what turned out not to be a river but a narrowing of Middle Harbour. Was this Manly? There was nothing here but a few boatsheds, a small shop and a long finger of land ending in a wharf with a funny-looking boat tied up to it. Like a barge, but bigger.

Margaret stood on the footpath, wondering what to do next as the other passengers walked briskly towards the wharf.

One of them, a kind-looking woman in a print dress and a big straw hat, advised her.

'You get the punt across, dear, and then the steam tram to Manly.'

A ferry. Well, that was no hardship. Margaret smiled at the woman and joined the stream of passengers walking through the open back gate of the punt. There was a horse and cart on there already, a brewer's cart by the look of it, full of barrels, pulled by a couple of creamy Clydesdales.

Margaret found a place to stand near the side, and watched as two men raised the gate and secured it. Then an engine started up and the punt began to move, as smoothly as if it were a toy boat in a bathtub.

Astonished, Margaret looked back to see a shining wet cable stretching from the side of the punt to the shore. She craned around – yes, the cable went the other way, too, to the Manly side. So, this boat winched itself backwards and forwards across this stretch of water.

Of course, they must have things like this in England, but she'd never seen one. It was like an adventure – and the presence of the patient horses, such a central part of the countryside of her childhood, just made it seem all the more alien. They were standing under a blazing sky, flicking away Australian flies with their tails, their coats positively gleaming in a way they would never do under the English sun, the backdrop of eucalyptus trees on the far shoreline a dull olive green, so different from the vibrancy of oaks and elms and beeches. She was, she admitted, disappointed in Australian trees, even after Jane and Tom had named a few for her. Scraggly, dull things, especially the she-oaks that climbed the hillside; they looked like dirty feather dusters. The only one she really liked was the angophora beneath her bedroom window.

Excitement fizzed in her blood. The telephone call out of the blue made her feel as though she really were in an adventure, as though the tide had turned for her. She wanted to *move*, to do something to let out some of this odd electric feeling – to do a cartwheel, as she used to do in the fields of home. And then she tried not to laugh at the image of passengers scattering in front of her on this tiny boat, scandalised and flapping.

The trip across was over too soon, and then another tram was waiting for them at a loop of track, its steam engine chuffing as it took them up another steep hill, and along another ridge. At the top of the hill, just before they plunged into the final descent, she could see a proper town. Quite a big one. Manly. It was spread along a spur of land between the ocean and the Harbour. The big hill on the other side must be North Head, where the *Borda* had anchored.

Margaret felt her head spin and then, almost with a flick, her mental map of the area settled and she knew where she was. It was a trick she'd developed when she worked with the railways – the complex train routes of troop trains and cargo were easier to understand if you had a good mental image of the countryside they traversed. She could probably draw a map of Britain with all the main stations and towns marked, from Land's End to John o'Groats.

At the tram terminus, which was near the ferry wharf, she asked a passing woman for directions. Belgrave Street led directly from the wharf, and number 44C was on a busy corner, with Raglan Street cutting across it.

She'd had no idea what an auctioneer's office would look like. It was plain brick on the outside, with one picture window with a placard: 'Estate sale on site, Saturday 10 am', and an address.

Inside was a foyer with a counter where a young clerk sat occupied with a couple of ledgers in front of him. Through a big door to the rear she could see a warehouse space, mostly empty, a utilitarian space with double garage doors at the back – they were open, and two men were loading a wardrobe onto a lorry just outside in a small yard. It all looked busy and respectable.

The young clerk directed her upstairs, where she entered a larger space that took up perhaps a third of the warehouse length. A bank of filing cabinets sat against the wall facing the street, and a couple of desks were arranged outside a partitioned-off room, which must be Mr Bertram's office. Prosperous but not luxurious. The door was open, so she tentatively went to the doorway.

'Mrs Dalton! Come in, come in! I'm John Bertram.'

Mr Bertram jumped up from his chair with automatic good manners and beckoned her in. He was younger than she had expected, only a few years older than she was. Twenty-six, maybe. He walked with a limp and a cane; a returned veteran, probably. He flourished the cane towards a chair facing his desk and thumped into his own chair, as if it were a game, and grinned at her.

She smiled back involuntarily.

'Right, now,' he consulted her application. 'The railways in England?'

'Yes, the office at Reading Station.'

He groaned, but theatrically. 'Oh, Reading Station! The hours we had to wait there before our troop train could go on.'

'The hospital trains had priority,' she said automatically, the standard excuse they'd always used.

'So they told us. No shorthand?'

'No, I'm afraid not. But I'm prepared to learn.'

'Might be useful,' he said. 'But we've never had anyone here who could do it, so we'll have to give that a try later. Typing speed?'

'Forty-five words a minute,' she said, and then felt impelled to add, 'when I'm in practice. I've been on a ship the past few weeks.'

'Ye-es.' He looked down at the application form, where she had formalised her lies. 'I'm sorry to hear about your husband.'

Margaret nodded. It was safer than saying something. Than saying anything, except the basics.

'Thank you.'

'Come and I'll show you around.'

He jumped up and grabbed his cane. She could see that he was a man who did things quickly, impulsively, impatiently; that could be a good thing or a bad, in a boss. Quick to anger, probably, but equally quick to forgive. He reminded her a little of her brother, David, who had also been quick on his feet. How he would have hated using a cane.

The long warehouse was half-full of furniture, farm equipment, odds and ends. The big doors at the end opened onto another street, where a cart stood and two men manhandled a tall hall stand off it onto a square of sacking. The lorry, with the wardrobe, had already gone.

'We're a general auctioneer,' Mr Bertram said. 'Don't do stock – that's animals – unless specially asked; say, if one of the stock auctioneers was sick. Mondays and Wednesdays, sometimes Saturdays, here in the saleroom. We do furniture, artworks, *objet d'arts.*'

So *that* was how you said it; she was grateful that she'd never said it aloud and made a fool of herself.

'Also,' Mr Bertram went on, 'house and land auctions, we're getting more and more of, and estate auctions, on the deceased person's premises. Bert Davids does most of those, but he's getting on a bit, so he works primarily from home. You'll barely see him. Young Donald down below does his paperwork.'

'You must be busy.'

'That's why we need you,' he said, and she realised that he'd already made up his mind. He beamed at her, all good nature. 'You'll have to work Saturdays until two, sometimes three if people are late picking up their items.'

'That's no problem,' she assured him. She could feel weight lifting off her, and realised it was fear going.

She had a job.

One of the men on the cart came up and stood, waiting to be noticed.

'And this is Joe, our delivery driver,' Mr Bertram said to her. 'Joe, this is Mrs Dalton, our new clerk.'

'Missus,' Joe nodded. He was a dark-haired, swarthy man with beautiful cheekbones. He reminded her of the son of the Italian greengrocer in Reading. 'This is the last one, boss,' he said to Mr Bertram.

'Jolly good.' Mr Bertram nodded. 'You can knock off after you've taken her back to the livery stable.'

A sudden smile flashed across Joe's face, lighting it up.

'A whole ten minutes early!'

'None of your cheek,' Mr Bertram said, also smiling, and turned back to Margaret as Joe walked away. 'You'll start tomorrow, nine o'clock, three pounds ten shillings a week to start, four pounds after three months, two weeks' holiday after a year. You'll have to look nice at all times, though,' he continued, looking her over, 'I can see that won't be a trouble to you. No make-up, hems well below the knee and no flirting with the customers.'

Easy, she thought. No more men, not ever.

'I don't think that will be a trouble, either.'

'Of course not, of course not,' he said, and she realised he was referring to her supposed widowhood; it made her uncomfortable, but what could she say?

He took her hand and pumped it enthusiastically.

'Welcome to Davids, Bertram and Co, Mrs Dalton.'

•

It was a beautiful day. Hot, yes, but with a cool breeze coming off the water. Now that she could relax, Margaret realised that she hadn't had lunch. Why not buy a sandwich and eat it by the sea as a kind of celebration?

By the time she found a sandwich shop and got her ham and cheese, it was after three, and the streets were filling up with schoolchildren, all of whom seemed to be heading for the beach.

It was only a short walk to the promenade, where benches were set under big trees. Some kind of pine, she thought, but exotic-looking. Instead of the pine needles sticking out from the stem, these had needles curved tightly into long fronds, almost woven together. She sat on a bench and played with one that had fallen to the ground. In one direction, it felt smooth – but slide your finger against the curve and the sharp points pricked your skin.

Like a lot of people: only prickly if you didn't go the right way about things.

The sea was a dark blue, with lighter patches of turquoise and aqua where there was no weed underneath. On the beach itself, a number of people sat in deckchairs watching the swimmers in the surf. She felt exhilaration rise in her: she had a job, and here she was, by the ocean.

All along the seafront people strolled. Anyone with real business or the need to go quickly walked behind her, on the other side of the road that hugged the shoreline. Before her, the promenade was edged with a sandstone wall, just low enough to see over if you sat down. Some young men, senior school students by the look of them, sat on the wall to eat their afternoon tea, more interested in the passers-by than the scenery. A few boys burst from a changing room a little to her left and jumped the wall, running for the surf. They were in swimming costumes: knitted one-pieces with singlet tops and formfitting shorts that came only halfway down their thighs. Far more revealing than anything she had seen in England. Not that she'd got to the beach, ever, but in Reading there was a men's and a separate women's swimming pool, and though she'd never been to them she had seen the costumes displayed in the local shops. Those were far more modest than these – they'd had shoulders and sleeves, for one thing, and the wool was much thicker.

Another thing she'd have to get used to, but she really didn't know where to look as they raced past her.

The boys were only young, thirteen or so. If they were free at this time of the afternoon they must be schoolboys, rather than juniors working around here. She envied them their education. She had left school at twelve, as most girls did around West Bromwich, and started working a week later at the greengrocer's on High Street. She'd studied typing at the

Business College at night (a big name for a couple of rooms over a shop where Miss Bean, career spinster, taught typing and filing).

The waves seemed too high for the boys, but they ran and dived with such expertise that her momentary anxiety turned into envy. How she would like to feel that cool water over her skin!

Margaret could hear girls' voices approaching from behind her, coming quickly and breathlessly as though the girls were running just as the boys had. They passed her in a group and she almost choked on her sandwich. They were wearing – good God – exactly the same kind of costumes as the boys!

Not a skerrick more. Singlet tops that showed every detail of their bosoms! Short legs, skin-tight, halfway up their thighs! Ah, not all of them. Some had little skirts instead of shorts, but still, so high up! And the tops. Even on the ones who had little cap sleeves instead of a singlet top, you could see their nipples clearly through the thin wool. Margaret's face flamed with embarrassment, and she looked away.

The young men on the wall stood up. Of course! *This* was why they'd been waiting there: for the chance to ogle these flibbertigibbets, for the chance to insult them.

But the boys lifted their hats as the girls went past and one called out, 'Training, Sylvia?'

'Can't beat those Bondi girls without practice!' one of the girls called back gaily, and waved. She was fifteen or sixteen, perhaps, with a lovely, open face. The face of a nice girl.

The girls went down the stone steps to the beach instead of jumping the wall, but they ran to the waves just as quickly, the young men watching them with – well, appreciation, but not the degrading lust Margaret had expected. The girls dived into a huge swell with smooth competence. Margaret could hear them laughing as they came up the other side.

'We're going to win this year for sure,' one of the young men said.

'Yep. Sylvia's a real Fanny Durack. Credit to the club,' replied another.

They walked off speaking quietly among themselves, and Margaret came back to herself and decided it was time to head home.

She felt shaken. The scene with the beach girls had unsettled her in a way nothing else had since she'd arrived in Australia. For the first time she really felt like she was in a foreign land – not just far away from England, but *different*.

Girls dressed – undressed! – like that in England would have been jeered at and jostled and had . . . well, indignities done to them. Even at the seaside.

She wasn't at all sure if the Australian way was an improvement. How any decent girl could dress like that!

•

'How else are they going to swim?' Jane demanded that night at dinner. 'If you wear one of those dress-thingies the current'll catch you and drag you right out.'

Margaret blinked at her vehemence.

'But they're so revealing!'

'This is the twentieth century, not the eighteenth,' Jane declared.

Margaret turned to Tom and Burnsie in mute appeal.

'I'm staying out of this one!' Tom said immediately. Burnsie smiled and patted Margaret's hand.

'I used to think the same way, dearie. But really, those big bathing dresses with all the frills just make more work for the lifesavers. I do think the girls ought to wear a robe until they get down to the water, though.'

No support there. 'But you wouldn't want Jane to wear one?'

'I *do* wear one, so stick that in your pipe and smoke it!' Jane shot back. 'And I'll bet you a pound that after you try to swim in the surf in one of those old-fashioned bags of a suit *you'll* wear one too!'

Margaret kept silent, but only because she didn't want to make a scene or make the others feel uncomfortable.

Jane grinned at her, all enmity vanished. 'Poor Margi,' she said. 'Don't worry, we won't let you stay a Pom for long. We'll turn you into a real Aussie.'

She knew 'Pom'. Frank had called her that, his 'Pommie girl'. It meant English, although it always sounded insulting to her; like 'pong'. Perhaps a cloud had passed over her face at the thought of Frank, because Tom intervened.

'Margi is fine just as she is, thank you all the same, miss.'

He turned the talk into calmer waters: his new job, the weather, and the upcoming State elections, which caused the whole table to join in with some enthusiasm.

Margaret didn't care who won. She didn't know enough about the various parties, and anyway, what was the point of getting upset about it when she couldn't even vote?

'This time is my first time voting,' Jane said, 'and I'm going to make it count!'

'You can vote?' Margaret couldn't believe it. Jane was nowhere near old enough! They all turned and looked at her with amazement.

'Of course I can,' Jane said. 'Don't girls vote in England?'

Margaret shook her head. That she was sure of. She'd fought often enough with her brother over it; he had been staunchly resistant to the idea, as most men were. Sad to think she couldn't write and tell him that she was living in a country that had decided she was right.

'In nineteen eighteen they allowed women over thirty who owned their own property to vote. But not girls, certainly not. It was only then that men who didn't own property were allowed to vote, as well.'

A row of shocked expressions faced her.

One of the students almost squealed. 'You mean ordinary blokes couldn't vote before?'

Margaret shook her head. 'Nor women.'

'That's so odd,' Jane said. 'We've had the vote for eighteen years now. Everyone over twenty-one. You'd think they'd be ashamed. Don't worry, we'll get you registered in time.'

Girls voting. Women in men's swimming costumes. Margaret had thought she was coming to a backwater, not a hotbed of revolutionary ideas.

All of a sudden, it was too much. For a moment she desperately wished Frank was here, to steer her through these unknown waters. She concentrated on her dessert, rice pudding, and ate it bit by bit, appetite gone. As soon as she decently could, she pushed back her chair and took her plate over to the draining board.

'I think I might turn in early tonight,' she said. 'Tomorrow's my first day.'

Tom looked disappointed, but he didn't say anything, just stood up as she left the room and the others said goodnight.

The image stayed with her as she climbed the stairs: the big redheaded man holding a napkin twisted in his fingers, his steady eyes watching her with concern.

9

The first day at work went better than Margaret could have hoped.

The office systems were beautifully organised. The woman who had done the job before her (gone to have a baby) had clearly been a hard-working, clear-thinking kind of girl.

It was easy enough to follow how the business worked. Items came in or were collected, and were given a receipt. Every hour a boy ran the carbon slips to her and she entered them in a ledger.

She typed letters from Mr Bertram's rough notes, following the pattern of earlier examples from the correspondence book. She answered the phone, although that first day she had to pass most of the queries through to the head clerk, Mr McDougall. But she listened as he answered customers' questions and knew that before long she'd be able to answer all but the trickiest of enquiries.

Mr Bertram was pleasant and full of energy, Mr McDougall, astonishingly, approved of young women working because 'it lends a nice tone to the establishment'. The men on the floor, who moved the lots around, treated her with respect, the errand boys with a cheerful friendliness that was somehow very Australian.

And being able to get a ferry to work was just the icing on the cake.

•

It was a blowy, gusty night, and Margaret found it hard to sleep. She got up eventually when she felt the pressure of her bladder. Too many cups of tea after dinner.

As she padded on bare feet back from the bathroom, she heard a groan, a muted cry. She froze. There had been pain in that sound; she should help, but she couldn't figure out where it had come from, or even if it was inside the house.

The noise came again – from further down the corridor, past the bathroom. Tom's room.

Barely breathing, she listened outside the door, not sure what to do. A low shout – not pain, but anger. And then a moan, a terrible sound, of despair and grief.

She closed her eyes tight as though that would help her hear, as though she could block out the meaning of the sounds. No matter how much she wanted to help, he would resent it if she went in. This nightmare wasn't the sort of thing a man would want to share. Slowly, with sorrow, she went back to bed.

So many of the men had come back carrying bad dreams tucked under their caps. She'd had one herself only recently, about a man on Platform 2 who'd gone wild and ripped all the bandages off the stump of his leg, clawing and scratching at the stitches until he'd begun to bleed, long spurts of blood arcing out from his leg. She'd run towards him, they all had, but he'd fought the closest nurse off, thrust her to the ground with the last of his strength, and had bled to death before anyone else got there. In her dream, she was running and running and not getting any closer, and the blood was spurting further and further, in huge arcs that finally hit her and covered her in hot red.

The first time she'd had that dream, she'd vomited when she woke up. But now she just lay still, shivering, before saying a prayer and going back to sleep.

Better to let Tom deal with his bad dreams in his own way.

At breakfast, she looked closely at him, but he seemed just the same as usual, which was a disquieting thought. Did that mean he had nightmares every night? Her image of him, of his quiet, sensible competence, was shaken into a new pattern. Competent and haunted, but not letting the night shadows influence the day.

'Have I got spinach in my teeth or something?' he quizzed her, laughing because she'd been staring. She blushed and prevaricated.

'A crumb on the side of your mouth,' she said, and reached to brush it off. His skin was softer than she'd thought. When their eyes met, her breath caught in her throat. She snatched her hand back and tried to pretend that nothing had happened.

•

After work on Thursday, Jane took Margaret into the city to enrol to vote at the main police station. It was easy – all she needed was her passport and a letter from Burnsie confirming her address.

Coming out, she tucked her purse under her arm and almost skipped down the stairs. Soon she would vote in an actual election. And her vote would be as important as – as the Prime Minister's! It was a heady thought.

'I told you it was worth it,' Jane said.

'I might never have got to vote in England.'

'Oh, votes for all women'll come there, too.'

'Maybe. But *I'm* voting now!'

They shared a glance, complicit in satisfaction.

'Better hurry up, or we'll miss dinner,' Jane said, smiling.

'Can't have that!'

Circular Quay was only a couple of blocks away. They headed down in a walk that almost broke into a run, the slope was so steep, the rushing descent matching her mood. She felt free to rush headlong into anything now.

On the ferry, as always, they sat up the front, watching the lights of Milson's Point – of home – coming closer.

'I met a girl today,' Jane said, 'up at the council. She was only a year older than me at school, but she got married just before the war, and now she's got five kids and another's on the way. Just think!'

'Five? That's quick work.'

'The first two were twins. But still . . . makes you wonder, doesn't it, what would have happened to you if the war hadn't come along?'

'I'm pretty sure I wouldn't be here,' Margaret said. She'd never considered travelling to Australia before she'd met Frank.

Jane stretched her legs out and regarded her neat little feet. 'Where would you be, then?'

'I don't know. Not in West Bromwich, I don't think. My mam was always telling me to get out, have a life.'

'Mine wants the opposite!'

'Oh, Jane, that's not true. She just wants . . .' Margaret floundered, helpless.

'She wants me to be safe and happy. I know.' Jane pulled her legs back in and glared at a man who'd been eyeing her. 'But what would – if you could be or do *anything*, what would you be?' It seemed to Margaret that there was something behind the question, but the problem itself distracted her. What did she want? No one had ever asked her that before, and she'd certainly never asked herself – not in this large, no-holds-barred way. It wasn't like she'd had any choice about who she was or what she could do. She'd taken the jobs that were offered and been thankful for them. What *did* she want?

There had been showers off and on all day, but the skies were clearing. She looked up at the high expanse of stars and felt rather like the sky: the clouds that had prevented her from having a clear view of her life were moving away, but she wasn't sure if she could see enough to answer that question.

'I like business,' she said. 'Maybe I'd like to run my own business. But I don't know in what. And where would the money come from? Might as well say I'd like to be a doctor.'

Sighing, Jane sat back and tucked her legs under the seat. 'Always comes down to that, doesn't it? Nice to be a man. They've got scholarships for returned soldiers.'

Margaret thought of the hospital trains that had gone through Reading Station, full of bandaged, or raving, or unconscious men. She thought of the boys who hadn't come back, and the men who had, silent and scarred.

'They've earned it.' She looked at Jane curiously. 'What about you? What would you do?'

Jane stood up and struck an attitude. 'Oh, I'd be a world famous star of stage and screen!' She laughed, a little bitterly.

Margaret stood up, too, and leaned back against the railing. 'At least you don't need a scholarship for that!'

Jane laughed again, more easily, and turned the talk to a new movie she wanted to see, *A Fighting Colleen*.

10

Gladys finished at two o'clock on Saturdays, so Frank picked up Violet from the neighbour who looked after her as soon as he got back from work.

The woman, Bea, answered the door looking harassed and visibly pregnant.

'Last day, eh?' she said to Frank. 'Well, I can't say I'm sorry. My two are enough, with the new one on the way.'

'Thanks,' Frank said, not knowing what to say. 'Yes, last day.'

Violet heard his voice and came rampaging up the corridor. 'Papa! Papapapapa!' She slipped between Bea's legs and barrelled into him.

Bea screwed her mouth to one side. 'You're never going to make a lady out of this one. A hoyden, she is.'

Frank swung Vi up into his arms. 'At least she's got a bit of spirit,' he said. Bea's children were behind her now, a couple of sharp-featured, pale-faced boys whose spirit, if they'd had any, was long gone. 'Do we owe you anything?'

'No, no, Glad fixed me up. You going to stick with her this time?' Her tone was belligerent.

'Reckon so,' Frank said. Violet flung herself backwards until she was upside down in Frank's arms, laughing happily. He couldn't help it, he laughed with her.

'If you don't put the strap to that one, there'll be no controlling her,' Bea advised, and shut the door in his face.

'Papapapa,' Violet said, and pulled herself up by hanging onto his arm, then kissed his cheek, and nuzzled into his neck with a big sigh.

'Hmph,' he said to the closed door. 'No one's going to strap a kid of mine.'

He had too many memories of being strapped himself in the orphanage. Strapped, belted, caned . . . and kept without food or somewhere to sleep for too long. His kids were going to get hugs, not beltings.

'Come on, bub, let's go get Mummy.'

Violet bounced in his arms until he put her down and they walked hand in hand to the tram stop on Parramatta Road. He would normally have just walked to the factory, but it was a bit far for Vi's little legs.

She loved the tram and the tram conductor grinned at her and clipped his ticket half a dozen times just to hear her squeal, 'Again!'

You always knew when it was the stop for the biscuit factory; the sweet scent wafted for a block or more. As soon as she smelled it, Violet clapped her hands together and said, 'Mummy!'

Frank carried her off the tram and down the side street to the staff door. They were a little early and he had to restrain Vi from just going inside to get her mum. She was halfway to a tantrum (and what would he do then?) when the door opened and the women came streaming out, Gladys included. The others kissed her goodbye, or waved, shouting, 'Keep in touch!' She waved back, then turned, smiling, to Frank and Violet.

'Are you being naughty for Papa?' she asked Vi, quite sternly.

Vi quietened immediately. 'No, Mummy.' Then Glad smiled and opened her arms and Vi launched herself into them.

'There's my good girl,' she said.

Vi pointed to the factory. 'Mummy work.'

'Not anymore, sweetheart,' Glad said with satisfaction. 'Now we're living with Papa. From now on, I'm going to be at home with you. All day, every day.'

Frank slid his arm around Gladys's shoulders. All day, every day. A home and family waiting for him, all day, every day. It wasn't the home he had planned with Margaret, but by God! it was better than a boarding house. And Gladys . . . the pre-war days when Glad was just a girl to go dancing with, to fall into bed with, they were long past. She was a born mother. It gave him a warm satisfaction to see her with Violet, loving their child the way a mother should.

'How about a milkshake?' he asked. 'Or maybe a lolly, to celebrate?'

'Lollollol!' Vi shouted, and they all laughed.

11

After lunch on Sunday, despite Jane's exhortations, Margaret hadn't dared go swimming. Jane had insisted on taking her to the beach – not to Manly, but to the smaller, quieter inlet of Fairlight, on the Harbour. A curve of smooth sand in a dip between sandstone headlands, Fairlight had attracted a number of families with children, many of the smallest running around naked except for their shirts, plump and pink from the sun, splashing in the shallows.

Margaret took off her shoes and stockings (blushing a little), tucked Mrs Shelley's good black skirt a little higher, and ventured down to the edge of the water. At least there weren't any big combers here. The small waves were barely taller than her knee, and broke just offshore, so she could walk in the shallows without even wetting her skirt.

The water was cool and delicious. Her feet sank into the sand as she just stood, watching Jane swim – actually swim the Australian crawl! – across the bay, out beyond the waves in the truly deep water. Margaret was full of admiration. There weren't many things she was afraid of, really, but to strike out so boldly! The sand shifted under her feet as a wave drew back, and she stumbled and righted herself, breathless. Time to sit on the sand and watch the endless waves.

When Jane sprinkled water down her back it caught her entirely by surprise.

It was beautifully cold.

'Jane! You wretch!'

'I don't know how you can stand out here and not want to try it,' Jane said, grinning. She at least reached for her robe and wrapped it around herself. Just as well – it had turned out that Jane's suit was made of knitted cotton, and was even more revealing than the wool ones when wet.

Margaret tipped her head back and closed her eyes, the sun making her eyelids turn red, filling her with energy and maybe some more gumption.

'Perhaps I will,' she said. 'But I want one of those suits with a skirt and sleeves.'

•

Monday was auction day, at two o'clock. Around one-thirty, Mr Bertram came up from the auction floor and beckoned to her.

'You're on the floor while the sale is going on. Bring the blue ledger.'

When they went downstairs, she was surprised by how many people were already there, strolling around the big room, leaning over or crouching down to get a better look at some of the items. Mr Bertram set her up at a desk to the right of the podium, complete with ledger and delivery slips. Mr McDougall sat next to her with the cash box.

'Well, lassie,' he said. 'Take a deep breath.'

It was good advice, because the next two hours were a whirlwind. At the lectern, auctioneer's wooden hammer in hand, Mr Bertram was transformed from a polite, genial man to a businesslike, get-on-with-it martinet. She could see why – there were so many lots to get through that there was no time for chatter. Today was a general auction: furniture, most of it old Victorian pieces that were too big and heavy for today's tastes, and household goods, which included everything from chipped crockery to egg beaters. Lawn mowers, ice chests, an elephant's foot umbrella stand, a couple of old mangles, a grindstone on its wheel . . . many were clumped together as 'assorted goods'. There were almost two hundred lots in total, and she was astonished at how fast Mr Bertram got through them.

She kept up – just. Once the hammer came down, one of the floor staff – Joe the delivery driver, in a different role today – gave the buyer of the item a red tag showing the lot number and the price. The buyer brought it to her, and she entered the details in the ledger. Mr McDougall took the money (or, in rare cases with a regular customer, a cheque). If the buyer wanted the goods delivered, Mr McDougall took the money while she made out the delivery slip.

Then on to the next one. And the next.

By the time she looked up to find that there was no one waiting, it was four-thirty.

She sat back in her chair, suddenly aware of an ache in her back, and let out a long breath. The floor was almost cleared of goods, excepting a few big pieces of furniture. Joe and his offsider were loading a Dutch dresser onto the firm's cart.

Mr Bertram came over and smiled at her, back to his friendly self.

'All right?' he said. It was a question to both of them. She tensed, waiting for Mr McDougall's verdict, aware that this first auction might be her last if she didn't measure up.

'It went very smoothly,' Mr McDougall said. 'She can keep her head.'

'Right!' Mr Bertram said, smiling at her. 'Tomorrow morning you calculate the sellers' payouts and make out the cheques, or make up the envelopes with the cash, whichever they prefer. It'll be on the file. Then we get ready for the next sale, on Wednesday.'

Margaret smiled. It had been exhilarating, in an odd way, racing to keep pace with Mr Bertram's swift dispatch of lot after lot. But she'd be glad to settle to some simple bookkeeping tomorrow.

•

Wednesday's auction was *objets d'art* and antiques. These were held only once a month, as were the auctions for jewellery and fine art. Fewer lots, but much higher prices. Folding seats set out for the buyers. Margaret helped Joe and the floor staff to set up. Not only seats, but tea and coffee were offered, and the big doors at the back were closed against the heat and glare.

Mr Bertram, like a chameleon, was a different auctioneer: urbane, witty, encouraging the buyers to spend more by lauding the qualities of each item with precise and informed praise.

'Now here, ladies and gentlemen,' he said, 'we have a lovely pair of Meissen statuettes, a shepherd and his shepherdess, circa eighteen fifteen, complete with the Meissen mark. Do I hear ten pounds?'

Margaret couldn't believe the amounts these little bits of china were selling for. It was another world. Even the High

House hadn't prepared her for either the beauty or the cost of some of the items.

This auction had a different rhythm, and a different feel, as though auctioneer and audience were united in one endeavour, and it took Margaret a while to work it out – it was the endeavour of culture. These were cultured people. The names Mr Bertram threw out: Meissen, Wedgwood, Moorcroft, Waterford; everyone in the room (except her, and maybe Joe) knew their significance, understood their meaning. As each piece was brought to the table by Joe and his offsider Dick, Margaret tried to figure out what was important in it; why it was valuable. Sometimes it was easy: silver, gilded, very old. But mostly the qualities escaped her. She didn't understand why a Meissen shepherdess commanded five times the price of a Royal Doulton one – they certainly didn't look any better, to her eyes. But these people knew. It was a select club, one she was locked out of.

There was no rushing the desk after each item, either. These buyers stayed in their seats. It seemed that the auction was a form of entertainment to them. Instead of having them queue at the desk to pay, Mr McDougall murmured the name of the buyer into her ear and she entered it into the ledger and then made out an invoice that would be posted to them. All of the buyers were known to Mr McDougall except one, who came and gave his details after it was all over. Several bought more than one item ('Antique shop owners,' Mr McDougall whispered to her), but most of the audience bought nothing at all.

'They just like to keep an eye on the market,' Mr McDougall said. 'So they know what prices are doing. They come here, they meet their friends, they see who's buying what. Wait until the jewellery sales!'

Afterwards, when the doors were set wide and the afternoon sun was mellow outside, Mr Bertram came over to her, and smiled as though he could read her mind.

'A bit different today, eh?'

'Yes,' was all she could manage. She'd never felt more working class in her life. But he grinned at her.

'Interested?'

'Very!'

'Good. I'll lend you some books. You'll soon get the hang of it.'

It seemed that Mr Bertram was willing to open up the door to the club and let her in. She didn't understand why, and said so.

'Might train you up as a valuer,' he said. 'I can see you having the touch with the old ladies. Business is expanding. I've got to plan for the future.'

'But my work here—'

He laughed. 'Don't rush. It'll take you years to get the expertise you'll need.'

•

Late that afternoon, Margaret met Jane at Circular Quay. She didn't mention Mr Bertram's astonishing suggestion, nor the fact that her bag was weighed down by a book on English potteries. Time enough to speculate. For now she was just happy to learn more about her job. But the image of herself as a New Woman, with a career instead of a job, was tantalising. She wouldn't even be an old maid, like most of them were. A widow making a career for herself was practically respectable. No need for a husband then. No need to put her life in someone else's hands. Independent and self-sufficient. Safe from heartache.

'Way's in Pitt Street have a sale on,' Jane said. 'Mark Foy's have a bigger selection, but Way's have the Canadian-style suits you want, and they're a whole shilling cheaper.'

So many stores she'd never heard of. All part of assimilating. She would come to know them, eventually, and be able to talk knowledgeably about them. She would have a map of the city in her head that included all these places, and more.

Jane led her off the tram and through a beautiful old Victorian arcade full of things far too expensive for either of them, 'but it doesn't cost anything to look,' as Jane said. The next street was Pitt Street. Way's was only a few doors down and here again Jane took charge, making Margaret get the lighter cotton suit instead of the wool, despite her misgivings about modesty, and she talked her out of the long-sleeved version for one with cap sleeves. But Margaret insisted on buying the stockings to go with it, and a rubberised bathing cap. And a Turkish towelling wrap. And some plimsolls. It made her nervous to spend so much money, but it would be worth it, she was sure.

'The sand'll get into your stockings,' Jane warned her on the ferry home, but she didn't care. She could get right down to the water in her wrap and then plunge under the waves and stay under.

'What are you smiling at?' Jane asked.

'Australia,' Margaret answered, and Jane grinned at her. The lights from the city were floating on the water as the stars came out, and the ferry was caught between the two, sailing across ink-black sea with an ink-black sky above. The warmth of the day was still caught in the wooden seats they sat on, and Margaret felt, for a moment, perfectly at peace, imagining her first venture into the water the next weekend.

Then she sat up, horror-struck. Her swimming costume was navy blue. It had been the cheapest.

'Oh no! Jane, how could you let me? I should have bought the black one!'

Jane stared at her, aghast. 'I never thought . . . Oh, look, don't worry. Once it's wet it'll look black enough. Anyway, no one'll know you're a widow.'

But *she* was supposed to know. *She* was supposed to *care*. She would never pull off this masquerade. Why had she let Tom talk her into it?

Jane was looking at her with deep concern, the light from inside the ferry cabin picking up the gold streaks in her hair, making her face seemed blanched with worry.

'It's all right,' Margaret said. 'I suppose it's . . . hard for me to believe it. I haven't seen him for so long . . .'

She felt wretched lying. Jane had been so kind to her.

'Not being at the funeral,' Jane nodded. 'Mrs Shelley was like that, after Major Shelley was killed on the Somme. Couldn't quite believe it. It takes a while to sink in. You only found out about it two weeks ago.'

Two weeks. It felt like months had passed. It felt like yesterday.

•

But on Friday, when Jane tried to persuade her to go with a party of friends to the dance at the Church Hall the next night, she absolutely refused.

'I'm a widow,' she said. 'It wouldn't be right.'

'You don't have to dance,' Jane wheedled.

'What good would it do her to go there and watch other people having a grand time?' Burnsie shook her head and Jane wilted, but then revived.

'She needs to get out of the house! She's hardly seen anything of the city.'

'Well, she won't see any more of the city in the Church Hall!' her mother said firmly.

Margaret met Tom's eyes over his teacup, and they both bit back smiles.

'How about I take Margi out for a sight-seeing tour on Sunday?' he asked.

'Don't I get a say in this?' Margaret asked.

'No,' Jane said. 'We'll all go.' She included the boys from the Conservatorium in her gesture, but they shook their heads.

'We have to practise for the Bush Week concert,' the cellist said. 'And we're playing at the dance on Saturday night, so Sunday we'll have to go like billy-o to catch up.'

'Just us three, then,' Margaret said, conscious of a faint disappointment that Jane would come with them.

'But on Saturday afternoon I'll teach you to swim!' Jane declared.

Heaven help her. She wasn't ready for that.

12

The water was cold at first. Startlingly cold as it reached her nether regions. It slapped against her almost as if it were playing. Around her, men and women and even children were jumping waves. A father swung a toddler so that his little feet slapped an incoming wavelet; the child gurgled and waved his arms, fearless.

'Come on!' Jane said. 'You can stand up a long way out.'

Margaret stood, paralysed, waist deep, waves breaking around her cloudy with sand. The surf tugged and pulled at her. Her feet sank deeper and she could feel sand creeping into her plimsolls. The whole world was moving: waves, sand, the clouds above. Her heart sped up; she didn't know if she was excited or terrified.

A warm hand touched her back at the waist.

'Come on,' Tom's voice said. 'It's all right. Just a little further and you'll be past the break.'

Carefully, she slid her foot forward. There was a dip in the sand and she stumbled, but Tom's arm came around her, holding her up. For a moment she was starkly aware of the band of heat from his skin through the thin cotton of her suit.

A blush swept over her and she took another step, another, to pull away from that sensation. A widow. She was supposed to be a widow, and it wasn't seemly for her to be supported by a single man. Especially when that man was clad in nothing but a singlet-topped bathing costume which came only to mid-thigh.

A curler came and broke right over her, over her shoulders, wetting her face, lifting her off her feet and setting her back down again. And again, another wave. The scale tipped over from fear to excitement; she laughed aloud, tasting salt on her lips.

'That's the spirit,' Jane said. She came back and took Margaret's hand, pulling her forward, past the break point.

Suddenly, it was easier to move. The tug and push of the waves was gentler, and she swayed easily with the pull. Tom came up level with her and grinned.

'You're doing well,' he said.

The scent of salt was so strong out here, away from every-thing. Smaller waves flowed past her, pulling and pushing her. Like being on a swing. Then a larger one came. As big as a horse. It would smother her—

'Jump!' Tom said and put his hand under her elbow, hoisting her easily. She tried to help, pushing off with her toes, and was astonished at the ease and lightness with which she floated up, was carried up, was lifted. Like flying!

Her feet came back down to the sand with a small jolt and she laughed. Tom grinned at her.

'Good-oh?'

She'd heard that word before, from Frank.

'Good-oh,' she said, smiling up at him.

Her moment's inattention cost her, as a wave slapped her face and water went into her ear and mouth. She spat it out, spluttering and laughing.

Jane had moved a little way away. Margaret couldn't work out what she was doing – standing there, arms forward but with her head turned back to watch the incoming rollers.

'Here's a good one, Jane!' Tom yelled. 'Ready, set, go! Jump, Margi!'

Jane dived into the water and began to swim frantically. The wave hit them and Tom hoicked Margaret up by her elbow. She felt again that magic, weightless sensation. When she came down and found her footing, Jane had disappeared.

'Jane? Where is she?'

Tom pointed to the shore, where Jane was hauling herself up from her belly on the sand, grinning widely, froth and bubbles around her feet.

'All that way? She ... she ...' Margaret didn't have the words to describe what Jane had done.

'She shot the surf,' Tom said. 'Jump!'

Absently, Margaret jumped, on her own this time, and was recalled to herself by the lovely push-and-float feeling.

'Shot the surf?'

'That's it. Surf shooting's the best fun you can have sober.'

Margaret blushed; Frank had used that expression for another activity altogether. For a moment she was overtaken by memory – Frank's hand on her thigh, his mouth on her shoulder ... A cold wave slapped at her and she was thankful for it.

Jane arrived back, full of energy.

'I'll watch her, Tommy,' she said. 'You have a go.'

'Sure?'

'I'll be fine,' Margaret said, uneasy but trying to be brave. 'You both go.'

'No fear,' Tom said. 'Not when you can't swim. Too dangerous. Jump!'

Margaret jumped and looked around. There were children of nine or ten happily jumping waves around her.

'Don't you be fooled,' Jane warned her. 'Those kiddies have been doing this all their lives. They can read the surf.'

'We'll both stay with you,' Tom said.

So they did. Jane taught her how to kick her legs and push her hands down as she jumped so she went even higher, her shoulders emerging at the top of the wave. The weightless feeling, the sense of flying, was even stronger.

Tom stayed nearby, ready with a steadying hand on her arm, her elbow, holding her hand for a moment, a second, warm and disturbing.

The world was a swirl of golden sun and green sea, blue sky and Tom's red hair, Jane's bright emerald costume; a swoosh of waves and children's laughter and her own panting, laughing breath. This was it. This was what she had wanted without knowing it, all those dreary grey days in the Black Country, all the nights nursing her mother and father before they died, all the cold dawns when the chilblains on her feet had made her limp to her shift at the Railways. Every time she'd shivered in her too-thin coat, every time she'd felt the rain slide chill into the flimsy stitching of her shoes, this was what she'd needed.

'Jump!' she shouted, and laughed.

•

Margaret felt far less self-conscious as she walked out of the water than she had walking in, despite the way her wet costume clung to her curves.

Jane pulled off her bathing cap and let her soaked hair tumble out to dry in the sun, as though a grown woman walking around with loose hair wasn't an invitation to – something.

Loose hair, loose woman, her mother used to say, but that was in England. How mortified her mother would be if she could see Margaret now.

But how could she be embarrassed when she was surrounded by forty or fifty other women dressed identically – in fact, perhaps not dressed quite so nicely as she and Jane? And the men weren't looking at her anyway – they were watching the men on the surfboards further down the beach.

'Wind's picking up,' Tom observed. 'Nice swell starting.'

The wind was pleasantly cool but Margaret was happy to wrap her Turkish robe around her when they reached their gear. She could feel that her skin had a touch of the sun; it wasn't burned, but it would be red tonight on her shoulders and forehead, and tomorrow she would have freckles across her nose. How lucky she was that she could tan, and that a light tan here wasn't so looked down on. At home, the only people who had browned skin were those who worked outdoors for a living – farmers and gardeners and navvies.

Poor Tom had slathered himself with coconut oil to ward off a burn – it was funny, his face and arms were weathered, but his body was pale, and there was a band of white across his forehead, where his hat sat.

'Too long in uniform,' he'd grinned. Now he stuck his oldest hat back on, as soon as they got back to their clothes. Second nature. She took a moment to look at him as he gazed at the surf. He'd taken her under his wing, that was certain, and he'd done it with a mixture of warmth and delicacy not often seen in a man, especially an Army sergeant.

Unlike a lot of men, out of his uniform he still looked manly, strong and tall and competent. She wondered if his interest in her was romantic, or merely the kindness a strong man might show to someone in trouble. He was the sort to take on a lame dog. The thought disquieted her. Of course, she didn't want a new romance . . . but she didn't want to be anyone's lame dog, either.

For a few moments they watched the surfers carve tracks through the waves. Astonishing! Like gymnasts or ballet dancers. They moved along their boards, crouched and turned with an exciting grace. Then, as one guided his board right into shore on a huge wave dwindling down to froth, Margaret gasped.

'That's a woman!'

A passer-by, a local by the look of his tanned shoulders and well-worn costume, turned and grinned at her.

'That's Isabel Letham. Best woman surfer in the world, I reckon.'

It was a new way of thinking. She would never have imagined that women could not only *physically* control the big wooden boards, but that people would actually approve. It was all of a piece with the heady, flying feeling of the surf. She felt herself shaking a little and tried to blame it on the chill of the wind, but underneath she was dizzy with possibilities. Voting, surfing – was nothing forbidden to Australian women?

Life at home had been ordered and predictable, once the war ended. But here, things seemed to still be changing, moving on rather than trying to bring back the pre-war days. It lit a flame in her, of anticipation. Who knew what she might become here? For a brief, laughing moment, she imagined herself out there on a surf board with Isabel Letham. There didn't seem to be anything stopping her except her own timidity. Certainly there was nothing stopping her learning to swim.

They threaded their way through a throng of what Jane scornfully called tourists to the bathing boxes that lined the street edge of the sand. Apparently locals did surf-shooting, and tourists surf-bathing – the kind of gentle wave-jumping that Margaret had so thoroughly enjoyed. Margaret was uncomfortably aware that she looked rather like a tourist, too, in her brand-new suit and shoes – none of the locals wore shoes in the water.

'Don't worry, pet,' Jane said. 'We'll have you shooting the breakers soon enough, eh, Tommy?'

'Too right. Next Saturday we'll teach you to swim.'

'And no shoes, I think, next time,' Margaret said.

'Or stockings!' Jane challenged her.

Margaret took a breath to steady herself. It felt more important than it surely was, this moment. As though she were a chick about to break out of its egg, or a snake shedding a skin.

'No stockings,' she agreed, and pulled off her bathing cap, shaking her hair loose down her back as Jane had done.

13

Frank and Gladys sat on a park bench and watched Violet run around on the grass, chasing a sparrow. Sunday afternoon and the park was full of families. And here he was, with his. There was warmth in his heart, even though his mind flicked momentarily to Margaret as a girl with brown curly hair walked by. The memory of desire kicked him in the gut, but he pushed it down. No good mooning over someone who didn't want you.

Glad wanted him. Loved him. He wished, he really did, that he loved her the same way, but he couldn't pretend to himself that he felt the same about her as he'd felt about Margaret. The first time he'd seen Margaret, with her vivid green eyes, it had been as though he'd turned into another man. Someone better, braver, stronger than he really was.

Still, Margaret wasn't here, was she? Australia wasn't good enough for her, apparently. He'd fallen on his feet, though.

'I bought you something,' he said shyly. Gladys looked at him with a questioning smile as he placed a box on her lap. A proper jeweller's box, although the ring itself was nothing to write home about.

Gladys opened it slowly, her eyes wide, and then the colour rushed up into her cheeks as she brought out the ring.

'Oh, Frank!'

A little thing, topaz, only nine carat gold. But it looked bonzer, shining in the sun. Gladys hesitated, the ring in her hand, as though she didn't know which finger to put it on. For the first time Frank realised he would have to choose. Friends or engaged? Well, it was a bit silly to call them friends when they already had a kid together. Engaged . . . well, he couldn't be engaged, could he? Not with a wife back in Blighty.

But Gladys deserved it. She'd been faithful to him, all that time he'd been away. Raising his daughter all by herself, and doing a great job. He wondered, briefly, if Margaret could have done as well – of course, *her* friends would have turned their noses up at an unmarried girl. Lucky Glad and he didn't move in those circles. He could only think of a couple of the girls at the biscuit factory who were married, but all of them had a fella. Except Glad. She'd just waited for him.

Even after he'd come home and told Gladys about Margaret, even then she hadn't gone off with some other bloke, and she'd have been well within her rights to.

He took the ring and slid it onto the third finger of Gladys's left hand. The engagement finger.

'There,' he said. 'Can't ask you to marry me, but that's the next best thing.'

'As long as we're together,' she said.

She leaned forward and kissed him, right out in front of everyone. She didn't care, he knew. All she cared about was him and Violet. Her lips were soft against his and he couldn't stop himself smiling.

'You'll do, my girl,' he said.

'I like being your girl, Frank.'

He put his arm around her shoulder and hugged her.

'So I should think!'

Violet ran towards them and flung herself into Frank's lap.

'Papa! Papa! Puppy!' She tugged at his hand and, laughing, he got up to go and see the puppy. He pulled Gladys with him as he went and they ran across the grass, the three of them, as happy as Larry.

•

That night he tucked Vi into bed.

'Story, Papa!' she demanded. He hesitated. What kind of story did you tell a little one? He'd never had any himself; bedtime at the orphanage had been a brutal, no-nonsense process policed by the older boys, who were more than happy to flick a belt around your legs if you weren't nippy enough getting under the covers.

'I don't know any stories,' he said. Violet looked at him in sheer disbelief.

'Mummy teach Papa. Sing!'

The lullaby of his childhood had been the homesick sobbing of the new kids.

He knew other songs, though. He rapidly sorted through the ones that were suitable for young ears.

Paddy wrote a letter to his Irish Molly-o
Sayin' if you don't receive it, write and let me know
And if I make mistakes in spelling, Molly dear, said he,
Remember it's the pen that's bad, don't blame the blame on me!
It's a long way to Tipperary, it's a long way to go . . .

He sang as softly as he could, and gradually her little eyes closed, but her hand remained firmly clasping his. Staring at her, it became harder and harder to keep singing; emotion rose in his throat and made him hoarse. She was so beautiful, his Vi, and so *happy*. He would make sure she stayed happy. That she would never, *never*, end up with a childhood like his.

'*It's a long, long way to Tipperary, but my heart's right there.*'

His heart was right here. He kissed her sleeping brow and carefully slid his hand out of hers. For the first time ever, he had a family. He could almost find it in him to be glad that Margaret hadn't come.

•

He slid into bed, careful not to wake Glad. Despite everything, this was the time when he thought about Margaret. He knew he shouldn't still love her, after what she'd done, but he couldn't help it. There was something about the memory of her clear green eyes, her soft mouth, those flyaway eyebrows . . . Glad was prettier, in some ways, but Margaret . . .

Well, he'd never lied to Gladys about how he felt. He cared about her, of course he did, and he cared more every day. But it was Margaret who came to him in his dreams.

14

Sunday morning was a big breakfast morning at Burnsie's. Bacon and eggs, chops, baked beans and fried kidneys. Mountains of toast.

It was a chattering, happy meal, and Burnsie was in her element, topping up teacups, urging everyone to have 'just one more'. It was hot in the kitchen, even this early, but Margaret didn't mind. It had been so long since she'd felt a part of anything, and this was almost like family.

'Come on, you lot,' Burnsie said, 'or I won't be finished the washing up in time for church.'

That was apparently a cue for everyone to say, 'We'll do the washing up.' Margaret joined in and found Burnsie fixing her with an assessing eye.

'Are you coming to church, Margi?'

Margaret blinked. She hadn't been a regular at church since 1915, when she'd started working at Reading Station. They'd worked a notional six-day week, on roster, but Sunday was the same as every other day to the war, and the troop trains travelled the same, so she'd had only every fifth Sunday off. And God forgive her, she mostly couldn't bring herself to spend any of that time in a dim and dismal church hearing the names of the parish dead read out, and prayers for those not yet fallen. For that one day, like her workmates and the soldiers they met, she wanted to have fun, to forget about war and death and evil. They never did really forget it, of course, but they tried: picnics and concerts and walks in the countryside, and of course the singalongs in the pub in the evenings.

And in West Bromwich, after her parents' deaths, she couldn't bear to go to the Methodist chapel that reminded her so vividly of them.

But there was no reason now not to go to church. Her mother and father would want her to go.

'Yes,' she said. One thing she had decided, during those war years, was that it didn't much matter what kind of Christian you were. It was the same God, after all. 'Yes, I'd like to go with you.'

Burnsie beamed at her. 'Right then,' she said. 'The rest of you can get stuck into the dishes while Margi and I get ready. Just put that big frying pan to soak, Tom.'

In Mrs Shelley's best black frock and hat and her own much dowdier black pumps, Margaret accompanied Burnsie up the steep hill to Lavender Street and along to Christ Church, the Anglican church.

'Jane . . . ?' she ventured. 'Is she not coming?'

Burnsie shrugged, unconcerned. 'Jane's a Free Thinker,' she said. 'She'll get over it. She's not a bad girl, or anything. But the war unsettled her.'

'It unsettled a lot of people,' Margaret said dryly, and Burnsie shot her a look of resigned humour.

'It did that. Here we are.'

Like many of the public buildings she had seen since her arrival, Christ Church was built of warm golden sandstone. Other than that, it was much like any Church of England church.

In Reading, the Methodist chapel had been a long way from her digs. When she did go to church, it was at the invitation of the other girls; not from Mary O'Grady, of course – there were limits, and Roman Catholicism was one of them. But she went to most of the others.

She'd found that there was less difference in the churches than you might think if you'd listened to her father. Different rituals, and there was no doubt that the Methodists were the best singers. But they all had Bible readings, and they all had sermons.

Margaret had a sudden memory of her father saying scornfully, 'No difference twixt Anglicans and the Papists, tha knows.' It seemed so long ago.

They went inside and saw children being shepherded out a side door by a young woman, presumably to Sunday School, and mothers with babies sitting in a group up the back, near the door, so they could take their little ones out if they cried. Because Australia hadn't had conscription, there were far more young men than you would find in an English church. The war hadn't killed off most of a generation here.

Burnsie picked up a couple of hymnbooks from a pile on a small table just inside the doors.

Each worshipper headed straight for a particular pew. Margaret hesitated, but Burnsie took her arm and led her to a pew halfway up on the right-hand side.

'Here we are,' she said. Margaret slid in beside her and looked around. It was lighter inside than she would have expected in a church – a combination of whitewashed walls and the strong

Australian sun beaming in. The room was alive with colour: the bright outline of each stained-glass window was cast on the white walls in vivid reds, blues and greens.

Mrs Shelley's hands had been smaller than Margaret's and her fingers were crushed into the inherited gloves. It made her feel even more a fraud, pretending to be a widow in the house of the Lord. She prayed for forgiveness, for understanding.

Then she prayed for Frank. Although she'd been angry with him, she couldn't help but care what happened to him. She didn't feel *vengeful*, just bewildered and sad and, still, unable to quite believe it all. They had been to church together, to the Methodist chapel, and he had seemed so sincere . . . Best not to think too much about that. Think of something else.

The doors closed behind them, cutting off a stream of light, as the vicar entered from the side, complete with vestments in green and gold, followed by altar boys.

They all stood up. A slice of light shot down the aisle as a latecomer entered, and a moment later Tom slid into the pew, breathing fast as though he'd been running.

'Just made it,' he whispered. He settled next to her, smelling of soap and heat, and picked up a hymnbook.

The service was different in specifics but familiar in purpose – more sitting down and standing up and kneeling than she was used to, and the singing was disappointing to one raised on the full-throated Wesleyan hymn-singing. But she felt, nonetheless, that she was reclaiming a part of herself that had been lost in the war, and by the end of the service she was full of an airy feeling that reminded her of jumping up into a wave.

The vicar stood at the door and spoke to everyone as they left. As Burnsie introduced him to Margaret and Tom, a man moving around them stopped.

'Sergeant McBride, isn't it? Bill Flynn.' He put out a hand and they pumped enthusiastically.

'Bill! Gosh, yes. But not so much of the "sergeant". It's Tom now. How are you? Didn't recognise you without all the mud.'

The two men dropped into the what's-happened-to-so-and-so talk of returned soldiers until Burnsie took Tom's elbow and pulled him out of the doorway so other people could leave the church.

'Oh, sorry,' Tom said, recollecting their existence, 'we've been prosing on and boring you.'

Margaret smiled at Bill and shook her head.

'Don't you fret about that,' she said. 'It's always nice to meet old friends.'

Bill's eyes warmed as he looked at her properly for the first time, and she looked away. She hadn't paid much attention to Jane telling her she looked good in black, but Bill's eyes were saying so much more stridently.

Tom moved a little, putting himself in front of her; just his shoulder, but it was enough for Bill to flick his eyes at Tom's face and then move back. Conceding ground. Acknowledging – what? It was over in a second, but Margaret had seen Frank do as Tom had done, and had known it for a movement of possession.

She was embarrassed and surprised. It was nice to know that she could still inspire that response, even if she was damaged goods.

Then another thought cut across that small spurt of pleasure and confidence. She couldn't give her happiness, her trust, into another man's hands. She couldn't. Couldn't bear to be betrayed again.

She moved away from Tom, turning her back on the men, and said to Burnsie, 'I think I'll head back.'

Burnsie came with her, uncharacteristically silent until they were almost home.

'He didn't mean anything by it,' she said quietly.

'Which one?'

'Tom. He was just . . . he . . .' It was odd, to see Burnsie stumble over words. 'He's a good man. He can't help feeling—'

'I'm in mourning,' Margaret said brusquely. The perfect excuse.

'I know.' Before Burnsie could say anything else, behind her, Tom's footsteps echoed. How did she know, without thinking, that they were his? He walked rapidly, but he went to Burnsie's side, not Margaret's, and that was good, that was just fine, because the last thing she wanted was to open herself up to hurt again.

'Bill's asked me to join Manly Life Saving,' he said happily, as though nothing had happened between them. And maybe nothing had, that he knew.

'Good idea,' Burnsie said. 'They could use a few more like you.'

The rest of the walk home was taken up discussing lifesaving training and the good it did.

'It'll be good,' Tom said, 'to *save* lives.'

That silenced all of them. Margaret couldn't help wondering how many lives he'd taken, not saved, but how could he even know? How could any soldier know?

•

Back home, Margaret washed her stockings and then wrote a letter to the Tooths, the family who were living in her parents' old house, telling them her new address. She didn't expect to get many letters, but there were some girls from the Reading Station days she'd like to stay in touch with. As the end of the war had approached, when they'd realised the office would be cut back to its normal staff and they'd all have to find other jobs, she'd given them her parents' address, but that was before her parents had caught the flu. Before she'd left to nurse them. Before. When she'd been cluelessly happy, naïvely gullible in her faith in Frank.

Even now she found it hard to believe. Some part of her still yearned for him, for his sweet smile and gentleness, for his warmth. For his touch. A wicked curiosity plagued her at odd moments: what did his real wife look like? His daughter? It was small-minded of her to hope that the wife had a squint and flat feet . . .

She sealed the envelope and put it in her purse so she could post it the next day. Still so hard to believe, that Frank – clear-eyed, straightforward Frank – had lied to her so viciously.

She must be a terrible judge of character.

After lunch, Tom and Jane waited for her expectantly at the front door. The sight-seeing tour. She'd forgotten all about it. It all seemed too much, all of a sudden.

'I don't think—'

'Come on, pet,' Jane said reaching for the purse, gloves and hat Margaret had placed on a side table when she'd come in from church. Jane held them out. 'It'll do you good.'

She could have resisted pushiness, but not kindness. Obediently, she pinned on her hat and put her gloves on, slid her purse handle over her arm.

'Ready, sergeant, ma'am.'

Jane grinned at her. 'That's the spirit.'

•

Sydney had a park named, inevitably, Hyde Park. So many things here were named after places from Home; Margaret wasn't sure if it was nostalgia or hubris that had inspired the colonists.

'Is the London Hyde Park like this?' Jane asked.

Margaret was embarrassed to admit she'd never been there. But how could any park in England be like this oasis drenched in sunlight, shadowed by gnarled trees she didn't recognise, with large shiny leaves that came to a sharp point?

'Moreton Bay figs,' Jane told her.

There was a band concert in a rotunda; they listened for a while to the 'Blue Danube Waltz' and then moved on, walking on close-mown grass to the edge where a brace of buildings confronted each other across William Street.

'The Cathedral,' Tom said.

'And the Australian Museum,' Jane said, pointing the other way to one of the solid temple-like buildings that were so popular in London, although there they didn't glow with golden sandstone under a hot sun. Margaret was conscious of the perspiration at her neck and arms.

They ought to go to the museum, she thought. She was a new arrival – it behoved her to learn as much about her new country as she could.

'A bit hot to go wandering around a stuffy old museum,' Jane declared. 'Let's go to Bondi and have ices.'

•

Tom insisted on buying their tickets for the tram, but when they found an ice-cream shop at Bondi Margaret overrode him and paid for them all.

'You're doing me the favour of showing me around,' she said, feeling quite bold and like a New Woman. 'It's the least I can do.'

He accepted with a good-humoured patience that made her wonder about his mother. He seemed used to women who were forthright. Perhaps he even preferred them? She put that thought away for later consideration.

They ate the ice creams on the beachfront, which was a great half-circle of a beach, as beautiful as everyone claimed, but otherwise much like Manly, with its promenade and stone balustrades and the park behind it where families picnicked and played.

Sitting on a bench in the afternoon sun, licking her ice cream, listening to Tom and Jane critique the lifesaving team that was practising launching its boat into the waves, she let all her worries stream away from her. Blue skies. Green water. Cool breeze almost lifting the hat from her head. Sweet cold on her tongue. Just breathe in and out and let tomorrow take care of itself. That was what she had done after her parents died. Trudge through the days, do what had to be done in each moment and let the next take care of itself.

That had been survival. This offered something more.

Tom pulled her to her feet with automatic strength, his hand warm against hers.

'Home?' he asked, smiling down at her, and she forgot everything she'd told herself that morning and smiled back.

They caught the tram right to Circular Quay, and managed to grab the front seat on the ferry, up in the bow where they could see the whole Harbour ahead of them. Jane went to the side to watch the ferry cut through the water and catch the spray on her face. Tom leaned his head back against the wheelhouse wall and sighed.

'Tired?'

'What?' He looked down at her and smiled. 'No fear. Just not looking forward to Monday.'

'You don't like your job?'

'Guess I could have done with a bit of a holiday in between the Army and work,' he said slowly. 'But the job was there, so I took it.'

'Well, you can't say no to work.'

'That's right. It just takes a while, getting used to civilian life.'

A buxom matron in her best Sunday suit sat down on Tom's left and he edged along the seat towards Margaret. His thigh touched hers, with that disturbing warmth. She'd sat like this next to strangers on the bus so many times, why should she be so aware of him? She cast around for a safe topic of conversation. 'Did you grow up in North Sydney?'

'No, I come from Queenscliff originally. The other end of Manly. Then my dad died when I was thirteen. My mum and I moved in with her sister in Annandale, and I left school and got a job over there in a timber yard. Worked my way up to foreman.'

'I'm sorry about your father.'

'No, that's all right. It was a long time ago but by Jove! didn't I miss the beach. You can swim in the Harbour over there, but I wouldn't recommend it. Too much shipping. Before the war I used to catch the tram to Bondi or the tram and ferry to Manly most Sundays. Scandalised my aunt, going swimming on the Sabbath, but my mum understood. As long as I went to church first.'

'And your mum? She's still in Annandale?'

'Oh, you couldn't pry her out of there with a winkle-picker!' he said cheerfully. 'I go for dinner every Thursday – it's the only day they don't have anything on. My aunty and Maree Hannan run the Red Cross from our house, and there's always knitting circles and sewing bees and the Lord knows what else happening.'

'She sounds like a very generous person, your aunt.'

'They both are,' he said. 'It's a family trait. Can't stand meanness.'

She'd never talked to Frank about his family, past that initial confession from him that he was an orphan. What else was there to say? She wondered whether it was his upbringing – or lack of it – that had turned Frank into a liar, a cheat. Perhaps if you never had a family to show you right from wrong, you never figured it out for yourself?

Tom's face turned serious, his hazel eyes firmly on her.

'It was nice of you to go to church with Burnsie, but I can take you up to St Mary's next week if you'd like.'

St Mary's. That sounded Catholic. Surely not.

'St Mary's?' she asked. Her voice sounded odd, she could hear the stiffness in it.

He did too. He frowned, puzzled.

'You're Catholic, aren't you?'

'No! Why would you think that?'

'Well . . . Frank. Frank Dalton. Francis Ignatius Dalton. Can't get much more Catholic than that. I just assumed . . .'

Frank had been raised in an Anglican orphanage. And Tom looked so Scottish, with his red hair and his height, *she'd* just assumed . . .

'And you are . . . ?'

He looked at her and nodded, his face losing all its good humour.

'Catholic,' he confirmed. 'Born and bred.'

Catholics weren't even supposed to go into other churches, she knew that. Certainly no Methodist would visit a Catholic church.

'But you went to the Anglican church with us.' Her heart was hammering hard in her chest. Ridiculous. It shouldn't matter this much.

Tom shrugged, but his eyes were intent upon her. 'All the churches pray to the same God.'

If he felt like that, perhaps it would be all right, she thought, carefully not specifying what 'it' might be, even to herself.

'Besides,' he said, 'High Anglican's a lot like Catholic, anyway. It's not like it's the Methodists.'

Impossible to feel cold in this hot sunshine, but a block of ice was solid under her breastbone.

'I'm Methodist.' She felt impelled to explain further. 'You're right, we all pray to the same God. So I went with Burnsie. But . . .'

'But,' he said. 'Protestants versus Catholics. It's an old fight.' His tone was grim.

'Yes.' She avoided his gaze. She couldn't help feeling almost . . . tricked. As though he'd become her friend under false pretences. An echo of Frank's betrayal made her uncomfortable, even though she knew it wasn't Tom's fault. They'd both been mistaken.

Still, she couldn't look at him quite the same, although that feeling made her ashamed.

Jane came back to them as the ferry drew into the wharf.

'What a topping day we've had!' she exclaimed. Margaret made herself smile. Yes. It had been a lovely day. Cling to the good things. Ignore the old prejudices. She and Tom could still be friends. Surely.

15

Tom hauled the last of the cut boards onto the trolley and trundled it across the yard to the storage shed. It was a relief to get out of the sun, even though the smell of pine and turpentine under the big tin roof almost choked him.

He whistled to one of the young offsiders, Bobby, and they stacked the newly cut lumber on the four-be-two shelf, then Tom left Bobby to daub the ends of the cut boards with red lead, to stop them cracking while they cured.

'Tom!'

It was Ernie, coming across the yard with a sheaf of papers in his hand. Orders, by the look of it.

'We've just had a call from McCliver's, down the road.' He jerked his head westward along the bay. 'They need some spotted gum planks for a fishing boat they're making. Some idiot spilt a batch of glue across the ones they had. Can you take a load down? Twenty four-be-ones. Get Bobby to help you. Bobby!'

Bobby poked his head out of the shed and Ernie shoved the order into Tom's hand. 'Sorry,' he said. 'Got a meeting in the office. You can handle it, right? Make sure it's top of the line.'

'No worries,' Tom said. He checked the order and marshalled Bobby into helping him load the spotted gum onto the trolley, then together they pushed the heavy load out the gate and left down the road. Boat-building sheds lined Berry's Bay. A couple were mostly chandlers with a small repair section, but the rest boasted full-size cradles and slipways, with boats in various stages of construction occupying them. The sound of hammers and the hiss of steam accompanied the men as they crested a small rise.

'This is it, boss,' Bobby said.

Tom grinned at the lad. He was a weedy thing, but stronger than he looked, and a willing worker. Tom supposed he must have looked much the same himself when he first went to work at Curry's Timber Merchants in Annandale. Except that Bobby had a head of black hair instead of his own bright red.

'I'm not a boss, Bob. Just one of the workers, that's me.'

Bobby threw him a look of disbelief, and it made him smile ruefully. Not so easy to give up being the one who gave the orders, and it showed.

They hauled the long trolley around and, with some backing and filling, made it through the gate. A short, stocky man in tar-smeared trousers and a once-white shirt came towards them.

'From Cobbin's?' he asked, and then answered himself, in a full Scottish brogue. 'Aye, a'course ye are. Over here, lads.'

He led them past a cradle on which sat the skeleton of a fishing boat – shaped a bit like a tug, it was shorter and squatter than Tom had imagined – and into an open shed much the same size as their own sawing shed.

There, on a smaller cradle, sat an altogether different kind of boat, with a couple of men working on her. Slimmer, sleeker, made to cut through the water fast and beautifully. A yacht, a ketch? He didn't know enough to name her. She was half-clad; the boards covered only her port side.

'Just stack 'em here,' the Scotsman said. They offloaded the timber and stacked it against the far side of the shed.

'Thankee, lads.' He regarded them with an experienced eye. 'A bit of a hot one, eh? Where's the bucket, Clarry?'

One of the men working on the boat, a half-bald man of about forty, brought over a metal bucket of water with a big lump of ice in it. Silently, he offered Tom an enamel mug. The water was beautifully cold. He drank deeply and then handed the mug to Bobby.

'Thanks, Mr McCliver,' Bobby said before dipping the mug in.

'That's a grand idea, Mr McCliver,' Tom said.

'Aye, it's no so bad,' McCliver said with satisfaction. 'We've got an ice chest in the office and the men get a lump of it every afternoon. Cuts down the complaints, I can tell ye! Have another.'

Tom did, sipping this time so he could watch the men. One was beginning to feed their spotted gum through a steamer, which Tom knew would soften the wood so it could be curved to the shape of the boat's skeleton. It was fascinating to watch while Bobby had another draught.

He could see the concentration on each man's face; it was dedication he saw, and satisfaction as the first of the boards was laid, curved and clamped, and then nailed.

Bobby shuffled his feet and Tom was recalled to the time they'd wasted.

'Thanks, Mr McCliver,' he said. He handed over the order and McCliver signed it with a pencil he plucked from behind his ear.

'Are ye a Scotsman?' he asked, eyeing Tom's height and red hair.

'Well, I'm a McBride,' Tom said. 'The story is my father's people came from Ayrshire, but my mother's people were Irish.'

'Och, I might have known. With the height on ye, ye couldn't be anything but a Scot!'

Tom grinned. 'I was posted with some Black Watch blokes at Ypres, and they said the same thing, but they never got me into a kilt!'

McCliver let out a bark of laughter and turned away, waving a hand in dismissal.

They pushed the trolley back to Cobbin's in good spirits, Bobby talking about his girl and where they planned to go that Saturday night, something about a new movie based on CJ Dennis's character Ginger Mick. Tom felt his heart lighten as he remembered the bald bloke's face as he smoothed and clamped the spotted gum in place. Nice to see someone enjoying their work.

He'd never thought of himself as a whinger, but he was finding it hard to drum up any vigour for this job. Nobody's fault but his own. The bosses were okay, as the American doughboys used to say. The men were just men, a mixture of bad and good, as they always were. The foreman, Ernie, was a solid young bloke. And wood was wood, after all was said and done, just the same as it always had been.

He was the one who had changed. He felt a deep restlessness, a desire to be up and doing, moving, getting *on* with things. But with what? They'd fought to preserve normal life at home; it was insane to be dissatisfied with normality now.

And today, after the wonderful afternoon with Margi and Jane had come to such a disastrous end, he was finding it even harder to rev himself up. The look of dismay – worse, of repulsion – when she'd found out he was Catholic had cut deep. Any vague ideas he'd had about courting her had withered with that look. He felt like getting into a fight – preferably with Frank Dalton. Why couldn't he have been named Wesley Knox? Then he wouldn't have even considered her a possible ... possible what? Ah, bugger it. Not worth thinking about now. Better get back to work, ignore that restlessness, go to lifesaving training tomorrow night and count himself lucky with what he had.

But the thought of throwing it all in, taking his savings and taking off across the world, was very tempting.

•

On the Tuesday night, he went to his first practice session with the Life Saving Club.

Bill Flynn introduced him around. One of the men, Vic Miller, recognised him from the old Queenscliff days, before his father had died and they'd moved to Annandale.

'Why didn't you join them?' he asked. 'You're a mick, aren't you?'

Even here, he thought, stabbed by the reminder of Margaret's dismay when she'd found out he was Catholic. Queenscliff club was Catholic. Manly had always been Protestant. He was sick of the old divisions; they were meaningless now, surely, after they'd all fought side by side.

'Bill and I are cobbers,' he said simply.

'Oh, right,' Vic said, nodding, and the other blokes nodded too. That word was a magic passport; having fought together cancelled all other loyalties.

Most of these blokes had served, too. As they stripped and put on their swimming costumes in the club house, he could see scars on more than one of them. It reminded him of being in the Army, this communal dressing. The scent of male sweat and shoe leather rose around them, a couple of the blokes were chiacking another, and underneath it all was a sense of purpose.

On the beach, they were split into teams, warming up with races on the sand and then practising rescues. He was a strong enough swimmer, but he didn't know the drill yet, so he was put into the line team – the men who fed out the rope to the man swimming the rescue. It was harder than it looked, to feed that line out in time with the others without snagging it, and he wasn't the only one who came a cropper. But no one criticised; they were all in it together.

The sense of teamwork, that was what he'd missed since being demobbed. Since France, really. Working together for something important. What could be more important than saving lives?

He thought, briefly, in a lull while they were packing up, that he'd like, someday, to have saved as many lives as he'd taken.

16

'Nothing nicer than a bath, eh, love?' Frank said. Firelight lit the colours in the rag rug under the bath and reflected on the polished andirons; by Jove, Glad was a good housekeeper.

Gladys smiled and poured warm water down his back from the big enamel jug. Sluicing the week away, he thought, all the hard work and the dirt. He liked working on the railways, but this week had been tough. Still warmish, in the eighties, but wet and windy. The kind of days that made you long for all the breakages to be in the shed, but they never were.

The railways were the backbone of the country. Any derailment, any washout of the lines, had to be fixed straightaway and no mistake.

In the country, it was the elite Flying Gang who went out, any time of day or night, no matter the weather.

In the city, it was Frank and a few fettlers and navvies. Their primary duty was supposed to be maintenance on the rolling stock, but there were too many emergencies for that to happen. So little maintenance had been done on the rolling stock during the war that all their chickens were coming home to roost at once. Couplings breaking left, right and centre. He'd had to take his portable forge out three times this week: Granville, Rookwood and even out to bloody Richmond.

Sighing, he eased himself into a better position in the old tin tub. Not that you could get comfortable in a hip bath. He remembered days in the Army when he would have killed for clean water to shave with, let alone hot water in a tub. He'd had it easier than a lot of blokes, he knew – in England for most of it, and only on the front line for a couple of months, and that time was all in summer, before the terrible winter cold and mud.

He'd had no trouble shooting at the enemy, either, unlike a lot of the blokes. All he had to do was imagine the man in the German uniform was old Foster, the head of the orphanage, the one who used the strap and the cane and put the boys in the punishment room for days on end without food. Then it was easy.

He'd even been mentioned in despatches, for the way he'd taken out a nest of German snipers, despite being wounded himself.

As though reminded, a twinge went through his shoulder. Bits of shrapnel still in there, the doctors said, but it didn't affect his ability to work. Yep, he'd been lucky all right. Had thought himself blessed by the gods, especially when he'd found Margaret. So beautiful, so *lovely*. Not just on the outside, either. There was a flame inside her, a light that shone out. He'd thought that light meant she was honest. More fool him. And more fool him for still dreaming about her, still wanting her. Not fair to Glad, either.

'Bad day?' Gladys asked, rubbing his back with a washcloth. Her hair smelled sweetly of biscuits. She wasn't working at the biscuit factory now they were a proper family, but she still liked to go down and buy a bag of broken bits and have a chat to her friends.

'Not now,' he said. She swooped down and kissed him, then poured the last of the water over him as he stood up, and handed him a towel. He wrapped it around his waist.

Violet was already in bed. She'd had the first bath, Gladys the second, and he, the dirtiest, the last of the warm water.

So, there was nothing to distract them. He stepped out of the tub and reached for her and she came, dressed just in her light cotton wrap. They kissed, Glad as sweet and supple in his arms as always. Then she pushed him away, just far enough so she could put her hands flat on his wet chest.

'I have some news,' she said.

He kissed the side of her neck and felt the little shiver that went through her.

'Mmm?'

'Frank. Look at me.'

He drew back. There was a look in her eyes. A bit of excitement, a bit of nervousness, something else – determination? He'd never seen Glad determined before.

'I'm expecting,' she said.

There was a moment when he didn't quite know what she meant. Expecting what? Then his brain caught up and he felt a welter of emotions go through him. Panic, wonder, understanding and, finally, joy. Why shouldn't he be joyful? They were a family now, weren't they, even if he and Glad weren't properly married? The more the merrier.

She was searching his face anxiously, so he hugged her (not too hard) and set her back down again.

'Well, that's just bonzer,' he said. Her face lit up. That was one of the things he loved about Gladys, the way everything she felt was right there, right on the surface. A man always knew where he stood with her. 'Might be a brother for Violet, eh?'

'You don't mind?'

'Mind! I should say not.' When he was a kid, in the orphanage, sometimes they'd pretend they were brothers. But they knew they weren't. He used to imagine being part of a big family where everyone – *everyone* – was blood related. No reason his kid – his *kids* – couldn't have that. 'The more the merrier,' he said out loud.

Gladys beamed. But then she took his hand and led him to the small table with its two chairs tucked in next to the parlour door. She sat down and tugged him into the other chair.

'Well,' she said. She took a breath. 'I've been thinking. There's no reason this one has to be a bastard.'

The word hit him. That's what he was. A bastard. He'd been left at the orphanage when he was a baby. Most likely his mother couldn't deal with the shame, he reckoned. And Violet, poor little Vi, she was a bastard too. Nothing to be done about that. If he and Glad were married . . .

'You're right,' he said slowly. 'No reason.' Why shouldn't they be married? It wasn't as though Margaret was going to change her mind. She'd have written to him care of the railways by now if there'd been a mistake. He'd written more than a year ago to tell her he'd got his old job back. The image of Margaret moved backwards in his mind, replaced by a picture of Gladys and the new baby.

'You could write to that woman and ask her for a divorce,' Glad said. Frank nodded.

'I have her parents' address,' he said. 'They'll know where to find her.' Pausing, he thought it over. He and Glad weren't the kind of people who'd be too embarrassed by a divorce – it wouldn't make any difference to their friends, quite a few of whom were living in sin, like he and Glad. But Glad was right. It was one thing to have a bit of fun when you were young, but if they were going to be together for good, they ought to be married. Getting married showed you meant to be in it for life. A sacred vow – *he* took it seriously, even if Margaret didn't.

But a divorce might cost a bit. 'I'll write to her. Maybe she can get it done over there, and then we won't have to pay for it.'

It gave him a small spurt of satisfaction. Let Margaret pay for breaking her promise, her solemn vow! Glad was worth ten of her. He kissed her, leaning forwards, urging her to come onto his lap, and she slid onto him still kissing, half-laughing, her robe falling open.

'Shh,' she said. 'Don't wake Vi.'

A proper family, he thought as she slid her cool hands against his wet skin. He kissed her harder, more hungrily, drunk with the thought of having what he'd always wanted.

He'd write first thing tomorrow.

17

On Friday night, Margaret met Tom and Jane after work at Circular Quay and they went to the cinema with some of Jane's friends to see *A Fighting Colleen*. It was a light-hearted story about a girl selling newspapers in New York City who defended her 'patch' by fist-fighting with her rivals, the newspaper boys.

Margaret sat in the dark, aware of Tom's bulk in the seat next to her. Jane, on her other side, laughed delightedly as the girl, Alannah, squared up to her rivals and began to punch, but Margaret found herself getting angrier and angrier, although she didn't know why.

Then she realised – the man on the piano who was playing along to the film was playing happy music with funny sounds when Alannah's punches hit. He was making fun of her. If this had been a fight between men, the music would have been different; darker, more solid. They said that one day the movies would have sound, and then it wouldn't be up to the piano player what kind of music to play along with the film.

She shook herself. People needed to laugh; it didn't matter what they laughed at. After the past five years everyone needed something to lift their heart. At least the movie took the girl seriously – it was her efforts that, at the end of the film, uncovered corruption by the town mayor. And Bessie Love was a wonderful actress, with such expressive eyes. Margaret wondered what her voice would sound like.

'I wouldn't mind seeing New York,' Tom said as they left. The thought sent a pang of dismay through her. She had so few friends here, she couldn't afford to lose one. Especially not Tom.

'I had enough of Americans in the hospital in France,' Clara said. Clara had nursed with Jane during the war in the VAD, although Clara had later gone to Europe while Jane stayed in Sydney.

The six of them walked through the city, looking in all the store windows. Jane's friends were a mixture of young men and women, all light-hearted and ready to laugh, although Margaret noted that one of the young men, Jonesy, walked with a limp and another had a scar across one hand.

Jonesy had the shadowed eyes of someone who didn't sleep much, and he flinched as a tram went past with a rattle like a machine-gun.

Jane flicked a glance at his sombre face and stole his cane out from his hand. She pretended to tap-dance like one of the vaudeville fellows until they were all laughing, even Jonesy. He joined in with her for a few steps, and sang a snatch of 'Daisy, Daisy, give me an answer do.'

'Now you've just got to work out what the question is,' Jane teased him. Their glance held for a moment, and then Jonesy smiled at her with unconcealed warmth. Jane smiled back, but Margaret couldn't see whether there was anything more than friendship in it.

They meandered towards Circular Quay and found a restaurant near the wharves where they ate heartily of roast beef and baked potatoes.

'Did you see her hair?' Clara asked while they were waiting for their dessert, flummery made with real pineapple.

'Bessie Love's?' Margaret had noticed it, and Jane nodded, but the men looked blank.

'She had a bob cut. All curls.' Mabel had frizzy light brown hair pulled loosely back into a bun at the nape of her neck. 'If I tried that my hair would stick straight out sideways!' She assessed Margaret. 'But you'd be all right. Yours would be nice and curly. You, too, Janey.'

'That's a great notion!' Jane said. 'No more waiting for four hours for my hair to dry after a swim.'

Men were renowned for disapproving of the bob cut. Margaret sneaked a look at Tom, but he seemed merely amused. In for a penny, in for a pound, she thought. A new life, a new look.

•

It was a rare Saturday – there was no auction on, which meant Margaret had the day off in lieu of working back on a couple of Wednesdays. Jane and Margaret found a hairdresser in North Sydney and stood outside, looking at the photographs of the cuts on offer. One of the photos was of Bessie Love with her trademark crop.

Margaret put her hand to the heavy bun at the nape of her neck.

'Having second thoughts?' Jane asked.

'No. No. It's just . . . I haven't cut my hair since my mother died. She used to trim it for me when I went home on leave. Since then, I haven't had the heart.'

Jane slid an arm through hers and held on tightly.

'Dad used to shine my school shoes,' she said. 'He'd get home every six weeks or so, whenever he finished a cattle drive. And he'd make them shine like mirrors. After . . . I drove Mum mad, I reckon. I wouldn't let her touch them, and I wouldn't do it myself. They stayed that way until I outgrew them.' She paused, looking down at her fashionably shod feet. 'I've still got them in the bottom of the wardrobe.'

Maybe that was why she and Jane had hit it off so quickly. They'd both suffered grief, but they'd both chosen to go on, to welcome the life they did have instead of dwell on what they'd lost.

'No time like the present, I suppose,' she said.

'That's my girl!'

Jane pushed open the door and they went in to find three barber's chairs but only one barber – a short, stout man with an enormous waxed moustache, sharpening a razor against a leather strop. They stopped dead.

'Ladies! *Bongiorno*!' Italian. Who would have expected an Italian hairdresser in Sydney?

'You've come for a bob, no?' He put aside the razor and gestured them in.

'Yes,' Jane said. 'Like Bessie Love's.'

'*Bene, bene* for you, *sì*, the American Girl bob. Sit here.' He flourished a cape and had Jane sitting hatless in front of the mirror in an instant. Then he came over to Margaret.

'But for your friend, the French bob!' He motioned for her to take her hair down.

Margaret took her hat off and laid it on the counter, and then pulled the pins from her hair. It fell to her waist. The hairdresser sighed.

'Oh, a shame. *Bella*. But all these bobs are good for business, no? You want to sell it?'

'Sell it?'

'But yes, for the wig-makers.'

'Oh.' Laughter bubbled up in her at the thought of someone else walking around wearing her hair. It was rather unpleasant but, after all, why not? It wasn't like she had any use for it. 'All right.'

'So,' he said. 'I cut your hair and your friend's for free, and I keep the hair, yes?'

'No,' Jane said.

He looked at her shrewdly, and she looked back, not at all abashed.

'It's worth more than that. Look how long it is. And in beautiful condition.'

'The hair, it is worth for me to sell to the maker – two pounds. The cuts, ten shillings each.'

'Strewth!' Jane said. Margaret, speechless, looked at the list of costs for men's haircuts. The most expensive was two and thruppence for a cut *and* shave.

'Ten shillings *each*,' Margaret managed to say.

'Oh, this is only for the first shaping of the hair, madame. Subsequent, four shillings only. I will give you credit for the next cut, for both of you.' He flourished, as though he were being generous.

Margaret and Jane exchanged glances, and burst out laughing.

'In for a penny, in for a pound,' Jane said.

•

Afterward, Margaret felt very strange. Her head was so light, as though it would float off her neck. She felt taller. And it was so cool! She ruffled the curls at the nape of her neck with something like glee. It was like being a child again.

'Let's go to the beach!' Jane said.

•

When they went back to the High House to get their beach things, Jane called some friends, and by the time they got to Manly, Margaret was part of a party with Tom and Jane and a few of Jane's friends, including Jonesy, who seemed to want to be Jane's *particular* friend. Again Margaret wasn't sure whether Jane felt the same way. For someone who seemed so open and spontaneous, Jane could keep her own counsel surprisingly well.

What a difference from her first visit! Today she wore no stockings or shoes into the water, and there was no shrinking back from the waves. She plunged in next to Jane, laughing in anticipation, Tom close behind.

It was like magic. And when she came up, laughing, she could shake her head and feel her lovely short hair swing free.

After a half-hour of swimming tuition, Jane and Tom stood in the shallows and debated earnestly whether Margaret could try to surf-shoot.

'Better take the chance,' Tom said, looking at the sky. 'This weather won't hold.'

It had surprised Margaret how accurate the Sydney people were with their weather predictions. The southerly buster, it seemed, came after a particular kind of day: this kind, when the air was heavy and humid and the heat made even her short hair seem a burden.

The surf was churning sand a long way out and the afternoon wind was picking up.

'I don't know,' Jane said. 'There's a few dumpers out there.'

Margaret had learned all the terms: dumpers were big waves that picked you up and slammed you down again; the rip was the current that could grab you and yank you out to sea; the undertow was like a rip, but it pulled you sideways along the beach before it, too, ferried you out to the open water.

'She might not get another chance this year,' Tom said.

'Don't I get a say in this?'

'No!' they said together. Tom smiled at her. 'Not until you can read the water better.'

'We'll stick with her,' Jane said.

'Yes. Righto. Come along, Margi.'

She strode in boldly. The water was sharp today, just a little colder than before.

'Current's turned,' Tom said. 'Autumn's coming.'

Margaret moved further out and discovered that the waves were rougher than she'd seen, breaking with a hard crash against her legs. But around her were children gaily jumping over them or riding them casually in to the shore. An old woman in an 1890s-style bathing costume, complete with mob-cap, happily floated just beyond the break, her stockinged toes peeping out of the water.

Out past the break Margaret, Jane and Tom paused, jumping waves together.

'Right,' Tom said. 'Get yourself set.'

They'd practised this on the beach. She stood facing the shore, half-turned to see the waves behind her.

'Start with a littlie,' Jane advised. 'Here. This one!'

'Go!' Tom grabbed her waist and pushed her off, and she began to swim madly. She seemed to go backwards for a moment as the wave sucked at her, and then it picked her up and moved her. For a brief moment she thought she'd done it, and then the wave outstripped her and left her behind in its wash, scrabbling to stand in the sand-clouded water.

She turned and waded hastily back to Tom and Jane, trying to get to them before the next wave.

Jane was laughing, but not unkindly. Tom's eyes crinkled at the corner as he tried not to chuckle.

'Didn't I tell you to keep your head down?' Jane asked.

'Yes, Mother.'

'Right. Then *do* it!'

A smallish wave slapped past them. Another, a big one, was right behind.

'Go!'

She swam. She put her head down, her face right in the water. She panicked for a moment – she couldn't see anything, didn't know where she was being taken – but she kept her face down. The wave picked her up as though she were weightless, as though she really were flying. It shot her towards the beach faster than she had expected. It was glorious! And then, somehow, she had got in front of the wave and it was smashing over her, tumbling her head over turkey until she slammed into the sand and rolled, salt water in her mouth and nose, sand everywhere. She dragged herself to her knees, coughing and coughing, wiping sand out of her eyes. It felt as though a bull had trampled her.

She was in the shallows. Next to her, a little boy regarded her with wise eyes.

'Got dumped,' he said with finality.

She got a full breath at last. 'Yes,' she said. 'I got dumped.' He nodded with satisfaction.

'You have to be *careful*.' She laughed, finding it hard to stop. Was it shock or simple relief? For a moment she had been so afraid . . .

Tom and Jane splashed up to her.

'Well, that was a dumper,' Jane said. 'Are you all right?'

Tom put a hand out and pulled her to her feet, checking her eyes. 'Did you bang your head?'

Margaret shook her head, conscious of sand caked right across her cheek. And everywhere else.

'Had enough?' he asked. His eyes were guarded. She looked down at the little boy and smiled.

'No fear,' she said, in her best imitation of an Australian accent. 'Let me at 'em.' The boy nodded with approval and she felt ridiculously proud.

'That's the girl,' Tom said. He was supporting her, one arm around her waist, so his face – his mouth – was close enough to touch.

'Won't be long until the change comes through,' Jane said. 'Better go if you're going.'

They dived and swam out, this time through even larger waves. Margaret wasn't at all sure she was brave enough to do it again, but she couldn't *not*, not after that look of pride in Tom's eyes.

The next wave was gentle, and took her halfway in to shore, but she pulled her head up again and lost it.

The wave after, a medium-sized comber, was perfect. Tom pushed her off strongly, and she kept her head down and kicked her feet, flying until her breasts and her thighs touched the shingle and she lifted her head to find that she'd come *all* the way in, right to the very edge of the water.

She flicked the hair back from her eyes and laughed, exhilarated beyond anything she had ever felt before. Alive. Tom landed beside her on the next wave, and Jane too.

They grinned at each other in simple triumph, then went and did it all again until the lifesavers took the flags down – sunset, although the sky still glowed with light.

Margaret realised how tired she was. She was starting to feel bruises coming up on her knees from when she'd been dumped. She and Tom sat watching while Jane and the others played around in the shallows, splashing each other and laughing.

Their hands were next to each other on the towel. Tom's little finger touched hers; just laid next to hers, not moving. She swallowed down some unnamed feeling; the warmth from that small touch swept through her, unstoppable. He looked across at her, and his mouth twisted awry, as though he'd tasted something bitter. But then he laughed, his eyes flattering her.

'It'd be nice if all our plans went to order, eh, Margi?'

What could he mean? She was aware of his liking for her, of perhaps more than that, but it seemed he was as reluctant as she was to act on it. The old Protestant/Catholic divide, perhaps. She didn't know what to say, nor what to feel.

Breaking the moment, a small boy rolled a hoop down the sand, his dog jumping through it as it rolled, first one way and then the other. The hoop came towards them, and the moment was broken as Tom, chuckling, fended off both dog and hoop and Margaret received the boy in her lap as he scrambled to get the hoop away from them.

Tom jumped to his feet and picked the boy up. Set him back on his feet.

'There you go, cobber.'

'Thanks, Bluey!'

'Off you go. You all right, Margi?'

She stood up, brushing sand off her legs. 'Oh, I'm just fine. Why did that boy call you Bluey?'

'Because of my red hair, of course!'

Of course. So Australian. Everything in opposites.

A bubble of mirth, of happiness, rose up in her and she was joyful and ashamed at the same time. How could she be so happy when everything she'd wanted, everything she'd dreamed about, had collapsed? Tom's hazel gaze was warm on her face. She smiled at him.

'I shouldn't be so happy,' she said, trying to sober herself.

'You deserve to be happy,' he said. 'If it's up to me, you will be.'

She hadn't expected that. Perhaps he hadn't either – he had flushed with embarrassment. Yearning rose up out of nowhere. How long had it been since she'd had anyone she could count on, anyone who took her welfare seriously? It had been a burden she hadn't even noticed until he offered to take it away from her.

'Now, then,' he said, brushing a tear away from her cheek with a sandy thumb. 'Now, then.'

Tremulous. That was the word for how she felt. Like a silly girl in a Victorian novel. She'd be having the vapours next. And how could she give her happiness into anyone's keeping, ever again? No more men, that was her motto.

The others came racing up.

'I'm starving!' Jane said. 'I told Mum we'd find our own dinner. Give her a night off.'

They changed and wandered down the Corso until they found a fish-and-chip shop and then took their parcels to the Harbour beach to eat. The others had laughed at Margaret when she'd asked for vinegar on her chips.

'You're not a Pommy now, you know,' Jonesy chided her.

She wrinkled her nose up at him and tucked in.

During the war there had been so little time for friends and picnic parties. The railways were the centre of the war effort, sending troops to the front and bringing home the wounded, conveying vital supplies to Army and Air Force bases and naval stations. Six-day weeks often turned into seven. There were jokes and good times at the pub after work, sometimes, but often she'd got out after closing time, and her boss had frowned on anything resembling merriment in the office itself.

'Lives depend on us getting it right!' he would declare, and of course that was true. Even in normal times, lives depended on the railway getting it right. 'Remember Quintinshill!' he'd boom, and every time she had shuddered. The Quintinshill disaster had happened just after she'd joined the railways. Two hundred and twenty-four people dead, as many injured. Five trains. A whole battalion of soldiers almost wiped out. Tragedies like Quintinshill were always at the back of their minds.

So, there were few jokes around the office, and she'd moved from girlhood to womanhood there without noticing the change.

Being with Jane and her friends made Margaret feel as though she were living her youth over again, but this time getting it right.

'Your hair is bonzer,' Tom said suddenly.

She looked up into his eyes, finding them full of admiration. She would have to decide what she was going to do about that. Later. Right now, she was tired of calling him Mr McBride in public.

'I quite like yours too, Bluey,' she said. He let out a crack of laughter.

'Oh, you're getting cheeky!' Jane said, grinning.

Jonesy doffed an imaginary hat to her and she thought: These people are my friends. This is my future being built around me.

18

Work was proving more than interesting. Margaret found herself fascinated by the variety of goods people sent to be auctioned. Most were what you might expect: furniture, the household contents of deceased estates, buggies, even motorcars. This week there was an auction of estate jewellery.

It discouraged her a little. She had been reading and reading about English pottery, and knew she had only scratched the surface. How could she possibly learn about everything else as well?

Step by step, she supposed. Better to know one thing really well than know a little about a lot.

That evening, at quitting time, she went back down to the auction floor, taking a copy of the catalogue, trying to understand exactly what the descriptions of each piece meant. Sometimes it was clear: rings were all round, and the stones they contained had names she knew: diamond, ruby, emerald. Other times she didn't even recognise the name of the piece. What was a parure? What was the difference between a mourning ring and a 'hair collar' ring? It took her longer than she expected to go through the whole sale, and it was almost dark outside before she went back to her desk to collect her purse.

Mr Bertram's door was open slightly. If he was working back, she should probably check he didn't need her before she left, so she knocked lightly on the door and pushed it open.

Mr Bertram was sitting on the edge of the desk and Joe, their delivery driver, was standing close to him. Joe sprang back as she came in and looked confused. Colour swept up Mr Bertram's face and he pulled his suit coat down as if making himself presentable.

She hesitated. Joe pushed past her, head down, mumbling something about getting on with work.

Margaret knew. Of course she knew. She thought immediately of her brother, David. Poor David. Sometimes she wondered if he'd died so heroically because the alternative was so hard.

The look on Mr Bertram's face was a mixture of defiance and fear. Of course, even a rumour would ruin him.

'Did you have anything you needed me to do before I left?' she said. He relaxed, just a little, but his face was still pink and his hands tense.

'No, thank you.'

She nodded. 'I'll see you tomorrow.'

Should she have said something? What could she have said? *Don't worry, I won't turn you in to the police?* Hardly. She couldn't talk like that to her boss, even though he must be worrying now that she would, or that she would gossip. He didn't know her well. Not well enough.

•

The fear in Joe's eyes kept her awake that night. He didn't know her at all, and she didn't have anything to lose by gossiping about him. He could be fairly sure she'd stay quiet about Mr Bertram, to protect her job, but Joe . . . he had nothing to protect him.

Her Methodist conscience was appalled at their behaviour. All the thundering from the pulpit she had ever heard came back to her: unnatural, obscene, an affront to God. But, as so often happened to her, the theory and the practice didn't seem to quite meet. She couldn't imagine Mr Bertram as an affront to God. She just couldn't. Because if he was, then so was her brother, and she *knew* that wasn't true.

It was like Tom being Catholic. Supposedly, all Catholics were under the evil sway of Rome, superstitious, idolatrous, ignorant sheep led by malicious shepherds. But no one could look at Tom McBride and think he was being led anywhere.

The rhetoric and the reality just didn't match.

Her father, she knew, had preferred the rhetoric, and pushed and shoved his reality until it fitted. She had come to realise that, although he'd been a good man, and a wonderful father, he had lived a small life. A simple life. One town, one church, the friends he'd grown up with, his friends until his death. An admirable life, in a way, but not one that had equipped him to deal with change. He would have been rendered mute and confused by her discovery about Mr Bertram.

She wished, painfully, that she could talk to her mother about it all.

She was heartily glad that her father had never found out about David. Her mother . . . it wouldn't have surprised her if her mother had suspected, at least, and come to some accommodation about it. She wished she knew what it was. Perhaps it was as simple as a mother's love.

It was in moments like these that she felt her grief most acutely. The moments when she would have given anything to be able to just sit at the kitchen table and talk, to feel her mother's hand touch hers lightly, as she'd always done, and have her say, 'It'll all come out in the wash, Margie.' Such a silly phrase, but in her childhood it had been the shield against all worry.

In the first months after they had died, every thought of them had brought back the terrible memories of their shared fever, their last, gasping breaths, the horror of wrapping them in the shrouds. And memories of David were overlain by what she knew to be true of the trenches and no-man's land in which he'd died: the terror and the mud and the everlasting bombardment of the shells.

Now, it seemed, she could go back further than that, and remember the other parts of them: their kindness, their love, their humour. Even her father's bigotry would be welcome right now; it was a solid wall to lean against, an unchanging thing in a shifting world.

It was a blessing to be rid of those haunting, horrible memories, but remembering the good times made her grief sharp all over again.

•

The next morning, when she arrived at work, Mr Bertram looked as though he hadn't slept much.

She went in to deliver the latest auction files, as normal, and her heart was wrung by the circles under his eyes, his pallor. She should have said something last night. She resolutely set her mind against guilt. It was as though she could perform one final favour for David, and she was happy she had the opportunity.

Time to put him out of his misery. What were the words David had told her, that night he had visited her in Reading, and confessed?

'I wish you could have met my brother, David,' she said. Mr Bertram blinked in surprise. 'I think you would have liked him. I always wanted to be an aunt one day, but I think David was a confirmed bachelor.'

He took a sharp breath in, of surprise and understanding, and relaxed. There was gratitude in his eyes.

'Is he back in England?'

'No,' she said. 'In France. He died on the Somme.'

'I'm sorry.'

She was sorry too. Sorry that David had never come home and found someone like John Bertram, or Joe the driver. Sorry that he'd been in love with someone who had hated what he was.

'I know he likes me,' David had said. 'I *know* he does. But all he'll talk about is the girl he's going to marry.'

He'd been killed going out to collect that man's body from no-man's land. Perhaps that was the best. It must be hard to live as Mr Bertram lived, constantly afraid of being discovered and put in gaol. Ruined forever, if he survived prison.

David's confession hadn't come as a shock to her. He had never been interested in girls, and she'd learned a thing or two about men and women since she'd started working at Reading.

One of the gnarly old sergeants who organised the catering for the troops who stopped at the station had said, almost as an aside one day, 'There's molly-boys in every unit. Not bad fighters, as long as you stay away from whoever they've got their eye on. But that's true of most men, eh?' She realised later that he was warning her about his offsider, a young, fresh-faced corporal from Devon who had befriended her. They'd become drinking chums, nonetheless, because he made her laugh and, after she and Frank were married and Frank had been shipped to the front, he was a safe companion.

So, by the time David had, with such difficulty, dragged the words out of some deep part of himself, she was able to hear his confession without revulsion or even much surprise.

She was glad that he'd trusted her enough to tell the truth, and she hoped that Mr Bertram had someone he trusted, too.

'Well, standing here won't get my filing done,' she said, moving to the door.

'Mrs Dalton,' he said. She turned to look at him. He was standing, now, leaning heavily on his cane. 'Thank you.'

Margaret smiled. 'It's only a bunch of files,' she said, gently. He smiled too, at last.

'Even so. Thank you.'

19

It was a scorcher of a day and the boss let them all go half an hour before quitting time.

'Wants to make the trots in time,' Ernie said to Tom, grinning.

'Don't care why, mate.'

'See you tomorrer.'

He lifted a hand in goodbye, but when he reached the gate he turned left instead of right, and went down to McCliver's. He didn't know why, but he had a fancy to watch the boat-builders again. Maybe it would take his mind off Margi and the stupid way he'd blurted out his feelings on Saturday. It had come out of nowhere – and the worst thing was, he'd meant it.

It had been like being coshed on the back of the head, a sudden blow of realisation and desire as their hands met, and then the words were out and he couldn't take them back.

At least she hadn't frozen him out.

Maybe it would have been simpler if she had. He couldn't quite imagine taking a Methodist girl home to meet his mother. *He* didn't care, exactly, but it would cause so much heartache for his family. He didn't want to break his mother's heart. It wasn't like he was in love with Margi. Not fully.

He wasn't even sure why he liked her. She was pretty, of course, and clever; he'd never had to explain a stray thought to her – she always understood. That was seductive, being understood.

He scuffed the toes of his boots in the gravel as he walked, thinking it over. He liked the way she was working to learn more, to *be* more. To swim, to surf-shoot, to learn about pottery, of all things. She was defying the betrayal in her past, picking up her burdens and marching on; courage that he admired.

Was that enough to justify setting his whole family at loggerheads? Was the way his pulse leaped when she smiled at him enough reason?

When he was with her, the restlessness inside him died down. As though she was enough, just in herself. When he was with her, a normal future felt attractive rather than constraining, desirable rather than imprisoning.

But even with her, could he stand the sameness of this life, every day? A life where nothing really mattered, nothing vital was at stake?

Thank God for the lifesaving. That was a job worth doing, working with other men to save lives. Even the training was satisfying. The selflessness and the teamwork – like the good part of the war.

He'd hated being in France, but he had to admit he missed the camaraderie of the trenches, the fellowship under fire. Lifesaving might be as close as he could come to that now, and his fellow lifesavers as close as he could find to the friends he'd made in France. The few mates who'd made it out alive were scattered now, all around Australia. He found himself thinking of them late at night, and remembering all the ones who didn't make it.

•

By the time he got down to the boatshed, most of the men were packing up to leave, but McCliver and a couple of men who looked like close relatives were still in the big shed, working on a long piece of wood that seemed more like a child's toy next to the three burly men.

Tom drifted in through the double doors, trying not to be obtrusive. McCliver flicked him a glance.

'Just watching,' Tom said.

McCliver grunted and went back to work. He was laying out the shape, measuring exactly and then drawing in the lines freehand. The younger men were following with chisels – one cutting in the lines roughly, the other coming behind him and putting an exact angle on the cut.

Perhaps it was a keel? Of a small boat, a sailing dinghy, maybe.

McCliver got to the end of the board and straightened up. 'If ye're looking for something to do, that centreboard over there needs sanding.'

The board he indicated was sitting on a bench to the side of the shed; a shaped and planed slice of oak, the thickest cross-section not quite as wide as his spread hand, thinning down to a point at the bottom. It was rough, but not too rough. He chose his sandpaper from a thing rather like a big letter rack, found a rag on a seat nearby, and got to work.

Rough paper, and then finer, and then finer still. He gave his attention completely to the task, caught by it in a way he didn't understand. He'd done a fair bit of woodwork over the years, but this arcane piece of oak drew him. Perhaps because it was beautiful, as all perfectly shaped things were.

The grain of the wood came clearer under his hands and each time he reached for the cloth to whisk away the wood dust, the curve of the wood grew more lovely. The restlessness in him was smoothed away with the sawdust.

When McCliver clapped him on the shoulder he was startled at how dark it had become outside.

'Let's have a look, then,' McCliver said. He ran his hands over the grain of the wood and grunted approval, then jerked his head over at the long piece of timber he and the others had been working on. Tom followed him to inspect it. Two long grooves – channels, really – interspersed with small square holes had been gouged into it and then finished off.

'Keel,' McCliver said. He pointed to the square gouges. 'That's where the framework sits.' The long channels: 'The lowest boards sit in this. Then we build it up, plank by plank.' There was a section cut out of it, right in the middle. 'That's where your centreboard'll go.'

'Clinker built?' Tom asked. Clinker boats had the planks overlapping. It made a strong boat, but it was heavy.

'Carvel,' McCliver said. So, the planks weren't to be overlapped; butted up against each other, the boat would be harder to make watertight, but much lighter in the water. Good for a sailing dinghy.

The younger of the three men came over, wiping his hands on a piece of rag. 'It's for m'cousin.' He had a Scottish accent, but it was weaker than McCliver's. Born here, probably.

'M'nephew Hamish,' McCliver said, waving a hand at him, and nodded towards the third man. 'M'son Andrew.'

'Tom McBride,' he said.

'She'll be a beauty when she gets going,' Andrew said, smoothing a hand down the upright end of the keel.

'Aye, well, time for dinner,' McCliver said.

Tom nodded and walked away with no more than a 'Good night'. He'd have to hurry or he'd be late for tea. Walking up Victoria Street, he lengthened his stride, refreshed by the time he'd spent with sandpaper and wood. A nice old man, McCliver – a bit rough with his tongue, but sound all through.

•

That night, he had the dream again. The sharp smell of mustard and garlic, rolling over the top of the trench, and him grabbing his gasmask just in time. The harsh sucking sound of his breath through the filters, the tunnel vision as the mask cut off his peripheral sight. Morry Fitz scrabbling for his mask. He leaped forward to help, but he didn't make it in time. In reality, Morry had taken only that one, terrible breath before Tom had got the gasmask on him, holding it there even though Morry was coughing and coughing and coughing. That one breath had killed him, twenty-four hours later, his lungs bubbling with blisters, unable to take a full breath.

In the dream, he didn't get the gasmask out at all, stood frozen while Morry breathed in the mustard gas, coughed and coughed and fell at his feet, his face blue around the lips but red everywhere else. In the dream, Tom kneeled beside him, careless of the ankle-high mud, and Morry reached up and dragged the mask off his face, left him helpless, trying not to breathe, trying not to breathe, not to die—

He slammed awake, bolt upright, scrabbling with the covers to get out, get away, as they'd done, the both of them, Tom half-carrying Morry, racing down the trench and then through the system of dug-out channels, far enough back that the gas hadn't caught them, crying *JesusMotherMaryJesus* as loudly as he could as though noise would attract Heaven's attention.

Tom listened; no one moving around. Perhaps he hadn't yelled too loudly, then. This was why he'd asked for the small bedroom up the back. With the bathroom between him and the other bedrooms, there was a better chance that his nightmares wouldn't keep anyone else awake.

Sometimes he thought he ought to give up any idea of marrying. What woman would want to lie next to him, listening to his grunting and groaning? Even awake, the memory was insistent.

He'd been lucky. Three blisters on his wrist – he'd been wearing leather gloves, which the gas couldn't penetrate. But Morry . . .

That was usually the second half of the dream: dying next to Morry, both gasping and struggling to breathe.

Better to stay awake the rest of the night than risk that. He put his bedside lamp on and grabbed the book on boatbuilding he'd found at the Mechanics' School of Arts library. There was something about the sweet, beautiful curves of a boat's hull that banished nightmares.

20

By the next Sunday Jane declared it was too cold for the beach, although it still seemed summer-like to Margaret. They spent a lazy day pottering around the garden instead. Tom visited his mother and aunt; Margaret wondered what, if anything, he'd told them about her.

Sunday evening was pot luck as far as dinner went, but there was always plenty in Burnsie's larder, and Jonesy arrived for the meal, having caught the same ferry as Tom. Afterwards they gathered in the front room. Jonesy, it seemed, could play the piano, and Jane sang for them, 'K-K-K-Katy', a song about a soldier leaving his sweetheart behind and trying to declare his love despite a stutter.

She had a lovely, clear voice, but it was her manner that made the song so funny. As it ended, she glanced at Jonesy and he slid effortlessly into a quieter tune, which made Burnsie beam.

She's only a bird in a gilded cage
A beautiful sight to see

You may think she's happy and free from care,
She's not, though she seems to be

There was something in her tone that made Margaret wonder if Jane herself felt caged in this pretty room, this loving home. She was standing in front of one of the Tiffany lamps, which turned her short hair into a golden helmet. Margaret realised that Jane was actually very good-looking – not pretty, but striking, with some quality in her that was brought out by the lights and the song. You couldn't help but look at her.

And her beauty was sold
For an old man's gold
She's a bird in a gilded cage . . .

Her voice sank into silence and Jonesy stared up at her with relinquishment in his eyes, as though he'd seen something too good for him. Margaret looked away from him only to find Tom staring at her with something of the same look in his eyes. Warmth fountained through her, but she looked away.

'Oh, I do like that one,' Burnsie said. 'How about a cuppa?'

'Thanks, Mrs Burns, but I think I'd better be getting back,' Jonesy replied. 'Don't want to miss the last ferry.'

The three of them walked Jonesy back to his ferry, through a cool night. An afternoon storm had moved on, but the sky was hazy with high cloud. They started out abreast, but as they came into Alfred Street, Margaret put a hand on Tom's arm to slow him, to let the others go ahead alone.

Tom tucked her hand in his arm and they strolled easily together down the hill, hearing Jane laugh, seeing her tilt her head towards Jonesy like an inquisitive bird. His voice was a low rumble in return. Margaret couldn't make out the words, but they quietened Jane. She took his arm and matched her steps to his halting ones.

'I'm glad you got your swim in last weekend,' Tom said suddenly, looking at the sky. 'I think we're in for another storm.'

A long bank of cloud was approaching from the south. It disconcerted Margaret; she still wasn't used to the way a change in weather came from the south. Lightning played over the underside of the cloud, creating strange reflections and an odd greenish light.

The wind began to pick up as they reached the ferry wharf, and the overhead wires rattled in the gusts. A late tram passed them as it began the long climb to North Sydney. They walked through the big tram shed to the wharf and saw a ferry churning through the waves towards them. Its lights winked red and green in the darkness, and its cabin was lit up; no one was inside.

'Better get off quick smart, mate,' Tom said. Jonesy nodded, looking rueful at having his farewell overtaken by the weather. He shook their hands and ran-hopped down the wharf into the glow of a streetlight. The ferry drew in and slowed. There was no one waiting to get off, and Jonesy waved to the ferry hand not to bother with the gangplank, instead leaping on board, and it turned smartly to make its way to the next stop, Kirribilli.

'I hope he gets back to Circular Quay before the worst of it hits.' Jane looked after the ferry with concern.

'Let's worry about getting ourselves home before,' Margaret said. The cloud was coming, and coming fast. Lightning always made her nervous, and right now she wanted to run home and bury her head in her pillow.

'Come on,' Tom said. He put a hand on each of their backs and urged them up the hill. Margaret took a look back: as the cloud came, so did a wall of rain. In an instant, the city was blanked out, its lights only smears of paleness. They went as fast as they could – as fast as she and Jane could go – but the clouds went faster.

At the top of Alfred Street, it hit them, like a slap on the back; in a mere moment Margaret was sopping wet. She couldn't believe it. This was worse than any English rain. It was like being hit by a wave. She turned to look back, but everything more than a few feet away was obscured by the downpour. The wind blew the rain at a strong slant and gusted around their legs.

She hated rain. Had always hated rain: cold, wet, dreary, mizzling stuff. But this rain was warm. It hit her hard, stinging a little. It felt more *real* than English rain. She turned her face up and felt a slither of excitement move up her spine. Lightning blinded her. Thunder boomed and echoed right over their heads, but she wasn't afraid.

'Come on, Margi!' Jane shouted. Tom's hand on her back was warm through her wet blouse. She turned and went with them, in a laughing scramble up the streets and onto the verandah, where Burnsie was waiting for them with towels. They took their shoes off so the floorboards wouldn't be marked and ran for their rooms.

'First in gets the bathroom!' Jane said and the three of them bounded up the stairs like children. Jane was quicker than either of them, and she slid into the bathroom and shut the door in their faces. Margaret was still laughing, breathless, when Tom pulled her against him, cold skin flaring into heat as they touched.

She looked up at him and felt her heart squeezed, that tug that made her breathe even faster. His eyes were fixed on her face, his mouth almost grim. She'd wanted to play, to laugh and be light and bright and uncaring for a while, but Tom McBride wasn't playing.

It was too fast. Only weeks. She'd made that mistake with Frank, married him quickly, as everyone did during the war, in case they never got another chance, in case the man never came back, in case, in case ... Her resolution never to trust anyone, ever again, faltered under his gaze.

'I'm supposed to be a widow,' she reminded him.

He shook his head. 'That's hard to remember.'

'Yes.'

He tightened his arms around her, his skin clinging to hers even through their clothes. His body was vividly alive against hers, his hand in her hair. For a long moment she let him hold her, her body urging her towards something she felt was inevitable but knew was dangerous. She pulled back on that thought. Not only a man, but a Catholic. Not only someone she'd just met, but a soldier; who knew how many girls he'd romanced?

'Get into some dry clothes,' she said. 'I'll meet you downstairs.'

He smiled wryly at her. 'Where it's safe?'

She raised her chin at him, not amused. Easy for him to laugh; he wasn't the one risking reputation and pregnancy if they went any further. Not to mention her heart. Could she survive having her heart broken again?

'Exactly.'

Letting her go, he stood for a moment with his hands by his sides. 'Safety isn't all it's cracked up to be.'

'It'll do for now.'

He took a breath in through his nose and let it out again. 'I think I'll turn in, then.'

His door closed behind him with a definite click. Silly to feel bereft. He was right; with their blood riding high like this it was foolish to spend time together. She was foolish to want to. She must put it out of her mind, forget the rushing pleasure and the fever in her blood.

In her room she stripped off her soaked clothes and piled them in her hand basin, astonished at how wet she'd become in such a short time. This country didn't do things by halves. Heat, wet, storms. Thunder boomed again, nearby. Why wasn't she nervous, as she always had been before? Her whole life. It couldn't just be that Tom was nearby. Something had changed in her. If it went on like this, she wouldn't recognise herself in a year's time. And would that be good or bad?

She towelled herself dry, wishing suddenly for someone she could gossip with, talk to about Tom, about storms, about how her life felt like it belonged to someone else. Her mother, or a friend. But how could she begin to talk about how she felt to Jane, when she was living so much of a lie?

This was horrible. She hated this secrecy and hole-in-the-corner skulking. She *hated* it. Jane's steps sounded, moving down the corridor from the bathroom. With sudden decision she opened her door and put out a hand to stop Jane going past.

'Come in for a sec.'

They sat on the bed.

''Fess up,' Jane said. 'What's going on with you and Tommy?'

'I don't know,' Margaret said. 'But I'm not a widow.'

The story came out haltingly. Jane's eyes got wider and wider. When she got to the part about Frank's daughter, Jane couldn't hold silent.

'Strewth! It's better than a movie! Sorry, go on.'

When Margaret had finished, Jane sat there and thought for a moment. She drew her legs up under her and settled herself against the pillows.

'I won't let on to Mum. Not yet, anyway. So, are you and Tommy going to . . . you and he, um . . . are you in love with him?'

That was the question, wasn't it? If she wasn't in love with him, or at least on the way to being in love, then to even consider a physical relationship was horrible. Dirty. But she didn't think she could bear to be in love with anyone, ever again. It opened you to so much hurt. How could she trust her judgement when she'd been so wrong about Frank?

'I don't know.'

'Better decide. Because I've known Tommy for a good long while now and I've never seen him fall like he has for you.'

'A while?'

Jane nodded solemnly. 'He was Captain Shelley's sergeant, you see. He brought the captain's personal effects home, just after the war. Only a week before Mrs Shelley died. Mum reckons it killed her. Once she'd seen his watch and his spectacles parcelled up like that . . . it was all real. Before then I think she'd tried to pretend it wasn't, you know?'

Yes. Lots of people had tried that. Margaret remembered trying to pretend herself, after her brother died.

'Anyway, Tommy came back to make sure she was all right, and he found us all at sixes and sevens, not knowing what to do because there weren't any relatives, and he helped. He had a couple of days' leave and he spent it here, with us, helping to nurse her, and, and—' her voice shook, 'after, he helped organise everything. And ever since he's kept an eye on Mum.

And me, I s'pose. Like a big brother.' She laughed shakily and wiped a tear away. 'He's a good man.'

'Yes. I can see that.'

She *could* see it, suddenly. Tom wasn't Frank, a man with no family, no connections, no history. If she'd *wanted* to check up on Frank, there'd been no way. She'd had to take his word for everything. But Tom had a history, a family, people who would vouch for him. She might not trust her own judgement, but she could trust Burnsie's and Jane's.

She felt relief pour into her like one of Manly's waves, and only then realised how unhappy it had made her to doubt him.

Although she'd wanted to marry Frank, she had felt that he'd rushed her into it, just a bit. Certainly it had been his desire to have her safely married before he went away that had set the date.

'I'm not taking the chance of you getting away from me,' he'd said, and she'd felt the glory of being wanted, of being special to someone.

She refused to let his real motivations disturb her today. Many war marriages were rushed, hurried things.

It didn't have to be like that with Tom.

21

'Here you go, bub.' Frank handed Violet the ball, a new red one he'd bought on the way home.

'Ball!' Violet grabbed it and ran, throwing it cack-handed and trying to catch it up, all the way across the backyard.

'Oh, Frank, you shouldn't have! You're spoiling her.' Gladys's words were hard, but her tone was indulgent. She slid her arm around his waist and leaned her head on his shoulder. They stood like that, just watching Vi try and fail to throw and catch the ball. Frank crouched down and called to her.

'Bring it here, bubby. I'll show you how.'

Violet brought him the ball, her eyes doubtful. He held out his own hands, cupped.

'Throw it to Papa.'

She tried, but it went sideways. He grabbed it with one hand, and laughed. Vi laughed too, her eyes lighting up.

'Now you,' he said. Gladys came behind Vi, reaching around to take her hands and put them together. Gently, he tossed the ball into Vi's outstretched palms. It bounced out, and her chin wobbled with disappointment.

'You've got to grab it when it comes,' Frank reassured her. 'Let's try again.'

This time, Vi managed to hold onto the ball, and she let out a cry of triumph.

'I wish you'd heard back from that woman,' Glad said. She sat down on a garden chair. Every time he looked at her Frank felt a great tenderness, thinking of the baby to come.

'It can't be that long before we hear. They might have had to send the letter on, to wherever she's living now.'

The thought of Margaret gave him a twinge, but then Violet threw the ball wildly back at him, right in the face.

He fell backwards from his crouch onto the mossy lawn, and then Vi was on top of him, tickling him, laughing like nothing would ever stop her.

Please God nothing ever would. He was swept by that astonishing mixture of thankfulness and fear he felt every time he looked at Vi. It was amazing that she was his, a wonder he'd never imagined. But so much could go wrong. So much could hurt a child.

Being prepared to kill anyone who hurt her wasn't enough. *He* had to not hurt her. He had to look after her with such gentleness, such strength that she would grow up keeping that open, lovely face. The face of absolute trust in Gladys, and in him.

He took her by the waist and set her on her feet, pretending to be a bear, growling. Squealing with excitement, she took off and he followed her on all fours, until she hid behind Gladys, peeking out, eyes alight.

'Bad Papa!' she said, laughing, but it still cut him.

'No, Violet,' Gladys said. 'Papa is a good Papa.'

'Good Papa!' Vi echoed. Frank sat back, transforming himself from bear to man, and she flung herself at him. 'Good Papa!' She kissed him, and he held her tight.

'The very best papa I can be,' he said. It was a solemn oath.

22

The next Friday, Jonesy came by to take Jane over to visit Clara for a sing-along night. He stood at the newel post of the stairs while he waited for Jane to get her coat and hat from her room. With his hand on the post and his head tilted up, he looked the very picture of the lovelorn swain. Margaret almost hated to disturb him, but she had to walk past him to get from the kitchen to the lounge.

'She won't be long,' Margaret reassured him.

He smiled, his long, dark face lighting up. He was more attractive than she had realised – a bit like Jane, it was animation that made him worth looking at.

'No, she's good like that.'

Out on the road, a car backfired, and he spun around, flinching, then relaxed and laughed shakily, passing a hand over his face before he turned to her.

'Sorry. Sorry, bad habit.'

'We all acquired some bad habits in the war,' she said, trying to make light of it. 'I can't bear the smell of a steam train – it takes me right back to Reading Station.'

'Oh, too bad,' he said, but it was an absent assent, a matter of form. His attention was still on the stairs, waiting.

'Maybe you'd be better off out of the city,' she ventured.

He looked up the stairs again, a quick glance. 'Can't leave the bright lights just yet,' he said.

'Or ever?' Perhaps it was pushy of her, nosy, but he looked at her properly and shrugged.

'See, it's all right when I'm with Jane. Or singing. While we're singing, there's nothing else in the world.'

Truth chimed in his words as clear as day. She worried about him. What if Jane didn't return this fervent loyalty?

Jane clattered down the stairs, pulling on her gloves.

'You've got long faces on!' she said. 'What's the matter?'

'Nothing now,' Jonesy said. He held out his arm and she slid her hand through it as they left, smiling up at him with a sunny, innocent smile.

Burnsie came from the kitchen as she heard the front door close.

'She'll be all right,' she said, misreading Margaret's expression. 'She's got her head on straight as far as men are concerned.'

●

So, it was only Margaret, Tom and Burnsie at dinner. Jane was off with Jonesy, and the others were who-knew-where.

They ate at the dining table instead of in the kitchen.

'Wouldn't let those harum-scarum boys eat in here,' Burnsie said, 'but it's nice to get out the good china occasionally, isn't it?'

She had made stuffed lamb hearts, 'since there's just the three of us, and they're only little things'. It had been years since Margaret had eaten them, and they made her nostalgic.

'My grandmother used to make these,' she said, 'but not as nice as this.'

'The lamb you get here's the best in the world,' Burnsie said. 'Well, and New Zealand lamb's pretty good too.'

They ate in silence for a while, and then Tom cleared his throat. Margaret jumped, looked up guiltily, and met his eyes. They both burst out laughing. Burnsie shook her head at them, smiling, but with eyes that missed nothing. Margaret suddenly realised that she was chaperoning them.

It was curiously intimate and at the same time strangely formal, sitting at one end of the big table on padded dining chairs, the Tiffany lamps glowing in the corners. Not as homely; Margaret wasn't sure she was cut out for the high life like this. At least she knew about cutlery; a nice lady on the war-bride ship had taught their whole table about silverware and which fork went with which course. She hadn't thought she'd ever have cause to use that knowledge, but when dessert came – fruit salad and cream – she was glad to know which spoon she should use.

They said Australia was a classless society. Perhaps this was what they meant; it didn't matter where you were from as long as you knew which spoon to use.

But you had to know.

After dinner, they helped Burnsie wash up – a much quicker process than usual – and then went into the drawing room while Burnsie disappeared upstairs with an 'I'll just go and powder my nose'.

Margaret settled on the sofa with one of her books on pottery, but Tom went to the victrola and wound it up, putting on a recording of 'Down By the Old Mill Stream'. She didn't recognise the singer – perhaps an Australian?

My darling, I am dreaming of the days gone by,
When you and I were sweethearts beneath the summer sky;
Your hair has turned to silver, the gold has faded too;
But still I will remember, where I first met you

•

The melody was pretty, but the words pricked at Margaret. All her dreams were gone. Frank, a home, family . . . gone. She had picked herself up and kept going, because what else was there to do? But, just as Tom had wished for a holiday between the Army and his new job, she wished she could have had a while to just cry and moan and complain about the blow Fate had handed her. And maybe get angry, too.

She'd made a new life for herself, but every so often a deluge of what-might-have-been swept over her, a dumper of a wave of disappointment and shame at how easily she'd been duped.

'No long faces!' Tom said. He held out a hand to her. 'Dance?'

'Methodists don't dance,' she said. Dancing led to immoral thoughts, and worse deeds. A tool of the devil, to tempt men into sin.

'Anglicans do.'

What was she? She might go to an Anglican church, but did that make her Anglican? What did she believe? She just didn't know anymore. It would hurt him if she refused.

She took his hand and he pulled her up and into his arms.

He was so tall. Taller and more solid than Frank, so she felt somehow protected in his arms. He was in shirtsleeves, and her hand, resting on his arm, felt the warmth of muscle through the thin cloth. His hand was tight on her waist, and he smiled down at her as he led her into a simple two-step, up and down the drawing room, around the furniture and out into the hall and back again.

She was breathless and laughing by the time the victrola ran out of steam and the music began to slow down. They slowed with it, until in the last few bars they were swaying, shuffling rather than romping. The music ended in a hissing silence as Margaret looked up into Tom's eyes.

She waited for him to let her go and move to the victrola, but he stood, gazing down at her, still holding her tightly. In the movement of the dance she hadn't been aware of his hold so much, but now everywhere he touched her was burningly evident. This was as close as they had ever been, closer even than when he had held her before. The Methodists were right; this was a temptation to sin.

The moment stretched out and she didn't know what to do. Pull away? Say something? She didn't know what she wanted. She didn't know if she still cared about him being Catholic. She didn't know anything.

His face was serious. He stared at her and then, finally, pulled his hand away from her waist and touched her cheek.

'No long faces,' he repeated.

Margaret felt jolted. She'd expected something else, she didn't know what. But she conjured up a smile, and he nodded, his eyes warming, not exactly smiling back.

'Only eight months,' he said. He let her go and went to the victrola, changing the record. She stayed where she was as he wound up the machine, surprised by the remark. Eight months took them to – November, the anniversary of when Frank was supposed to have died. The end of her official mourning. And then what? Did he mean that in November he'd do more than look at her? More than cheer her up or dance with her?

Anger flooded her. She was tired of men organising her life, changing it with no reference to what she wanted. Frank, who had lied to her and betrayed her; the factory owner who had thrown her out of her family home as soon as her father was dead, because the house was wanted for other workers; the station-master at Reading who had given away her job; her father, forbidding her to have anything to do with Catholics; even Tom, who had hauled her off to that hostel without so much as a by-your-leave. She had thought he was leaving it to her to set the pace, and it annoyed her intensely that that might not be true.

She went to him where he was bending over the victrola and pulled his arm so that he straightened up and looked at her.

'I haven't seen that rotter for more than two years. Who knows what he got up to when he came home? Whatever I can do in eight months I can do now!'

He was surprised; his whole body showed it. But then a sudden fierceness came on his face, and he bent and grabbed her, kissed her, body to body, mouth to mouth.

Not a tentative kiss. First kisses were supposed to be romantic and gentle; but they weren't kids.

It wasn't love, but it was need. She understood need. Need was honest. No deceptions, no lies, no pretence. She kissed him back, one hand in his short hair, the other clutching his collar. He was shaking. Something exulted in her. Oh yes, desire was as honest as a mirror.

Burnsie came clumping down the stairs and they were apart. She wasn't even sure which of them had moved first. Tom bent over the victrola and she snatched up her book and sat, breathing fast.

'Put something nice on, love,' Burnsie said, sitting opposite Margaret in the big armchair by the fireplace.

'How about this?' Tom said, straightening, apparently in control of himself. The record hissed and started. 'Brahms' Lullaby'. Margaret started to laugh. She didn't know why, but the images of babies and sleep the music conjured were so far from what had just happened.

'Not that nice!' Burnsie said. 'Don't want to put us all to sleep, eh, Margi?'

Tom turned and grinned at her before changing the record, and she felt a stab of desire in her abdomen. Not so far removed, she thought with a wry smile, and she'd do well to remember that. Need was all very well, but the last thing she needed was a baby. She'd acted like a harlot. A brazen hussy. Her mother would have slapped her face for behaving like that.

She couldn't concentrate on Josiah Wedgwood and English porcelain. Her workbox was on the side table. Darning. Nice and uncomplicated. Stitch by stitch she rescued her old stocking, and wished she could stitch her life back into shape as easily.

What should she do? What should *they* do? Her body seemed to hold the memory of his touch; her mouth, her back, her arms were warm from it. The next step was . . . much more of a risk.

Nothing had to be decided now, though. It wasn't like it had been with Frank, a quick and sketchy courtship because of the war. She didn't have to trust without proof, without evidence. She could let their relationship unfold gradually, the way courting was supposed to happen.

They had time. They had all the time in the world.

23

On Friday when Tom went to the post office to deposit his pay, his passbook came back with an extra sixty-two pounds and five shillings: his demob money had come through. With his own savings, that meant he had more than a hundred and fifty pounds, not counting the money his mother had saved for him. Three hundred, if you counted that. That was enough to buy land and build a house.

He walked back to Burnsie's house in a mood that wavered between satisfaction and restlessness.

He had money. He had a job. He had, perhaps, a future with Margaret. He ought to be on top of the world. But one kiss, no matter how passionate, wasn't a guarantee of anything.

On Blue's Point Road, a tram rattled by and he winced. He loved the Harbour, but the noise of the city was hard to bear. That was one of the reasons he fretted about his job, he reckoned. Noisy. Too many reminders of shells and explosions. It set his nerves on edge and he was always having to control his temper.

God, he'd love to get away from things for a while. Take Margi with him. He let his mind dwell pleasantly on that for a moment, but there was little chance of it happening. He couldn't ruin her reputation, after all, even if she'd come.

In a week it was Easter. Four days off. Now, he might just give John Bradley from the Quartermaster's office a call . . .

When he got home, after saying hello to Burnsie, he rang John, thanking his lucky stars that Mrs Shelley had put the phone on early in the war and Burnsie had decided to keep it.

'Quartermaster's office,' Bradley answered.

'John, it's Tom McBride.'

'Sergeant! Nice to hear from you. What can I do you for?'

'You mentioned a while back that the surplus stores were coming up for sale . . .'

'Yep. Starting soon, as a matter of fact.'

'Any chance of buying a few tents?'

'Strewth yes! We've got them coming out of our ears. How many do you want?'

Tom thought. Margaret and Jane. Burnsie, if she came. Him and Jonesy. Maybe a couple of Jane's friends.

'Better make it four,' he said. 'And ground cloths. Half a dozen blankets, too.'

'Mounting an expedition, eh?'

'Thought we might go camping over Easter.'

'Half your luck. I'm on duty. Tell you what, I'll have a look and pick you out some good ones. Have to do a proper request, though. Paperwork.' He said it with the obligatory groan in his voice, although Tom knew that he revelled in forms in triplicate.

'Can I pick them up Wednesday?'

'Oh, yerse, no worries. She'll be sorted by then. Tell you what, I'll get them dropped off to you.'

The door opened as he hung up the handpiece and Margaret came in, taking off her hat as she shut the door. She hadn't seen him yet. He enjoyed the simple pleasure of looking at her: her ruffled brown hair, her lithe, graceful body, the freckles kissing her nose. When she turned and saw him, her face lit up and he felt a rush of tenderness. A fierce fondness. Was that love?

He'd thought himself in love a couple of times before, and each time had been different. Helen, the VAD nurse he'd been engaged to, had been happy and bouncy and a good chum, and he'd wanted to bed her with all the lust of a young man, but of course there'd been no funny business. They might have made a good enough marriage, if he hadn't fallen for a married woman, and Helen hadn't found a wounded major who needed her more than he ever would.

The married woman, Ruby, well, he still didn't know what to think about that. He'd been a fool; she'd never made any secret of how much she loved her husband. But she'd been so beautiful, and so *present*, there every day at work, where she was the bookkeeper. Brave and beautiful. Those were the qualities Margaret had, too. But Margaret had something else, and he didn't know what it was, exactly. A hunger for life, maybe. A willingness to take risks, to laugh and live life to the full. You only had to see her in the surf to know she was reaching out for life with both hands. After four years of death and destruction, he was in the mood to live like that himself, and damn the consequences.

Maybe it was that simple. Ruby was the one he had loved before he went to war, but he needed something different now. Ruby had been the evening star, but Margaret was the morning sun.

He moved towards her and pulled her into his arms.

'Tom!' she protested. 'Not here.'

But she kissed him anyway, her mouth soft, her hands in his hair.

'I've never felt this way about anyone,' he said. And meant it.

'Oh, Tom . . .' Her green eyes filled with tears, and he castigated himself for a brute. She wasn't ready for this. Not after that cur Dalton had treated her so badly. She touched his cheek hesitantly.

'Sorry.' He took a breath in and stood back from her, making his hands drop away from her waist. 'I didn't mean to put you on the spot.'

A smile broke across her face. 'You can't *apologise* for saying *that*!'

Suddenly they were both laughing and he felt a great relief. No dramas with Margaret. No dark emotional storms. He could trust her for that. She took his arm.

'We'll talk later. Somewhere else.'

'Yes, ma'am.'

'That's right. You bow to a greater authority.' But she was smiling as she said it and she gave his arm a little squeeze before letting go so she could walk into the kitchen ahead of him.

'Hello love,' Burnsie said. 'Put the kettle on, will you?'

As Margaret busied herself with the kettle, Tom leaned against the doorframe.

'So,' he said. 'How do you feel about an adventure?'

•

It took a bit of organisation, but he did it. On Holy Thursday afternoon, there they all were, waiting for him on the verandah as he rolled up in the truck from work. He'd asked if he could hire it and the boss, Mr Cobbin, had said, 'Just fill up the tank after you're done,' and thrown him the keys. He must have shown his surprise, because Mr Cobbin had chuckled.

'You're only young once,' he said.

'Thank you, sir!'

'Off you go. Don't crack the sump.'

Now for the next surprise, but this time he was the one giving it.

He pulled up at the gate and double-checked the handbrake before he got down to help load. He left the engine running, though. No need to crank it up again.

The girls were dressed for camping, all right. Jane had had a hand in that, he reckoned – he doubted that Margaret had left England with dungarees and elastic-sided boots. For once, she'd put aside that pretty straw hat she wore everywhere and had an old beaten-up wide-brimmed felt hat on her head – she looked like a kid playing dress-ups.

He hadn't told them where they were going. Just that they'd be camping and coming back on Monday afternoon. Burnsie had laid in boxes of food and unearthed a brace of old billies and a camp oven. He and Jonesy hoisted them into the truck and laid the blankets on top to form rough seats. The truck had high wooden slat sides, so they'd be safe enough riding there. That done, he helped Margaret, and then Burnsie, up into the cab.

'I could drive, you know,' Jane said. She could too. Part of her VAD work had been ambulance driving.

'Don't think my boss would like that, thanks all the same.' He grinned at her and jerked his head towards Jonesy, waiting to hand Jane up into the back of the truck. She poked her tongue out at him and went back. Four more of her friends, two girls and two brothers who he thought might be twins, made up the party. No doubt he'd sort all their names out in time. One was Clara, he knew that.

He swung up into the cab next to Margaret and felt his heart lift as she smiled at him with all the excitement of a kid off on an adventure. No matter how dark his mood, that smile could lift him right up. At the moment he felt so good that it was lifting him right up to the mountaintops.

'You've *never* been camping before?'

'I was a bit old for Girl Guides when they started, and wherever else was I going to camp? The closest was staying out late in summer on the common. The boys used to sleep out, but girls weren't allowed.'

'I haven't been much lately,' he admitted. 'If you don't count France, that is.'

'Let's not count that.' She moved her right hand so that it fitted down between their bodies. He could feel it there, connecting them.

'Right, Burnsie?'

'Tally-ho!' Burnsie said, beaming. 'Isn't that what they say at Home, Margi?'

'Tally-ho!' they all shouted, and set off.

•

Their destination was Clareville, a small waterfront suburb on Pittwater, a huge inlet north of Sydney. On the right side of a peninsula were the northern beaches: Manly, Curl Curl, Dee Why, Collaroy, Narrabeen, Warriewood, Mona Vale, Newport, Bilgola, all the way up to Palm Beach at the very top. On the left side, the Pittwater harbour reached down about a third of the way from Palm Beach. And Clareville was halfway along Pittwater, level with Avalon on the ocean side.

It took almost two hours to reach it. The first hour was reasonable driving – the road was paved until The Spit punt and after that was in all-right condition considering the rain they'd had that summer.

But past Collaroy it was little more than a country track, half-corduroy and half-mud.

Tom nursed the truck over the rough bits, especially going up the Bilgola Plateau, which seemed to rear over them darkly as the sun went down behind it. When they came out on the top and could see the last of the sun disappearing, gilding Pittwater into a glaring shield of bronze, it was like coming out of the Valley of the Shadow.

'Huzzah!' he heard the boys in the back yell.

He grinned, but down was always trickier. He turned on the headlamps and made his way cautiously down the winding track. It was a fair way away from anywhere, that was for sure, despite the occasional houses they glimpsed between the gum trees. Up Plateau Road and down Bilambee Avenue, and then he had to get the map out and give it to Margaret, along with his electric torch.

She was good at map reading, a bit to his surprise, and got them there without a single wrong turn. Every moment he was with her, he fell more in love; a simple thing like map reading felt enormously important, as though she were showing her true self, her deepest spirit. He laughed at himself. What a booby he was.

They found Hudson Parade as the sun was finally disappearing, but there was enough light to unpack the truck.

They piled out, exclaiming at the view across the tops of the trees to the water. The block, next to a reserve on one side and several empty blocks of land on the other, was steeper than he'd thought it would be. Tough to build on this.

But as he scrambled down the slope with a tent under each arm, he could see the water between the trees. There was a bit of flat land at the bottom – more than enough to camp on – and he paused, enjoying the salt breeze and the sense of peace. A kookaburra farewelled the sun, wood pigeons cooed, wattlebirds squawked an alarm at their invasion. Other than that, the only noise was the hiss of small waves on the sand.

This'd be a bonzer place to bring up kiddies.

24

Margaret carried Burnsie's bags as Burnsie came down the hill with Tom on one side and one of the twins, Alf, on the other. Burnsie was swearing under her breath and digging her heels in as she came.

The land was what Australians called 'bush' – a mixture of gum trees and shrubs, knee-high bracken and bright yellow wildflowers. Leaf litter and curls of bark were thick underfoot. It was as though no one had ever set foot here before.

'I'm not going back up that thing until we go home!' Burnsie said breathlessly, at the bottom. But then they looked around. The sand glimmered and the water reflected the pink and orange of the high clouds. As they watched, the boys went up the hill again to lug down the food and the moon rose behind them, edging up over Bilgola Plateau.

Margaret turned and looked up at it through the trees. It was almost full, impossibly golden and huge. She would never get used to the fact that the Man in the Moon didn't show his face the same way here. What did Australian mothers tell their children about the moon?

She asked Burnsie.

'Can't you see? That's the mother rabbit putting her little rabbits to bed.'

As she waited for the moon to clear the trees so she could inspect it, she helped the boys put up the tents while Tom started a fire and Jonesy took the tomahawk off into some thick bushes, limping less than he had been. He came back with some poles shorter than the ones the twins were using as tent poles. Two longish and four short with forks at their ends.

'Here you go, Burnsie,' he said. 'I'll make you a bed.'

And he did – he lashed the short poles together into two X shapes with a Y at the top of each stick, then put the long ones through two hessian sacks. The ends of the long poles went into the Ys on the short poles.

'Voila!' he said. 'A camp bed.'

'You get an extra piece of fruitcake for that, dearie,' she said gratefully. 'I'm a bit old to rest my bones on the ground.'

'How did you find this place, mate?' Jonesy asked.

'It belonged to a cobber of mine in the battalion,' Tom said. 'He didn't make it back.' There was a moment of silence, then Tom moved his shoulders as though shaking off the memory, and went on. 'His brother's putting it up for sale. I'm thinking of buying it. Building a holiday house.'

He turned and looked at Margaret and she smiled tentatively back. A holiday house. Only *rich* people had a holiday house. In England it was 'a house in the country', but they were the preserve of the entitled. It would never have occurred to her that an ordinary man might have a spare house. An image of her and Tom here, some time in the future, rose up: a quick picture of the two of them helping a couple of redheaded children build a sandcastle . . .

Now that was just rushing things. She turned her attention to unpacking the food.

The boys finished putting up the tents while she, Burnsie, Jane and Clara began to get food ready: a cold collation, the cookbooks would have called it. Salad and corned beef and even some ham. Bread and butter. And fruitcake to finish.

As they sat around the fire eating off tin plates and drinking tea out of tin mugs, Margaret turned her gaze back to the moon. She *could* just see the rabbit ears, and she supposed the rest was imagination, just like with the Man in the Moon.

She was aware of every shift of Tom's body, every breath he took, and made an effort to talk to the others without looking at him, although she was also aware of his gaze on her throughout the meal.

It turned out that the twins were Clara's brothers; and by the look of things, both were sweet on her friend Sissie. The four of them clustered.

The boys seemed incredibly young compared to Tom and Jonesy. She'd noticed this at work; there was a big gap between those who'd gone to war and those who hadn't, even if only a year or two separated them in age.

•

Tom took a torch and tomahawk and went to look for more firewood.

Margaret followed, another torch in hand. It was easy to spot him. He was a tall, solidly built man, but he seemed even bigger out here, even in the growing dark, as though he'd expanded in the open air to his proper size.

She realised, with a flicker of unease, that it was hard to look away from him. Hard to think about anything, anyone, else.

He had found a fallen, long-dead tree between a couple of big boulders and was chopping off its brittle branches.

'Can I help?' she asked, knowing what the answer would be.

'Yes,' he said, surprising her. He stuck the tomahawk into the trunk of the tree and slid his arms around her.

Part of her was laughing at the 'romance' of it – kissing over the firewood! The other part, the traitorous, languorous part, swayed her towards him and turned her mouth up to his. As they kissed she shifted backwards until a boulder stopped her and then he pressed against her. Was it wrong that she exulted in his desire? The rock behind her was only to waist height, and he lifted her up to sit on it so their faces were on a level then she slid her hands under his arms and up to his shoulders, holding on tightly. A small movement of his knees and he was standing between her legs.

For a small, sane moment she knew she ought to pull back. That it was her job, her duty, to pull back. It was always the woman's job to set the boundaries, even when she wasn't a virgin anymore. Instead, she wrapped her legs around him, feeling him push against her immediately, ready for her. He made a noise deep in his throat and said her name—

A shout went up from the campfire and he pulled away, looking dazed.

She probably looked the same.

Her mouth was throbbing and the rest of her – God, the way the rest of her felt!

His breath was ragged but the dark was closing in and she could barely see his face. She desperately wanted to see his expression. Did he think her fast? Was he repulsed by her wantonness?

Was she in love with him? Could she make love to him if she wasn't? That would be the worst kind of sin, surely? True fornication. She felt herself suspended between two equally frightening options: to want him without loving him was lust, a deadly sin; to love him was dangerous, putting her heart into his hands. The sensible *and* the moral thing to do was to walk away from him, right now.

He kissed her again, and she knew she couldn't walk away.

He raised a hand to her face. 'Later,' he breathed, and went back to chopping, hitting the wood with extra force.

She tried to walk back to the campfire nonchalantly, as if nothing had happened, but she didn't think she'd fooled Burnsie.

Later, he'd said, and she knew that she would go to him then.

•

Later was much later. After the fire had burned down. After everyone had crawled into their tents. After she'd waited, quietly, blood fizzing, until Jane was asleep.

She'd got out of her dungarees to go to bed, and was sleeping in nothing but a slip. Silently, she pulled an old, loose, print dress over her head and slid out of the tent.

She was acting like a scarlet woman. She knew that. But. All her life she'd been told to keep herself for marriage, to keep her virginity for her husband.

And she had. Oh, she had.

Now, what was she? Not a virgin. Not a wife. Not a widow. Vulnerable as all women were to an unwanted pregnancy, but with only a fabricated, lying reputation to lose. If God had wanted her to stay a virgin he should have protected her from Frank.

She'd done what was expected of her all her twenty-two years, and got nothing for it – no, not nothing, because she had got to come to Australia. That brought thoughts of surf-shooting, of that wild exultation she felt as the wave took her. Those moments had shown her a side of herself she'd never suspected.

It was that side that was compelling her out of the tent. Lust, or love, she didn't care. It was as though it didn't matter. Whatever the risk was, he was worth it.

The almost-full moon lit the shore and the waves as though the sun had turned silver. She found him down the beach, away from the camp in the opposite direction to the latrine. Good. No one would see them if they got up in the middle of the night to pee.

He was leaning against a big rock, looking up at the moon, red hair washed into blond by the moonlight, face like a statue, strong and male. The side with the scar was away from her, and for the first time she realised how good-looking he had been, before.

On bare feet she walked down the sand, her short hair lifted by a small wind.

He sensed her coming, although she was sure she hadn't made a sound. He turned and she ran the last few steps to him. Then he pulled her into his arms, bending his head, blocking out the moonlight, leaving her in a dizzying darkness.

They moved, locked together, around to the other side of the rock, where no one could see them, and there he'd laid out a groundsheet. For a moment he pressed her back against the rock, as he had earlier that evening, and she felt the same shock of desire. But this rock was too tall for her to sit on as she had then, so they subsided, still in each other's arms, onto the groundsheet. It wasn't comfortable; the ground underneath was uneven, and hard.

She didn't care.

Their kisses were frantic. His hand on her hip, pulling her closer. His other arm under her, hand on her back, holding her so tightly. She slid her leg up over his and instantly he pulled back.

Had she done something wrong? Shame swept over her. He thought she was a slut – but his hand slid into her hair and tilted her face up to him.

'Are you sure?' His voice was unsteady. 'I'll try to get off at Redfern, but I can't promise . . .' He groaned and buried his head in her neck. 'I can't promise.'

She had no idea what he was talking about, but it didn't seem like he was shocked by her need of him.

'I'm sure,' she said. Greatly daring, far more daring than she'd ever been with Frank, she took his hand and slid it up under her skirt to her bottom, so he could feel that, underneath her slip, she was bare.

A sound came out of him that she'd never heard, as though she'd pushed him past any resistance, any control. It sent a spear of triumph through her. *Yes.* He should feel like that about her. Unable to resist her, as she was unable to resist him.

His mouth came down on hers and then there was nothing but heat and flesh and desire. It was all new. She'd thought that every touch would bring back memories of Frank, but Tom was so different – every movement, every touch, the smell and the feel and the tenderness were so different it was as though this was an entirely new thing she was doing.

They were doing. Blindly seeking his mouth, she thought, that's the difference. This was something *they* were doing. With Frank, it had been something he was doing to her.

She was astonished at how good it felt.

•

They lay dozing for a while afterwards, wrapped in each other's arms, a blanket pulled up over them. For the first time, she thought that Frank might have done her a favour by lying to her; it had led her here.

Tom lifted strands of her hair and let them drop, over and over, gently.

'I love you,' he said. 'I know you're supposed to say that beforehand, but . . .'

She put a finger against his lips.

'Shh.' The world around them was beginning to grey, the clear grey before dawn. His face was becoming clearer to her, and his eyes had a question in them. No doubt what he wanted to hear: that she loved him too.

Did she?

It was so hard to separate the needs of her body from her feelings for him, and that alone made her blush. She looked into his eyes; those steady, warm, lovely hazel eyes, and a surge of some feeling she'd never known filled her so completely that tears were forced from her eyes.

It wasn't what she had felt for Frank. This was softer, deeper, more dangerous. This could destroy her if she wasn't careful.

'Yes,' she said. 'I love you too.'

She'd expected his face to change – to show happiness, at least. But instead she saw a reflection of the same surge of feeling: something soft and deep and dangerous filled his gaze. He didn't say anything. He didn't kiss her. But he gathered her tightly to him, her head under his chin, his arms wrapped completely around her, hers around him, as though they were trying to merge into one body, one complete being.

'Only seven months,' he muttered against her hair.

'Seven months,' she agreed.

'Then we get married.'

He pulled back and looked at her, just for confirmation, clearly assuming that she would say yes.

A small fillip of pain, the last bit of pain Frank would cause her, set her heart beating. She was angry that the memory of him would intrude on this moment. Stupid to fall in love so fast; stupid to give herself to Tom so fast; stupid to remarry so quickly – that's what that flick of pain said to her. It told her to slow down, to be careful, not to make any more mistakes. It said she couldn't see through Frank, so how did she know Tom was any different? It said stop, think, be sensible. Protect yourself. He's Catholic, you can't marry a Catholic. An image of the wave lifting her, shooting her forwards, swept across her mind.

She kissed him gently. 'Ask me again when I can say yes with a clear conscience.'

25

The rest of the weekend was surprising in more ways than one. The next day was Good Friday, so Burnsie sent the boys out fishing from the rocks on the point. Fish on Fridays again. High Church Anglicans were quite strange, really.

Jane, Clara, Sissie and Margaret swam and walked along the beach. At one point, Margaret and Jane found themselves floating in the small swell while Sissie and Clara made a sandcastle on the beach.

'Janey, what does "get off at Redfern" mean?'

Jane spluttered and dropped her feet to the sand, looking at her in astonishment.

'Where did you hear that?'

'Um . . . the men at work were talking. I don't think I was meant to overhear.'

'I should say not!' Jane grinned at her, but she looked a little embarrassed, all the same. Jane *never* looked embarrassed. 'It means . . . well, Redfern is the station before the Central Station country platforms. The station before the end of the line.'

'Yes?' Clearly there was some meaning here she wasn't getting. Jane sighed and spoke carefully.

'So . . . if, for example, a man was . . . was on a journey . . . his destination would be Central.'

'Yes . . .'

'So, if he got off at Redfern, he'd be, er, stopping the journey before he got to the, the . . . end.'

For a moment, she stared at Jane in bewilderment. Then the penny dropped and she blushed hard, feeling the red sweep up over her face.

'Oh,' she said inadequately. '*That* kind of journey.'

'Exactly,' Jane said, relieved she understood. 'But don't you ever believe them. They *say* they'll get off at Redfern, but they don't.'

That was the voice of experience talking. Margaret thought back to Tom's attempt to promise last night. Poor lamb. He'd had no hope at all of getting off at Redfern. She and Jane shared a complicit glance, and then started to laugh.

•

She and Tom had no more chance to be alone together. When she tried to crawl out of the tent that night, Jane woke.

'Just going to the latrine,' Margaret said.

'I'll come with you.'

Margaret had a suspicion that Jane was protecting her from herself; that she hadn't believed for a minute that mythical conversation from work. Margaret wasn't sure whether to be thankful to her or not. Her whole body demanded Tom's, and it would be a long time before they could be together again. But a baby at this point would be disastrous.

Frank had used condoms; so she wouldn't be left raising a child on her own while he was at the front, he'd said. Now she wondered if it had been because *he* didn't want to be lumbered with an illegitimate child. She and Tom could use condoms, too. In fact, she felt a little indignant that he hadn't brought any with him.

Then she thought that she would have been indignant if he had; if he'd made assumptions about her.

Condoms weren't good for men, she knew. It made it less pleasant for them, or something. Too bad. Seven months was far too long for them to risk 'getting off at Redfern'. Even if Tom *could* do it.

As she crawled back into her sleeping bag, she resigned herself to more days of frustration.

Stolen kisses behind the rocks. A hand touch as they both helped prepare breakfast. Swimming together, cool flesh gliding across cool flesh as their legs touched.

It was agony.

It was wonderful.

Jane's friends were remarkable for their lack of judgement of her – a widow keeping company with a single man. Although it quickly became Jane and Jonesy, Margi and Tom, and then the foursome of Clara, Sissie and the twins, none of them raised an eyebrow. Burnsie kept her own counsel, brooding over it by the fire in a bush chair the boys had made out of saplings and a couple of flour bags. She swam, too, in an ancient bathing costume that covered every single bit of her body except her face.

In the water, she was as good a swimmer as Jane, striking out across to the next bay without hesitation and then riding the current back towards them.

It just showed you never knew with people.

Margaret pushed down that flick of unease she had felt the night before. She didn't *care* if she was wrong about Tom. It was better to live the life she wanted now, rather than be afraid all the time that she was making a mistake. She had waited and waited for the war to be over, and waited again to be reunited with Frank. She wasn't going to wait any longer.

•

On the Sunday afternoon, they managed to get some time alone – at least, out of earshot of the others, who were playing quoits on the beach. Not *actually* alone, not enough even to kiss. But together, sitting on a blanket under a tree large enough that both of them could lean back against it.

Tom brought out the coconut oil and began to smooth it on his arms and face. He worked it well in to his scar, with no change of expression, as though he didn't even notice it anymore.

Margaret reached out hesitantly and touched the jagged white line.

'Does it still hurt?'

'No.' Tom's response was instant, reassuring, then he paused. 'Well, it feels stretched sometimes.' He looked down at the bottle of oil in his hands. 'I suppose you want to know how I got it?'

'Only if you want to tell me.' She'd heard a lot of soldiers' tales over the years, but she wasn't sure if she wanted to know this one. She did, because she wanted to know everything about him; she didn't, because she didn't want to think of him in pain.

'It was a night raid,' he said, his voice carefully neutral, his eyes still on his hands. 'We went over the top. The brass laid down a smokescreen. The Krauts couldn't see us, but we couldn't see either. Couldn't find our way.' He paused, then pushed the cork back into the bottle with some force. 'Two hours. Two hours of fumbling around, blind as bats. Then our subbie called the retreat. I tell you, I was glad to hear it.' She put her hand over his, and he put the bottle down and laced his fingers through hers. 'We thought we were home clear, thought we were retracing our steps, but the smoke had us turned around. Sanderson stepped on a land mine.'

His hand gripped hers suddenly, so hard it hurt, and then let go.

'Well, that was it. I got a bit of shrapnel.' His voice was dismissive.

She didn't know what to say, so she touched the scar again. 'It looks like it was pretty bad.'

'They thought I'd lose the eye,' he said. For a moment he looked away from her, letting go of her hand, and her heart clenched. If he couldn't look at her, couldn't share this terrible memory in any way but words, what hope did they have for a future? She felt as shut out as she had that night she'd stood outside his bedroom door and heard him crying out for help that didn't come.

He looked back, letting her see the fear that had ridden him then, and the grief. 'That was the worst part. That and Sandy copping it. He was a mate of mine. For a while there I wanted to go too.'

She cupped his face with one hand, the tips of her fingers lightly touching the scar. 'I'm sorry,' she said. 'But I'm glad you didn't. I'm *so* glad.' A mixture of compassion and gratitude twisted within her that he had turned back to face her. She wanted to kiss him, but the others could see. Instead she found his hand and held it so tightly she could barely feel his skin against hers.

'Yeah, I'm glad too. Now.' He grimaced, looking down at their clenched hands. 'The worst of it was, it was for nothing. We didn't sight the enemy all night.'

'Come on,' Margaret said, standing up and pulling him up after her. 'We need a swim.'

'Is that your answer for everything?'

'Why not?' She smiled, trying for light-heartedness. 'I'm an Aussie now, aren't I?'

He smiled slowly at her. 'You certainly are.'

●

They drove home after lunch on Easter Monday. Sticky with salt, sunburned and in high spirits, they sang 'It's a Long Way to Tipperary' and 'Pack Up Your Troubles in Your Old Kit Bag' at the top of their voices on the way home.

The songs brought back memories of other friends, mostly dead, but it was as though this happy rendering washed those memories cleaner than they had been – allowed them to remember the high points of those friendships as they should be remembered, with gratitude and a lighter heart.

Tom swung Burnsie down from the cab of the truck and then lifted Margaret out, his hands lingering for a warm moment on her waist. He quirked the side of his mouth at her and she smiled back, impossibly happy, and sashayed up the steps in her print dress, knowing he would be remembering.

She lugged empty baskets into the kitchen and set them down on the table. Burnsie was already putting the kettle on.

As Margaret turned to go, Burnsie put out a hand to stop her.

'You and Tom,' Burnsie said quietly. 'None of my business, but I wouldn't like to see him get hurt.'

'Him?'

Burnsie looked at her steadily. 'You've lost someone, I understand that. And sometimes, when death comes and stares at us, we reach out hard for life. Later on, you might regret it.' She hesitated. 'It happened to me, when my Eddy died.'

'I'm sorry,' Margaret said. What could she say? She was full of revulsion at her own deceit. It was wrong to lie to this good woman. No more of it. 'But it's not the same. I'm not a widow.'

Burnsie sat down in her chair, blinking.

'My husband – he was already married. I didn't find out until I got to Australia.' It all came out in a rush, as if she'd rehearsed. 'All my papers are in his name. All my work references. Tom thought it would be easier to pretend—'

'*Tom* thought?'

Margaret nodded. Burnsie took a deep breath.

'Don't know if I'm Arthur or Martha,' she said. 'That came out of the blue. Tom handled all this when he was in the Army, eh?'

She nodded again. Her heart was tight in her chest. Burnsie would be within her rights to throw her out of the house, particularly after what had happened at Clareville. The kettle whistled into the silence.

'Well.' Burnsie got up to turn off the gas, and poured the steaming water into the teapot. She took her time, putting the teapot on the table next to the waiting cups, sitting down, then looking up at Margaret. 'I'm not sure that's any better, my lady. Finding out your husband . . . that might be worse than losing him, to my mind.'

Margaret's head moved sharply in negation before she even thought. 'No. Nothing's worse than that.'

Burnsie's eyes narrowed for a moment, and then her face relaxed. 'Yes . . . we've all seen a bit of death, I reckon, and you're right. While there's life there's hope.'

Margaret wasn't sure whether Burnsie was giving approval or merely withholding judgement. She turned back in the doorway and saw that Burnsie was sitting still, both hands flat on the table, looking like a judge, her face shuttered.

'I'll keep your secret,' she said, 'until I see a reason not to.'

The rush of relief was immense. 'Thank you,' Margaret said and turned to go, her hands shaking, realising how precious this house was, this port in her storm.

'But no funny business under my roof!'

She leaned against the doorway and laughed helplessly, not even knowing what was funny. Burnsie smiled dourly, as if she knew.

'No,' Margaret said. 'No funny business.'

Part of her was glad. She didn't *want* to be a loose woman. Having Burnsie at her back gave her a sense of solidity, almost a sense of being in a family again.

•

That night the students were rehearsing and Mr Lewis had retired early, so it was just the four of them.

They sat in the parlour and Jane played the piano, moving between snatches of popular songs and classical pieces. She was very good, and when she hummed along to the tune her voice was so sweet that Margaret couldn't help watching her, still surprised that such an ethereal sound could come out of plain-spoken Jane.

Tom sat across from Margaret, staring at nothing. Occasionally his gaze would focus on her, and he would smile.

It was a quiet, happy little interlude, and she wished it could last longer.

On the way up to bed, Tom stopped her on the stairs, his hand on her wrist.

'I promised Burnsie—' she began, but he nodded.

'Not that. I'd like you to meet my mother and my aunt.'

Dread washed through her with stunning force and she spoke without thinking. 'Your mother? Oh, no, I can't do that.'

'Why not?' He frowned, clearly surprised and disappointed.

'I can't lie to your mother. I can't turn up there in widow's weeds. I just *can't*, Tom.'

Her whole body revolted against the idea. Absolutely not. Not on your nellie.

'We can tell her—'

'Oh, no! You can't turn up with this woman and say, "Oh, she's just pretending to be a war widow because her husband was a bigamist." What would she think of me?'

His face gentled into amusement. 'She's more likely to think something about Dalton than you. She has very advanced ideas, my mother. All for women's power, she is.'

The idea of confessing to his mother – his *mother* – made her frantic. She didn't know why, exactly. But how could she present herself as a desirable daughter-in-law when she was damaged goods? She could just imagine what her own mother would have said if David had brought someone like her home.

For the first time since Clareville, she doubted that she and Tom should be together. He deserved better than her.

'No argument,' he said. '*I'll* tell her the story before you get there.'

'No! No. I'll tell her. But not yet. Not just yet.'

Burnsie was coming down the hallway. She would turn onto the stairs any second.

'All right,' he said. 'But we're not going to wait too long.'

It had all seemed so simple, back on that groundsheet. Now she'd thrown her cap over the windmill, and how it would all end was anybody's guess.

She'd just have to trust Tom.

26

'So, you've been lying to me, young feller-me-lad?'

It was a harsh question, but Burnsie's voice was gentle. Tom felt a blush start under his shirt collar and climb up his cheeks.

'Not lying, Burnsie!' he protested.

'Did you or did you not tell me that Margaret Dalton was a widow? I should throw both of you out.'

He heaved the washing basket, full of wet clothes, off the laundry tub and took it out to the line, stalling for time. He'd been glad when Margaret had told him that Burnsie knew the truth, but he hadn't been looking forward to this conversation.

Burnsie followed him in silence, peg bag in hand.

'Even her passport's in his name,' he said. 'It would have taken her months to get it all sorted out.'

'That's as may be. But she's in it up to her neck, now, and you with her.'

Mrs Shelley, as with everything in her house, had put in the best washing line. A strong post at each end, a full nine feet high, and each good hardwood cross-beam held in place by a six-inch bolt that went right through so that the cross-beams could be tilted easily, bringing one line and then the other down to the pegger-outer.

He grinned at that. 'I hope so!' He took out the wooden props that held the line up so that the nearer side of the two lines canted down while the other side went up.

Burnsie picked up a sheet and flicked it out and over the low-hanging line.

'Easy to laugh, lad, but you don't think you'll just waltz in like nothing's ever happened, do you, no matter what went on at Clareville? Once bitten, twice shy.'

That sobered him. He'd thought occasionally that Margi was holding back from him, reserving something of herself. She was alive, vivid, sparkling in a way he'd never seen in a girl, with sudden moments of sweetness and passion. But despite their intimacy, and though they'd talked long and easily, and he'd heard all about her parents' death, her brother's, her own war work, still there was something held back. She would give him her passion, but not her trust. He couldn't help remembering that moment of silence after he'd mentioned marriage, her equivocal answer.

'Can't blame her,' he said, frowning. 'He treated her pretty badly.'

'Yes.' Burnsie kept flicking and pegging, and he automatically pushed the line up once she had filled it so she could begin on the other side. It reminded him of helping his aunt do the washing back home in Annandale. Yes, time to take Margi home, prove to her that he had nothing to hide.

'Thing is,' Burnsie said, 'when someone fools you, you don't only blame them. You blame yourself for being fool enough to be taken in.' He looked at her, puzzled, and she sighed with exasperation. 'It's not only *men* she doesn't trust. It's her own judgement.'

She'd finished pegging out the washing. He put the props back under the line securely, so the white sheets wouldn't drag across the ground if a wind came up.

'I can't do anything about that,' Tom said. 'All I can do is not let her down.'

'Hmph. Just make sure she doesn't let *you* down. And like I told her, no funny business in my house.'

Burnsie stumped back into the house, washing basket on her hip.

Margaret might be gun shy, but he had nothing but time, and no stains on his conscience. She could trust him, and he would show her that. By November, she'd trust him enough that when he did ask her again, she'd say yes. He just had to go slowly.

Tom looked up. He could see his own window, but not Margi's. He imagined her up there, getting ready for work. Burnsie had been up at dawn to get the first load of washing in the copper, so it was still quite early, though hot enough.

She would be dressing, putting on one of her blasted widow's outfits. The fact that she shone in them like a pearl in a black oyster didn't make it any better. It stopped them doing so much. Social conventions weren't as strict as they used to be, but a recent widow who socialised with a single man . . . they were stretching the limits by going for a walk together. Only the smokescreen of Jane's friends had allowed them to go to the cinema.

This pretence drove him crazy, and he cursed Dalton under his breath.

Just as well the war was long gone. Because if the killing days weren't over, he'd be inclined to go and find Mr Frank Dalton and give him a few scars to remember Margaret by.

•

Even if Margaret wasn't ready yet to meet his mother, he knew he'd better tell them about her. They'd be very hurt if they found out he'd been serious about a girl and kept it from them. He went that night to have tea with them. It was hard to start; they'd got to dessert before he mentioned her name.

'She was raised Methodist—' he started to explain.

'They hate Catholics!' his aunt said. 'They're all teetotallers and wowsers – no drinking, no dancing, no fun at all! You can't bring your kiddies up like that!'

'*Will* she bring the kiddies up Catholic?' his mother asked. That was the question.

'I – we haven't talked about it.'

'Well, you need to talk about it, and soon,' his aunt said decisively. 'You can't marry her otherwise.'

'Well, now—' he said.

'No "well, now" about it! You can't deprive your children of the sacraments. The Holy Eucharist. This woman can't be worth condemning your own children to Hell!'

His mother said nothing, but she looked troubled.

They believed it. And deep inside, maybe he did, too. He loved them, and he hated disappointing them. But he didn't have to listen to this litany of reproach. He pushed back from the table, but he didn't get up. There were too many emotions struggling to get free.

'In the trenches,' he said, looking down at his Sunday shoes, 'when the shells were falling and you were up to your hips in mud, every man in that trench was praying. And we were all praying to the same God.' He looked up briefly, to meet their eyes, and then looked out the window. 'When you come out of that, all these little differences don't add up to much.'

There was a flicker of understanding in his mother's eyes, but his aunt snorted her disbelief.

'It's the only true faith, and so you know, Thomas Paul McBride! You can tell yourself these pretty stories if you like, but you know in your heart you're wrong. Well, I'll tell you now, and I'll tell you only once: if she won't bring the children up Catholic, Father Ford won't marry you. And if you're not married in a Catholic church, I won't be there and neither will your mother. You'll be cut off from your religion for the rest of your life.'

His mother was deeply distressed, trying not to cry. 'You're a grown man, and you can make your own decisions, Tom, but you can't deny salvation to your *children*!'

He stood up and found his hat.

'I – I'll talk to her,' he said. 'But I can't promise anything.'

They clustered at the door as he left, fretting, and it poisoned his gut to be the cause of any worry for either of them. They'd given him so much, done without so much for him. Didn't he have a duty to live up to the standards they set?

As he walked down to the ferry on Rozelle Bay, he couldn't avoid the thought that wanting to marry Margaret was piling up problems, pushing him into decisions and a way of life he'd never in a million years have picked for himself. Not raising his children Catholic, not being married properly, in front of the altar, maybe not even in a Catholic church . . . he'd clung to his rosary beads in France; the only good thing about being there was being able to go to Mass in the local churches, the familiar Latin phrases about the only comfort there was then, the Eucharist a blessing and a source of hope. Could he give that up for good? Could he steal it from his children?

He didn't think that a Methodist child was any less likely to get into heaven, but there was no doubt in his mind that the sacraments brought with them a grace that made it easier to do the right thing with your life. Going to Mass had kept him out of the brothels, for one thing – that and the ever-present reality of VD.

He'd go to Margaret and explain it all to her. Maybe she'd let the children do both – Catholic one week, Methodist or Anglican the next – so they could choose for themselves later.

Just for a moment, a flicker of time, he wished someone else had been on duty the day the *Borda* had sailed into Sydney Harbour. He rejected that thought as soon as it had formed, remembered instead the way she had felt in his arms only a few days ago. Remembered her sweet, trusting, loving face. Was there anything he wouldn't give up for her?

No. If it was a choice between being Catholic and being Margaret's husband, he knew which he'd pick, no matter how hard it would be.

27

Tom's mother wrote to her.

Dear Mrs Dalton,

We would be so pleased if you could join us for afternoon tea next Sunday. I'm sure Tom would be happy to escort you.

Yours truly,

Pauline McBride (Mrs)

'I didn't put her up to it!' Tom protested when she showed him. Jane was laughing at the two of them. She sat down at the piano and played a short, comical fanfare – the sort of music that preceded a disaster in a comedy film.

'Very funny,' Margaret said to her. She regarded Tom, but it was obvious he was as surprised by this summons as she was. 'All right. I'll go.' It had to be faced some time, after all. She sat down at the writing desk in the corner and penned a short acceptance, then gave it to Tom to post.

'Have you met Tom's mother, Jane?'

'Oh, yes. I was summonsed too, when he first started spending time with us. But they saw pretty quick that I wasn't marriage material.'

'Why do you say that?' Jane was excellent marriage material, Margaret would have thought.

'Oh, Tommy's like my big brother. No chance of a romance there.'

Burnsie came in from the kitchen smelling of liver and onions. 'She's waiting for Prince Charming, this one is. Wouldn't know a good man from a crab-apple tree.'

A crab-apple tree? Jane shrugged. But she turned a small ring on her right hand thoughtfully. It was a Celtic friendship ring, showing two hands clasped together, and she'd been wearing it a lot lately. Jonesy, perhaps?

'Give her time,' Margaret said. 'So, what are they like?'

Jane's face lit up with mischief. 'Oh, no! You can find out for yourself. Don't worry. You'll be fine.'

•

On the way, on the ferry, Tom cleared his throat.

'They're worried that, er, if we get married, you won't let the children be brought up Catholic.'

She blinked. 'Jumping the gun a bit, aren't they?'

'It's serious stuff for them,' he said. 'I told them how I feel about you.'

'Well . . .' Margaret didn't know what to say. It was all happening so fast. From friends to lovers to – what, engaged? – in only a few days. 'We can think about it later, surely.'

'But you're not ruling it out?'

His expression was worried. She wished she knew what she intended, but she didn't. So many expectations. And her own family; was it right that they didn't get a say just because they were dead?

'No,' she said. 'I wouldn't rule it *out*. But I'm not too keen on the idea, to be honest.'

He nodded. 'They'll have to take what they can get, then.'

It sounded good, but he wore a frown still.

Tom's aunt's house was a single-storey terrace house on a tree-lined street in Annandale. Nice, with a bay window and a box hedge. Her mother had always yearned after a bay window and a front garden, the real proof of middle-class respectability. Their old front door had opened straight onto the street.

He didn't knock, just opened the door and called, 'Yoo-hoo!' as he ushered her through, down a corridor past a couple of closed doors to the parlour in the middle of the house. This was a fine room, with a sofa and two armchairs arranged around the fireplace, and a dining table against a wall. Two women came through from the kitchen, both with aprons on. Otherwise, as different as sisters could be. One was tall, thin, her brown hair streaked with grey caught back in a bun. She was wearing a simple print frock under her coverall. The other was short and plump with hair as red as Tom's own piled on top of her head in a confusion of curls. It was an old-fashioned hairstyle, but it suited her, as did her tailored skirt and blouse.

'Mum, Aunty Theresa, this is Margaret. Margaret, my mother and my aunty, Mrs Cartwright.'

'How d'you do,' they said. Surprisingly, the brunette was Tom's mother.

Two shrewd pairs of hazel eyes assessed her, costed every item she had on, checked that her shoes were shined and her hem straight and not too high, and then smiled, as one.

'Come and sit down. I've just popped some scones in the oven,' Tom's mother said. 'They'll be done in a minute.'

Acknowledging the greater right of the mother to question her first, Mrs Cartwright went back to the kitchen where the kettle was beginning to whistle. The noise went on for a while, growing louder. Mrs McBride made a face.

'Theresa likes to have the water on the full boil. Now, tell me all about yourself.'

It was an experienced interrogation, gently done and without malice, but it turned her inside out and back to front. Before it got well started, Mrs Cartwright brought the tea things in, and the questions and answers, so civilised, were accompanied by fresh scones with raspberry jam and piping hot tea.

'And then you arrived in Sydney and found out your husband had passed? What a terrible shock,' Mrs Cartwright said gently.

Margaret took a deep breath. She liked these women. Liked their straightforwardness, their care for Tom, the humour that showed around their mouths and eyes. She wouldn't lie to them.

'No,' she said. 'He's not dead. But he's not my husband, either.'

They both blinked, and sat very still. Tom sat forward and took her hand reassuringly. Tom's mother flicked a look at him, and then concentrated fully on her. The story poured out, unfiltered, unpolished. The only thing she didn't tell them was Clareville, and what had happened there.

'Well, praise God and pass the ammunition!' Mrs Cartwright said at last. 'Sounds like you've had a real escape.'

Escape? That wasn't a word she would have used.

'Yes indeed,' Tom's mother said. 'A man like that, he might have kept on deceiving you. Thank God he came to his senses and stayed with his wife and child.'

She'd never thought of it like that – of Frank having done the *right* thing by abandoning her. But it was true. Marriage was for life; she could blame him for deceiving her, but she shouldn't blame him for going back to his wife, where he belonged. The thought made her cheerful. It lifted some darkness from her that she hadn't even been aware she was carrying. It *felt* better to think of Frank as a man who'd made a mistake but corrected it. It fitted far better with the Frank she had known, the man she had married, whom she still had trouble thinking of as a liar and a cad.

'Now, I see that you have to pretend to be in mourning,' Mrs Cartwright said. 'That's a pity. But a year is soon past.'

'November,' Tom said.

They nodded their heads like Chinese dolls, and cast quick glances at each other.

'Have you thought about after that?' his mother asked.

'No,' Margaret said firmly. She couldn't think that far ahead. She wouldn't. 'Once I'm out of mourning, we can decide what we want to do.'

'Fair enough,' his aunt said. She poured Margaret another cup of tea. 'But remember, when you're thinking, that Tom has more to lose than you do.'

'Aunty Tess!' Tom said.

'I'm just doing my job,' she answered. 'I'm your godmother, remember.'

Margaret could feel herself stiffen, no matter how much she tried to sit normally. Tom's mother put one hand over hers.

'We'd like to be able to welcome you into the family, Margaret. But you do understand, if you don't agree to bring the children up Catholic, we can't approve. You wouldn't even be allowed to get married in the Church.'

'Yes, I see.' She could hear her tone was flat, and she wished she could reassure them.

The two women looked swiftly at each other, clearly concerned. Margaret felt as though she'd failed some kind of test, but what else was she supposed to say? She wasn't at all sure that she was ready to marry Tom and bring her children up as Romans.

He loved her, and she loved him, and she'd be prepared to give up a lot for him. But she'd been sure she loved Frank, too, and look where that had got her. Perhaps this fierce desire was just bodily; she had to be much surer of them both before she committed herself to a house at Clareville and crucifixes on the walls. All this talk of marriage and family felt too much, too fast. Hemming her in.

Still, what a lovely image it presented: she and Tom and a gaggle of redheaded children cavorting in the sea together. That was a life she could live, no matter what his mother thought.

•

On the ferry to Circular Quay, they sat at the stern, alone. With just the two of them there, all the stiffness and reluctance and worry fell away. When they were together, everything seemed easy.

Tom smoothed an unruly curl behind her ear. 'Thanks for being so good about the two of them. They're enough to make a saint swear sometimes.'

'They love you. They're worried about you. It's only natural.'

'You're a good woman, Margaret,' he said, and bent to kiss her.

Making a spectacle of yourself, her father would have said. But they had so little time together. Tom's face was scratchy under her gloves, so she took them off (another scandal!) and slid her hands up against his cheeks as they kissed.

What she *wanted* to do was press her body against his, lift his hand to her breast . . . She stifled a laugh, imagining the reaction of the other passengers.

'What's funny?' Tom asked, rubbing his thumb along her bottom lip, leaving a trail of pins and needles and heat.

She buried her head in his arm. 'If I told you, I'd have to do it, and then we'd probably be arrested!'

His shout of laughter turned heads, but it sparked an answering laugh in her, and then she was composed enough to sit next to him, although her blood was as wild as . . . she didn't know what it was like, but she knew that sitting still was a kind of agony.

Tom fidgeted beside her, his knee jiggling in a shared impatience.

'I just wish there was somewhere we could *go*!' he burst out.

'Five months,' she said. 'I can get out of my blacks at the beginning of November.'

He sighed, a heartfelt sound. 'Yes. Maybe we can go camping again, once the weather warms up.'

Margaret laughed. 'It's warm now!'

'You won't convince Burnsie of that, and without her . . .'

Without Burnsie as chaperone, she couldn't go.

'We can survive three or four months,' she said. 'Even five, if we have to.'

'Speak for yourself!' he moaned, but he was laughing as he leaned in to kiss her again, and again.

Happiness fountained inside her. She had cleared the decks – no more lying to anyone important. Jane, Burnsie, Tom's family, all knew the truth. She could simply live, now, without being afraid of being found out. She could grasp the future with both hands. Tom's kiss was like a huge wave and she was surf-shooting it, riding the strength and the delirious pleasure of it into shore.

28

On Wednesday, there was a letter from England waiting for her. She didn't recognise the writing, but the postmark was West Bromwich, so it was probably someone she'd gone to school with.

She took it up to her room, put away her coat, hat, gloves and bag, and then sat on her bed to open it. It was strange, getting a letter from home. Her life there was so far away, so long ago, like it happened to another person.

Inside the envelope was another envelope, and a notecard that said, 'Forwarding this but please inform your correspondents of your correct address. Postage to Australia isn't cheap, you know!' It was from the man who'd taken over her family's cottage after her parents died.

The envelope inside was addressed to Mrs Frank Dalton, and she recognised that handwriting immediately. It was Frank's.

She stared at it for some time. Best not to open it, she thought. Best to throw it in the fire. What could he have to say to her? And how dare he address it to her using that lie of a name!

That anger gave her the strength to rip it open.

Dear Margaret,

As you might expect, since you decided not to come to Australia, I have gone on and made a life for myself.

What? What was he talking about?

I told you I hadn't been a saint. Well, after we got married I found out that my lady friend from before the war, Gladys Mortimer, had had my baby, a little girl, Violet.

After they got married. After.

When you didn't come on the Waimana, *I went back to her and now we are living together like a proper family.*

The *Waimana*? Cold dread began to creep through her. The *Waimana* was the ship she had first boarded, the one that was in such bad condition that General Monash had moved all the war brides to the *Borda*. But everyone was supposed to have been told about that. All the other men got the message and turned up to collect their wives.

I want you to know, Margaret, that I was faithful to you all the time, right up until they told me at the ship that you weren't on board. That you'd decided not to come. I was absolutely faithful to you the whole time. I hope you were to me, too, but I suppose that's not likely, otherwise you would be here.

Faithful. An image of Frank's face rose up in her mind. That honest, open face she'd trusted so blindly. Had she been right to trust it, or was this letter a lie, too? She felt sick.

Anyway, enough about that. I wasn't good enough for you, and I can't blame you for realising it. But now Gladys is expecting again, and we want this baby to have properly married parents. So I'd like a divorce. I don't care what grounds you want to use — you can say I've been unfaithful to you if you want. Glad and I will send letters for the court if you need them. But since you're the one who ended the marriage, I think it should be you who gets the divorce.

I wish I could say I wish you all the best. I just hope you were true to me while I was at the front.

Yours,

Frank

An address was underneath, a house in Denison Street, Camperdown. In Sydney.

She started to shake. Nothing made sense. It all made terrible sense. The past tore itself into pieces and rearranged itself in a new pattern.

Frank hadn't lied to her.

Frank had met the wrong ship. He thought she'd never left England.

'Lady friend'. Not wife. This Gladys was a lady friend.

Frank hadn't known about the baby until *after* they were married.

Married.

She was married. Properly, legally married.

His lady friend was pregnant again.

She was married. She and Tom had committed adultery.

She ran to the washstand and was ill in the basin.

Cold raced through her. She had been a slut, after all, fornicating, committing adultery. If only she'd been chaste, she could have met Frank with a clear conscience.

What was she going to tell Tom?

Sitting back on the bed was harder than it ought to be, she was shaking so badly. What a horrible, horrible mistake! Such a simple mix-up, and what pain it had caused – was going to cause. Tom . . . it would hurt him so much. And this Gladys woman, with her second baby. What was *she* going to do?

Yet, there was a terrible satisfaction brewing in her. She *hadn't* been a fool. He *hadn't* tricked and deceived her. Her judgement *hadn't* been bad. A segment of herself slipped back into place; she could rely on her own judgement again, without questioning herself about everything.

Frank. She was married to Frank. She stared at her wedding ring. She'd been so proud of it, so sure of her love for him. And she'd been right. That understanding was slowly seeping through her. She'd been right to trust him. Right to come to Australia. Right to love him.

Love him.

The past few months and her belief that he had deceived her had ripped her love for him out of her heart and shredded it. But that belief had been wrong. Frank wasn't the deceiver she had thought. He was the honest, faithful man she had believed him to be. She couldn't allow this awful misunderstanding to deceive her *now*. She had to rebuild that image of him, that love she had had for him.

Because they were married, and that was that.

In her mind Frank had become shadowy, unreal. She had to see him, desperately *needed* to see him immediately, to test with her own eyes what he was really like.

She'd grown up enough to know that she wouldn't see him the same way she had when she was twenty, when he had seemed like her knight in shining armour. But he wasn't the demon of her recent imagination either. She had to see him, to meet him, to judge for herself if he *was* the man she had married, or if this was some kind of trick, some attempt to get something more from her.

It was so hard to let go of suspicion. There *were* two children, after all.

What was she going to tell Tom?

Adultery. Every time she thought of Tom, the word tolled in her mind, like a death knell. Her body was frozen with the sound of it.

Was it still adultery if you didn't know you were married? It would be if they ever were together again, even a touch of the hand, a kiss. The Bible was clear: 'Whosoever looketh upon a woman to lust after her hath committed adultery with her already in his heart.' That went for women, too.

She'd have to stay well away from Tom. Tell him what had happened, and then stay away. Move. Find another boarding house. Never see him again.

Tears welled up. A new pain, a new confusion. She couldn't bear never to see him again. She couldn't be near him without wanting him. She hadn't realised just how much he meant to her until this very moment.

Her love for him didn't matter, balanced against her solemn vow to Frank. She *had* to go back to Frank.

Tom's eyes when he had said, 'I love you.' How could she look into his eyes and tell him the truth? It would break her heart to see his hurt.

Now, she thought. Do it now. Right now, before you falter.

Unsteadily, she pushed herself to her feet, ignoring the tears that snaked down her face and spotted her dress. She went out, down the corridor, and knocked on Tom's door.

His face lit up at the sight of her, and then darkened, concerned, as he saw her expression.

Before he could speak she thrust the letter into his hand, then turned and ran back to her own room. She couldn't look at his face as he read it. Couldn't watch as his hopes and his love crashed against the rocks of the truth.

She curled up on the bed and clutched a pillow to her stomach and rocked backwards and forwards.

She didn't know what to hope for. Frank might be the man she had loved and she might find that she still loved him just as much. She *should* hope for that. It shouldn't feel like a betrayal of Tom. It did. It felt as though a huge section of her self was being dragged out of her and thrown away.

A knock on the door.

'Margi?' Tom's voice. He hesitated. 'Margaret?'

She went to the door, her feet dragging, but she didn't open it. She placed her hand flat on the surface, about where she thought his knuckles might have touched, and leaned her head on her hand.

'Margi?' His voice was so low, so worried.

'I – I can't.'

'Are you all right?'

She laughed hysterically, almost a cackle. 'Never better.'

'I'm getting Burnsie—'

'No!' She didn't want anyone. No one but Tom, and Tom she couldn't have, ever again.

'Margi . . .' His voice pleaded with her to let him in. But that would be adultery.

'I'll go and see him tomorrow,' she said. 'After work.'

'I'll come with you.'

That was a bad idea, but she couldn't argue with him. He deserved to look his nemesis in the face.

'All right.'

The letter slipped under the door, spotted with her tears. She bent and picked it up, noticing for the first time the cheap notepaper it was written on, the blots and awkward script of a man who seldom wrote. Poor Frank.

She was smitten with compassion for him; he had gone through the same horrible process that she had, believing that his wife had abandoned him, perhaps that she had never meant to come, or that she had found someone else. He had gone through the same disbelief, the same feeling that his judgement had been faulty, that he had made a terrible mistake. And now he would find out that he'd been wrong, that she had meant everything she'd ever said to him.

She didn't know if she wanted him to be glad of that or not.

'Goodnight,' she said. No more words of love. No more 'sweetheart', or 'dearest'. Not with Tom.

'Goodnight, my dear,' he said.

My dear. It was the kind of thing a father might say to his daughter.

In the middle of the room, it was as though she'd forgotten how to walk. A mixture of grief and excitement, relief and confusion held her to the spot. Memories of Frank: the way he'd laughed at a Fatty Arbuckle movie, giving his whole body to the guffaw, which had made her laugh more than the movie had. His brown eyes, warming whenever he looked at her. The tiny specks of coal dust and grease in the creases of his big hands; no amount of scrubbing could get them out. His hand on hers as they made their wedding vows. Tears swamped her. She had loved him so much.

The day he'd told her about being an orphan. On the riverbank, a sparkling spring day. They were having a picnic lunch before she went to work the late shift. Pork pies and strawberries – a strange combination but they didn't care; any food would do as long as they were together. On a blanket Frank had scrounged up from somewhere, she sitting like a lady should, he lying, propped up on one elbow. His dark hair had shone in the sunlight.

'I don't have family,' Frank had said. 'Someone left me on the orphanage steps when I was a baby. Newborn. They used the obituary columns to name us. I was lucky. My mate got Jebediah Blenkingthorpe.'

He'd grinned at her and she'd smiled back, but she'd put her hand on his shoulder because she could see that the memories weren't all happy.

'Tell me about it,' she said.

Haltingly, looking down at his linked hands, he skimmed over the details, but the broad outlines were horrible enough. Beatings, little food, casual cruelty in the name of 'building character'. No love, except between the children themselves. The ones who'd had fathers and mothers taught the others about family.

'We looked after our own,' Frank had said. 'Shared food, no dobbing. Some got adopted, but mostly it was the girls, the pretty ones. No one wants a boy, not after they're school age.'

There was a litany of rejection behind that. So many people choosing not to love him. Impulsively, although they hadn't known each other very long, she had put her arms around him and hugged him, wanting to assuage that young boy's loneliness and sense of worthlessness.

He had hugged her back with delighted surprise, and then kissed her.

Their first kiss.

Not her first, but it felt like it; it felt new, thrilling, with a queer heartache in the middle of it, from the compassion she felt for the abandoned baby, the unloved boy. She had yearned to make it up to him.

Now, she had the chance after all. The yearning flooded her again, but this time it had to break around the rocks of the past six months. Of Tom. The thought of him pierced her through the breastbone, a real pain as though a sharp thorn had been rammed into her. Or an ivory dagger, not quite reaching her heart.

She wanted both of them, Frank and Tom, the life she'd planned and the life she was living. Impossible.

Margaret sat back on the bed and stared unseeing out the window, not thinking, not moving, barely breathing, until the sky outside grew pale and the kookaburras laughed at her from the angophora tree.

29

She realised, halfway through a day in which each simple task seemed like climbing a mountain, that turning up on Frank's doorstep unannounced wouldn't be fair to him or to his Gladys.

Not to mention the little girl. She must be, what, almost three now? The thought troubled her. Frank had been back in Australia more than two years and, whether or not he'd been faithful to her before, he would have been a father to that little girl. She knew his desire for a family well enough to be sure of that. What would happen now?

At lunchtime she stayed at her desk and wrote him a letter.

Dear Frank,

I was very surprised to get your letter.

Surprised. Yes. She burned to see him, to get it all sorted out, to see for herself if she could trust him again. What if this was all another ruse – maybe to get money out of her for a supposed divorce? Could she trust him at all?

I am in Sydney – I came out on the SS Borda, *just as we had arranged. The* Waimana *hadn't been refitted properly, so General Monash transferred all the war brides to the* Borda. *I've been here since January. When you didn't meet the ship, the Army tried to find you, but the address you had given wasn't—*

Wasn't what? Good? Correct?

wasn't current. Since you had put Gladys down in your Army record as your wife, I—

This was much harder than she had thought it would be. Just telling him the story made her relive that terrible time.

I was told that my marriage to you wasn't legal.

Apparently that has happened quite a few times, according to the Army sergeant. I suppose you didn't get the letter telling you I'd been moved to the Borda. *What a terrible mix-up.*

Now what?

You can imagine my surprise at your letter.

I'll come to visit you on Saturday afternoon, if that's all right. Around 4? If I don't hear from you before then I'll assume that's all right.

Should she say that she had been faithful to him while she thought they were married? No. No. Leave it until they were face to face.

Yours,

Margaret

Now, should she put her address? She had to give him some way of contacting her, but she felt a real reluctance to give him her address. She didn't want him turning up there and upsetting Burnsie. Or Tom.

In the end she put her work address and telephone number.

The pit of her stomach was heavy with dread. She ought to be *happy*. And part of her was. The part that had missed Frank for those two years and four months was uplifted with joy and relief, impatient for Saturday, wanting to see him, wanting to talk it all through.

She posted the letter straightaway and looked up from the posting box to find that the weather had changed again; high pearly clouds covered the sun but the wind had dropped and it was almost warm. Warm enough not to have her heavy coat on. She had avoided breakfast, not wanting to see Tom, so hadn't eaten anything all day, but she couldn't face Burnsie's cheese and pickle. Nothing so solid. There was a cake shop on the Corso, and she bought a cream bun and enjoyed the sweetness. Cream buns had been a real treat in her childhood, bought only for birthdays or special occasions. She supposed this was special.

When she went back to work, Mr Bertram stopped by her desk, to give her back a letter she had typed – full of mistakes.

'Is everything all right, Mrs Dalton?'

'Yes. Yes. I just had some news from home yesterday and I'm afraid I've been rather distracted. I'm sorry. It won't happen again.'

'Bad news?' he asked sympathetically.

How did she answer that?

'Not exactly. More a shock than bad news.'

He nodded and went back into his office. Thank God he wasn't the nosy type. She retyped the letter and took it into him and tried to pretend that everything was normal.

She was in a new life, that was for sure. The one she and Tom had planned had vanished like mist at noontime. The one Frank and she had planned – she remembered how she'd felt sailing into Sydney Harbour, how perfectly joyful she had felt. Would she feel like that again once she had seen her husband? It couldn't be as simple as just taking up as though she'd arrived in Australia yesterday, could it?

No. Not with two children involved. And this Gladys person. She imagined some brassy blonde with a big bosom, painted face and sharp eyes. Frank was just honest enough to get taken in by someone like that.

Well. Saturday would tell.

•

Tom insisted on meeting her after work on Saturday and taking her to Camperdown.

'It's a rough area,' he said as they waited for the ferry. 'I'm not letting you go alone.'

'But you'll have to stay outside. I have to see him – them – alone first.'

His hands were clenched into fists, but he nodded. Margaret made sure she stayed well apart from him; no need to make this harder by an accidental brush of the hands.

The tram to Camperdown was crowded and they almost missed their stop because the conductor forgot to tell them until the last moment. They sprang off as the tram started up Parramatta Road again, and found themselves only a few yards from Denison Street.

It was what journalists in England called a 'mean street' – full of tiny terraced workers' cottages. Different from England, though, because these were one storey, and each had a small porch across the front. No more than twelve feet wide, she thought. About the same width as her family's cottage in West Bromwich.

If Frank had brought her here when she'd first arrived, she would have accepted it gladly. But after the High House, these cottages seemed cramped and uninviting. She'd been spoiled.

They were a few minutes early, but she couldn't bear to wait. Tom held back and let her go alone the last few yards to the door. It was freshly painted, dark blue. There was a knocker, a simple ring. She knocked.

Frank opened the door.

She thought she was prepared, but at the sight of him all the air went out of her lungs. It was like being kicked in the stomach.

Somehow she'd built up a picture in her head, all these months of believing that he'd deceived her. A picture of a sneering, lying cad of a man. But here he was, her own Frank, just as he'd been the last time she'd seen him. Brown eyes, brown hair, open, honest face. He was even in a khaki shirt, as so many working men were these days, as they used up their Army clothes.

He smiled, and it was the smile she'd fallen in love with.

'Margaret.' His voice was full of simple joy at seeing her. He moved back and she went in, then he closed the door behind her and opened his arms wide. Her body was in turmoil and her mind as well. She felt transported back, more than just two years. Before her father and mother had died. Before David had died. Before. When Frank was the centre of things, and the only thing wrong was the war. She walked into his embrace and laid her head on his shoulder.

He was wiry rather than muscular and her arms reached further around him than they did around Tom. He smelled different, too, a smell of coal and steam and iron, the scent of her working day at Reading. But her body remembered his, and warmed as he held her.

The past rushed over her and settled into the feel of his hands on her back, his mouth against her hair.

'I've missed you,' he said, awkward as he always was with sentiment.

She pulled back to look at him and realised that she was crying, the tears rolling down her cheeks unchecked.

'Hey, what's all this, eh? No need for tears.' He hugged her reassuringly, and then bent to kiss her.

The gesture was so familiar, so ordinary, so strange. He was her husband; he had the right to kiss her.

His mouth was soft. The clenched fist inside her loosened. This was Frank, and they had loved each other, and married, and lain together. Memories flickered past, desire and enjoyment, need and touch. Her mouth softened and his kiss grew stronger, but she pulled back, uncertain.

'Margaret? What's the matter?'

She laughed out of pure nerves. 'I don't know. I'm just getting used to all this again . . .'

Those brown eyes were confused, but then he smiled. 'Come and have a cuppa.'

He led the way through to the parlour, holding her hand, his fingers rough and warm against hers. The furniture was old and a bit tatty, the kind of furniture she'd grown up with. But the place was scrupulously clean; even the window gleamed in the late afternoon sun.

Frank kept going, into the small kitchen – well, it wasn't that small, no smaller than the one she'd grown up with. She felt a sudden chill, realising how thoroughly the High House had changed her perspective. Too big for her boots, she thought, just as her father had always said.

The kettle was ready, already steaming a little, on the compact gas stove. Frank put a match to it and turned to smile at her again, shaking his head. He was buoyed up with excitement, and she couldn't help but be flattered by it, reassured that he really loved her and had always done so. In his place, feeling so rejected, she might have gone back to the old familiar love too, especially when a child was involved. There'd been no deliberate lying on his part. No real unfaithfulness. The acid thread that betrayal had woven through her mind and spirit dissolved in his smile.

'I can't believe it. Just can't believe it.'

'I know,' Margaret said. She sat at the small table, set for two: neat white cloth, cups and saucers, a plate of biscuits, even a little posy vase with some native Australian flower in it. Bottlebrush? That's what it looked like, although she'd never seen a bottlebrush that was bright pink. It was a curiously feminine table setting; she realised, with pain in her heart, that Gladys must have got this ready. She wasn't sure she could have done the same if their positions were reversed.

'Where is . . . where is your . . .' She didn't quite know how to describe the woman, but Frank showed no embarrassment.

'Glad's taken Vi to the park,' he said, pouring boiling water into a brown ceramic teapot and bringing it to the table. His face was a little flushed – was he embarrassed after all? But he smiled at her as he sat.

'You can play mother,' he added, touching her hand. She was ashamed that his happiness didn't call up an answering happiness in her; it just added to her confusion. It had all felt simple until she had seen that afternoon tea table, but now it was back to being horribly complicated.

She poured in silence for both of them, and automatically sugared his cup. He grinned at her, and despite her best intentions to remain calm, she blushed.

'Gladys,' she said.

He looked troubled, raising one hand to rub the back of his head, the gesture so familiar it made her breath catch.

'We were, you know, together, before I enlisted. But it was never *serious*. We had a good time, that's all.'

A good time. She remembered her own words to him: 'You don't expect men to have been saints.' She'd been happy enough with the idea of his 'experience' until it had a name.

'The baby . . .'

Now he did look embarrassed.

'Well, Vi was an accident. I used . . . you know . . . protection, but it broke. It was on my last night of leave before I embarked. And, Marge, I can't say I'm sorry about that even now.' His expression was stubborn, ready for her to object. 'She's such a ripper of a kid. I can't be sorry about her.'

'No,' Margaret said. 'I can understand that.'

'It's not the way I wanted it to be, when we got married. I wanted everything to be perfect for us. I'm sorry it's all turned out such a mess for you.'

She didn't know what to say. She felt that she *ought* to know. Ought to throw herself into his arms, perhaps, or else be angry and affronted. But none of that seemed right. It was all too complicated for easy answers.

'I always loved you.' Frank leaned forward and put his hand over hers. 'Always. When I came back – Glad never had a look-in until I thought you'd given me the brush.'

His voice, his face, everything about him was earnest and true. He loved her, he really did, and the old Margaret, the one from West Bromwich, she loved him right back. Emotions flooded her. She couldn't name them all, but affection was one of them, a real fondness for this simple, honest man.

'But you didn't tell me about your daughter.'

The worry on his face cleared, as though they were back in friendly territory. 'I didn't know about Vi until after we'd been married. Got Glad's letter when I was already on the front line.'

232

'You didn't write to tell me.' She could hear the reproach in her voice, but why shouldn't she reproach him? He'd deceived her, by omission if nothing else.

He looked down at his cup. 'I'm not much of a one for writing. A foxhole's no place to write something important, I can tell you. With the shells, and the smell . . . It was a bit hard to explain, too, so I thought I'd leave it until I could do it face to face. And, to tell you the God's honest, I didn't think I'd get out of there. They were going down like flies all around. I did write a letter for you, in case—'

'But you left your will in Violet's favour.'

That stubborn look returned to his face. 'What would you have done? If I was gone, there was Glad, all alone with the baby. She'd have needed it more than you did. You had a job and you were doing all right. I had to look after them.'

Yes. She nodded. It all made sense, given those terrible, haunting times. It was even noble, if you looked at it from the right direction. He relaxed back into his chair and took a long, sighing breath.

'But then I got winged, and they sent me back to Sydney, and there we were.'

'You and Gladys.'

He looked startled, sitting up and throwing one hand out as though to stop the idea.

'No! Gawdstrewth, no! I saw them, of course. Got to know Vi. Spent time with her, like a father should. And I'd been paying her way ever since I found out, and I kept paying. But I was faithful to you, Marge. Always. I was so looking forward to you coming. Until . . .'

'Until the mix-up over the ships.'

They stared at each other, both stunned for a moment at the calamity caused by a simple mistake.

'It must have been hard for you,' he said, 'thinking that I'd – that I'd been a lying bastard, excuse my French.'

'Yes. It was hard. Hard for you too.'

'Hardest thing ever.' A memory of pain passed over his face.

Outside, sudden in the silence, rain started; one of those Sydney downpours that drenched you to the bone. She thought fleetingly of Tom, out in the street somewhere, but Frank claimed her attention. He leaned forward and took her hand again.

'If I'd stayed in the boarding house, got that second letter, none of this would have happened, I guess. But I just wanted to make a life for us in a nice house.' He gestured around him. It gave her a jolt, realising that he had brought Gladys to the house he had prepared for her. A squirm of nausea pulsed through her at the thought.

But what else was he supposed to do? No doubt he'd already taken a lease on the place. He couldn't afford to walk away from it. Who could?

'I told you I hadn't been a saint, Marge.'

Yes. Yes, he'd told her. And possibly, if he'd known earlier, and he'd explained his daughter away as a youthful mistake, she would have accepted it and married him anyway— no. No, she really wouldn't have done that. She would have expected him to marry the mother of his child, and no mistake about it.

'But now we can be together.' His face was alight with love for her.

'*Gladys*,' she said again.

He stood and paced to the door and back, sticking his hands in his pockets with sudden force. 'Yes. It's a bad thing

234

for her. I've been thinking and thinking over it. I don't know what's best to do, really.'

'You're supporting her?'

'Well, I have been these past few months. Since your ship . . . Before that, I paid for Violet, and Glad worked at the biscuit factory.' He was worried, frowning. 'The thing is, I can't afford to keep this house on *and* pay for somewhere for us. But we'll help, won't we? Like I was doing before. That's only right.'

'You're just going to . . .' She didn't know how to put it. Abandon her? Cast her off? She was carefully not thinking about that 'somewhere for us'. She wasn't sure how she felt about that.

He came up beside her and squatted down in that way Australian men did, bringing his face just under hers. His dark eyes were almost black with worry. 'There's no good answer that I can find. I'll do right by her. She's a lovely girl, Gladys, and she deserves better than this. I feel bad, I can tell you. But – we're married.'

'I don't see why you care so much about marriage when you're happy to – to—' She waved her hand, taking in the house and all it stood for.

He blushed, looking about fifteen. That pang of compassionate affection went through her, as it had so often, and for the first time she wondered if wanting to look after someone was really adult love.

'That's different. It's one thing to just . . . you know. Nobody around here worries much about that. It's not like we're posh.'

It made her realise how different their upbringings had been. In her neighbourhood, respectability was almost as important as God-fearing. Her parents would have been appalled at the thought of divorce, let alone living in sin as Frank and Gladys did. She wondered what other differences there were, that she hadn't known about when they married.

'I may not follow all the Commandments, but I wouldn't break a solemn vow,' he added. 'That's why being married *means* something. It's one thing to live together, but if you get *married*, well, that means you're in it for good. For life.'

Yes. He was right. Marriage was for life. A tumble of feelings swept over her. The longer she stayed with Frank the less she felt she knew him – or, rather, knew who she was when she was with him. She longed to just throw herself into his arms; she didn't want to touch him. She wanted him to kiss her again; she remembered Tom's mouth on hers and yearned for him instead. But Frank was her husband, and surely there was enough left of their love to make a marriage? At least there would be no problems about religion, or family.

'Besides,' he said. 'I love *you*. Staying with Glad when I feel the way I do . . . that wouldn't be right, either.'

She touched his upturned face.

The back door opened and she snatched her hand back, wondering for a panicked second if it were Tom, come to make sure she was all right.

A young woman came in, shepherding a little girl. Gladys. Not the brassy blonde of her imagination. Slight, with mousy smooth hair, a pretty heart-shaped face. Dressed in a simple floral dress, quite modest, longer than the fashion. Just noticeably pregnant, although if Frank were telling the truth, she couldn't be more than five months along. Five and a half at the most.

Smiling an apology at Frank, Gladys shook an umbrella out the back door and set it up against the wall. As Frank rose the little girl ran and threw herself into his arms.

'It rained *rocks*, Papa! Little rocks that jumped!'

'I know we were supposed to stay away,' Gladys said, in a soft, gentle voice, 'but it started hailing, so . . .'

'Of course,' Margaret said quickly. 'Of course you were right to bring her home.'

Frank swept Violet – it had to be Violet – up in his arms and tossed her in the air, both of them laughing. Margaret had a sudden memory of her own father doing the same thing to her, and felt tears start in her eyes, as though her feelings had been overloaded by that one recollection.

She blinked them away.

'I'd better go,' she said, rising.

'No, hold on—' Frank said, settling Violet on his hip.

'Oh, no—' Gladys exclaimed at the same time. They both stopped and looked at each other, sharing a small smile, an automatic intimacy neither seemed aware of. It made Margaret sharply aware that this was a family house, and they had been living together as man and wife, in effect. Had lived together that way far longer than she and Frank had.

'Bikkies!' Violet said, squirming down from Frank and running to the table.

Gladys put out a restraining hand. 'Wait. What do you say?'

Violet looked up at Margaret with big brown eyes. Frank's eyes. 'May I, please?'

Margaret smiled. How could she not? 'Of course you may.' She picked up her bag. 'But I'll be going.'

'I'll see you out,' Frank said. She nodded at Gladys, not knowing what to say, and was struck by her expression; as though watching Frank walk away was tearing out her heart. That couldn't be right. It couldn't.

As she and Frank walked down the corridor, his hand warm under her elbow, he said, 'You know, since I got your letter, I've been sleeping on the couch.'

'Yes. I see.'

He sighed, relieved, and hugged her with one arm as he opened the door. 'I knew you'd understand. So, we'll go looking for a new place for them next weekend, and then you can move in. Or if you'd rather, Gladys can stay here and we'll find a new place. Money might be a bit tight if we do it that way, though. Either way, we'll be together.'

A shudder went through her, but she knew he was right. Wasn't he? They were married. No way out of that, and did she even want a way? If only there wasn't a child involved . . . two children . . .

They stepped outside and he shut the door behind them. The sudden squall had passed and blue sky was breaking through above, the setting sun gilding his face and turning his eyes to shadow. He slid his hands up her arms, holding her tight, and again she felt that rush of familiar emotion, again felt the past settling down over her like a warm blanket. She was aware of a spark of optimism; perhaps they really could recover their old feelings for each other.

He raised a hand to touch her face. Out of the corner of her eye she saw Tom, standing in front of the neighbouring house. And there was Gladys, just inside. She moved back a half step.

'Let's not rush into anything,' she said. 'Let's take some time to get to know each other again.'

His face clouded, both bereft and confused.

'Margaret . . . you're my wife. I love you.' There was an unasked question there. Did she love him? She hadn't said it yet. It hurt her that she didn't know how to answer him.

Tom moved forward, and Frank half-turned as he realised Tom wasn't just walking by. Tom just stood there, face expressionless. Waiting for the verdict, Margaret realised.

Frank looked from Margaret to Tom, and stiffened.

'So, is that it?' he asked. 'You've found someone else?'

The sharp hurt in his voice almost undid her. Tears rose to her eyes.

'I thought we weren't married. I thought you'd lied to me.' It sounded weak in her own ears, but it wasn't. Her voice grew stronger. 'I have to think!'

'There's nothing to think about.' He touched her cheek again. 'I know you thought I was a rotter, love, but I wasn't. I'm still the man you married. Anything else that's happened . . .' He cast a look at Tom. 'That's in the past. Like me and Glad. It's all in the past.'

'I – I . . .' Everything she had ever believed in urged her to say, 'I love you too, Frank,' and submit to being his wife, as God intended. The Margaret of Reading Station couldn't believe she didn't just throw herself into his arms.

'It takes a bit of getting used to,' she said finally. 'I'll be in touch.'

Tom had begun to move back, giving her room to say goodbye. He was such a generous man; but so was Frank, in his own way.

She couldn't look back as she walked away. She didn't want to see Frank's face as she fell into step with Tom.

'He says marriage is for life,' she said. There was a long silence.

'He's right.' Tom's face was set, the muscles around his mouth tight, the scar standing out pale and ridged.

It was getting dark and there was still rain close by; she could smell it. Gusts of wind pushed papers in the gutter into a whirl. Dead leaves clogged the drains. The beach and the surf and the golden days of summer seemed a long way away. It was hard to remember Clareville and the happy certainty she had felt.

'I ought to go back to him. I would, I'd *have* to, if it were just him and me and you to consider.'

At that, he looked at her sharply. 'The child?'

'Not just her. Gladys, and the new one. She's a nice girl, Tom. She doesn't deserve to be dropped like a hot potato just because . . .'

'Because you're married,' he said.

And that was that. What else was there to say?

Frank had asked for a divorce, but he wouldn't give her one now. And he had to agree, or the judge wouldn't grant the decree. She couldn't divorce him for abandonment, not under the circumstances, not when he wanted them to be together again, and a wife couldn't divorce a husband without infidelity – and he hadn't really *been* unfaithful, had he?

What a mess.

Despite herself, she remembered the heat in Frank's eyes as he'd gazed at her. He loved her. She didn't doubt that. As for his relations with Gladys . . . she'd be on firmer ground criticising that if she hadn't had the same kind of relations with Tom. No children, but that was more good luck than good management. As for what Gladys deserved now – she could hear her grandmother's voice in her ear: *That one's no better than she ought to be. Don't waste sympathy on her.* She couldn't stop her sympathy, though, or a kind of fellow feeling. Gladys had seemed very alone, and she knew how frightening that could be. Whether or not she loved Frank . . . oh, it was all so hard to think about!

Frank had known they were legally married, but . . . she couldn't condemn him for going back to the mother of his child when he'd thought she had tossed him aside. And she couldn't criticise him for wanting to honour his marriage vows now.

All her life she had believed that marriage was a sacred vow, never to be broken. She thought of the women she'd known back in West Bromwich. The baker's wife had come to the shop with black eyes sometimes, but she'd never even thought about divorcing him, nor even leaving, as far as Margaret had known. 'You makes your bed and then you lie in it,' she used to say. The greengrocer had kept a mistress – everyone knew, including his wife, but it didn't seem to affect his standing in the town, and certainly everyone would have been scandalised if the wife had sued for divorce. Her own father's offsider, Taffy Johnson, had 'stepped out' on his wife a few times. He'd even tried it on with her, after the funeral, for God's sake. His wife had come across them when Taffy had her backed into a corner. 'Give him a good knee in the bollocks, love,' she'd said, and whacked Taffy over the back of the head, but there hadn't been any malice in it, and barely any anger, just resignation.

Compared to those men, Frank was a saint. The dreams of a life in Australia she had once had came back to her, now; she could have them all, just as she had planned. But she wasn't the same person she had been even six months ago. Her dreams had shifted. The question was, could she create new ones that she and Frank could share? Deep in her belly she felt a warmth, left from the way Frank had looked at her, the way he'd been so *happy* to see her. She could melt into that warmth, if she tried, and the old Margaret very much wanted to try.

On the tram back to Circular Quay, she and Tom sat in silence, a careful couple of inches between them.

'In the Catholic Church, even if you get divorced, you can't get remarried,' he said suddenly.

'I thought you didn't care about Catholic versus Protestant anymore.'

'No,' he said. 'Not for myself. But things stick with you, you know?'

Yes. She knew.

She'd thought she had a choice between Tom and Frank, between following God's laws or her own heart, if she even knew what that heart wanted. But perhaps she didn't have a choice. Perhaps Tom wouldn't marry a divorced woman. The thought was leaden in her mind.

•

She couldn't eat her dinner, despite it being lamb chops. Afterwards, she went upstairs to think it out.

The one thing she knew was that she couldn't make this decision based on how she felt about Tom. That would be adultery, plain and simple. She couldn't allow her own inclinations to matter at all. She had to do what was right, if she could work out what that was.

She could take the easy course, the course everyone would approve of: go back to Frank, live as his wife, bear his children . . . all the things she had planned so joyfully when she left England.

Frank probably didn't surf.

Her hands were shaking. For the first time since she came to Australia she felt cold to her bones. Frank's honesty; Tom's slow smile. Frank's blatant adoration; Tom's passion. Her memory licked her with images of both of them, touching her, kissing her: Frank had been so sure of himself, so gentle, helping her cope with the first time; Tom had ignited desire in her she hadn't known she had. Now that she knew, could she find the same passion with her husband?

She had been sure she loved Frank and planned their future with simple faith. She knew with a different, more mature surety that she loved Tom – but with him, who knew what the future would bring?

She sat in a chair by the window, watching the rain slant down in the streetlight and the angophora tree swish and groan in the shadows.

What would her mother have done? That was easy. She couldn't imagine anyone in her family thinking that Gladys had any claim on Frank. 'Sow the wind, reap the whirlwind,' her parents would say. 'Deserves what she got.'

Did she have the right to put Gladys's needs in opposition to everyday morals and God-given law? Gladys's and the children's?

Margaret didn't know. The only thing she could think was that she had to see Gladys again. To talk it out with her. She'd have to take a day off work. Tuesday. She'd tell Mr Bertram there was a family problem.

Surely this counted as a family problem, if ever there was one?

30

On Tuesday morning she left at her normal time, and headed down to the ferry. For once, she went inside, away from the sharp wind and blowing foam. The waves were up and the ferry struggled up and thumped down each one, its engine grinding. But the sky was blue, an astonishing clear blue that seemed far higher than any blue sky she had ever seen.

Perhaps that was a good omen.

The tram from Circular Quay was packed with people off to work, but once they'd passed Town Hall it emptied out a bit and she could perch on a seat, hands clenched around her purse. Today she had to decide. It wasn't fair to anyone – especially Gladys – if she waited too long.

The house in Denison Street seemed to shine, the newly painted door reflecting the morning sun. She felt like Jack and the Beanstalk going into the Giant's castle, but that was silly. Anyone less likely to *fee fi fo fum* than Gladys was impossible to imagine.

Margaret knocked firmly.

When Gladys opened the door, Margaret could see that she was shocked, but she moved back immediately and ushered her in. Not to the kitchen this time, but to the 'good' room, the parlour.

They sat and stared at each other for a moment. Gladys clearly wasn't going to start the conversation, nor offer her a cup of tea.

'I don't know what to do,' Margaret said. 'I've thought and thought and thought and I don't know what to do.'

Gladys leaned forward, intent.

'Do you love him? Seems to me if you loved him, you'd know what you wanted.'

Margaret looked down at her hands. Her gloves had picked up smudges from somewhere – the handrail on the ferry gangplank, probably.

'I don't know. I *did* love him.' But had she really? Had she loved him the way she loved Tom, with that feeling of having come home, of being completed? Looking back, she wasn't sure. 'I was only a kid, you know. Nineteen when we met. I haven't seen him for so long . . . I don't know what I feel about him, and that's the truth.'

'Then you don't love him,' Gladys stated with perfect simplicity. 'If you did, you'd know.'

But marriage wasn't only about love, about feelings. It was about solemn, sacred vows.

'*I* love him,' Gladys said. 'I always have. While he was away, there was no one else for me. I didn't even *think* about being with someone else.'

No doubt about it, Frank must have told her about Tom, and Gladys was condemning her for taking up with another man. It nettled Margaret.

'*I* thought Frank had lied to me. Abandoned me. Married me *bigamously*.'

Gladys didn't look impressed.

'He should have married *you*,' Margaret said. 'Even if he didn't know about the baby.'

Gladys's dark eyes filled with tears. 'It's not his fault. We weren't – we weren't that serious, because we knew he was going to join up. I didn't write to him until after she was born. I'd had a couple of slips, you see, and I didn't want to tell him until I knew the baby was all right. It's all my fault. If I'd written as soon as I knew, none of this would have happened!'

'You think that's true? You think that if he'd known about the baby, he wouldn't have married me?'

Gladys seemed faintly shocked that she could even ask. 'Of course not! He's a good man, Frank. He loves Violet. He would have wanted to do the right thing. He always wants to do the right thing.'

So simple. Perhaps it was simple. Perhaps it was *glaringly* simple.

'If marrying you was the right thing then, it has to be the right thing now,' Margaret said slowly. She gestured at Gladys's pregnancy.

'Frank won't think so. He's always loved you more.'

'And you want him anyway?' Margaret couldn't keep the incredulity out of her voice. Gladys smiled at her wryly, an oddly knowing look on her face.

'If you were really in love with him, you'd understand. Especially if you'd had his baby.' She put her hand on her belly protectively, and Margaret felt a surge of envy. 'Besides, Frank's the nicest fella I've ever met. He's never hit me, not *once*. Even before he moved us in here, he was paying for Violet, all that he could. He's the most decent man I know. So, if I have to be second-best for a while, I will. He'll come round.'

Underneath that soft, gentle voice was a thread of steel and a surprising knowledge of pain. Gladys had seen more than she should have, Margaret thought, and lived through things it was best not to ask about. She felt a dawning respect for her, and a kind of shame, because next to how Gladys felt about Frank, her own affection for him was like a penny candle to the sun.

'Right, then,' Margaret said. 'We're agreed. Frank should be with his children. With his family.'

Gladys's whole face lit up. 'You mean it? Truly really?'

Not trusting her voice, Margaret nodded. The die was cast.

'But you'll have to persuade him to give me a divorce. I can't do it without him.'

'They're expensive, aren't they?'

'I don't know. I'll find out.' Margaret hesitated. 'Gladys, I . . . I'll have to name you as co-respondent. That's the easiest way to get it done.'

'Oh, don't worry about that!' Gladys waved away the shocking idea as though it meant nothing. Perhaps it didn't – after all, she'd been happy enough to live in sin with Frank. Again Margaret was confronted by a completely different way of looking at life. Frank and Gladys clearly shared the same attitude to having relations before marriage; and she couldn't look down on them for it, not after Clareville. Gladys hoisted herself to her feet. 'I'll put the kettle on. Violet, you can come out now. Come and say hello to Aunty Margaret!'

Violet peeped around the door to the kitchen. She was such a sweet little thing, with Gladys's fragility of bone structure and Frank's colouring. Margaret patted the couch next to her and Violet immediately ran and launched herself into Margaret's lap.

'Smell nice!' she said, patting Margaret's face. 'Aunty Mar-Mar!'

'So do you.' It was true; she smelled of small child, that lovely, fugitive fragrance. Margaret gave her a cuddle and Violet giggled and produced a doll from behind her back.

They played with the doll, called Judy, until the tea was ready, and then they went hand in hand to the kitchen. Violet sat in her lap while she and Gladys drank tea and ate pieces of biscuit ('you get them cheaper if they're broken') and discussed ways and means and what Frank would say.

'Frank is Papa!' Violet interrupted.

'Yes,' Margaret said. 'That's right. Frank is Papa.' She and Gladys locked gazes and they both nodded. 'That's what's important. Frank is Papa.'

•

It didn't seem worth going home and then traipsing back again, so Margaret spent the day with them, waiting for Frank to come home. Besides, Gladys was grateful for the help. She hadn't been able to finish the washing on Monday because of the weather, so they did it together, Margaret taking all the hard jobs including hoicking the hot sheets out of the boiling copper and into the cement sink. It was an up-to-date laundry, with a mangle on a pivot so you could swing it over the tubs. Frank had gone all out when he picked this place for them to live.

At lunchtime they walked up to a pie cart on the corner, outside the pub. Margaret's treat. Violet skipped the whole way, and all the way back as well, running literal rings around Gladys's slow stroll.

'She must keep you busy,' Margaret said.

Gladys laughed. 'Doesn't she what! She's a good kid, though.'

Violet skipped back to them and held up her hands to Margaret, to be picked up.

'Don't bother Aunty Margaret,' Gladys scolded, but Margaret laughed and swung her up.

'She's no bother.' Better than no bother. Violet was a sweetheart, full of joy and energy and affection. It was a long time since Margaret had been around children – the *Borda* had been full of them, and she'd helped out the beleaguered mothers as much as she could, enjoying the company of the little ones and dreaming about the babies she and Frank would have, someday soon. She'd been filled with the desire to learn as much as she could about babies; at the back of her mind was the knowledge that she'd have no support in this new country, no easy network of mother and aunts and cousins to advise and help out. She'd be on her own. As Gladys was. She discovered that Gladys was an orphan, like Frank, and wondered if that had drawn them together. But it meant she had no one to turn to, either. No one to help, except Frank.

•

When Frank came through the front door, he was startled enough by Margaret's presence in the parlour to say, 'Strewth! What are you doing here?'

'I came to talk it over with Gladys,' Margaret said. She got up from the couch where she'd been playing dolls with Violet. She faced him, and Gladys came to stand beside her.

Her chest and stomach thrummed with tension, as though her heart had sped up so fast that individual beats could no longer be distinguished.

'I – we, we've had a talk, and I think it's best if we go on with the divorce.'

All colour drained from his face. He even swayed a little, as if he were going to faint. But then he recovered, putting a hand out to the wall to steady himself.

'Do you now?'

'For Violet's sake. And the new baby's.'

Violet was hanging on his trouser leg by this time, hugging him. He looked down at her and she smiled up beatifically.

''Lo Papa!' she waved.

'So we can be a family,' Gladys said, her voice as soft as ever.

Frank picked up Violet and kissed her. Then he looked at them.

'Ganging up on me.' His voice was flat.

'No!' Gladys cried.

'Yes,' Margaret said. She bit her lip and glanced at Gladys's shocked face, then went on, pushing down her nerves. 'You told me, in England, that all you'd ever wanted was a proper family. And on Saturday you said that families should stay together.' He nodded, automatically, acknowledging the memory. She gestured around the room: at Gladys, and her pregnancy, at Violet, at the neat little house. 'This is your *family*, Frank. And you can't desert them. It wouldn't be right.' She took a breath and let it out again. 'No matter what you or I might want.' Let him take that as he might. It wasn't as though she *knew* what she wanted.

His eyes flickered and he looked down at his boots, then up again.

'So, you reckon it's the – the *right* thing to do? Don't see how it could be, seeing as how we're married.'

'If you'd known Gladys was expecting before you left Australia, would you have married her?'

'Of course I would!' he said immediately.

'Exactly,' she said. 'Marrying me was – was a mistake. Just a mistake. Because you didn't have all the facts.'

'No mistake,' he said, his face white, staring at her. 'Best thing I ever did.'

'Staying married might be the worst thing you could ever do.'

For the first time, he looked straight at Gladys. 'And you want me to, as well? Knowing I'm married? Knowing I – I love Margaret.'

There were tears in Gladys's eyes. 'I only want what's best for Violet and, and the new one.' She laid her hand over her belly, the way pregnant women did. 'I want them to have a *real* father. Not like us.' There was a deep yearning in her voice for the father she'd never had.

He flinched, jiggling Violet in his arms without thinking about it. She was trying to poke her doll's hand into his ear, and he jerked his head away and tried to put her down.

'No, Papa!' she scolded. 'Violet up!'

For a moment, Frank's eyes met Violet's, and then she smiled and kissed him, throwing her arms around his neck. He straightened slowly, burying his face in her hair, turning his back on them as though he didn't want them to see whatever emotion he was feeling.

'It's the best thing for Violet,' Margaret said quietly. Gladys went to Frank and put her hand on his arm.

'We're a family, Frank.' She took his hand from Violet's shoulder and put it on her belly. 'The four of us.'

Frank turned to face Margaret, his eyes wet. He looked from her to Gladys, his face unreadable. Then he took his hand from Gladys's belly and touched her face, gently.

'All right,' he said. 'All right.' Relief flooded Margaret, but it came with a blade of pain as she let go of all those dreams yet again. There was no good way out, there was only the way that was best for the children.

Gladys slid her arm around his waist and he patted her back. 'I suppose you'll have to apply for it, tell them I'm unfaithful. Send me whatever I have to sign.'

Margaret nodded. He guided Gladys away from the door and helped her to sit in an armchair, Violet in her lap. Gladys smiled up at Margaret, a wobbly smile with tears not too far away.

'Thank you.'

Frank jerked his head in the direction of the door and Margaret went, feeling quite close to tears herself. Had she done the right thing? The moral thing? Would she look back on this moment and curse her stupidity and her soft-heartedness?

She nodded to them both, waved to Violet, and left.

Walking back to the tram in the winter sun, Margaret felt herself begin to shake. She remembered a night, early in the war, when she and a few of the girls from Reading went up to London to see a show at the Lyceum Theatre. In the interval, she and her friend Patty walked to the pub behind the theatre after agreeing that the lemonade on offer at the theatre really wasn't enough to tide them over until they made it back to their digs. As they'd rounded the corner, the earth seemed to shake and there was a noise so loud she couldn't hear it. That was what it had felt like – being physically pushed by a wall of noise. She couldn't hear, but she could see, around her, people screaming, women and men both, even the men in uniform, and there was a hole in the wall of the pub. Bodies, and people staggering out of the pub over the top of them. Blood. And above them, criss-crossing the night sky, the anti-aircraft spotlights revealed a whale, a shining golden thing just floating, impossibly. A zeppelin.

She saw another bomb fall in the distance, but she couldn't hear it land.

At that moment she had begun to shake, realising that if she and Patty had walked just a little faster, had left the theatre a minute earlier, they would have been in that pub, would have been one of those bodies . . .

She hadn't thought about that night for years; it had been buried under more recent ordeals. But that was how it felt now. As though she had avoided some terrible disaster.

She was going against everything she had ever believed in, everything she had ever been taught, but she was pretty sure God cared more about Violet than he did about her own reputation. And Violet needed her father.

No matter what happened with Tom, she could survive. She had learned that she could survive when Frank hadn't appeared at the ship. Even if she never married, she would survive. And Violet and the new baby would be all right.

•

Margaret decided that it was best not to tell Tom about the divorce until she was sure she could get one. Deep down, she didn't want to tell him, in case he said that it didn't matter, he couldn't marry a divorced woman.

But as she closed the front door of the High House behind her, he came out from the kitchen, where the others were having dinner.

He just looked at her.

'Gladys and I have convinced Frank that it's not fair to the children if the two of them don't get married.'

He nodded, face unreadable, and turned away, then turned back.

'Where did *you* get married?' he asked abruptly.

'What? What difference does it make?'

'Maybe none. Maybe a lot.'

'At Reading Registry Office.' She'd wanted a church wedding, but they hadn't had time to call the banns for three weeks running; who knew when Frank would be posted to the front? So, they had gone to the registry office, like so many young couples in those days.

Tom's face broke open in a wide smile. He grabbed her upper arms and jiggled her on the spot as if in celebration.

'That's wonderful! That doesn't count!'

'What?'

'As far as the Church is concerned. Registry-office marriages don't count. So, if you get a divorce, it'll be all right.'

'Oh. Good.' Perhaps her tone showed how little she thought of that distinction. He touched her cheek gently.

'*I* wouldn't care, but my mum would have.'

He grinned at her again and went back to the kitchen, whistling jauntily.

She felt both affronted and relieved. One thing she didn't have to worry about, at least, but how ridiculous a rule! One marriage, in an office, another, next door at the church. The same people, the same vows, the same emotions . . . but one counted and one didn't? All her father's imprecations about Popish idolatry and Jesuitical lies came back to her. Still, Tom's mother's scruples were the least of her worries at the moment. (Although, she thought, no child of mine is growing up Catholic.)

She had to find a lawyer. And it was time to come clean to Burnsie and Jane.

•

With characteristic efficiency, Burnsie listened to the story, snorted and said, 'You're born to trouble, Margaret Dalton,' and then wrote a letter of introduction to the lawyer who had looked after Mrs Shelley's estate. Valentine Quinn.

'Not as daft as his name,' she said. 'He'll see you right.'

Jane went up to Margaret's room with her and sat on the bed, not saying anything at first.

'My life's a mess,' Margaret said.

'Well, it's a bit of a dog's breakfast, that's for sure. But it'll sort itself out.'

'Do you think I'm doing the right thing?'

'Not sure there is a right thing to do in this situation.' Jane ran her hands through her hair as though it would help her find an answer. 'You've got to go with your gut, I reckon. I'll come to the lawyer's with you.'

If she'd found nothing else in Australia, she'd found a friend in Jane.

31

On the Thursday evening, Margaret and Jane made their way to Valentine Quinn's office in the city.

The office was daunting, and Margaret was thankful Jane was with her as they pushed open the carved cedar doors with their shining brass handles.

Inside it was more of the same: panelled walls, Turkish carpets, Chesterfield sofas in dark green leather. All top quality. She recognised a pair of Meissen figurines on a shelf and was quietly pleased with herself. She wouldn't have known the value of any of it six months ago.

There was a desk, and behind it sat a male secretary, or maybe a clerk – lawyers had clerks, didn't they? A tall pale blond with a supercilious mouth who looked them up and down and almost sneered at Jane's cheap navy suit. Her own clothes – courtesy of Mrs Shelley – received more respect, and his manner thawed.

'May I help you?'

'Mrs Dalton to see Mr Quinn,' she managed to say, handing over the letter of introduction. For the first time since she had

arrived in Australia, she drew on all the elocution lessons her
mother had slaved to pay for. It worked. He nodded quite
respectfully.

'I'll see if Mr Quinn is ready for you.'

They waited while he went through to the inner sanctum.
It was rather like being in a grand house where the butler
announced you – just like in the theatre.

He opened the inner door and announced, 'Mrs Dalton
and . . . companion, Mr Quinn.'

'Thank you, Lucas,' a deep voice answered.

They almost crept in; but Mr Quinn bounced out of his seat
and came to greet them, smiling warmly, shaking their hands
and guiding them to visitors' armchairs upholstered in the same
green leather as the sofas. He sat down himself and beamed at
them as Mr Lucas shut the door silently behind himself.

'Mrs Dalton – and Miss Burns, how nice to see you again!
Come in, come in, sit down. How can I be of assistance?'

He was around fifty, a roly-poly of a man with white at his
temples and brown hair slicked down ruthlessly on the rest of
his head. A ruddy face, with a slight suggestion of a drinker's
nose, but nothing so obvious that he seemed untrustworthy.
He was full of bonhomie, a genial, smiling man.

Margaret smiled back, nervously. This was the moment
where she broke with all the tenets of her upbringing.

'I need a divorce, Mr Quinn.'

The smile was wiped off his face by both surprise and dismay.

'Well, well, that's . . . that's sad news, for such a young
woman. Are you – are you *sure*?'

She could back out. Right now, she could back out. In his
eyes was a warning, and she'd be a fool not to pay attention to it.

'This is a very grave step, a very grave step indeed,' he went on. 'The repercussions are serious. Are you sure there is no hope of a reconciliation?'

She knew what he meant by repercussions. There was no way to keep this quiet. Divorces were reported on in the press, and this story – oh, her story was too much like bad melodrama for the press to refrain. She'd be shamed and shunned by respectable people for the rest of her life. The women at church would turn away from her. She might even lose her job.

Was it worth it?

Not for her, or for Frank. But it was for Violet and the new baby.

'I'm afraid not,' she said softly. Slowly, so he could make notes, she told the story, leaving out Tom altogether but emphasising the two children.

'Hmm, hmm,' he said after she'd finished. 'It's a pretty pickle, I see that. But still, Mrs Dalton, it's not as though he has been *deliberately* unfaithful . . . I'm not sure we could prove adultery and abandonment . . .'

'He's still living with her now,' Jane put in. 'What's that, then?'

'Yes. Yes, that's true. Well. If you're determined . . .'

Margaret brought out her strongest argument. 'I wouldn't have married him if I'd known about this woman beforehand.'

His shrewd eyes, a surprising shade of light grey, searched her face.

'And if you do divorce. Is there . . . someone else for you?' He tilted his head at her like a bird. 'Now, don't be offended. But if the other side finds out, it may derail things.'

'There is a man I was keeping company with before I knew . . . before I knew the truth of what had happened. But of course we're not now.'

'Tom McBride,' Jane put in. 'You remember, from Mrs Shelley's funeral?'

'Sergeant McBride?' Mr Quinn brightened. 'Oh, a fine man, a fine man. Good. We can depend on him to keep a level head. But you shouldn't see anything of him until this case is concluded.'

'They both live with us,' Jane said.

'Oh, no, that won't do. He'll have to move out. It's good for you to have a chaperone like Mrs Burns, my dear, but he can't be under the same roof, no. That wouldn't be at all wise. You *must* present to the judge as beyond reproach.'

Margaret's resolve faltered. To go without Tom's support, to not see him for so long . . . the months ahead would be grey and dreary without him. She wasn't sure she could deal with all this on her own.

'I'll ask him, but I can't guarantee—'

'*I* can,' Jane said. 'He'll go back to his mum's house, probably. Don't you worry about that, Margi. I'll sort it out.'

What a good friend Jane was! Practical and generous. Margaret stiffened her spine. She could cope. She'd have to, even though this legal process felt so alien, so *posh*. Just like something on the stage, and she had to play her part.

'Now, the other thing which is *imperative* is that you have no contact with the other parties at all. We must avoid any appearance of collusion, or the application will be rejected.'

'All right. But I'll have to let them know—'

'No, no, my dear. All communications from now on must go through this office. No speaking to or seeing either the respondent or the co-respondent from the moment you leave this office. I must have your promise on that, or we might as well forget the whole thing.'

Margaret let out a long breath. It was a relief, in some ways, to have all the decisions taken away from her. She hadn't been looking forward to seeing Frank again anyway.

'The costs . . .' she murmured.

'Well, they can be considerable,' Mr Quinn admitted. 'But since this is not being contested, it shouldn't cost more than, say, fifty pounds. Perhaps not so much, but it's best to be prepared. We'll get someone strong to appear for us in court.'

Margaret just stopped herself from gasping. Fifty pounds. More than four months' pay. All the money she'd saved up in England, plus the stipend the Army had been paying her. (Would she have to give that back now? It was the first time that had occurred to her, and it filled her with dismay.) She wasn't sure she *had* fifty pounds. Not quite.

'Now, don't be alarmed. In divorce cases the respondent generally has to pay costs. It will cost *you* very little.' He patted her hand with avuncular reassurance.

That wasn't right, but this wasn't the place to say so. She and Frank could sort it all out later.

'We'll need a retainer – ten pounds will be plenty – and then we'll get started. Have you brought your documents?'

Wordlessly, she handed over her marriage lines, her birth certificate and her passport.

'Excellent. Now, I don't suppose you have anything that shows you are domiciled in New South Wales?' Another shrewd glance saw her bewilderment. 'That is, something that shows you live here permanently.'

'I'm on the electoral roll,' she said faintly. Did that count?

'Very well done, Mrs Dalton. Excellent. I'll have my clerk get a notarised statement from the Electoral Board. Good. Now. Details of the respondent and co-respondent.'

She had typed up Frank's and Gladys's details and the list of relevant dates on the machine at work, after hours the day before. At least she didn't have to be ashamed of her paperwork.

'You are a very businesslike young lady, aren't you?' Mr Quinn said, looking over the information. She tried to believe he was entirely approving of her efficiency, but there was an edge to his voice that reminded her that a divorced woman, by definition, was 'fast'. Or a failure as a wife. As a woman. A blush was creeping up over her face as she felt the warmth of embarrassment flow over her. How had she come to this moment? It didn't seem real.

She might as well get used to it.

Her blush brought out real approval from Mr Quinn. Perhaps he thought embarrassment was more seemly than efficiency for a woman seeking a divorce. Perhaps he was right.

'Now, Mrs Dalton, don't you worry. Leave it all to me, and in a year or so we'll have your divorce.'

'A year!' Jane exclaimed.

'Since it's not being contested. We'll get the decree nisi in six months or so, if we're lucky, and then the decree absolute six months after that court date. It very rarely goes longer than eighteen months.'

He stood, beaming at them, as if he'd given them good news. Margaret stood up slowly. Fifty pounds and eighteen months. She'd known it was complicated, but still . . .

Jane took her arm and squeezed.

'Thanks, Mr Quinn,' she said. 'Come along, Margi.'

Obediently, Margaret followed her out into the office.

'Now, if you'll just give Mr Lucas here a cheque for ten pounds, we'll get everything underway. Start a new file, Lucas. Dalton versus Dalton.'

A cheque? Rich men and businesses had cheque accounts, not working women. She'd brought twenty pounds, just in case, but she felt more awkward than ever before as she said, 'I'm afraid I don't have a cheque account. Will cash do?'

'Silly of me,' Mr Quinn said. 'Of course you don't. Cash will be fine. Or you could drop a money order around any time. Now I'm afraid I must rush off. Another meeting . . .'

He bowed, a formal little bow that made Margaret want to curtsey like a child, and then disappeared back into his office.

Mr Lucas held her two five-pound notes with the tips of his fingers, as though mortified to take money from her. He wrote out the receipt neatly enough, but his smile as he handed it to her was perfunctory. 'Dalton versus Dalton' had removed any respect.

'We'll be in touch,' he said.

They walked out into darkness and cold. The wind off the water slid up Phillip Street and sliced right through them. For a few moments, they walked down the hill in silence towards the lights of Circular Quay.

'Well,' Jane said. 'Have you *got* fifty quid?'

'Almost. Frank will pay half, I'm sure.'

They kept walking.

'I feel like a scarlet woman,' Margaret said. 'Dirty.'

'That bloody Quinn. *And* that snooty clerk of his. Don't you mind them, Margi.'

'Everyone will treat me like that.' Tears scalded her eyes and she dashed them away before they could fall. Dalton versus Dalton. Damning.

'Not us. Not the people who know you.'

Jane slid her hand through Margaret's arm and again squeezed comfortingly.

'You're a good friend, Janey.'

'Hah. I know when I'm onto a good thing. You're the right sort, Margaret Dalton, and don't you forget it.'

But all the way back on the ferry Margaret couldn't get the memory of Mr Lucas's disdain from her mind. That was the way of the world: no matter what the man had done, a woman who divorced her husband was looked down upon. She refused to feel ashamed of herself. Mr Lucas could take his disdain and, and . . . blow it out his arse. That's what her grandma used to say.

32

'What d'you mean, I have to move out?' Tom glared at Jane, but she put her tip-tilted nose up in the air and ignored his anger, carrying on with the washing up as if they were discussing what brand of soap to use. After dinner, which had been later than usual because of the girls' trip into the city, Jane had shooed away everyone else and insisted that he and she could do the dishes themselves. Now he knew why.

'Do you *want* Margi to get free and clear of Dalton?'

Did he? Finding out that Margi was actually married had shaken him more than he liked to admit. It was too much like the past; why did he have this problem with married women? He had no luck at all with girls. But yes, he *did* want Margi to be free. It had been a bad few days when he'd thought he'd have to choose between her and the Church he'd grown up in. The last time he'd felt that much relief was when he'd woken up in hospital after he'd been wounded.

'Yes,' he said shortly. Jane put another plate on the dish rack and he picked it up and dried it.

'Well, the lawyer cove says no breath of scandal can come near Margi until after the decree. No more trips to the cinema, mate, and no more kisses and cuddles, either.'

'How long?'

'Six months,' she said, although she didn't look him in the eye.

'Six months and?'

'Six months to the decree nisi,' she said reluctantly. 'Another six after that before the decree absolute. But I don't think it's as much of a problem then. Just until the first court date.'

Six months without seeing Margaret every day. Without their brief meetings, their stolen moments, the few 'kisses and cuddles' they'd managed to snatch since they came back from Clareville. A lump in his chest grabbed tightly; his heart felt like it was being squeezed. How could he let her go for that long?

'Six months now or you lose her forever,' Jane admonished. She knew him too well, like a little sister. 'Move back with your mum for a while – she'd love that.'

'No,' Tom said. 'I'll get another billet near here somewhere. Annandale's too much of a trek, morning and night.' He hesitated. 'Does your mother know?'

Jane grinned at him and slid a tangle of knives and forks onto the drainer. 'Yes, don't worry. She's not happy to lose you, but she'll go along with it.'

He put one arm around her shoulders and hugged her. 'You're a good one, Janey.'

'Mmm.' She looked down, studiously swirling the dish mop over another plate. 'I might need a favour myself one day, you never know.'

'What have you got planned?'

She shrugged. 'Not planned. But you know, I'm not cut out to be a tea lady forever.'

He looked at her afresh. The bright golden hair, snapping blue eyes, the shapely figure and something else . . . some essence of Janeness that made the room light up with a sense of fun whenever she entered. He realised, with a little surprise, that she was damned good-looking. Not pretty, like Margi, but striking. Attractive. She certainly didn't look like a tea lady.

'Well, I'll back you, but give me warning if it's going to be bad.'

Jane laughed, a delighted gurgle, and he had to grin along with her. That was just how it was when Janey laughed.

'Don't worry, I'll give you a cooee ahead of time.'

•

He called Bill Flynn. He and Bill were on the same lifesaving team now, and they practised their drills winter as well as summer, although the hours the beach was patrolled were cut back in winter. You still had some idiots go out in a swell no one should swim in, despite the weather.

Flynn lived in a flat with another bloke, Ben Needham, in North Sydney, just a few blocks away.

'Reckon you could fit me in on the sofa for six months or so?' Tom asked.

'I can do better than that,' Bill said. 'Ben's getting married in a month. You can have his room.'

Wonderful. He finally got a place he could take Margaret for some privacy, and he couldn't go near her.

'I'll move in tomorrow after work, if that's all right.'

'Copacetic.'

'You're not sharing a trench with Yankee doughboys now, mate.'

Bill laughed. 'Fine. No worries.'

Tom grinned. 'That's better.' He was a nice bloke, Bill. Even-tempered, which was all to the good, as God knew he himself was likely to be a bit irascible over the next while. It was hard to imagine not seeing Margaret for six whole months . . . for a moment, he wondered how Frank Dalton had felt, not seeing her for more than two years, only to be told that she'd abandoned him. Despite himself, he felt a flicker of pity.

Still, he'd got a girl pregnant, and if Margi had to divorce him so he could do the right thing . . . whatever the right thing was in this situation. He'd be blowed if he knew. He wanted Margi too much to be sure of his own morals. He was just lucky she felt so strongly about the children needing their father. If Dalton had been single, with no ties . . . Margaret loved him, Tom was sure, but whether that love could have withstood every claim of God and man . . . He felt like thanking that Gladys woman for getting pregnant again.

In the parlour, Burnsie was sitting in her favourite armchair, knitting, while Jane and Margaret were going through the victrola records.

'Bill Flynn's mate Ben is getting married, so he's offered me Ben's bed in the flat,' he said. It was a good excuse to move. An easily explained thing, if anyone came nosing around Margaret's business.

'We'll be sorry to lose you,' Burnsie stated, with a quick look up at him. He couldn't tell if she approved or disapproved. Margaret was staring at him with wide eyes. Wounded eyes. He was ashamed that he felt a dark satisfaction knowing that she would find the separation as hard as he did.

He wished she'd never met Dalton – but then she wouldn't have come out to Australia, so what good would that have done him? He wished that he was the one she'd met, that instead of a fishing boat he'd spent his leave stranded at Reading Station.

If wishes were horses, beggars would ride, his aunty would say.

'I'll be sorry to go,' he said, ostensibly to Burnsie, but looking at Margaret. She turned her head away, blinking back tears, and it was all he could do to stop himself going to her and pulling her into his arms.

But the two students came in from the kitchen and one sat down at the piano.

'Sing us a song, Jane,' he said, playing an arpeggio down the keys.

She began to sing 'Let Me Call You Sweetheart' and he picked up the melody immediately; they'd sung it together before. This time, she looked around at them all as she got to the chorus, and motioned for them to join in.

Let me call you 'Sweetheart', I'm in love with you.
Let me hear you whisper that you love me too.
Keep the love-light glowing in your eyes so true.
Let me call you 'Sweetheart', I'm in love with you.

He couldn't help it; he gazed at Margaret all through the yearning words, the sweet music conveying everything he couldn't say. He saw tears in her eyes again as she tried to sing along, and he was glad of them, glad she felt the same way.

Margaret was true blue. Six months was nothing. If he could get through six months at Ypres, through the mud and the terror and the cold, the mustard gas and the shells, he could get through six months without her.

Then he could court her properly, and they could get married as soon as the decree absolute came through.

•

The next morning he packed up his kit – he didn't have much, yet – and stacked it next to his door, ready for after work, then went down to have a last early breakfast with Burnsie.

He was glad to find her alone.

'Well,' she said, dishing out bacon and eggs and toast, 'you think you've got it all sorted, do you?'

So, she didn't approve.

'It was only a registry-office wedding, Burnsie,' he said. Burnsie was High Anglican – the rules for them were pretty much the same as for Catholics. She paused in mid-pour of his tea.

'That so? Well, that still doesn't make it right. Makes it better, but not right.'

'Not right for those two kiddies not to have a father, either.'

'If it wasn't for those children I wouldn't be having anything to do with this. Marriage is a sacred institution.'

'Yes.'

Tom didn't know what else to say, but it seemed to be enough. She sniffed loudly, but she finished pouring his tea and even pushed the sugar over to him.

They ate in silence, and then he got up to take her plate and his over to the sink.

He bent and kissed her cheek, and she lifted a hand to touch his shoulder in a kind of blessing. Walking down to the harbourside with his lunch bag in his hand, he hoped she'd never have cause to be ashamed of him.

•

Margaret was waiting for him when he went back to get his bag. She just stood next to his open bedroom door, her hands gripping her elbows as if to support herself.

Tom went through into the room and pulled her behind him, closing the door.

She slid into his arms without a word, raising her mouth to his.

A mixture of desire and triumph swept through him as he kissed her. She was *his*, and bedamned to Dalton and the lawyer and everyone who wanted to keep them apart.

He kissed her as he'd never kissed anyone before; with desperation and longing and need. For a moment she stilled, as though he had surprised her, and then she matched him, breath for breath, touch for touch, need for need. Her passion thrilled him and made him want to weep as well as crush her to him. He hadn't realised it, but he'd been afraid she had changed towards him.

They couldn't do more, not here, not at Burnsie's, and they both knew it, so he pulled back reluctantly, the sweet underside of her lip clinging to his and making him kiss her just once, just once more.

Then he stepped away from her and stood still, knowing his love for her was marked in every line of his face. But that was all right, because she looked the same.

'Six months,' he said, his voice husky. She nodded wordlessly. 'I don't like it, but I'll do it. Off you go, now.'

Instead, she stepped forward and touched his cheek. 'I love you, Tom McBride.'

She slipped away to the door before he could reply, and slid out with only a single look back at him.

He sat on the bed and put his head in his hands, waiting until he was calm enough to go downstairs and say goodbye to Burnsie. She had already stripped the bed; damn, he'd meant to do that for her before he left.

Deep breath in, and out . . . soon enough he'd pick up his duffel bag, say his goodbyes, pay his shot and leave. He'd been happy here, even if he'd been unsettled. The first time he'd been happy in a very long time.

It was odd to think that, if all went well, he'd only ever enter this house again as a guest.

33

Frank decided to make a cot for the new baby. A friend of Glad's let him measure up her baby's cot, and he went to the timber yard in Annandale to get the materials and set up in the backyard on the next fine Sunday.

He had his own tools, of course. He'd sold his kit when he enlisted, not having anywhere to store it while he was away, and he'd kept that money sacred, no matter what, and added to it a bit whenever he could, so that the day after he was demobbed he could go to the pawnshop and kit himself out. Nothing fancy: hammer, mallet, screwdrivers, a plane, rasps and a few good chisels of high-carbon steel. A wood saw and a hacksaw. Carpenter's pencils, chalk, twine, a folding rule, a level, a plumb bob, an awl. The bare minimum, really, and yet he could make or mend almost anything with those few items. His blacksmithing tools he kept at work.

Metal was his first love, and he was a bit cack-handed with wood, but he managed.

Working with his hands kept him from thinking too much. Allowed him to concentrate on the baby. To not think about Margaret.

He'd been so uplifted when he'd found out she was here; that she hadn't abandoned him, hadn't lied to or cheated on him. He was worried about Gladys, yes, and guilty for leaving her in the lurch, but it had been a good moment, getting Margaret's letter and realising it was all a mix-up, that he hadn't been tossed aside, not even worth a letter explaining things. Having her tell him he should stay with Glad . . . that had been a bad time. One of the worst.

If he hadn't seen that redheaded bloke with her, he might have believed her when she said it was all for the kiddies.

Jealousy gnawed at him.

But he believed her, in the end, because it was Margaret, who was truthful as the day was long. And because there was Vi, tugging at his leg, loving him, *needing* him. Gladys and the new one needed him too.

It was good to be needed; not something he was used to.

Cutting the pieces to size was easy, and he wasn't fool enough to try dovetailing the joints – it would have to be dowelling and glue holding it together. But he spent a long time sanding each piece down to silky smoothness, so no part would catch on a baby's tender skin.

It took him two Sundays, and then he was ready to paint it.

'It's lovely, Frank,' Gladys said. She handed him a mug of tea and he took it gratefully. Hot, smelly work, painting outside.

The cot stood gleaming white in the afternoon sun. Simple but sturdy. It would last for this baby, and maybe for more. He imagined it becoming an heirloom. Maybe one day this baby's baby would lie in it. His grandchildren. Great-grandchildren, even.

He slid his arm around Glad's shoulders and they stood looking at it. He grinned. Watching paint dry. He'd never thought it could be so satisfying.

34

When their case came to court, she would have to tell Mr Bertram about it. Margaret didn't want him to be informed when a customer demanded to know why he employed a scandalous divorcée. But sufficient unto the day.

A week after her visit to Mr Quinn, she received papers to sign and return to him by registered mail. She did as he asked, then waited.

Two weeks later he wrote to say that Frank had been served his papers and the proceedings had been lodged with the court. Now they had to wait for a court date.

Time to tell Mr Bertram, and find out if she still had a job.

She waited until it was quiet – their mid-week lull, Thursday afternoon – and sat down in his visitor's chair, her heart thudding.

He listened to the whole story (minus Tom) without comment, staring down at his blotter, only his quick fingers playing with a pen showing any sign of his disquiet.

'Divorce . . .' he said when she finally fell silent. 'Our customers won't like that.'

'They may not find out.'

He laughed shortly. 'Oh, they'll find out. Mrs Gascoigne, for one, goes through the newspaper divorce lists with a fine-toothed comb.'

Mrs Gascoigne was a woman of around sixty, whose main entertainment appeared to be auctions and gossip. But she was a person of influence in the area, and could damn the business if she chose.

What could she say? He was right. She felt social disapproval pressing down on her like a physical weight. Perhaps it was better if she just did nothing. Left Frank and Gladys alone. Never married Tom. The thought was a sharp pain in her abdomen. Gladys and the babies came first. That was all she could cling to.

'Do I need to find another job, Mr Bertram?'

He slid a quick glance her way and returned his gaze to the blotter, holding his fountain pen in the middle and flicking it backwards and forwards fast so that each end hit the paper, like a drum roll.

She had kept his secret, but she didn't think that gave her a claim on him; any decent person would have done the same.

'No,' he said, throwing the pen down as if in disgust at his own thoughts. 'No. Times are changing. I read the other day that divorce rates are climbing sky-high. We can't cut everyone out of society who – who's made a mistake.'

Her legs were trembling. The old fear of being out of work had made her weaker than she realised.

'Besides,' he said, trying to laugh. 'With households splitting up, surely there'll be extra work for auctioneers!'

She smiled with difficulty.

'It's a bad case, Mrs Dalton. But we'll get through it, I'm sure.'

'Thank you, Mr Bertram.' She'd never said anything she meant more.

'Right, then. Do you have Monday's figures?'

She did. They returned to work with marked relief on both sides. One hurdle crossed.

•

Now that Tom wasn't there, she and Jane took a nightly stroll. They kept to the well-lit streets and didn't linger, as much because of the weather as because of any fears for their safety.

The cold winter that Tom had promised her had arrived. The wind from the south cut through her jacket, so that she pulled out the English coat she'd put in mothballs, blithely assuming that she'd never need it again.

'It's a lazy wind,' Jane laughed. 'Too lazy to go around you so it goes straight through.'

The first weekend in July it stormed and raged, gale-force winds breaking branches off trees. And yet, two days later the skies were sunny; out of the wind she could sit in shirtsleeves, turn her face up to the sun, close her eyes and imagine it was an English summer's day. Would she ever get used to the weather here?

The next afternoon, Jane insisted the two of them go through Mrs Shelley's old clothes and pick Margaret out a new spring wardrobe.

'You can't keep the mourning up now. Once they publish the divorce in the paper, well, it's all up. Might as well spike their guns. How about this one?'

She held out a green art silk dress with big cuffs on the sleeves and a lovely contrasting sash across the hips in deep blue. It felt smooth against her skin as she slid it on; inevitably she was reminded of Tom's touch, and her face flamed. She bent over to fiddle with her garter to disguise it.

'Oh, you look smashing!' Jane clapped her hands.

'Wouldn't this fit you? You look lovely in green.'

'Not that dark green, it washes me right out. Besides, I've tried on every dress in here, believe me! They're all too small across the bust.'

'Couldn't they be remade?' She hesitated. 'I'm not sure your mother would approve of this right now. She's not very happy with me at the moment.'

Jane picked up a delicate silk shawl and let it drop back onto the bed in a puddle of gleaming gold. She didn't meet Margaret's eyes.

'She likes *you*. She just doesn't like the mess you're in.' She flicked a quick, mischievous glance at Margaret. 'Besides, she'll have more to worry about than you soon enough.'

'Jane. What are you planning?'

Jane threw herself back across the bed, arms outstretched above her head as though reaching for – something. Then she bounced back up and onto her feet.

'I'm going on the halls. Jonesy and I have an audition on Saturday afternoon, up at Clay's Coliseum.'

Margaret knew the building; it was in North Sydney, up the road a piece from the train station. She also knew that it was in poor condition – she doubted it had seen a lick of paint since before the war. If it was an example of the industry Jane wanted to join, it wasn't an impressive one, but saying so wouldn't be helpful.

'Jonesy?' she asked, grasping at the one thing that didn't make sense. 'How can he . . . with his leg?'

'Oh, he's a lot better, haven't you noticed? Besides, we'll mostly be singing, and then we've got a bit of patter, and a little dance.'

'Are you sure you're . . . good enough?' She *had* to ask. Better her now than some director or whatever they had in the theatre laughing at them. But Jane laughed at *her*.

'You've never really heard me sing, Margi. I can't let loose in a little room. I've been having voice lessons since I was seven. Mrs Shelley paid for them. She said I had a God-given talent and it was a sin to waste it. Although, I admit, she mainly wanted me for the church choir.' Excitement fell from her face as though someone had turned the gas mantle down. 'You don't think I'm a fool, do you, Margi?'

'I think you're lucky.' Margaret looked around the beautiful room, which was only the third-best bedroom in this palatial house. 'You'll never have to worry about having a roof over your head in your old age.'

Jane stared as though this thought had never occurred to her. Margaret smiled wryly at her. 'That's why most people don't try things like this, Jane. They're afraid of a dark, grim, hungry future.'

'You too?'

Margaret forced herself to grin. Better not to dampen Jane's enthusiasm with her own terror of poverty and unemployment, when Jane would never have to face them. Besides, who was she to criticise anyone's choices? 'You're looking at the girl who came halfway around the world for a man she'd only known for eight weeks, remember? If this is what you want to do—'

'Oh, it is! I've always wanted to, but Mum . . . she thinks all actresses are, are – disreputable women. Besides, she lived through the Depression of the nineties, and she's never got over it. Get a government job and keep it was all she ever wanted for me.'

Yes, she spoke with the thoughtlessness of someone who'd never known hunger or fear. And she was right to. Her ambition was uplifting; Margaret felt ennobled by it, made braver and more able to face her own future – more Margi than Margaret.

'Good luck to you, I say!'

'Oh, no, you'll jinx me! Theatre people don't say "Good luck", they say "Break a leg!"'

Margaret hugged her. 'Then, "Break a leg!"'

'But mind, I'm not telling Mum until *after* I get the job!'

Jane danced her around the room and then, when Margaret's wind failed, kept dancing herself. She *was* a wonderful dancer, and singer. But was she good enough for the professional theatre? She hoped with all her heart that Jane wasn't heading for a fall.

•

She girded her loins the next day and went to work in a pale blue dress.

It was a sale day, and Mrs Gascoigne arrived, as she always did, early. She blinked when she saw Margaret, and came over to the desk where Margaret was setting out the ledgers and cash box.

'You're out of mourning then, Mrs Dalton?' she asked.

Margaret took a deep breath. This was the moment she had to confess, and Mrs Gascoigne was the one to confess to. Once she was told, everyone else would know within hours. Which didn't mean the truth couldn't be shaded, just a little.

'Well, I don't mind telling *you*, Mrs Gascoigne,' she said, leaning forward and lowering her voice. 'But it turned out that my husband wasn't dead after all.'

'No!' Mrs Gascoigne's eyes widened, and she settled her silk coat around her more comfortably to listen, as if she were an old granny by the fire.

'He'd just . . .' She could feel the blush rising, but this time it was all to the good. 'He'd just gone off with someone else and . . . well, the Army got it wrong.'

'Oh, my dear!' A salacious glint in her eye, the old bat.

'So, I'm divorcing him.' There. Make or break. 'He's got this other woman and, well, she's expecting, you see.'

A hissing indrawn breath and a moment's consideration. Which way would she go? Accept or shun? Was it possible to push her the right way?

'I'm sure you understand, Mrs Gascoigne, that I couldn't put up with that kind of behaviour. Not when my own conduct has been above reproach.' There was the lie, but too bad. She had Mr Bertram to think of as well as herself.

Mrs Gascoigne nodded and patted her shoulder with a heavy hand.

'I'm sure you're doing the right thing. The war pushed such unsuitable people together – and how could you tell them apart in uniform? My dear, you're well rid of him.'

She sailed off to her usual seat and spent the next ten minutes speaking in low and urgent tones to her companions, women of influence like herself. They cast shocked and speculative glances towards Margaret, but at the end of the auction, when they were paying for the few baubles they had bought, a couple of them were careful to smile at her before they left. Like priests bestowing a blessing. More put their noses in the air and only spoke to Mr McDougall. The cold shoulder.

But they all nodded or spoke to Mr Bertram on the way out, which meant that he, at least, wasn't being blamed for her disgrace.

She clung to that comfort. It wasn't until you lost respect-ability that you realised how reassuring it was. How much of a bulwark against the world.

35

Clay's Coliseum was a rickety old building that had been the tram shed for the North Sydney line until they changed the tracks some years ago, according to Jane. If you looked closely you could see the dilapidation – but it was gaudy with posters and promise.

The left-hand door of the back-of-lobby doors was open, and Jane, Jonesy, Margaret and Clara let themselves in.

'One day I'm going to dine out on the story of how I watched Jane and Jonesy's first audition!' Clara grinned with simple confidence and it buoyed all their spirits.

An empty theatre is an uncanny place, full of shadows and the smell of dust and limelight. Margaret followed Jane down the centre aisle, but stopped halfway, where she and Clara slid into plush red seats and watched the two performers go the rest of the way.

The stage was set with tonight's first-act backdrop: a rather drab-looking garden setting with only a couple of small lights on it. An upright piano was being wheeled on by a lackadaisical boy. At the front of the seats, a couple of men and a woman taking notes sat, talking earnestly.

Jane and Jonesy walked up to them with assumed confidence. Jane had gone all out in a shortish white dress with a flippy skirt, adorned with sequins sewn around the hem. Jonesy was dapper in a slick tan suit with a boater hat. His limp was barely noticeable.

With her customary breeziness, Jane walked around and stood in front of the two men, Jonesy at her back. They exchanged a quick smile and Jane said, 'Jane and Jones, for our audition.'

She seemed to have such confidence – which, Margaret thought, after the whirlwind of nerves she had been while getting dressed, should alone get her the job. Even the meagre lights on the stage made her blonde hair glow like gold.

'Up you go, then,' one of the men said in a North Country accent. Margaret was always surprised to hear an English accent, despite the number of Britons who'd emigrated here over the past fifty years, and earlier. This time, something about the voice made her sharply homesick. She yearned to be among people who spoke like that or, better yet, be in a Black Country pub surrounded by the sounds of home. She wanted fish and chips with malt vinegar, and black pudding with her scrambled eggs, and warm beer in a snug with both men and women sitting and drinking instead of this Australian custom of separating the two.

Perhaps it was the theatre; theatres were theatres the world over, and this one had exactly the same smell as the one to which her parents had once taken her and David to see a pantomime.

All three dead now.

How many of the audience from that night were still alive? Most of the young boys dead in France, many of the others dead from the Spanish Flu, and probably some others, too, from natural causes or accidents or plain old age.

Life was a privilege. Even being homesick was a privilege; it proved your heart was still beating.

Jane was up on stage now. Margaret dragged her attention back to the present.

Jonesy handed some sheet music to the man at the piano, and they began, with Jane looking around the stage for Jonesy and he evading her. He sang the verse and she the chorus:

Kelly and his sweetheart wore a very pleasant smile,
And sent upon a holiday they went from Mona's Isle,
They landed safe in London but alas it's sad to say,
For Kelly lost his little girl up Piccadilly way.
She searched for him in vain and then of course began to fret,
And this is the appeal she made to everyone she met:

Has anybody here seen Kelly?
K-E-double-L-Y.
Has anybody here seen Kelly?
Find him if you can!
He's as bad as old Antonio,
Left me on my own-ee-o,
Has anybody here seen Kelly?
Kelly from the Isle of Man!

Even though she'd seen them sing it before, Margaret couldn't help but laugh. On stage, the actions and facial expressions that had seemed so overdone at home were perfectly judged.

They broke into a soft-shoe shuffle halfway, and then the song went to the chorus, with Jane finally 'finding' Jonesy.

Margaret didn't know if she should applaud. She and Clara exchanged glances and decided not to; it would have felt too much like special pleading. Jane and Jonesy came to the edge of the stage.

'Got anything else?' the North Country man asked.

'You bet!' Jonesy said. He nodded to the man at the piano, who turned to a new page and began to play.

This one was romantic, a lyrical, swaying melody.

Meet me tonight in dreamland,
under the silvery moon;
Meet me tonight in dreamland,
where love's sweet roses bloom.
Come with the love-light gleaming
in your dear eyes so true;
Meet me in dreamland,
sweet dreamy dreamland;
There let my dreams come true

They sang it as a duet, and by the end of it Margaret was convinced they really were in love. Their voices blended so perfectly, tenor and soprano. She did have a beautiful voice. It was as though it wasn't Jane and Jonesy up there, but some other, classier, more *expensive* version of them. She understood Burnsie's fears better; you couldn't look at Jane up there and think she'd be satisfied with a normal job ever again.

'Orright, then. You can start in the middle of the first act, after the performing dogs. One song this week, see how you go. Do the duet. Six nights a week plus matinees. Start Tuesday fortnight. Mondays we're dark.'

'Bloody beauty!' Jonesy exclaimed. Jane said nothing, just nodded, her face barely smiling, but with so much excitement held in she looked like she might fly up to the ceiling and burst like a lost balloon.

'See Cec about your pay,' the man said, waving them over to another man, sitting towards the side.

Margaret and Clara went outside to wait for them. It wasn't long before Jane rushed out and flung herself into Margaret's arms.

'Did you *see*? Did you hear? We're in!'

They all did a little dance of celebration, right there on Miller Street. Margaret wished Tom could have danced with them. Every moment like this, of joy or wonder or even sorrow, was lessened by his absence.

•

When they got home, Burnsie was sitting at the kitchen table, peeling potatoes. She took one look at Jane and snorted.

'You look like the cat that ate the canary. What've you done?'

'Jonesy and I are in the show at Clay's.' Jane blurted it out and then stood there, looking about five years old, waiting for the onslaught. Burnsie's mouth tightened, but she didn't say anything for a moment, and then she sighed.

'Just like your father,' she said.

'Dad? He was a drover.'

'Yerse. Always off to see something new. Never satisfied with what he had. Well, all that got him was drowning in a flash flood. I hope you don't tread the same path.'

Her shoulders were bowed. Jane went around the table and hugged her, and for a moment Margaret could see how alike they were, how pretty Burnsie must have been twenty-five years earlier.

'Ah, get away with you!' Burnsie said. 'All honey and kisses now you've got what you wanted.' But she patted Jane's hand as she got up to put the potatoes in their saucepan. She flicked a glance at Margaret. 'And what about you, young lady? I suppose you've known about this all along the way? What other mischief are you going to get Jane into?'

'That's not fair, Mum,' Jane said quietly.

'Isn't it? You two are a good pair. Never know when you're well off. Always wanting something more. In my day if a girl got a respectable tradesman for a husband she counted herself lucky. *Or* a government job. You girls today don't know what's what.'

'Maybe we know too much,' Margaret said quietly. She felt the justice of Burnsie's criticisms, and yet . . . 'Maybe we've seen too much death to be satisfied with being half-alive.'

Burnsie stopped and looked at her, saucepan still in her hand.

'Maybe,' she said, nodding as if it cost her something to admit it. Then she stiffened her back. 'Or maybe that's just your excuse for being flibbertigibbets.'

As Margaret went up the stairs to her room, leaving Jane and Burnsie talking quietly in the kitchen, she wondered how it could seem that both were true; that they *were* flibbertigibbets *and* that they wanted more than the old pre-war life had offered them. It was as though she had two pairs of eyes, one she'd inherited from her parents and their parents before them, and the other new-found, not during the war, but on the instant peace was declared and they could start *wanting* things again. She suspected that neither pair of eyes saw clearly. But neither was entirely blind. It was just that they looked out onto different worlds.

36

The court date was set for the twelfth of October. Margaret warned Mr Bertram.

'A Tuesday,' he said.

She shrugged apologetically. 'I think it's best if I take the week off, sir. Mr Quinn wants to have a meeting with the barrister on the Monday, and who knows how long the case will take?'

He did his trick of flicking his pen rapidly up and down against the blotter, and then nodded. 'Yes. Well, you've got the time owing to you. You can take a week of holiday pay.'

That was more than she had expected. Usually you didn't get leave until after you'd been in a place for a year. 'Thank you, sir! That's very kind of you.'

He waved her thanks away. 'But you'd better train someone in how to note down the auction results before then, or we'll all be in trouble!' He paused, and flicked a glance towards the stairs to the warehouse. 'It's all *objets d'art* and household items that week. Small things. We won't be needing the lorry much.'

Avoiding her eye, he fiddled again with the pen, then put it down resolutely and looked up at her. 'Or the driver.'

'I could train Joe, then, do you think?' she asked.

Almost apologetically, he nodded. 'He *is* quite bright, really.'

'Yes,' she said, dryly. 'I've noticed that.'

He grinned at her, looking no more than a boy. 'He wants something a bit better than driving a lorry. If you can train him up, he can get a job away from here.'

'And that would be best for everyone,' she said. His happiness faded and a terrible hopelessness came into his eyes.

'Yes,' he said. 'As best as we can manage, anyway.'

She didn't quite like the idea that she and Mr Bertram were in a conspiracy to attack all the moral foundations of respectability, but she supposed they were, really.

At least she'd have her time off. Joe came up to see her just before what she had learned to call smoko, at eleven, his flat cap in his hand and his fingernails scrubbed clean.

'Boss says you're going to teach me bookkeeping, missus.'

'Well, I'm going to teach you how the books work *here*, anyway.' They looked steadily at each other and nodded. Yes, it was a conspiracy. A fight against unthinking prejudice and everything that stood in the way of love. Well, Methodists never backed away from a fight.

'Get yourself a chair and we'll begin,' she said.

•

Waiting for the court date was harder than Margaret had thought it would be. She was almost glad that there was so much to do to prepare for a fundraising concert for the Life Saving Club. They were lucky – The Sunshine Company, a popular music hall troupe, had agreed to do a short version of their act, bulked out by a recitation from a local elocution teacher and a song and dance from Jane and Jonesy.

Normally, their fundraisers were on Saturday nights, but the Sunshine Company was only available on Mondays, when the theatres were dark. At least she'd get to see Tom there, even if they couldn't go together.

•

On Monday evening, the first act was Corrie and Baker, a singing, talking and dancing team. This was what Jane and Jonesy aspired to, Margaret realised, watching a breathtaking tango that used every inch of the small stage. Then Miss Corrie sang.

'Jane could out-sing that one,' Burnsie whispered, and Margaret had to agree. Burnsie didn't usually come to the fundraising events, but she had casually told Margaret she 'quite fancied' seeing the Sunshine Company, as if it had nothing to do with the fact that Jane was performing.

After Corrie and Baker came Clemo and Brady, jugglers and tumblers, who elicited gasps from the audience, and then Bert Devine, a tenor with such a mellow, velvety voice that some of the young ladies almost swooned.

'Bet he never has to sleep alone,' she heard one of the lifesavers say to a mate, and managed to not laugh or show that she'd heard. It was true that a voice like that would be very hard to say no to. Involuntarily, her eyes went to Tom. He'd stood up to give his seat to an elderly lady and now propped up the side wall, arms folded. He met her glance, and smiled; not a full smile, but a softening of his eyes, a small curl of his mouth, as involuntary as her glance. It was as though he had kissed her.

She looked back to the stage knowing she was blushing.

Then came Jane and Jonesy, announced as 'the new attraction at Clay's Coliseum'.

Jane looked lovely in the costume she'd had made for Clay's, a white handkerchief-hem dress with sequins that sparkled in the spotlight. Jonesy sprang up onto the stage with a young man's leap, his limp seemingly completely gone. They sang the funny song they'd performed at the audition, which was a good choice – if she'd been Jonesy, she wouldn't have wanted to try singing seriously right after Bert Devine.

The applause for them, the local act, was just as loud as for Corrie and Baker. As Jane took her bows as though she were being fed manna from heaven, Margaret stole a look at Burnsie; she had tucked the corners of her mouth in as though she were trying to stop herself grinning, but nothing could disguise the pride in her eyes. She even clapped.

There was a recitation of *The Man from Snowy River* by a woman who probably had never even see a horse close up, and then the Sunshine Company and Jane and Jonesy came back to lead the audience in singing 'Waltzing Matilda'.

The best part of the evening, though, was watching Jane on the way home in a special celebratory taxi. Changed into her normal clothes but still carrying the scent of greasepaint, she was uplifted, eyes shining, fingers tapping out the refrain of their song. Burnsie watched her indulgently.

'We weren't too bad, were we, Margi?' she asked suddenly.

Margaret laughed. 'You were wonderful!'

'We weren't bad, eh? As good as Corrie and Baker?' Her eyes were suddenly sharp.

'As good in the singing. But I don't think your dancing is up to their level yet,' Margaret admitted.

Jane drew in a deep breath, nodding. 'It will be. Jonesy's leg's getting better every day.'

Margaret couldn't resist asking. 'What did you think, Burnsie?'

Burnsie shot her a look, but she answered readily. 'Yes, you did well enough. I daresay I won't have to be ashamed of you when you perform at that devil's hole of a theatre.'

Jane laughed and hugged her. 'Oh, Mum!'

•

Burnsie refused to go to Jane's opening night, but the rest of them were there, and Margaret got to sit next to Tom, hoping the size of their group would disinfect any contact they had in the eyes of the law. They laid their arms together on the arm rest, the touch distracting her from everything. In the silences between the songs and laughter she could hear him breathe, feel the rise and fall of his chest, the tension in his thighs. He sat unnaturally still, and she knew he was resisting the urge to take her hand.

At interval, Tom bought her a lemonade and they stood on the edge of the group of Jane's friends, sipping genteelly. Nothing was said that the judge couldn't have listened to, but Tom's eyes spoke for him, reminding her of Clareville nights. His breath came a little shorter, and heat slid through her blood as he took the empty glass from her, touching her fingers in passing. When they went back into the theatre, Tom let Clara sit next to Margaret, with a quick glance to make sure she understood why.

She understood, all right. Why torture themselves? But all the length of her arm, from elbow to wrist, where his arm had touched, felt cold for the rest of the night.

Yet it was a wonderful night. Jane and Jonesy sang like nightingales, the other acts were only just barely as good, and they all went home very late, laughing and satisfied.

Jane lingered on the verandah when they got home, and Margaret stayed with her. It was a crisp, cold night with a gusty wind and the stars were out. Not a pleasant place to stay for long, but exhilarating for a while.

'I thought,' Jane said, one hand on the verandah post, leaning back and rocking from side to side, 'that it might be disappointing.' She came upright and turned fully to look at Margaret. 'You know. You get what you want after a long time, and it's not as good as you thought it would be.'

'Yes,' Margaret said, thinking of her own dreams of coming to Australia to a life with Frank.

'But it wasn't like that at all. It was even *better* than I thought it would be. It was good last night, but they were all people I've known forever. Tonight it was *strangers* clapping us!' She leaned back against the post, the light from the transom streaming out to colour her like a patchwork. She looked like a stranger. Like someone too beautiful, too glamorous to be Margaret's friend.

For the first time, Margaret felt the same fear she saw in Burnsie's eyes whenever Jane's performing was mentioned. She was afraid for Jane, yes, that she'd be injured or seduced or disappointed. But she was also afraid for herself, that this new Jane wouldn't have any room in her life for home and family.

A long moment of silence allowed that fear to bite sharply. She realised how much she'd come to depend on Jane's honesty and common sense, on her friendship. She wouldn't want to hold Jane back, but she wondered if Jane could possibly maintain her old ties once she'd moved fully into this new world.

The wind gusted and sent the boughs of the trees waving wildly.

'Ah well,' Jane said. 'Back to Earth. Must be nippy enough even for you, eh, Margi?'

She moved to the door and Margaret followed her. 'This? This is nothing. Not even a flake of snow!'

They went in to find hot cocoa and raisin toast waiting for them; Burnsie was going to ensure, Margaret realised, that Jane found coming home just as pleasant as she could make it.

It made her eyes prickle with tears. She didn't think about her own parents much, because it hurt so, but it was times like this that she missed them the most.

37

All the next day Tom wrestled with the need to see Margaret. Being with her, even in a crowd, just seemed to feed his desire for her – not just physical desire, but a bone-deep ache to be in her presence, to feel those green eyes upon him, that vibrant smile warm him.

He dallied at knocking-off time, tidying up the tool shed, half-hoping to bump into her on his way home; but then he realised how dangerous that might be. He'd be better off making sure they *didn't* meet, if he wanted that divorce to go through on time.

So when the boss closed the gates, he turned left instead of right, down Victoria Street to McCliver's, the nor-easterly wind at his back bringing the scent of the ocean.

Old man McCliver and his family never paid much attention to knocking-off time. They were to be found at all hours, putting in more hours than God gave on their beloved yachts. They made punts and barges for pay, but they loved their racing yachts.

Since moving out of Burnsie's, Tom had taken to dropping in a couple of times a week, silently lending a hand where one was needed, taking in everything they did and trying to figure out why they did it.

He found the quiet, turpentine-scented shed felt more like a church once the hands had knocked off; a place for quiet contemplation and deliberate action. Each movement was purposeful. The light of the lamps shone along the sleek hulls as though blessing both them and him.

This evening, only the old man was in the big shed, to the side, working on a little sailboat. Too small to be called a yacht, it was a one-man skiff with a centre mast. It was a repair job, brought in with a sprung board the week before and put aside, 'until we have time to have a look at it' young McCliver, Hamish, had told him.

McCliver looked up when Tom came in and gave a jerk of the head – his normal greeting. A jovial man outside the shed, once he put his hand to the work he retreated into silence. Wordlessly, he pointed at a pot of varnish sitting on a side bench. Tom brought it over.

McCliver was sanding a recently replaced board. Tom took a rag and wiped off the dust after him, the two of them finding a rhythm that was as soothing as a lullaby.

Taking up the varnish, McCliver paused and then handed it to Tom.

'You've got the touch for it, I'm thinkin',' he said. 'Let's see what kind of job ye make of it.'

It was a test. Before he started, he looked at the grain of the rest of the hull, the way the varnish had been laid on it, and tried to match the almost invisible brush strokes. The old man watched for a few moments, grunted, and walked away.

Afterwards, when Tom was washing up, McCliver brought over two tin mugs and tacitly invited him to sit on an upturned barrel. He took another barrel himself. The tang of whisky came up from the mug and they shared a silent toast.

It was a good moment; the best in a while. What would it be like to work here full-time? To make, instead of destroy? Like the lifesaving, it spoke to a part of himself that had been stripped bare by the war. He was so sick of destruction.

With each stroke of the brush along the grain, Tom had felt something settling in him. He'd always loved work, until the war, and he'd missed the simple pleasure of doing a job well, a job that was worth doing. Losing that feeling had hit him harder than he'd admitted to himself until now, when he felt it again. This was a job worth doing, and the doing of it not only reclaimed the part of himself he'd lost, it opened up possibilities for who he might become.

The painstaking craft sang to him, like a promise of peace. To work, moment by moment, towards something beautiful and useful – that was a life he yearned towards almost as strongly as he wanted Margi.

What the hell. It couldn't hurt to ask.

'You wouldn't have a job going, would you, sir?'

McCliver eyed him shrewdly. 'Mebbe. I'm losing my journeyman – my nephew Hamish, he's got a mind to go to the auld country, work with my cousin a while in Aberdeen. He'll be off in a week, and Home for Christmas. I could bring ye in as a fourth-year apprentice to take his place. I had a mind to ask you, but I didn't think ye'd take to apprentice wages.'

'Fourth year? I don't know enough.'

'Ye don't know much more than young Jacko at the boat end of things. But ye know wood, don't ye?'

'Yes.'

'And ye're smart enough. More than that, ye've got the feel of it. Can't teach that.'

'So . . .'

'You'd do a year's apprenticeship. Money's bad, but after that ye'd have your papers.'

'Could I learn it all in a year?'

'If ye try.' He chuckled and lifted his mug to Tom. 'Well, what d'ye say?'

He should discuss this with Margaret. But McCliver wasn't the kind of man who'd understand needing to consult a woman. And besides, by the time the divorce came through he'd be halfway through his apprenticeship. Tom clinked his mug against McCliver's.

•

He stopped at the corner of the street that led to the High House. If only he could tell her the good news, share the jubilation that was gradually fizzing through him. Not seeing her was a constant pain; an actual pain, like an old wound that ached in bad weather, like the scar on his face that hurt sometimes when he smiled. If she hadn't come so faithfully to watch the lifesaving practice, he wouldn't have been able to stand it.

No use going there now. He continued on to the flat, thinking about boats.

A boat-builder. That was a good, respectable job, a *beautiful* trade. Part of him had been a bit ashamed to offer Margaret no more than a leading hand at a sawmill. It would have been different if he'd been a foreman. This was better. Better all round, even if money would be a bit tight at the start.

He smacked his hand against the wall in sheer good spirits and bounded up the stairs to tell Bill all about it.

38

Now life had a new rhythm, with Jane no longer available for nightly walks, and Tom never to be seen. Margaret kept her head down and did what she had to do. Went to work, studied her books about pottery and furniture, and helped Burnsie with cooking and cleaning, trying to step into Jane's shoes at least that much so Burnsie didn't have to do everything herself.

Once a fortnight or so, she, Clara and Sissie went up to see Jane and Jonesy perform. They got free tickets sometimes, which helped the budget, as Margaret was still saving frantically to pay for the divorce.

She waited, those nights, and she and Jane went home together, getting the last tram down the hill.

'When you and Jonesy sing that love song,' she said, one Friday night, as they walked from the tram stop, 'you really make us believe you're in love.'

Jane glanced at her and smiled wryly. It was hard to see her in the dark; even the streetlights just lit her pale head and left her face in shadow.

'You mean, am I in love with him?'

'I know it's none of my business . . .'

'No, fair enough, I asked you about Tom.' Jane paused for a long moment, pulling her shawl closer around her. 'I'm waiting to make up my mind.'

'What for?'

'You know how I met Jonesy?'

Margaret had heard the story. Jonesy had been a patient at the Repat Hospital while Jane was a VAD nurse.

'The men . . . When you nurse someone back to health, specially someone who's been as sick as Jonesy, sometimes they kind of *fix* on you. A bit like a baby duckling when it comes out of the egg. As though you're their link to staying alive.'

'And Jonesy was like that?' It explained a lot.

'Mmm. He's changing, now we're partners. Maybe what he feels won't last, once his leg is fully healed and he's back to being his own man. Maybe it will.'

'But what do *you* want?'

Jane flicked a smile at her. 'I'm damned if I know myself. Sometimes I think he's the love of my life, and sometimes I think I'd be a fool if I let myself care for him. So, I'm waiting. And in the meantime, I'm having fun.'

Waiting. Margaret was waiting too.

It was a strange, suspended time. She was neither flesh nor fowl nor good red herring for real, now. Not a wife, not a widow, not a divorcée, not a single woman. Long weeks went by without word from Mr Quinn – he had engaged a barrister for the court date and now there was nothing to be done until then.

She put Frank out of her mind. That was a different life. It was behind her now.

Australian winter days were wonderfully long. There was none of the getting-up-in-the-dark and leaving-work-in-the-dark she'd known in English winters. Day after day of brilliant sunshine made it hard to believe it was winter – until that wind hit you. Still, when the days started to get longer, she was glad.

Soon it would be warm enough to swim again.

She went to bed each night promising herself to go to sleep quickly, but every night she found herself remembering Tom, wondering where he was, how he was. If he missed her as much as she was missing him.

Thank God for patrol training. Even in winter, the lifesavers practised on Tuesdays and Wednesdays.

She sat on the beach as the afternoon slid into evening and watched the lifesaving team practise their rescues. Margaret was fascinated as always by the way the lifesavers used a belt attached to a line to make sure they made it back to shore, even in heavy seas. The team on the sand fed the line out from a reel, and there were several men between the reel and the rescuer, making sure the line didn't snag. It was a complex and strangely compelling sight, to see the rescuer towing the person in distress back to shore, with such fervent support from the other men. Even in practice there was great tension, and she could only imagine how everyone would feel when the danger was real.

Tom wasn't asked to swim a rescue, not yet. As a new member of the team, he was one of the men who kept the line clear of snags and then pulled heartily on it to bring the others home. The sun was setting by this time, and it turned the waves and the lifesavers a golden brown, as though they'd been captured in bronze; muscles taut and bodies leaning back against the undertow, focused on helping. On life.

And Tom was there, practising as hard as the others. They wore woollen guernseys over their swimming costumes, but their legs must have been freezing. His legs were strong; she couldn't help it, she drank in every glimpse of him she could.

The training sessions got her through the week. And maybe made it easier for him, too; she knew he saw her, huddled up at the foot of the promenade wall, wrapped in her coat, watching. Shameless.

They couldn't talk in public. But sometimes she waited until the men were streaming past her to the clubhouse. Then he would linger, last in line, and they would look at each other, hungry for a glance, before he had to go in.

Meagre, but it seemed enough fuel to keep her love for him blazing.

She hoped the same was true of him.

Sundays were the oasis they returned to: she and Jane both home for the day, everything the way it had always been, except for Tom's absence. She and Jane walked a little around the bay, sometimes went to a concert, darned their stockings, read, wrote letters. Margaret had received mail from girls she had worked with during the war, and she picked up her correspondence with them manfully, like a burden. But once she had written the first letter, admitting her circumstances and telling them about the divorce, those few who wrote back became a lifeline, reminding her of who she had been and where she came from, that she hadn't just been washed up like sea-wrack on Manly Beach.

Her birthday was in mid September, on a spring day that seemed to bring a whiff of summer with it. The wattle was out, and daffodils and tulips were still waving in Burnsie's garden.

Margaret was touched to find that all of the residents had laid presents at her place for breakfast: the students, some sheet music; Mr Lewis, lavender soap; Burnsie, a new scarf she had knitted herself, in soft shades of blue and green. Jane's present was delayed. 'Come up to Clay's tonight and I'll give it to you backstage afterwards.'

Margaret had been backstage a couple of times, each time amused by the contrast between the gilded velvet opulence of the theatre and the bare boards and unpainted walls of behind-the-scenes.

She found the women's dressing room easily enough after the show was over. Jane and Jonesy had been moved up to the second half of the programme, right before the finale, which was quite a promotion, apparently, so Jane had only had a moment or two to take off her make-up and get into her street clothes before Margaret arrived.

Margaret tapped on the door and a couple of chorus girls came out, giggling, still in their robes. One of them flicked Margaret on the arm and said, 'Save some for me!' 'There's enough to go around,' another girl said, which produced more laughter from the others.

Perhaps there was cake. That would be like Jane. Margaret pushed the door open and Jane confronted her.

'Now, don't go mad at me. No one here will tell on you, and you know this was what you *really* wanted for your birthday.'

She slipped out and held the door open for Margaret, bewildered, to go through.

Tom was waiting for her, looking enormous in the tiny room, and completely out of place among the boas and lace and spangles.

She was in his arms before Jane had closed the door.

•

That night she had trouble sleeping, and woke early, when the clouds were flooded with gold and rose and the palest of pinks. Margaret sat by the window and tried not to think too much about Tom. Not to yearn for him, not to dissolve with love and loneliness for him. She wasn't sure if Jane had done them a favour or not. It felt doubly hard to be without him this morning.

It was warm again. Perhaps this weekend they could go surf-shooting, could once again fly in an ecstasy of foam and movement. The idea seemed impossibly far away. She remembered this; it was the way the idea of peacetime had seemed in the middle of the war. A colleague would say, 'When this is all over', and everyone would nod, and in their heads would be a sunlit image of green fields and happiness; but the images never had any substance – they were more like the memory of a dream.

It was hard to piece together how she had come to this: in a foreign country, waiting for the next day and the day after that, until she could testify in her own divorce hearing. A possibility she would have laughed at even a year ago.

What was the first step to ending up here? Marrying Frank so quickly because he persuaded her to, in case he was killed on the front? Or further back . . . when her friend Queenie had said, 'Come out with my Ted and some of his mates', and she had met Frank for the first time? Or even further . . . she remembered her mother, wrapped in one of her eternal print pinafores, in the middle of their kitchen, drying off the carving knife and saying, 'Don't you let yourself get stuck in this place, love. You go down and register for war work. Who knows where you'll end up?' And before that, the elocution lessons. And before that? Maybe just that look in her mother's eyes, the sad, hungry look that gave Margaret the determination to be more than a West Bromwich housewife.

That was the past. She yearned to be able to see ahead, to have the decree absolute in her hand, to stand on that precipice of the future and see the life in store.

That seemed a long way off, like the green fields and happiness of a dream.

•

A week later, as Friday afternoon slid down into another gusty golden sunset, Burnsie called her in from the verandah where she had been drying her hair.

'Telephone, love!'

The hall seemed dark after the brightness outside, and she fumbled picking up the earpiece and the speaking set.

'Hello?'

'Margaret? Oh, thank God.'

'Frank?' She couldn't be mistaken in that voice. 'You're not supposed to contact me—'

'It's Glad! She's in the Women's Hospital. Something about high blood pressure.'

'Oh no, Frank, I'm so sorry.'

'Thing is, I have to work this weekend. All day tomorrow anyway, and maybe Sunday.'

'I can visit her, if that's what—'

'It's Violet, see? I don't have anyone to leave her with. I know it's a cheek, but could you . . .'

The lawyers would disapprove, but she could hear his desperation, and his fear for Gladys.

'I work in the mornings, Saturday, too, Frank . . . hold on a minute.'

Jane was on the stairs, her eyebrows raised. Margaret covered the mouthpiece and whispered, 'Gladys is in hospital and he wants me to take Violet tomorrow.'

'I'll take her for the morning,' Jane said immediately. She was salt of the earth, Jane.

'Look, Frank, if you can get her here tomorrow morning, we'll sort something out.'

'Thank Christ. All right. I'll see you tomorrow morning.'

She hung up slowly, worried now. Gladys was so slight, it wasn't hard to believe she was ill.

'It's very kind of you, Jane . . .' she began.

'Poor little blighter,' Jane said. 'She's only three, isn't she? We'll be all right. I'll take her to the Coogee Aquarium, and then we can meet you here after work.'

'I'll take her over to see her mum afterwards, then, and Frank can pick her up there.'

She hoped with all her heart that this moment of kindness wouldn't derail the divorce. But none of this was Frank's fault; and although she'd fallen on her feet here, with Burnsie and Jane to lean on, she remembered all too well what it was like to live alone, with no family left, and no one to turn to if things went bad.

There had been a time, when she was working at Reading Station, when she'd caught the first wave of Spanish Flu and spent the next eight days in her bedsit wondering if she was going to die, and so ill that she half-hoped she would. If the baker and the milkman hadn't delivered as usual, she'd have died of starvation. As it was, she lived on bread and milk and eggs until she was well enough to get dressed and stumble out to the shops.

Her landlady wouldn't come near her for fear of catching the flu, and she hadn't known any of the other tenants well enough to ask them for help. That had been a dark time.

She had to help Gladys if she could.

39

The house Margaret was living in was so posh Frank was almost afraid to knock at the front door. Maybe he should go round the back? But he couldn't see how to get down the side of the house, so he grasped Vi's hand more firmly and headed up the brick path.

An older lady opened the door, and he relaxed as he saw her print dress and apron.

'So, you're Frank Dalton, are you?' she asked, looking him up and down like he was a side of meat.

'Yes, missus.' Then she gazed down at Violet and her eyes softened.

'Come on in, then. I'm Mrs Burns. I'll bet you're hungry, are you?' she asked Violet.

The hallway was even grander than he'd expected, and he kept his free hand in his pocket so he wouldn't put dirt on anything. At least Vi was clean, dressed in her best gingham frock and blue jumper and white socks with almost-new shoes.

Kitchens were always friendly places. And there was Margaret, standing by the counter, hastily eating a slice of toast. And another woman, a good-looking girl with blonde hair.

'Hello, Violet!' Margaret said. She came around the table and squatted down to smile into Violet's eyes. 'Remember me?'

'Aunty Mar-Mar,' Vi whispered.

And then Margaret smiled that lovely warm smile of hers. It was that smile that had made him fall in love with her in the first place, but he found that his heart didn't turn over as it once had. He was too worried about Glad.

'That's right. And this is Aunty Jane. She's going to look after you this morning while I work, and then we're going to go and see Mummy.'

'They won't let kids in the wards,' Frank said. 'That's why I couldn't leave her there.'

'Well, I'll see Mummy for you and then you'll know she's all right. How about that?'

Frank watched as Violet nodded. She was always shy, but she took Margaret's hand easily and went quite happily to sit on a chair at the table and have breakfast with Jane. Margaret tucked a strand of hair behind Violet's ear, and Vi looked up and beamed at her. Marge would be a bloody good mother. He pushed that thought out of his mind and concentrated on Vi.

'Bye, baby,' Frank said, kissing her.

'Bye bye, Papa.' Violet waved a little chubby hand. He loved her so much that it cast whatever he felt for Margaret right out of him. Vi was what mattered – the women were right about that, even if he hadn't liked the idea of a divorce much at first.

Margaret walked out with him to the verandah.

'I'll take her over to the hospital this afternoon and you can pick her up from me there. Then bring her over tomorrow morning and I'll have her for the day.'

'Thanks, Marge.' He took a deep breath and settled himself. Underneath all the worry about Violet and the disturbance of seeing Margaret again was a bone-deep fear about Glad and the new baby.

'Listen, when you go to the hospital, see if you can get anything out of the nurses, will you? They won't tell us men anything.'

She nodded reassuringly. 'I'll see you there – what, about five?'

'Yes. Easily by five. Thanks.'

He didn't know what else to say, so he turned and walked away.

•

He spent the day worrying in turn about Gladys and Violet, and made a run for it as soon as the bell rang to end the day. A quick wash up in the locker room and he was off. One thing about working at Eveleigh Railway Yard was that the train was right there. He hopped on a slow-mover as it left Macdonaldtown station, hauling himself up into the open door, and rode the door into Central. Then trams to the Royal Women's. Every leg of the journey seemed to take forever.

The nurse let him into Gladys's ward reluctantly, as though his working clothes made him unfit for a hospital visit. The poor ward, as it was called, had a dozen beds in it, mostly filled with heavily pregnant women. But the staff had done what they could to make it nice – there were big windows, and down the centre of the ward, where the nurses' desk was, stood a row of palms in pots. Gladys's bed was in the middle, opposite one of the palms.

Glad looked a shocker: pale, dark circles under her eyes, but with a hectic flush on her cheeks.

She opened her eyes when he touched her hand, and smiled. It made him want to cry a bit, she was so brave. A bonzer girl, Glad. He was lucky to have her.

'Vi?' she whispered.

'She's with Margaret. They'll be here soon.'

She half-nodded and closed her eyes again. Her hands seemed swollen. Was that normal? He held her hand and sat back in the visitor's chair and closed his eyes, too. He wished he still believed in prayers, but that belief had been knocked out of him in the trenches.

A quiet footfall some time later made him open his eyes. Margaret, with the light from the window behind her turning her red-brown hair into a flame. She had Violet by the hand, and a doctor in a white coat was following her.

'This is Doctor Carmichael,' she said quietly. 'Doctor, this is Frank, Gladys's husband. Now, Vi, you sit in Papa's chair and say hello to Mummy.'

Gladys smiled wanly as Vi scrambled up into the chair and grabbed hold of her arm.

The doctor tilted his head and they moved away from the bed to the middle of the room. Frank could feel a palm frond prickling against his leg.

'We're not happy with Mrs Dalton's condition, Mr Dalton, as I've just been telling your sister.' Sister? Margaret was a clever one.

'What's wrong?'

'It's a condition that has recently been named preeclampsia. No need to go into the details, but it's very serious. We're going to start labour early.'

'Can you do that?'

The doctor stroked a thin ginger moustache and smiled, looking down his nose even though he was two inches shorter than Frank. Frank pushed down the impulse to punch his lights out. As if that would help.

'Oh yes. And we have a very good success rate here at the Royal. But I have to warn you, nonetheless, that there is a risk. More of a risk if we just sit and wait, however.'

'I see . . .'

The doctor seemed to take pity on him. 'I'm telling you to say whatever you want to say to her now, man. Just in case.'

Frank felt the blood drain from his face, and he must have swayed, because the doctor caught him by the arm.

'Come, come, none of that! You have to be strong for her and the child. Buck up, man!'

'Yes. Yes, I'm all right.'

'I should think so. Very well. I'll be back in half an hour to start the procedure.'

Hesitantly, Frank approached the bed. Gladys was sitting up now, smiling at Violet who was cuddled up against her shoulder, and talking; her soft, sweet voice a little fainter than usual. Frank went to the other side of the bed and took her hand. It felt odd under his fingers, the swollen flesh neither soft nor hard.

'They say they're going to bring the baby on early,' he said.

'Yes, the nurse told me. Can't be early enough for me.'

Margaret smiled at her. 'I'll leave the three of you to chat,' she said. 'Violet, I'll see you tomorrow, won't I? We might go to the zoo, how about that?'

'Thanks, Margaret,' Gladys said. 'I know she'll be safe with you.'

They exchanged a look and Margaret nodded, as if sealing a bargain, then kissed Violet's cheek and left.

Frank cleared his throat. Say what you want to say, the doctor had said, but he didn't know what that was. Better to say what he *ought* to say. What he should have said long since.

'I love you, Glad.'

Her little face lit up and her eyes filled with tears. The fear the doctor had brought him flared up almost into panic, and made the words true. He did love her. Not the same way he had loved Margaret, but truly, and deeply. He didn't dare think about losing her, or the baby.

'Oh, and I love you too, Frank! So much.'

He bent to gently kiss her lips, but Violet pulled his head over to her so that the three of them touched foreheads. It was like being in a small, dark, happy cave; he and Glad both kissed Violet, and that was all right. That was how it ought to be.

40

Not for the first time, Margaret was thankful for the peace and calm of the ferry ride. She went to the front of the boat and let the cold spray refresh her.

It was strange, how quickly she and Gladys had become friends. Allies. Only two meetings. And yet, that afternoon in the hospital, when Gladys had looked at her with a plea in her eyes, she had known what was coming.

'The nurse told me to say my goodbyes, just in case,' Gladys had said. Margaret must have flinched, because Gladys patted her hand. 'It's all right, it might not happen. But if it does . . .'

Violet was playing with Gladys's hair, sliding her little fingers through its ominously dull strands. Gladys flicked her eyes up at her, then looked significantly at Margaret.

'If . . . you know, *if* . . .' Margaret nodded wordlessly, but she took Gladys's hand and held it tightly. '*If*, then she'll need someone. A woman. A *nice* woman.' What could she do? She nodded. 'Frank's a good dad, but . . . but I'll feel better if I know . . .'

She forced herself to speak.

'Don't worry. I'll keep an eye on her. I'll always be there if she needs me.'

Gladys's eyes filled with tears.

'Don't cry, Mummy!' Violet said, almost scolding her. 'Be a good girl.'

Gladys and Margaret both laughed helplessly.

'All right, darling, I'll be a good girl. And you be a good girl too, for Papa and Aunty Margaret.'

And then Frank had come back and she'd left as soon as she decently could.

•

The next morning, when Frank didn't come to drop Violet off, she knew she had to go to the hospital.

She wished with all her heart that she could call Tom and say, 'Come with me.' Say, 'I'm afraid. I won't know what to say or do if the worst has happened.' Say, 'I won't be able to look Violet in the face. Come and hold my hand.' She longed to feel the comfort of his arms around her.

Jane was out with a party of friends, so Margaret went to the hospital on her own, carrying a bag of Anzac biscuits Burnsie had made, 'for the little girl'.

When she saw that Gladys's bed was empty, she asked the nurse.

'Mrs Dalton's still in the delivery room. She's had a hard night of it, I'm afraid.'

Still. Labour took time, she knew, but . . . Gladys was so slight, so thin. How could she have the stamina to keep going for so long?

The delivery rooms were upstairs. There was a waiting room; and there were Frank and Violet. He looked shocking – he probably hadn't had any sleep at all – and Violet was bouncing with boredom.

'Aunty Mar-Mar!' She ran and threw herself into Margaret's arms for a cuddle. Over her head Margaret asked Frank a silent question. He shrugged, looking defeated.

'See what I have for you, lamb?' Margaret said, handing over a biscuit.

'Bikkie!' Obeying some rule of her mother's, Violet handed the biscuit back to Margaret, struggled up onto one of the hard chairs that lined the room until her back was firmly against it, and held her hand out. Margaret gave the biscuit to her and she nodded a grave thanks before biting into it with gusto. Such a sweet little girl, so much like her mother. Children were so easy to love; they got under your skin in a moment and then they were there for life. She kissed Violet's forehead and sat next to her, arm around her shoulders. The little body nestled into hers.

'Will you stay for a while?' Frank asked. His voice was husky with tiredness. She had to say yes. Anything else would have been cruel. And everyone here thought she was Frank's sister. She'd better keep her gloves on so no one saw her wedding ring.

An hour later she was trying to teach Violet how to play cat's cradle with an old piece of string Frank had found in his pocket, and Frank was pacing up and down. They were no further along; two other fathers were waiting nervously. It was only looking at them that she realised how young Frank was. They were all just boys, really, not even twenty-five. If it hadn't been for the war, they might not have thought about marriage or children for a good long while.

Occasionally, a nurse would come in to announce, 'Not long now!' to one or other of them and, once, 'It's a girl!'

Around lunchtime, when Margaret was considering taking Violet out into the fresh air to find something to eat, a big Italian family came in, the mother and sisters of the pregnant woman demanding to be allowed into the delivery room while the nursing staff stood united against them. The young father simply sat in a corner and left the women to it, staring into his hands as though the answer to all life's mysteries was there.

The Italian women were loud and demonstrative and waved their hands around a lot. Violet found them very entertaining, chuckling whenever one of them shouted. Margaret wondered why the nurses didn't just let them in. Most women gave birth at home, surrounded by their female relatives, so why not?

She was so caught up in the little drama that she failed to notice the doctor come into the room until he was almost in front of them. The doctor, still in his surgical gown. It couldn't be good if the doctor came himself instead of sending a nurse.

'Mr Dalton?'

Frank forced himself to his feet. She steadied him when he almost stumbled.

'I'm sorry, Mr Dalton, we did everything we could.'

'Gladys?'

'I'm sorry.'

Frank seemed blank, as if he couldn't quite understand. Margaret felt his pain as a knife under her own ribs. She had to ask, because he didn't seem able to.

'The baby?'

The doctor sighed, looking at her with undisguised weariness and a touch of shame. 'I'm sorry. He was stillborn.'

'He . . .' Frank said. His eyelids flickered, and he passed his hands over his eyes. 'It was a boy?'

'I'm sorry. Your wife's condition meant that he was born blue. It's better that he didn't survive.'

They understood him. Deformity, feeble-mindedness, physical incapacity; it was all there implicit in his tone. Better this way.

Frank just stood there, as if he hadn't taken it in. Violet was playing hide and seek with one of the Italian children.

'Well, I've got another one starting. I must be getting back. Sister will give you the paperwork.' The doctor put his hand out to Frank and Frank shook it automatically. 'I'm very sorry, Mr Dalton.'

As though the doctor's departure had flipped a switch, Frank sat down on the edge of his chair. He took long, wavering breaths: one, another . . . on the third his eyes filled and he began to cry. Soundlessly, shoulders shaking but eyes staring blankly straight ahead. His hands trembled.

Margaret sat next to him and took his hands, racked with compassion.

It was so hard to see him like this; the affection she still felt was stronger than she'd realised. He'd tried so hard to do the right thing.

She pressed a handkerchief into his hand. It was only a small square of linen, clearly inadequate, but it was all she had. He looked down at the dainty white cloth and pushed it back at her, as though worried he would dirty it. He fished a big blue-and-white kerchief out of his pocket and buried his face in it, blowing his nose like a little boy.

It was impossible that Gladys should be gone. Impossible. She was so gentle, so honest. Perhaps the most simply honest person Margaret had ever met. Her throat was as hard as a stone; she could barely breathe, fighting tears. She didn't have the right to cry.

'What's matter, Papa? Where's my baby? Want my baby!'

Frank snatched Violet up and held her tight, his face buried in her tummy. She wrapped her arms around his neck and kissed the top of his head. 'Papa sad. Kiss it better.'

He began to sob. Margaret could only just catch his muttering. 'Didn't know. Didn't know how much . . .'

She stroked Violet's hair, and patted Frank's back. There was nothing that was worth saying. The other fathers avoided them, as if they would bring bad luck, but the Italian mother came over and detached Violet from Frank with the kind efficiency of someone who had raised a brood of children.

'Come along, bambina, come have some chocolata. You let your papa alone for a while.'

'Choc!' Violet said, clapping her hands, and went willingly.

After a few moments, Frank's sobs quietened and he wiped his face with his kerchief.

'Sorry. Sorry about that.'

'There's nothing to be sorry for. Do you . . . do you want me to see the sister about . . . the paperwork?'

'Thanks. Yes, thanks.'

Her steps were reluctant, as though until she held the official document Gladys's life wasn't formally over. But it was the only thing she could do for Frank right now.

She found the sister in charge of the ward and received the death certificate. The paper crackled under her hands, so she forced herself to relax her grip.

'She'll be kept here at the hospital until you've made arrangements. As soon as possible, please.' Perhaps Margaret's expression showed shock, because the nurse added, 'I know that sounds harsh but it's been a hard winter and we've had several cases . . . we did everything possible, you know.'

But sometimes, everything possible wasn't enough.

41

The funeral was at St Stephen's, the closest church to Gladys and Frank's home, on Wednesday, an inappropriately fine day, although the air was cool and the wind brisk. A short service, followed by a graveside prayer and the committal of the body. Bodies. Gladys was buried with her son in the same coffin. Margaret couldn't help but picture her, lying with her arms around her little boy, the two of them so alone, but united.

The rector seemed genuinely saddened. Gladys, it appeared, had been a regular church-goer, despite her unconventional living arrangements, and was known at the church as Mrs Mortimer.

Margaret was touched when Tom turned up; saying nothing, not coming near her, but there where she could see him and call him if she needed him. Despite the cold wind, she was filled with warmth, and tried to put all that she felt into her expression as she glanced at him. Perhaps she was successful. The tight lines around his mouth eased, and he returned her smile.

Margaret was surprised by the number of people there. Gladys's friends from the biscuit factory, she thought, made up most of them, the ones who were quietly crying or watching red-eyed. One was expecting, and she kept her hands protectively over her abdomen the whole time, and cast anxious glances at the sky, where clouds were gathering.

When it was over, and the rector had announced that there would be refreshments served back at Denison Street, she went to Frank, sure that Tom would wait for her until after she had made her respects.

Frank seemed dazed, emptied out by grief. Hands shaking. He kept looking down as if to find Violet, and then remembering that she wasn't there.

'Vi's with the neighbour,' he told her, reassuring himself.

'She'll be fine there, I'm sure. I'm so sorry, Frank.'

'Mmm. Yes. Do you think I did the right thing, putting them together?' He blurted it out, as though it had been torturing him and she was the first person he could ask.

'Yes, I'm absolutely sure. It's what Gladys would have wanted. She would have wanted to keep him close.'

He nodded, his eyes full of tears, and kept nodding until she put a hand on his arm.

He put his own hand over it. 'I'm so glad I've got you to turn to, Margaret. I don't know what I'd do if I didn't. But at least I don't have to worry about Violet.'

She pulled her hand away slowly, feeling a sudden, deep chill. 'Frank, what are you talking about?'

'Violet.' His voice was puzzled. He spoke slowly, as though she were a stupid child and he were the teacher. 'Now the divorce is off, you'll be able to look after Violet.'

Her mind went blank. She stared at him for so long that he shuffled his feet and blinked. Tom moved closer; she was aware of him, at her shoulder, as though her body tracked him even when her back was turned.

'You know,' Frank said, not even glancing at Tom. 'The divorce, all that, was all for the kiddies. So they'd have proper parents.'

'But—' It was all she could say. He was right. That was the reason – the only reason – she'd given him. For the children, she'd said. The fact that since then she'd fallen even deeper in love with Tom McBride . . . Frank didn't know or care about that, and why should he?

Frank looked at her in confusion mixed with concern.

'I agreed to that divorce so Glad and I could be married and make things right for the kids. That was it. Now you and I – we're all the parents Violet has. We *have* to look after her.'

The reminder of her promise to Gladys was like a jab in the stomach. But they couldn't discuss it here. People were looking; Tom was standing right behind her and she could sense him getting ready to speak.

'We'll talk about it later. This isn't the place or the time.' She hesitated. 'I have to get back to work.'

'Come over after work, then,' Frank said. He turned to greet other mourners, people he knew, probably knew better than he knew her.

She and Tom walked away together, in silence.

•

On the tram, sitting together inside while the heavens opened around them, she slid her hand down between them and tucked her fingers into his. It was unwise, but Tom was the only secure point in a whirling universe. It had not occurred to her that Frank would want to derail the divorce. How hardened had she become, that she hadn't known immediately that it was now her duty to return to him? How caught up in her love, her need, for Tom?

'I don't know what to do,' she said, very quietly.

Tom's fingers tightened around hers. 'I don't know either,' he said.

She was surprised. Part of her had counted on him talking her out of her marriage; part of her had wanted him to succeed. But he was a good, honourable man. He wouldn't do that.

'If I hadn't met you . . .' That was the truth, she supposed. If she hadn't met Tom, she would have gone back to Frank. She had convinced herself that she was being noble, that she was considering only the needs of the children and of Gladys, but that wasn't true.

Oh, all her concern for Gladys had been true. But it wasn't the only thing driving her decision. Underneath had been this dark, passionate desire for Tom.

Which made her no better than a common-or-garden adulteress.

'I wouldn't have married him if I'd known about Violet.'

And that was true, too, and had to be considered. Or did it? Plenty of women found out horror stories about their husband's past, but they didn't divorce over it.

'He's got a hide,' Tom said with force, 'expecting you to look after that little girl.'

That was an aspect she hadn't considered, and she dismissed it. It wasn't Violet's fault that her birth was bad. That was the parents' sin, both of them. Unbidden, though, she remembered Gladys's pale face, and how she herself had promised to 'keep an eye' on Violet.

Margaret imagined, for a moment, living in that little house in Denison Street, alone with Violet, waiting for Frank to come home.

Eight months ago – yes, almost to the day, it was eight months and two days since she'd arrived in Sydney – that life was all she had wanted. All she had dreamed of. A little house, children, Frank. And the big blue Australian sky over all of it.

A squall of rain hit the tram windows and the unseasonable cold swept up her legs. About the only rule of life she'd found true was that you never got what you expected.

Again she conjured up the picture of her possible future: Frank and Violet and maybe another little baby, a family happy and content and together. Loving. Was it possible? He thought it was. She could love Violet easily enough, and enjoy being her mother. But Frank . . .

She'd loved him once. Couldn't she love him again? He hadn't changed.

No, but she had. Not just Tom; the war, the death of her parents, surviving on her own for those long months until she could get a berth on a war-bride ship, the experience of being abandoned and having to manage her own life in this new country. All those things, and more, had changed her. If she'd met Frank now, would she have fallen in love with him?

She wasn't sure that, now, Frank's honesty and simple admiration – and, be honest, good looks – would be enough. What she felt for Tom cut through every bit of moral teaching she'd ever had. She was ashamed of herself. And more ashamed that part of her exulted in the strength of it, the deep, basic need she had for him.

She didn't have to give in to that need. She could be better than her own base instincts. Surely.

'I don't think I can do it,' she said to Tom. 'Even if we don't get a divorce, I don't think I can go back to him.'

Tom was silent. She glanced at him and found him frowning.

'I think,' he said slowly, 'you have to give it a chance.'

'What?'

'Not go back to him,' he added hastily. 'Not go and . . . and live with him. But maybe give him a chance. Get to know him again.'

Whatever she had expected, this wasn't it. She couldn't breathe. Tom was supposed to, to . . .

'I thought—'

He turned quickly and held her hand tighter. 'If you were free, I'd marry you tomorrow.' He slowed, forcing words out quietly. The drumming of the rain on the tram roof, the clack of the tracks, almost drowned him out. She moved closer to hear him. 'I don't . . . I know what I want, but I don't know what's right.'

'Neither do I,' she whispered. Her eyes filled, and Tom brushed the tears away with his fingertips. She could feel his skin, rough from hard work. He was such a good man; she had dirtied him by dragging him through this mire.

'Whatever you decide, I'll stand by,' he said. 'If you get a divorce, I'll marry you the day after it's granted. If you don't . . . I won't reproach you.' Her tears overflowed and he gave her his handkerchief and waited silently while she wiped her eyes, bent over her in concern.

The tram jolted to a stop.

'Allll out allll change please!' the conductor shouted. Circular Quay.

They moved apart as though caught in a conspiracy and walked quickly through the crowd to the ferry wharf.

Together they waited, silently, and together they boarded the ferry when it came. They stayed inside, out of the squalls that howled against the windows. October was only a week away, and that was supposed to be swimming season. But today was a far cry from the golden days of summer when all she had to worry about was pretending to be a widow.

At Milson's Point they set off up the hill, the rain and wind pushing them from behind with cold hands.

Tom saw her to the front gate and then paused.

'Do you want to come in?' she asked.

'No,' he said. 'Better safe than sorry.'

He was so much taller than she that his umbrella overshadowed hers easily. He moved closer and put a hand against her cheek; the cold skin warmed instantly at his touch.

'I should go,' he said, but he didn't move. Margaret wanted to beg him to stay. To come in, to move back in, to – she didn't know what. Anything but tell her to give Frank a chance. She needed Frank and Tom to be on opposite sides, to give her a clear choice. Otherwise, she was lost.

'Tom—'

He bent and kissed her, his hand still warm on her face. She slid her arms around his neck, letting her umbrella and purse fall, uncaring. Who knew what the next days would bring? Since Gladys's death she had lived from moment to moment, and this moment was the best of them.

Warm, strong . . . she kissed him as though it were the last time, as though it were the first time. His hand moved into her short hair and gathered it together, pulled her head back gently; their bodies clung desperately.

The noise of horses' hooves coming down the street broke them apart. Tom picked up her things and handed them to her.

'Burnsie has my address. Let me know how things go.' He touched her cheek.

She nodded, then turned her face into his hand for a brief moment of comfort before moving inside, not looking back.

42

'Dalton, in here.' The boss, Maguire, was a big beefy Irishman with a loud voice and a hard fist. When he called, you went.

Frank put down his hammer, wiped his hands on the rag he kept hanging from his back pocket, and walked the length of the train shed to Maguire's small office: a cubicle of wood with one small window through which Maguire kept an eagle eye on the work in the shed. At the moment, though, he was standing in the doorway in his shirtsleeves, hands in his pockets.

'Yes, boss?'

'Got some good news for you.' The tone was jovial. Maguire put his thumbs under his braces and rocked back on his heels.

'Yerse?'

'Old Danny Hughes, in the Flying Gang, you know him?'

'Course. He trained me up.'

'That's right. He's retiring next month and he's given you the nod to take over from him as the ganger.'

Maguire beamed at him. It was an honour, no doubt about that, and he expected Frank to be overjoyed. The Flying Gang was the top-notch group – they went all over the state, repairing tracks and train stock wherever there was an emergency. Higher pay as the ganger – and lots of overtime, danger money, the works. He'd make twice what he made now. But he'd be away for weeks at a time, and no notice – the Gang got called and they went, no delays, no excuses. He couldn't look after Vi and be in the Gang.

What bloody bad timing.

Maguire was staring at him, frowning as he realised that Frank wasn't reacting with delight.

'What's the matter with you?'

'You know my old lady just . . . I only buried her yesterday.'

Maguire's face softened, a smidgen. 'Yeah, I heard. Sorry about that.'

'I've got this little girl. She's only three . . .'

'Well, you better find someone to look after her when you're away – or else you can find yourself another job. I've already got someone taking yours.'

'But—'

'No buts. You want to stay here, you work on the Gang. Twenty-fifth of October, morning shift.'

He turned on his heel and shut the door behind him. Frank could feel his gaze through the window all the long walk back.

•

That evening, after he picked up Vi from the neighbours, he managed to cook some mince on toast. Vi was listless, picking at her food, so different from the bright, happy little girl she had been that it broke his heart.

'Come on, love, eat your tea.' He picked up a spoon and fed her some mince, but she turned her head away after a couple of mouthfuls, her chin wobbling.

He picked her up and sat on the lounge with her in his lap, rocking her gently.

'Want Mummy,' she said, starting to cry.

'I know, love,' he said. 'I miss her too. But Mummy's gone to visit God.'

'Get her!'

'I wish I could, bub.' He buried his face in her hair and they cried a little, together, until Vi fell asleep. Frank let his head fall backwards to rest on the wall, staring up at a crack in the ceiling until his vision blurred.

A knock at the door. Probably another neighbour with a casserole or something. They'd been good like that.

He carried Vi into her little bed and went to the door.

A man stood there, with a woman behind him. Both in navy suits, both in their forties, the woman with her hair in a tight bun. Oh, no. He really didn't need any God-botherers right now.

'Mr Dalton?' the man asked.

'Yes, I'm Frank Dalton.'

'Child Protection.'

He felt the blood drain from his face, and had to clutch the doorframe to stay upright. No. *No.* He wasn't going to let them take Vi.

'It's all right, Mr Dalton,' the woman said. 'It's just a routine check-up. May we come in?'

He wanted to bar the door and never open it again, but he let them in, grudgingly. He knew better than to get them offside. Half his mates in the orphanage had been put there by Child Protection.

'Come through,' he said. He led them to the lounge room and they all sat. They looked around with unabashed judgement, taking in the mess, the uncleared dishes on a side table, the general air of frowstiness.

'Violet's asleep,' he cautioned them. Keep your voices low, he meant, and they nodded.

'We're just here to make sure you're coping,' the man said. 'That your daughter's all right. It can be hard for a man on his own.'

'We're doing fine.'

'We've been called in by the young woman who used to look after Violet, when your . . . when the child's mother was still working. She's worried that you don't have anyone to care for her during the day.' The woman looked sympathetic, but he knew that was a trap. Never show any weakness to them.

'The lady next door is looking after her,' he said. No need to tell them that she'd said he had to get someone else, quick smart. Or about the Flying Gang. 'And in the long term, my wife—' What to say that wouldn't sound insane? 'She'll be arriving from England. We got married during the war over there.'

They looked at each other, a swift, troubled glance. 'And she'll take on . . . er, another woman's child?'

'She loves kiddies,' Frank said. 'She knows all about Violet. Violet was conceived before I met Margaret.' All that was true.

'I see,' the woman said slowly. She scribbled something in her notebook. 'When is she arriving?'

He had to give himself a bit of leeway.

'The twenty-fifth of October,' he said. The day he started at the Flying Gang. If Margaret wasn't here by then it was all over anyway.

'We'll pop back again after that, shall we?' the woman said. He hated the way they made it sound like a social occasion, as though it was nothing, as though it wasn't about them stealing his daughter and locking her away.

'Yes,' he said. 'That'd be fine.'

He saw them to the door and closed it behind them with a shaking hand. Panic hit him.

He had to get Margaret back. For Violet. Because otherwise . . . he couldn't bear to think of Violet in an orphanage. Just like him. He'd be damned in hell before he did that.

They'd take her if he lost his job. Say he was 'incapable'. If he got booted out of the Railways – and Maguire wouldn't give him a reference, not him – what could he do? He'd never done anything else his whole working life but repair rolling stock and rails. Even in the Army, he'd spent most of his time doing the same. And there was only one Railways. There were no other jobs out there, not now. All the demobbed blokes were fighting over every vacancy.

But to keep his job, he had to go on the Gang, and then he'd be in the same position. Even if he found someone to look after her during the day, they wouldn't take her on for weeks at a time. No one would. And how could he trust them, anyway, strangers as they'd have to be? The woman who'd turned them in wasn't prepared to take Vi back even for working days, let alone nights. Oh, no, but she was prepared to open her big mouth to Child Protection. Everyone *knew* you didn't do that.

Violet needed a mother. She needed Margaret. She *loved* Margaret already, which didn't surprise him. She'd be such a good mother.

He paced back and forth across the small room, memories of the orphanage overwhelming him. The cold, uncaring staff. The bullying big boys. The scanty food and the total, complete, absence of any love. The panic he used to feel when the superintendent shut him in the punishment room overwhelmed him, and he sank to the floor, head in his hands.

Margaret was the only solution. She belonged with him; a wife belonged with her husband. He'd lost sight of that, but now . . . Once Margaret was away from that redheaded bloke, she would remember how much she'd loved him. He clung to that thought, to the memory of Margaret smiling at him as she said her wedding vows. That feeling, that love, couldn't have disappeared forever.

A sudden stab of grief for Gladys caught his breath away. *She* had known how to love, known better than any of them. He kept expecting her to walk through the door, to be there when he came home from work, to touch his shoulder in passing the way she used to do. When Vi did something precious he would look up to share a smile with her; but she wasn't there, and each time it happened was like a turn of the knife. It was worse than when he thought Margaret had abandoned him. Much worse.

If he felt like this, imagine how Violet felt. She needed a mother, someone to cuddle and soothe her and fill that terrible gap.

Margaret.

43

Margaret caught the tram to work. It was so rough on the Harbour that she couldn't face the ferry. She had thought that she wouldn't be able to concentrate, but once she was safely at her desk she found it was a relief to dive into the everyday details of lot, reserve and estimated value.

In the afternoon she took the tram again to avoid alighting at Circular Quay and having to make the decision about whether to get on a tram to Camperdown and Frank, or a ferry for home.

Not today. She just couldn't face Frank today.

The next afternoon, at work, he called her.

'Margaret?'

'Yes, Frank.' Her whole body tensed.

'Margaret, I need you back here as soon as you can. I've got no one to leave Violet with. Please.'

She was his wife, and supposedly his problems were hers. In West Bromwich, if a woman died leaving children behind, someone would look after them; a cousin, a grandmother, an aunt – there would always be someone. Maybe he'd have to pay them a little bit, but not much. Everyone knew everyone else, everyone had relatives in the area. Maybe it was the same here, but not for Frank. Frank had no one. No one at all, except Violet, and her.

She fell silent, conscious of his breathing, quick and upset on the other end of the line.

'Margaret, you're still my wife. I'm in trouble now and I need your help!'

There it was. Stark and incontestable. He was being reasonable – indeed, few men would have been as generous. They were married, and he was grieving for Gladys, even if he didn't realise it. And poor little Violet . . .

'I can help pay for someone to look after Violet,' she said desperately. 'Until we can sort things out.'

'I can't leave her with a stranger. She's so upset, missing Glad. And she loves you.'

'Frank—' she said, all her hesitation in her voice.

'So much for "this divorce is all about the kiddies".' He hung up gently enough, but still the shock of it rang in her ears.

Her father used to say, 'You're getting too big for your boots, lass,' before he brought out the strap for a pailing across her legs. She knew that he would urge her to go back to the safety and security – the sacredness – of marriage with a good man.

Was she too big for her boots?

Or – and this was a radical thought, one she couldn't have dreamed of before she came to Australia – were her boots too small for her?

She had imagined that a life with Frank was all she could ever desire. But her imagination had grown stronger since then, big enough to encompass her much stronger love for Tom.

She went back home on the ferry that afternoon, without having given in her notice as she would have to do were she to go home to Frank, trying not to think about it, not sure what she could do to make the situation better. To go back to Frank, to leave Violet in the lurch – she couldn't bear to do either. She would have to convince Frank to let her help pay for someone to look after Vi. What else could she do?

The weather was still cloudy and chilly, so the inside of the ferry was crowded, the smell of wool and damp leather almost overpowering. The click of umbrella points on the deck as passengers used them to steady themselves against the swell maddened her.

She stood in the doorway to get away from it all, gazing out through salt-clouded glass at grey seas and greyer skies. Even the seagulls had taken shelter. Perhaps she should, too.

•

That evening, Mr Quinn called.

'I'm afraid I have bad news, Mrs Dalton. Your husband has decided to contest the divorce.'

It wasn't a surprise, and yet it hit her like a blow.

'Mrs Dalton?'

'Yes. Yes, I'm here. Will he— Can we—'

'We have Miss Mortimer's deposition. We have the testimony of the doctor and the nurse at the Royal Women's as to him being the father of the second child. There's no doubt that he committed adultery. I think we'll be fine.'

'Gladys's death doesn't change things?'

'No, not in any material way. Don't worry, Mrs Dalton. It will all be fine.'

But she felt as though disaster loomed over her like a storm cloud.

•

The next day was Saturday, and she had to decide if she was going to go to Camperdown after work. She wanted to check on Violet, but dreaded an argument with Frank. The very idea of it made her feel dragged down. If only Tom could come with her.

She went home to Burnsie's – she told herself it was to change into a frock that was less susceptible to Violet's dirty fingers. As she approached the High House, on the verandah, sitting on the bench seat with Violet on his knee, was Frank, with Burnsie watching from the open front door.

Margaret walked up the steps slowly, not knowing what to say. Violet wriggled down from her father's lap and ran to her for a cuddle.

'Aunty Mar-Mar!'

'Hello, tiddler,' she said, gathering her in. Violet looked thinner, and had dark circles under her eyes. 'How are you?'

'Mummy with God,' she said solemnly. What did you say to that?

'Yes, cuckoo, I know.' She hugged Violet tightly and then put her down.

'She's been having trouble sleeping,' Frank said tiredly, getting up. 'I thought an outing might do her good.'

An outing in this weather? It wasn't raining right at this moment, but it had been squally on and off all day, although it wasn't cold – at least, Margaret's English blood didn't find it cold.

'You should take her for a walk down the foreshore,' Burnsie said, her tone kind but her face implacable. It was clear she wasn't going to let them in. Fair dealing, Margaret supposed. Not the sort of meeting a landlady should have to deal with.

'Yes, come on, lamb, let's go visit the seagulls.' She held out her hand and Violet took it. The three of them walked out the front gate and headed down towards the Harbour. As they walked, the skies began to clear, grey clouds gradually shredded away on the wind.

At the small park that overlooked the Harbour, Violet pulled away from them and chased after a couple of bedraggled seagulls, waving her arms to make them fly. Some were gathered out of the wind in a wooden picnic hut, and Violet chased them out and then pulled herself up onto the seat and walked along it.

'Well, Margaret?' She had imagined him shouting at her, berating her, but his tone was almost flat. Despairing.

'You really want an unwilling wife?'

'I won't force you. I can't,' he said. 'But . . . But . . . Work's putting me on the Flying Gang, and I either take the job or I'm out. I'm supposed to start in three weeks.'

His whole body was tense. His hands twisted together.

'What's the Flying Gang?'

'It's the railway repair gang. If a bridge is washed out or the line comes up or something, they go out on a special fast train to do repairs.'

Margaret didn't see why that was going to change things. 'So . . .'

'I'll be away weeks at a time,' Frank said. 'I haven't got anyone to look after Vi while I'm gone. Child Protection have already been nosing around, threatening to take her away. Put her into a home.' He glared at her fiercely. 'I won't let them do that! You don't know what it's like, growing up in one of those places!'

A shudder went through her. Everyone knew stories about Child Protection, though in West Bromwich it was called The Welfare. It would be the same here. Children taken away and never seen again. No appeal, no recourse. And the way the children were treated . . . No wonder Frank was desperate.

'You could get another job.' She was clutching at straws, it seemed, to try to avoid this terrible responsibility that settled on her like a lead cape.

'Where? My whole working life's been spent on the railways. I'm not fit for anything else. I can't risk it. If it was just me, but . . .'

Frank turned to her, openly pleading. 'Come back to me, Marge. *Please*. Even if it's just for long enough for me to find another job, and someone to look after Violet in the daytime.'

Could she do that? To keep Violet out of an orphanage? Her promise to Gladys weighed down on her until she could hardly breathe. Give up her job. Give up her hopes of an immediate future with Tom – possibly *all* hopes of a future with him.

It wasn't right to condemn Violet to a horrible, love-starved life, but nor was it right to live with a man she didn't love, or to hurt and abandon the one she did.

Margaret started to tremble, her whole body shrinking in on itself. She was trapped and she didn't know what to do. Violet ran back to them and tugged on her dress.

'Aunty Mar-Mar! Up! Up!'

Blindly, Margaret bent and picked her up. Violet's little arms came around her neck, and she knew without any doubt that she couldn't abandon her.

Frank saw her weakness. 'All I ever wanted for her was a proper family. A mother and a father. That's what Gladys wanted, too.'

So, this was it. This was the moment she had to decide.

For Margaret, everything seemed to be ranged on Frank's side: God, society, Violet, and Margaret's own promise to Gladys.

Margaret couldn't help but remember what she had felt for Frank when they married, and his initial devotion and fidelity, his honesty and constancy, his love before all the confusion set in. What a woman in her circumstances ought to do: stick with her husband through thick and thin, be a helpmate, a supporter, a crutch if necessary.

And on the other, what? A few months' friendship with Tom and one night at Clareville. How she felt when she was with him. How much did her own need and desire and love count?

More seagulls descended and Violet wriggled down.

'Birdies!' she said, flapping her arms like wings.

'Margaret?' Frank said, his voice despondent.

She should go with him, now. Going back to her husband was the only right thing to do. She could put her own feelings aside for Violet's sake.

She raised her eyes to Frank's face to say so and saw, past his shoulder, a group of men coming out of a yard gate, further along from where Tom worked. One of the boat-builders' workshops. The newly revealed sun was striking a dazzling silver from the wet streets, so that the men were all silhouettes. They were laughing and joking among themselves, as if they'd had a couple of drinks. Behind them, taller than all of them, a dark-hatted man she couldn't mistake for anyone else. The sight of Tom took away all thought, all ability to be reasonable and sensible. She couldn't breathe.

The group came along the laneway and passed them, turning up Victoria Street. Tom saw her and Frank, and Violet, and he stopped for a moment, his mouth pressed together as if to prevent himself from speaking. It seemed as though he understood her decision, because he nodded at Frank as she had seen football teams nod to the winning players. His eyes were bleak.

Tom turned to follow the other men up the street. The sight of his back turned to her filled her with panic. Her soul was being wrenched in two, and half of it was moving away from her.

'Tom!' she called. 'Tom, wait!'

He didn't stop, although he hesitated a moment.

She ran. Five steps to the edge of the park, five, ten, twenty to catch up with him, running as hard as she'd ever run in her life, breath coming short, heart jittering, so fast she couldn't stop in time on the wet road and cannoned into him, sending him staggering.

He turned and grabbed her upper arms, steadying them both, and stared down at her.

'Don't go,' she panted.

He looked over her head, to Frank, and then back down at her.

'Are you sure?' His eyes were dark and his mouth still tight with doubt and pain.

'I can't be without you,' she said. 'I just can't.'

Tom's hands tightened on her arms, and she saw the muscles around his eyes loosen with relief, his mouth relax before he firmed it, and nodded.

Frank's footsteps echoed on the hard road behind her. She turned to face him, knowing how much she was about to hurt him.

'I'm sorry,' she said.

All her life she had tried to do what was right, what was expected of her. But now she was in a place where expectations collided. There *was* no proper thing to do. This was new territory, and she had to make her own path. She could hurt Frank, but she couldn't sacrifice Violet. Automatically, she checked: Violet was happily running after some pigeons.

She let go of Tom's hand and spoke to Frank, eye to eye. Only the truth could save them now.

'Tell me the truth. If you could have Gladys back, would you still want me?'

He jerked back as though she'd slapped his face, and then stilled.

'Violet—'

'No, not Violet. If Vi was out of the picture. Who would you rather have as your wife? Gladys or me? Who do you really think you'd be happiest with? Who do you really *love*, Frank?'

He stared at her and then his eyes went blank, as though he were looking back, looking into a past that had escaped him. His lips trembled, once, and he turned his head sharply away to hide his expression. A moment, and then he took a deep breath and turned back to face her.

'Glad,' he said tightly.

Tears were hurting her eyes; she blinked them away. Tom stood beside her, but she looked only at Frank. It was a big thing he'd admitted, and it had hurt him to say it.

'Sometimes you make a mistake about who you love,' she said. 'I think we both made a mistake.'

He stared at her with a terrible determination.

'Vi!' she called, walking back to the park. The men followed as if on a string. Violet ran to her and Margaret crouched to hug her, then swung her up onto her hip.

'I'll look after Violet, Frank,' she said. A shudder passed right through Tom, and he closed his eyes for a moment. Frank let out a sigh and rubbed his eyes. '*But*,' she went on, 'I'll only do that if you don't contest the divorce.'

'But—' Frank said.

'Margi—' Tom said.

'Tom, I'll marry you, or live with you, or whatever it is we can do in the end. But if you want me, you'll have to take Violet too.'

The two men were staring at her with identical expressions of astonishment.

Then Tom's face changed. She held her breath. It was a lot to ask of him, to take on another man's child. But he nodded to her solemnly. A promise. Her heart cracked open and she knew in that instant that she would love him forever, with no doubt and nothing held back, and that he loved her the same way. It was too deep to speak about; she would never have words for it.

She tightened her grip on Violet, who was happily playing with the beads around her neck, and turned to Frank.

'You said all you ever wanted was a proper family for Violet,' she said, trying to speak gently. 'Even if I did go back to you, it wouldn't be a proper family. You need love to make a family, Frank. I *reckon*,' she used the Australian word deliberately, because she was Australian now, 'I reckon she'd be miserable and confused and sad, growing up with a father who was never there and a mother who wanted to be someplace else. Tom and I can give her a real home.'

'But I'm her father,' Frank said. He sounded dazed. No wonder. It wasn't the solution he'd hoped for, or the one he'd dreaded. But it could work; the more she thought about it, the surer she was.

Tom placed a hand on her shoulder. With that support she could face anything.

'I'll look after her, Dalton,' he said. 'Don't worry about that.'

Frank was looking at Violet as if at his last glimpse of heaven. 'I'll pay for her keep,' he said. 'Maybe later, if I get remarried . . . she can come back . . .'

'That's not fair to her,' Tom said. 'She needs a proper home. One home.'

Margaret's heart clenched at Frank's misery. It made her feel like an assassin; or a thief, stealing away all that was good in his life, but Violet's welfare had to be their guide, as it was before. She made her voice as reassuring as she could.

'It'll be a lot better than an orphanage, Frank,' Margaret said. 'You can see her whenever you want. Like family,'

Frank's face changed at the word 'family', and he nodded.

'Of course,' Tom said. 'It might be an odd family, but you'll be part of it.'

Tears rose in her eyes; he was such a generous, such a good man. Frank shook his hand looking, if not happy, then reassured. He held out his arms to Vi.

Margaret kissed Violet and handed her over, disentangling the little hands from her necklace.

'Want!' Violet said. Her voice was choked with tears and temper; her face had turned woebegone again, and it caught at Margaret's heart. She could do with a little spoiling. Margaret smiled at her and smoothed the hair away from her face.

'All right, poppet.' She took off the beads and looped them around Violet's neck.

'Ta,' Violet said, absorbed in her new toy.

Margaret turned to Frank. His eyes were red with unshed tears. He raised a shaking hand to touch Violet's hair. She wrinkled her nose at him and bounced in his arms, happy with her beads. He clutched at her blindly. 'I guess some people just aren't meant to have families,' he said.

'We wouldn't have suited in the long run, even if . . . even if it had all gone the way we planned.'

A rueful flicker of a smile went across Frank's face.

'No way to tell now, is there?'

'Aunty Mar-Mar!' Violet said, and tried to lunge back to Margaret.

'None of that, now,' Frank said. 'You're going to be a very lucky girl, Vi. Pretty soon you're going to have a nice long holiday with Aunty Margaret.' A tear fell onto his cheek; he wiped it away with the back of his hand, quickly.

Violet clapped her hands. 'Ice keem!' she said. Frank jiggled Violet on his hip in a practised manner, a father to his bones, and turned his face into her hair, as he had done once before, to hide his anguish.

He walked away, still holding Violet tightly.

Tom put out a hand to stop her following. She wanted to collapse against him, but not here. She rested a hand on his arm.

'Thank you.' She tried to put everything she felt into it: her trust, her love, her admiration for this good, generous man.

He smiled – the sweet, slow smile that had first attracted her – and put his hand over hers.

A long moment of silence, as they watched Frank and Violet out of sight. The men from the boat-builders were gone, too, so they stood alone in the wet, shining world, handfast.

She turned into Tom's arms and held him tightly. His arms came around her and they stood, stock still in the middle of the road.

There was a lump in her throat, which was ridiculous. She should be happy. She *was* happy. If only Frank hadn't looked so devastated.

Tom kissed her then, a kiss full of tenderness and promise that brought more tears to her eyes. She clung to him, feeling foolish and alive, shaking just a little.

They went to sit in the picnic hut, hand in hand, and sat for a while, discussing how Violet would fit into their lives, and all that would happen next. It was a sober talk, but underneath there was a singing happiness in both of them, and the knowledge that they had finally found the right road.

'Just over a week until the divorce hearing,' she said. 'After that, at least we'll be able to be seen together in public.'

Tom lifted her hand and brushed his lips across it. 'Can't come soon enough for me.'

Margaret kissed him one last time, and went out, to where the high blue Australian sky was waiting.

EPILOGUE

November 1923

'Right, get yourself set,' Tom instructed. Violet posed herself, arms forward, hands one on top of the other, head twisted back to watch as the waves came. 'Go!' Tom yelled, and she launched herself and swam, arms flailing, trying to keep in front of the wave long enough.

Margi laughed with sympathy when the wave passed her and left her in the sandy shallows. She jiggled Davy on her hip, and he gurgled and waved his little hands in the air in delight.

'Try again!' Margi shouted to Vi. She slid Davy across her and let him down so his feet could dance along the top of the waves – they were right at the edge of the water, and the biggest wave wouldn't even wet his bottom. He loved the water, splashing noisily and babbling the whole time, as if he were having a conversation with the hissing wavelets.

Violet scrambled back to her father; Tom was waiting for her at the limit of where she could stand up, grinning widely. There was nothing he liked better than teaching Vi to surf. She looked like Gladys – all her mother's loveliness and charm, with an extra helping of cheekiness and confidence. They kept her hair short, though, so she could swim more easily, and sometimes, in profile, a resemblance to Frank would jump out at Margaret, a jolt to the heart that would probably never go away.

Later this afternoon they would take the sailing dinghy out on Pittwater, taking turns with it, Tom and Vi, then her and Vi, one of them waiting on their own little beach with Davy. The house at Clareville had been finished just in time for Davy's birth; during the week they lived in a flat at Lavender Bay, but on weekends they were here, on the beach at Avalon or sailing on Pittwater.

The flat was getting a bit small for them, now that Davy was out of long skirts and too big for his cradle. He and Vi were sharing the second bedroom equably enough, but if they had more children . . . and Vi was going to school next year, so they had to choose soon.

'Look, Marmar!' Vi shouted, along with a dozen other children, all showing off for their parents. Margaret waved, and waved Davy's hand too.

Moving house to the other side of the Harbour would make it easier for them to take Davy and Vi to visit Tom's mother and aunt. Margaret had agreed to raise the children as Catholics (how could she not, when Tom had been so wonderful?). They had forgiven her, mostly, for being Methodist, and taken Violet into the clan without a second thought.

It would be easier for Frank, too, who visited whenever he was in Sydney, every six or eight weeks. Violet seemed quite content to have a 'Papa' and a 'Daddy'. No doubt one day she would ask questions, but she hadn't yet.

There had been tears enough from Violet at first, but she had adapted. Burnsie was like a grandmother to her now, and Jane a beloved aunt. Margaret was glad Frank could visit; he always left Violet with troubled eyes, but he walked more strongly, refreshed by seeing her. It was odd, sometimes, having her divorced husband and her real husband sitting at the dinner table, but they all coped. Frank had started seeing a nice woman, a war widow, in one of the country towns the Gang went to. It was a slow courtship, though, as he didn't get out there often.

Violet jumped on Tom's back and the two of them surged through the waves to her, Tom swinging Vi down at Margi's feet.

'My turn!' she said. He grinned and held out his arms for Davy. 'One, two, *threeee*,' she sang and sailed him over, kicking and laughing, into Tom's strong hands. The touch was enough to remind her that a new baby wasn't at all unlikely.

She let her hand trail across his shoulders as she and Vi went past.

'Come on, tiddler!' she said to Vi. They held hands and ran out to where the waves were breaking, diving under the next wave as one and laughing as they came up.

'You go first and wait for me,' Margi said. Seriously, Vi poised herself ready and launched just before the next wave. 'Go! Go!' Margi shouted. This time, Vi rode it all the way in; the waves were breaking just right.

She jumped up. 'Did you see me, Dad? Did you see, Marmar?' and waved. Margi waved back before moving into deeper water.

This was the best moment. She waited, heart pounding, and pushed off, swam, felt the wave pick her up and carry her, frothing and joyous, wild and fearless, flying towards the ones she loved the most in the world.

ACKNOWLEDGEMENTS

My first thanks go to Queenie Sunderland, who at 95 wrote her autobiography, *Bride of an Anzac*. From her I first heard about a Margaret who, arriving on a war-bride ship, found that her husband had abandoned her. My Margaret's job at Reading Station was originally Queenie's.

My mother-in-law, Doris Hart, hails from West Bromwich, and from her I learned about what Margaret's early life would have been like (though she was born several years after Margaret left for Australia, I hasten to say!).

The change in shipping from the *Waimana* to the *Borda* did in fact happen, and caused quite a widely reported scandal at the time. After a rat got into a cradle and bit a baby, the women who were supposed to sail on the *Waimana* petitioned General Monash, who organised for them to move to the *Borda*. There is a wonderful series of photographs of the voyage out. It took severe restraint on my part to not start the story at Tilbury and use these photos to inspire a story of travel; but Margaret's plight doesn't really start until she arrives in Sydney, so I controlled myself! (You'll find the whole story, with pictures, on my website, <www.pamela-hart.com>).

David Gist at the Australian War Memorial was terrifically helpful in getting me details about the post-1918 demobilisation process.

Great thanks go to Ray Moran at Manly Life Saving Club, who most kindly allowed me access to their archives and personally conducted me through their wonderful records.

Susan Gardiner at the King Street Court House was very generous with her time and expertise – it's not her fault that the scenes set in the Court House were cut from the final draft!

North Sydney Library's Local Studies section was full of wonderful information about boat-building in Berry's Bay. And, as always, the trove.nla.gov.au website of the National Library of Australia is an historical writer's best friend.

My gratitude also goes to my beta readers, especially Judith Ridge, who taught me about being a Methodist.

Finally, I would like to thank Rebecca Saunders, Karen Ward and all the team at Hachette. This last year has been very difficult personally, and they gently shepherded me through the editing process with enormous compassion and expertise.

ALSO BY PAMELA HART

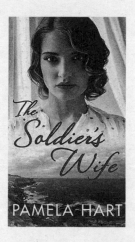

Sydney, 1915. Newlyweds Ruby and Jimmy Hawkins are sure their love will survive the trauma and tragedy of war. As the months of Jimmy's stay in Gallipoli slip by, Ruby must forge a new life in this man's world. Taking a job in a city timber merchant's yard, she faces complications as the lives around her begin to shatter . . .

Inspired by the author's family history, *The Soldier's Wife* is a heart-soaring story of love and loss and learning how to live when all you hold dear is threatened.

'*Evokes WWI Sydney to the point where the reader can almost feel the salty wind blowing off the harbour as the troops are shipped out through the Heads.*' **Books+Publishing**

'*Deeply insightful into the lives of the women left behind. Hart skilfully builds up suspense in this poignant novel and its dramatic conclusion is breathtaking.*' **Better Reading**